The HITHERTO SECRET EXPERIMENTS of Marie Curie

The HITHERTO SECRET EXPERIMENTS of Marie Curie

edited by

BRYAN THOMAS SCHMIDT & HENRY HERZ

BLACK STONE

PUBLISHING

Printed in the United States of America

First edition: 2023
ISBN 978-1-6650-4703-6
Young Adult Fiction / Horror

Version 1

Blackstone Publishing
31 Mistletoe Rd.
Ashland, OR 97520

www.BlackstonePublishing.com

Bryan dedicates this volume to:
A bright star in the future of STEM,
following in Marie Curie's footsteps,
Vienna Tran,
whose enthusiasm for serving others is an inspiration.
And to
Glenda Schmidt,
the strong woman who raised me.
Giving up nursing to stay home with the kids,
she put her heart and soul into becoming an advocate
for her ADHD son so that no limitations and no barriers
would keep him from success and living his dreams.
And lastly,
for May Restullas, who can do anything, I truly believe.

Henry dedicates this volume to:
My parents, my wife Julie,
my sons Josh and Harrison, and the Author of all things.

CONTENTS

INTRODUCTION

Marya Salomea Skłodowska (a.k.a. Marie Curie) is inarguably one of the most famous female scientists in world history: a double Nobel winner whose discoveries changed science and our understanding of it forever. But who was Marya when she was growing up—a young teenager mourning the loss of her mother and sister as she struggled to come into her own in Russian-ruled schools? Schools where women were told to know their place, which was anywhere but science . . .

The Hitherto Secret Experiments of Marie Curie sets out to imagine just that using Marya and speculative, fantastical ideas and elements to imagine what it might have been like, rather than representing actual events. Here are sixteen original stories, entirely fictional though sometimes based on snippets of history, imagining what Marya's young life in the late 1800s and Marya herself might have been like. The late nineteenth century, after all, was still an age where superstitions and myths were often held in just as high regard or even higher than science—although scientific research and discoveries were ever growing, they were still something a great portion of the public found mysterious and regarded with skepticism. As such, the period lends itself to exploration of both the connection and juxtaposition of science and folklore, and our authors herein have fun with that. From an obsession with conquering death and disease to facing dragons, rat kings, and demons in many forms, even debating with her peers over science versus magic and imagining what her life might have been like had she taken a darker turn, these stories are filled with tales of the triumph of spirit and ingenuity and rising above oppressive circumstances. For simplification, we have chosen to refer to her throughout by her Polish given name rather than her more famous westernized moniker.

Although much has been written about Marya, this younger period of her life is vaguely known, and so our writers take liberties for the sake of entertainment. Many of the characters are fictional in these stories, but her historical best friend Kazia and family members recur throughout. This should not in any way be seen as disrespect, for we all hold Marya in the highest regard. In fact, over one hundred years later, when women are still struggling to be taken seriously in STEM, stories about heroes like Marya are as important as ever.

It is our hope that these sixteen thought-provoking adventures inspire the next generation of upcoming Maryas to reach further so they too can become world-changing scientists in the mold of Marie Curie. If our stories play any small part in that, we would forever be humbled, grateful, and in awe.

For those who may know Marie Curie by name but not much else about her, my coeditor Henry Herz has provided a brief historical overview following this introduction, about Marya/Marie, her accomplishments, and the world in which she lived. This gives context to the stories that follow and serves as a reminder of a great woman who deserves to be celebrated by generations to come.

So here now from some of the top writers in horror, science fiction, fantasy, and young adult literature working today, are sixteen inspirational stories and four poems of the fictional (and fantastical) misadventures of young Marya. We hope they inspire you to dream, just as Marie Curie continues to inspire women all over the world to never give up in their quest to conquer scientific mysteries and change the world.

Bryan Thomas Schmidt
Ottawa, KS

HISTORICAL OVERVIEW: *Marie Curie*

by
HENRY HERZ

Best known by her married name, Marya Salomea Skłodowska (a.k.a. Marie Curie) was one of the most influential and well-known scientists in history. Her higher education began at Warsaw's clandestine Flying University. She then earned master's degrees in physics and mathematical sciences and a doctorate of science in physics from the Sorbonne in Paris. A brilliant scientist who spoke five languages, she was the first woman to win a Nobel Prize and the first person to win them in two different fields. Her awards included:

Nobel Prize in Physics (1903, with her husband Pierre Curie
    and Henri Becquerel)
Davy Medal (1903, with Pierre)
Matteucci Medal (1904, with Pierre)
Actonian Prize (1907)
Elliott Cresson Medal (1909)
Nobel Prize in Chemistry (1911)
Franklin Medal of the American Philosophical Society (1921)

Marie Curie at the 1927 Solvay Conference on Quantum Mechanics among the other gods of science, including Erwin Schrödinger, Wolfgang Pauli, Werner Heisenberg, Paul Dirac, Arthur Compton, Louis de Broglie, Max Born, Niels Bohr, Max Planck, and Albert Einstein. Photograph by Benjamin Couprie, Institut International de Physique Solvay, Brussels, Belgium.

Marya Salomea Skłodowska was born in Warsaw, Poland, then part of the Russian Empire, on November 7, 1867, to Bronisława and Władysław Skłodowski. Marya (nicknamed *Manya*) was the youngest of five children. Her siblings were Zofia (five years Marya's senior, nicknamed *Zosia*), Józef (six years, *Józio*), Bronisława (eight years, *Bronia* or *Brounia*), and Helena (nine years, *Hela*). As a child, Marya was plump with fair, unruly hair.

Marya's father had a scruffy beard, fiery eyes, and a deep, warm voice. Learned in mathematics and physics, he moved with vigor and had a playful nature. Shortly after Marya's birth, Władysław was appointed assistant director of a Russian gymnasium (high school) in western Warsaw. The family moved to an apartment on Nowolipki Street, where they lived for twenty years. In 1873, he was demoted by a resentful Russian boss. The reduction in income forced the Skłodowskis to convert their home into a boarding school. After Russian authorities eliminated laboratory instruction from Polish schools, Władysław brought some of the equipment home and instructed his children in its use.

Marya's mother was delicate and tall, with hair sometimes worn in perfectly coiled braids around her ears. She played piano. A director of a private girls' school in central Warsaw, she eventually found the commute and taking care of her family too taxing and resigned from her position.

Marya suffered more than her share of childhood tragedy. Her mother, a devout Roman Catholic, began showing signs of tuberculosis when Marya was four. She traveled to Hall, Austria, and Nice, France, accompanied by Zosia to "take the cure." Marya's Aunt Ludwika (*Lucia*) helped Marya's father care for the other four children. When Marya was eight, Zosia died of typhus. A little over a year later, her mother finally succumbed to tuberculosis. Marya suffered deep depression, abandoned her musical studies, and became agnostic. Her mother and sister were buried at Powązki cemetery.

Highly intelligent with a great memory, Marya began attending public Gymnasium Number Three at age ten. The school was housed in the second story of a former convent of the adjacent Church of St. Joseph of the Visitationists, commonly known as the Visitationist Church, located off the broad north-south-running street, Krakowskie Przedmieście. A watch shop run by the kindly Mr. Wosinski occupied the first floor. Russian control made school an oppressive place. Girls were treated as second-class students, and everyone was forced to speak Russian rather than Polish in the classrooms. A bright spot for Marya was her good friend, Kazia Pryzborowska, daughter of the librarian to Count Zamoyski. Kazia lived with her parents at the Count's residence, the Blue Palace, located near the Saxon Gardens. Marya graduated high school, first in her class, before turning sixteen.

In Russian-controlled Poland, women could not continue their education past high school. Those interested in higher learning sought it in other countries, an option initially not available to Marya due to her father's limited financial resources. In 1883, Polish progressives established a clandestine academy to offer women a way to advance their education and promote the goal of a free Poland. When the Russians discovered the academy, sending many of the teachers into exile, the Poles adapted, with instructors teaching a "Floating (or Flying) University" in their homes. Marya and her sister Brounia participated. Marya took full-time employment to help pay for Brounia to study medicine in Paris.

When circumstances finally permitted it in 1891, Marya left to study in Paris, where she adopted the name Marie. She met her future husband, Pierre Curie, in 1894. They married the following year and had two children, Ève and Irène. Marya became the first woman to become a professor at the University of Paris in 1906. Irène followed in Marya's footsteps, winning a Nobel Prize in Chemistry with her husband in 1935. But Marya's life remained a mixture of triumph and tragedy, as her husband was killed in a traffic accident that same year.

Marya deduced that radioactivity does not depend on how atoms are arranged into molecules, but rather that it originates within the atoms themselves. She proved that the atom is not indivisible. She discovered polonium and radium. As director of the Red Cross Radiology Service during World War I, she treated over a million soldiers with her X-ray machines. Her work contributed to finding treatments for cancer.

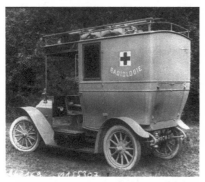

Mobile x-ray unit (Bibliothèque Nationale de France, département Estampes et photographie)

The humble and generous Marya observed a modest lifestyle, giving away much of her first Nobel Prize money to friends, family, and research associates. She chose not to patent the radium-isolation process, enabling the scientific community to do further research without that financial barrier. Marya often shared monetary gifts with the scientific institutions with which she was affiliated.

Marya died in 1934 from the ravaging effects of exposure to ionizing radiation during her experiments. She became the first woman to be entombed on her own merits in Paris's Panthéon mausoleum. Marya was originally buried in a lead-lined casket to prevent radium and polonium radiation from her body harming others. The Curies' personal effects—scientific notes, cookbooks, even furniture—are still radioactive to this day. France's Bibliothèque Nationale keeps Curie's notes in lead-lined boxes.

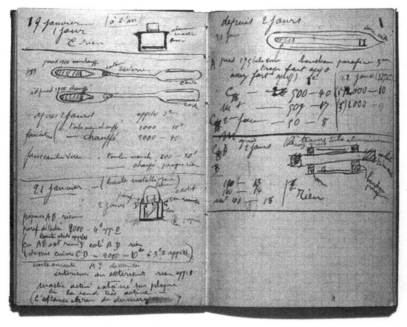

Marie Curie's notebook (Wellcome Library, London)

Marya continues to be honored long after her passing. A 2009 poll by *New Scientist* found her the "most inspirational woman in science." Poland declared 2011 as the Year of Marie Curie. Three radioactive minerals are named after the Curies: curite, sklodowskite, and cuprosklodowskite. The curie (Ci) is a unit of radioactivity. The element Curium (atomic number 96) was also named for her. Marya's likeness has appeared on banknotes, stamps, and coins around the world.

DARK LADY,
Salomea

by
JANE YOLEN

"Nothing in life is to be feared,
it is only to be understood."

—Marie Curie

O, collector of firsts,
Noble lady, Nobel lady.
First female professor in Paris,
First woman to die the dark death.
Do the scales balance?
You, bringer of demonic power,
that fierce light of radium,
speeding your way
to publication?
Do the lives lost, gained,
weigh equal in your heart?
Or do you just polish
the medals and move on,
researching in the heaven
you do not believe in,
while the rest of us
pickaxe the coals of hell,
trying to stay safe,
trying to stay warm.

UNCROWNED *Kings*

by

SEANAN McGUIRE

It is easier to watch over one hundred fleas than one young girl.

—Polish proverb.

1876

They buried Zosia yesterday.

She never hurt anyone in her life, which was barely long enough to serve as a sentence, much less a story; she was born, she lived, she loved her family, she got sick, and she left in the night, hand in hand with tall, fair Death, the woman in white and the girl in gray walking away into the streets of Warsaw, leaving her weary, worn-out body behind.

It wasn't right. Mama and Papa said that it was God's will working through the world, but Maria couldn't see how God's will wasn't an affront to His own creation if he thought killing a fifteen-year-old girl was somehow the right and kindly thing to do. As if it were just. Zosia had been bright and sweet and kind. She had been of an age when her eyes trended toward the boys in their parish, and when her cheeks flared red if one of them brushed her hand in passing at the market or commented on her hair ribbons. She had been old enough to fall in love if God's will hadn't ordered her to wait until marriage or if she hadn't been so bound and determined to be a good, obedient daughter and bring neither attention nor shame to her family name.

Instead, she had brought bills from the physic, treatments that were not enough to save her, and sleepless nights for all of them when her coughing stole sleep away. Maria was ashamed to remember how weary she had been, so angry at her oldest sister, as if Zosia had somehow chosen her illness, had chosen to keep her family awake as she wheezed and struggled for each and every breath.

By the end the coughing had been a welcome confirmation that Zosia was still alive. The doctors had stopped taking Papa's money two days before, saying that it would be a crime in thought if not in deed to let him continue to pay when they already knew they couldn't save her. He wept more when they pressed the bills back into his hand than when the coughing had finally, horribly, mercifully, brutally come to an end.

Maria had been lying awake when Zosia had finally stopped coughing. She had almost drifted off to sleep by the time her mother's scream split the air into two tidy halves: the world in which she had an eldest sister named Zosia, stubborn, sensitive, tender, terrible, and all the things an eldest sister ought to be to be worthy of the title, and the world in which Bronisława was now the eldest of them and always would be. Bronia was an excellent sister, and Maria loved her fiercely, but she wasn't meant to be the eldest. She was meant to have someone to set herself against, someone to serve as a magnifying lens for her own brilliance and to sharpen her the way she, Józio, and Hela, sharpened Maria. Without Zosia, how would Bronia ever be sharpened as she was meant to be? How would she shine?

How would *any* of them shine? Maria had lain in the dark, consumed by the sound of her mother's screams and by the weight of her own grief which had seemed so big it would devour the world. She had known two things to go with the two halves of the world. She no longer had a Zosia to hold and love and call her very own; and someone would have to pay for this. She would find a way to make someone pay for this. She would see Zosia avenged if it was the last thing she did.

After Zosia's death, the priest had come to the house to see the body and talk in low, hushed tones with Maria's father, not noticing the young girl with the tight-drawn face who watched them from the corner of the room, motionless, as if she were a part of the furnishings. Her mother had walked through the day like a ghost herself, covering mirrors and opening windows, following the old traditions before the priest could arrive and tell them that God had everything well in hand. It wasn't worth the argument.

Her mother said that God had things well in hand, but there was still virtue to following the rituals they knew so well, the ones that had been passed down from parent to child for generations. God might want Zosia home with Him in the mansions of Heaven, but would He open all the windows between her spirit and the heights of his domain? Or was that something so small that He would leave it to the people He had created, trusting them to do what needed doing?

God had a plan. Everyone said so. But if a dog died in the street and no one hauled it away, it would bloat and rot where it lay, and maggots would pick the flesh from its bones, and the hand of God would never come down to lift it into the sky. Zosia was not a dead dog. But if a dead dog might require some intervention by human hands, it only made sense for a dead child to require the same.

So the house had been prepared before the priest's arrival. He had come to murmur softly to Maria's parents, their voices low to keep the eager ears of children from drinking in forbidden knowledge. Maria held her tongue until the moment she saw her mother sway, knees buckling, dropping her to the floor. Then, and only then, Maria had rushed forward, glaring at the priest, who had down looked at the little girl in silent assessment.

"What did you say?" Her demand had been loud enough to crack the air, forming another divide in the world. The world *before* Maria had raised her voice to a man of God and the world that existed after.

Her father took a step back, eyes wide, clearly too surprised to speak.

The priest looked down at her with infinite patience, not a flicker of frustration in his placid face, and in that moment, she hated him, and it, more than she could possibly have said. She wanted to hook her fingers into claws and scratch at his smooth, rounded cheeks, which had never been hollowed with hunger, never pocked with frost or sickness of any kind. He was too perfect to have suffered, and how could a man who'd never known anything but the kind of plenty that could inspire a voluntary vow of privation. She had never been able to understand how priests could pledge to have less so that the Church, which already owned the world, could have more. Maybe they could do it because, for all their pledges and promises, they remained the richest men in Warsaw. Their stomachs were always full, even if their pockets were empty.

That is its own form of wealth, to know that if you stumble, the people will catch you, and that if you leap, God will be there to stop you from hitting the ground. And she hated him for that wealth, hated him so much it felt as if his answer must not matter because she would hate him all the same.

And he looked at her with those kindly eyes, with that kindly face, and said, "I told her that had she not allowed an ungodly man to room in her home, with her children, her Zosia would not have fallen ill, nor been taken from us so quickly."

Her mother gave an agonized wail, like the cry of a seabird with a broken wing, and Maria knew hatred like she had never known before in her short life. She narrowed her eyes, and she glared at the priest so fiercely that if she had believed in Hell—and she was increasingly sure that she didn't believe in Hell in the least; if God had wanted them to suffer eternally, He would simply have made life an eternal state, and never allowed them any hope of Heaven—she would have been consigned there in an instant.

"And had the Church not set the tithes so high, we might have had the money to support ourselves without the taking of lodgers," she said, voice sharp, and stepped away from him.

He met her anger with an expression of deep sympathy. "You are a child," he said. "You know not what you say."

"Maria," said her mother, keening finally coming to an end. "Maria, behave. Do not vex the priest."

Maria shot a scandalized glance at her mother, who would take this man's side after he had said such a horribly unforgivable thing to her. Then she slumped, stepped back, and said, "The house is prepared for the mourning period. I know it's inappropriate for me to go out and play right now, but may I go and tell Zosia's friends of her passing? They'll be waiting for her by the fountain."

"Go, go," said her mother, willing to ignore the possibility that Maria would break her mourning with levity if it meant that she was no longer antagonizing the priest.

Maria turned and fled.

Bronia was waiting by the door. She looked over with interest as Maria approached and frowned when she saw her little sister taking her coat down from its hook. There was only a year between them, but from the vaunted height of ten years old, Bronisława felt as if it was her duty to protect the baby of the family from the dangers of the wide, wild world.

"What are you doing?" she asked, voice low out of respect for the priest, who was only a room away, and might take normal volume for impudence. "You know we mustn't go out to play until the *Pusta Noc* is done."

As if three days of mourning could possibly be enough for them to cry all the tears that Zosia deserved. Three days mourning, and then the funeral, and then Zosia forever in the ground, under a headstone that would say Zosia Skłodowska and two dates, with none of the years between. Her favorite food, the little songs she sang when she tied her shoes, the way she brushed her hair, the crushes she harbored, and the hopes that she hid; they'd all go with her, and no one would put them on her headstone.

The thought was enough to make Maria's stomach ache. So she raised her head, looked along her nose at Bronia, and said, "I'm going to tell Zosia's friends that she passed away in the night and the funeral will be held in three days' time. Mother permitted me. You can come along, if you'd like."

Secretly she hoped that Bronia would say yes. It was better to go walking with a sister, whether it was a walk of merriment or sorrow. And so, when Bronia reached for her coat, she had to fight the traitorous smile that wanted to rise through her grief to replace the miserable twist that contorted her mouth.

"All right," said Bronia. "But only out and back. We're not going to play."

"No," agreed Maria, and opened the door.

It was a beautiful day, which felt shameful, sinful even, and as they stepped out into the sunlight, all Maria could think was that Zosia would never feel the sun. Not ever again.

That was four days ago, and they buried Zosia yesterday. When the sun rose, the period of mourning would be over, and normal living would be expected to resume. They'd have to sit through their lessons, and Papa would have to go to work, and everyone would go on with the business of being alive. Everyone except for Zosia, who would never have the experience of being alive ever again. She would not grow or change or see the people her siblings would become in her absence. She would only go to the dirt and the worms, and to the halls of Heaven, of which Maria had never seen any proof and doubted further every day that she ever would.

Zosia was in the ground. Zosia was in the past. Maria took a deep breath, raised her chin, and tried to think of a future when she would be grown and grand and clever, and everything would be different. She would find a way to make sure of it.

1882

Zosia had been dead for six years. Maria was a grownup girl of fifteen, still looking toward the future, spending her days at the gymnasium and her afternoons at the Flying University. She was learning from instructors who believed as she did that her sex—which she had had no say in but had been granted to her by God or by nature, bundling a clever mind and a diminutive form like one must by definition inform the other—should not in any way restrict her, nor deny her the opportunity for greatness. It was not a belief shared by all. Far too many of the men she knew thought her body was a commandment in and of itself, like she had somehow been sentenced to an inescapable prison before she was even born.

Well, she was having none of it. None of it, and none of them, mewling men who still believed in the hand of a loving, almighty God, could take their preconceptions and the preordinations and hang for all she cared.

She had just stepped outside the school gates when she heard a commotion from the walkway and turned to see Bronia hurrying toward her, spilling smaller students to either side in her rush. She stopped when she reached Maria, clasping the sides of the younger girl's face and studying her with hungry eyes before letting out a sigh of relief.

Maria, who was not accustomed to such wild behavior from her staid older sibling, frowned and wrenched her face away. "Have I done something for you to embarrass me so in front of my classmates?" she asked, taking a step back from her sister's reach.

"You said I was to tell you at once if anyone came ill," said Bronia.

Maria froze, feeling a physical chill wrap around her bones. "Józio?"

"Hela," said Bronia. "She shows all the signs of . . ." Her voice dropped, all too aware of what even a rumor of illness could do to their family but unable to contain the knowledge a moment longer than she must: "of typhus."

"But we've had neither beasts nor boarders in the home!"

Typhus came through two channels—through lice carried on the bodies of the afflicted, most often the traveling or the unclean. However, Maria knew from her youth that lice could affix themselves to anyone unlucky enough to be exposed and from fleas carried on the bodies of beasts. The fleas of cats did not have the right qualities for passing the disease along, so a cat in the home could keep the second type of typhus away. The first was mainly a matter of hygiene and care, both of which were well present in the Skłodowski home.

Maria frowned. When Zosia had taken ill, the Church had blamed their family's most recent boarder, for there were no rats in the home, and the family cat was fat and lazy in the kitchen. But the man had been clean and taken care with his own washing, and it had never settled well with her.

"Have there been other cases among our neighbors?" Maria asked, beginning to walk briskly in the direction of their home, forcing Bronia to rush to keep up.

"Three, I suspect," said Bronia. "Jakob has been out of school for three days. Szymon lingers unwell."

Children. All children, again, as it had been six years before when the Church blamed Zosia's illness on their mother. Maria no longer believed in even the hope of a Heaven, but at times she wished she could, so that her mother could have been reunited with lost Zosia and thus reassured she served her daughter well.

Still, it was strange for typhus to move so through a small area and to afflict only children when adults had so much more hair upon their bodies to house and harbor lice. Maria thought it so when Zosia died but had been too taken in her grieving to think further until the summer had turned, and it had been far too late.

She proceeded straight home, Bronia beside her, and barged into the house, thundering along the hall to the room where Hela malingered. Their sister huddled in her bed, clearly miserable, blankets clutched high under her chin. Maria almost regretted what she was about to do. Not enough to change her course, but enough to feel somewhat sorry for doing it.

"Take off your clothes," she said, voice carrying.

Hela stared at her. "I'm *cold*," she said, voice a thin whine of protest.

"Yes, and I'm trying to save your life," snapped Maria. "Take. Off. Your. Clothes."

Hela, like Bronia, was accustomed to the sometimes incomprehensible demands of her scientifically-minded youngest sister. Still staring, she shuffled from beneath the covers and removed her shirt, submitting to a close inspection of the hair growing in her armpits, groin, and the nape of her neck, after which Maria shook her head and declared, "No signs of lice. Several bites, as might come from a flea. Have they been itching?"

"Yes, awfully," said Hela. "May I put my nightdress back on?"

"Yes," said Maria, and left the room, Bronia behind her.

"What was that?" asked Bronia, becoming alarmed as she saw that Maria was heading for the door, pausing only to retrieve a bottle of bleach from the closet where their mother kept her cleaning supplies. "You can't intend to ask the others to remove their clothes! Jakob and Szymon are boys! It would be indecent for you to see them—"

"In the eyes of a God I no longer put any faith in, perhaps," said Maria. "But no, I will be good, and polite, and ask only if anything has bitten them in these last days. I can be a pious child when I feel the need."

Bronia eyed her dubiously. "I'm coming with you," she said, and the two girls proceeded into the street.

One by one, Maria knocked at the doors her sister had identified, and at each was told that the ailing children *had* been bitten by insects recently, for all that each of them had a cat, and none had been exposed to, or complained of, lice. Then their parents closed the doors and returned to the task of caring for, and fretting over, their ailing offspring. Typhus was a monster that carried children away in the night, and none wanted to believe it could be stalking them.

Bronia watched her sister warily as Maria walked down the street in seeming serenity. "Now where are you going?"

"Fleas don't come from the ether," said Maria. "They must be carried, and for them to be seeking out only children means they must be carried from a place where few adults would go. The boys and Hela all spend time by the fishing pond, down near the mouth of the old sewer, yes?"

"Why do you ask when you know the answer?"

"Because you're more likely to stay with me if you feel included, and I don't want to do this alone." Maria shot her sister a surprisingly vulnerable look. "Zosia played there too. The week before she sickened."

"I remember."

"The doctors said she had taken ill because of lice from our boarder, but they never found any, and none of the rest of us were afflicted. And none of the rest of us spent any time there."

"You think something is attacking them?"

"I think something is wrong and not behaving according to the scientific principles of disease as Dr. John Snow has recorded them; if only those who favor a certain location are afflicted, then something in that location is causing the troubles. It is less illness than exposure to some terrible malevolence."

"So you want to expose *yourself* to it?"

"Not alone."

Bronia was not a timid child. Even so, she preferred to stay close to home to avoid attracting attention or taking needless risks. But she loved her family very well, and she loved her youngest sister most of all, and she was unwilling to let Maria march off into the possibility of danger by herself. "Not alone you either," she said sharply.

Maria smiled. "I thought you'd say that," she said, and they walked on.

The sewers of Warsaw were marvels of architecture, large enough to drain not only sewage but storms safely away from the city, built to last for century upon century. They were meant to be barred off from people, save for those whose job it was to go down into their depths. But "meant" was not always an accurate reflection of reality; every child in the city knew the places where the sewers could be accessed, where a toy lost down a grate might be retrieved if the rains had been heavy enough, or where a frog might be pursued into the shadows and caught in eager hands. One such opening let out near the small fishing pond frequented by the city's children, too small to interest adults, large enough that the occasional carp or eel could be snared.

Maria and Bronia picked their way through the weeds toward the pond's edge, Bronia complaining quietly the whole way, as if her objections could possibly change her sister's mind at this stage.

"Shush," said Maria once, sharply. "This is our sister."

"You can't expect to find something in the water that would make her well again!"

"I'm not looking in the water."

Bronia followed Maria's gaze to the sewer opening and paled.

"Maria, no."

"We must."

"You have no way of—"

"Adults come to the pond. They do not linger. Every child who sickens has been here, by these waters, and however obedient they are to their parents, they have gone at some point into the shadows. There was mud on Zosia's shoes."

Bronia's face softened. "Maria—"

"There was mud on her shoes," repeated Maria, anguished.

"This is still about her? You can't bring her back."

"No, but I might save Hela."

Bronia sighed.

They continued toward the opening into the sewer, toward the dark.

There were footprints in the mud at the sewer's edge. Footprints, and paw prints, and a strange long mark, like someone had dragged a rope along the ground. Maria stepped up, Bronia close behind her. The air inside was cold and clammy, heavy with murk and with the slow rot that came to dark places. Maria continued forward, slow, and cautious.

When the light began to fade behind them, she stopped, and yelled into the echoing channel ahead of them: "I know you're here! Show yourself!"

The sound of her voice rolled down the corridor like a bell, catching on the brick, bouncing through the open space. Bronia caught her breath, moving behind Maria as the sound of something heavy came scraping along the ground. Maria narrowed her eyes.

"There you are," she said. "I don't believe in religion, and I don't believe in God, and I don't believe in *you*, but sometimes when I don't believe a thing, it keeps on existing anyway. I can't disbelieve so hard that it changes the world." There was a challenge in her tone, like she fully expected the world to change on her command one day, when she got older, when she got better at disbelieving.

The scraping sound grew louder until something massive and unspeakable heaved its bulk into the sewer hall. It had more than a dozen heads, each of them with two bright red eyes and a mouth open in a hissing snarl. Its body was made up of smaller bodies piled up on top of each other in a terrible construct of paws, tails, and backs.

And those tails. They were braided together, locked in a terrible knot, impossible to sever, glued into a single unit by filth and feces until they became a single cord connected to the multiplicit singularity of the Rat King the rodents had become.

Bronia screamed.

Maria smiled.

"There you are," she all but cooed. "I heard the stories. We all did. The sickness without a source, the monster that feeds on children, the mouths too small to feed the body they supposedly serve. You need the children. You need their vitality. You need their *lives*. And what you do looks so much like typhus that someone who doesn't know better—someone who was looking before Dr. Snow's studies changed the way we understand such things—would take it for natural disease. You come out to feed only when you need to and when conditions are right. But you made two mistakes."

The Rat King hissed.

"You came to my city."

It dragged itself closer to the two girls.

Maria pulled back her arm and hurled the bottle of bleach, lid already loosened, into the center of the mass. It splashed open on impact, eating away at the shell binding the Rat King's tails together. The Rat King screamed a sound that echoed like thunder in the hallway, bouncing off the walls until it was church bells on Christmas, until it was the wail of a woman whose only child had just died, until it was the end of the world.

Through it all, Maria stood serene, not flinching, even as Bronia wept behind her.

When the Rat King dissolved, a tide of ordinary rats rushed in all directions through the sewer from the place where it had been. Maria exhaled.

"They'll recover now," she said, turning to Bronia. "We can go home."

"How did you—why did you—what did you . . . ?"

"You've heard the stories too. When a thing makes no sense, look to the data people have left behind. If it still makes no sense, the fault is either yours, or the world's. There are too many tales of Rat Kings for them not to have a drop of truth inside them."

"But the bleach . . ."

"A Rat King is born when ordinary rats become bound together by their own waste. They can no longer forage as rats should and so grow dark and terrible and strong in the shadows. Eliminate the waste, eliminate the threat."

Bronia hesitated. "And you're sure the sickness will pass?"

"I am. The stories say it will if someone slays the king." Maria offered her hand. "Hela will be feeling better soon. We should be there when she does."

Bronia took her hand, and the two sisters walked, side by side, out of the dark tunnel that smelled of bleach and decay and back into the light.

MARYA'S Monster

by

ALETHEA KONTIS

Candle in one hand and key in the other, Marya slowly exhaled and steadied herself.

Someone on the sofa giggled.

"Shh, Doina! Marya's trying to concentrate."

Since Kazia was her best friend—and Doina a renowned chatterbox—Marya didn't say it would be far easier to focus without an earful of her scolding. Truth be told, the entire task at hand would have been made simpler had Elżbieta done a better job of removing the wax from the key after taking her turn. Exhaling once more, Marya tipped the candle. A thin stream of hot wax fell straight through the hole in the key and into the bowl of cold water below.

The other three girls all clapped at once.

"Well done, Marya!" Kazia cheered.

"I wish I'd poured half so well," said Elżbieta.

"Hold it up! Hold it up!" Doina chanted. "What do you see?"

Marya set down the key and fished in the bowl for the now-solid wax. She pulled it out of the water and held it up to the light. "It looks like . . . a great lump."

"*Jędza!*" Elżbieta accused sarcastically. "I got the great lump first! How dare you fall in love with my husband."

Marya shrugged. "The spirit of Andrzejki has spoken. Destiny is destiny."

Doina giggled again.

Marya grinned despite herself; Doina's joy was contagious.

"Here, let me see."

Marya turned the candle and lump over to Kazia and grabbed a *pączek* from the tray on the table.

Her best friend moved closer to the wall to better see the shadow cast by the wax. "You know, it almost looks like . . ."

"Nothing," Marya took another bite of fruit pastry. Trying to read patterns in wax was as silly as pretending a cloud was a rabbit. But it was the tradition for young girls to try and catch some clue about their future husband on St. Andrew's Eve, and Kazia's mother had gone to the trouble of inviting a few of Kazia's closest friends to the Blue Palace for the occasion, so Marya played along. Father dismissed such frivolity, but best friends did not come around as often as books and making them was not as easy as passing tests.

" . . . like a wolf," Kazia finished.

Doina's giggle turned to a gasp. "Kazia! Don't even joke about that."

"I'm not joking," said Kazia. "Look. This is the open mouth, right? And this could be the body—"

"Stopstopstop!" Doina waved her arms frantically. "My *babcia* says that on St. Andrew's Eve, wolves can eat anyone they want."

"Can't they anyway?" Elżbieta asked.

"I'm being serious!" Doina's fat brown curls bounced when she huffed. It was tough to take Doina seriously when she looked like a red-faced doll dressed for a tea party and spouted old Romanian wives' tales about wolves. "St. Andrew is the only one who can ward them off. Buni says that on this night, wolves can speak to humans."

Kazia laughed. "Wouldn't that be something?"

"No it would not!" Doina's wide, dark eyes seemed genuinely concerned. "Anyone who hears a wolf speak will die! Right there on the spot!"

Marya took the wax back from Kazia. "It still just looks like a lump to me," she said calmly. "But I promise, if my future husband turns out to be a wolf, I will run the other way."

"Or chop his head off," said Kazia.

"Or both!" Elżbieta shouted, and the room dissolved into giggles again.

Doina doubled over, arms wrapped around her stomach as she laughed. "I would be so scared!"

"Not our Marya," Kazia said proudly. "She's not afraid of anything."

Elżbieta held up a *pączek*. "Marya the Unafraid!"

Doina held up a piece of cheese. "Marya the Mighty!"

Kazia lifted her teacup. "Marya the Brave!"

Marya held her teacup aloft in solidarity. Her friends called her these things when all she had done was continue to breathe when others—her sister, her mother—had not. They didn't know that a Great Sorrow had moved into Marya's body and set up residence. But here in this salon, surrounded by laughing friends, Marya almost believed that one day she could defeat it.

Frivolous or not, it was a pleasant evening. Marya treasured her time with Kazia. She also treasured the walk home. After saying good night, she wandered the Saxon Gardens for a while. The quiet dark was a balm to her soul, unlike the constant din of the boarding school Father had made of their house.

The garden's patterned plots were bare of flowers, and the fountains were still, but the air was crisp and misty. She could make out no stars, but a crescent moon shone brightly through the haze. Shadow limbs of bare trees stretched out at her feet, and the statues looked down from high on their plinths.

The Russians had removed many works of art from Warsaw over the years, but they'd left the Saxon Gardens' sandstone muses. These great women towered over pedestrians, bearing books, snakes, cups, and globes. Marya moved so that, on the path, it looked as if she held the shadow hand of the nearest statue. She could almost imagine this goddess was her mother: beautiful and benevolent, a paragon of learning. Now equally as untouchable. And cold.

A darkness swept over her that had nothing to do with the night. Tears threatened her eyes. Marya snapped her hand away and hurried down the gaslit streets toward home. Marya Skłodowska wasn't afraid of anything, but she refused to let the goddesses—or Mama—see her cry.

She slipped into the boisterous house without a word to anyone; she'd been social enough this evening. None of her sisters were in their shared bedroom. Marya lit only one small candle as she changed out of her good skirt and into her nightdress. As she approached the bed, she realized that hiding under the sheets wouldn't work for long. Bronya and Hela would join her all too soon.

Right now Marya needed a place to herself where she could feel her feelings, however inappropriate. There always seemed to be a proper time and place for emotions, and she had the bad luck of always having them at the wrong times and in the wrong places. She regretted coming home from the gardens so quickly. Between her siblings and the students father boarded in order to make ends meet, there wasn't much solitude to be had here. Without another thought, she grabbed the threadbare blanket from the chair in the corner, blew out the candle, and slid under the bed.

There was room beneath the slats for her to lay her head on a bit of the blanket and cover herself with the rest; she hadn't grown much since Mama died. Hela was the only other one who might have been small enough to join her here, but Hela still believed that monsters lived under beds. So much the better for Marya.

She sneezed, a rare thing in this oft-used hiding place. She curled into a ball and sneezed again into her blanket, a squeak, almost as if she was asking a question.

Somewhere in the shadows between her and the wall, a growl answered.

Marya froze. She suspected there had been a mouse under the bed once, but never anything large enough to growl. Had Father taken in a new lodger with a pet? Not that he would have allowed such a thing; he could barely afford to feed the human mouths beneath this roof. Well, she might be small, but she was a great deal larger than a mouse. To a mouse, she was a veritable sandstone muse. She shot out a foot to kick the wall—anything in front of or behind it should promptly scurry away with the thud.

Her foot collided with something long before it reached the wall.

There was no thud, only another low growl and two glowing yellow eyes that appeared in front of her face.

The blood in Marya's veins turned to ice. The fine hairs all over her body stood at attention. But she refused to show fear. Instead, she closed her own eyes for a moment, not trusting them, and let her other senses tell her what shared the space with her. The growl was deep, as if it had come from a large chest. But how large a chest could fit beneath this bed? Whatever her foot had hit felt like muscle and sinew over bone, and possibly fur, like an animal. Her nose agreed with the fur assessment, and she sneezed again. She could hear breathing now, low and slow and warm.

She opened her eyes again, but apart from those yellow irises and black pupils, there was nothing but darkness. Marya parted her lips in an attempt to speak, but nothing emerged. She closed her mouth, took a deep breath, and tried again. "Are you a wolf?" she whispered.

Another low growl answered her. The rumble echoed in her chest. She closed her eyes once more, knowing what she wanted to say next. If Doina's *babcia* was to be believed, when she spoke, there would be no more school and no more books. No more statues in the gardens or *pączki* by the fire. No more of Kazia's scolding or Elżbieta's goading. No more Tata or Józio or Bronya or Hela. No more cold or hot or dust or sneezing or breath. A tear slid down her cheek. But soon there would be no more tears. No more Great Sorrow. No more hiding. No more Marya.

She would be with her mother again, able to hug her, hold her, and learn from her. Marya had once offered her life up to God in exchange for her mother's, but God had ignored her. Foolish, illogical God. Perhaps this wolf would not do the same. Could not.

"If you are a wolf, I order you to speak to me," Marya said, her voice unwavering. "I am ready to die." She clenched her fists so tightly that her fingernails bit into her palms. Apparently, not all of her was ready to die right here on the spot, but the wolf didn't need to know that.

This time there was not a growl, but a huff. "I am no wolf."

What struck Marya first was not the flash of teeth or the haunting words that resonated in her bones. "You speak Polish?"

Another huff. "It seems I do."

"We're not even allowed to speak Polish at school," she explained. "It's against the rules."

The words this time were accompanied by more of a grumble. "Such rules do not apply to me."

But other rules did? Marya held her tongue before it carried her away, but questions flooded her mind at breakneck speed. *What manner of man or beast was this?* (She chose "man" based on the timbre of his voice, but even that was suspect.) *How did he come to be here? And if he didn't intend to attack or kill her, what did he want?*

The next round of thoughts that flew into her brain like a murmuration of starlings were scenes from the books Father read to them every week and the twisted Romanian tales from Doina's precious *babcia*.

"Are you a prince?" asked Marya the Mighty. "There's an old Polish tale of a monster who tried to scare a girl, but he was really a prince in disguise."

"So you want my castle and throne of gold?"

"Bah. I don't care about being rich; I care about being smart." Marya focused on those eyes. "Tell me what you are, then."

Two huffs. "I am no prince. Just a monster here to scare you."

"I am not scared of you," said Marya the Unafraid.

"Then I have two more nights in which to try," said the monster.

Marya noted this as one rule he did have to follow. "And if you do not succeed?"

"I will go away forever."

This part did sound like the fairy tale. The heroine had to remain fearless for three nights; a test Marya could easily pass. But . . . "What about tonight? Will you go away now too?"

"I will if you want," said the monster. "Do you want me to go away?"

"No," said Marya the Brave.

The answer neither of them had been expecting lay in the darkness between them. He closed his bright eyes, returning Marya to the solitude she was no longer sure she wanted. Marya tried to get a sense of him without reaching out. Had he vanished? Well, if he was still with her, perhaps he would respond. "Define monster. What are you, *exactly*?"

The glowing yellow orbs returned. "I am nothing."

This time, Marya huffed. "You are definitely something."

"Then I am a something."

Marya laughed, the very opposite of the monster's goal. She felt a little bad about that. "My sister Bronya is always saying she wants to be 'something' when she grows up. Maybe she will grow up to be a something like you."

A brow furrowed over the yellow eyes, angling them in a sinister way. "Monsters do not grow up or down. We just are. Or we are not."

He hadn't liked her question. Marya hid her discomfort by adjusting the blanket beneath her head. Her fists were not clenched anymore, nor was her chest as tight. The monster's presence had erased the chill from the hard floor. Even the glow of his eyes didn't seem as menacing as it once had. Perhaps she had imagined that feeling. Minds were powerful things, especially hers. Perhaps she was imagining all of this. But even if she were, here under this bed right now was the safest she'd felt in so long. She didn't want to think about it.

Marya took in a long, slow breath because she could and tried to recall what one said to new people when one wanted to be liked. She didn't know why she wanted the monster to like her, but she did all the same. "Where are you from?"

"I am from the darkness, and to the darkness I shall return."

"What is it like there?"

"Darkness is darkness."

Ugh, he was worse than Elżbieta. "But what do you *do* there?" Marya persisted. "What do monsters do when they're not scaring people?"

"It is always dark somewhere," the monster said dryly. "There is no peace for the wicked."

She blinked at the familiar phrase. Surely he wasn't trying to make her smile? Marya smiled anyway. An overabundance of work was definitely something she knew about. "Life isn't easy, is it? For humans or monsters."

The responding huff was almost a laugh. When he spoke again, it sounded like he, too, was grinning. "Tell me what scares you, brave girl, if I do not."

Marya shrugged. Could he see the gesture? Would he know what it meant? "I would say 'changing schools,' but I did that. I would say 'the

Russians,' but my new school is Russian. I would say losing a sister, but I've already lost one. I would have said losing Mama, but . . ." Her voice betrayed her, and she was unable to finish the sentence.

"Does it frighten you to think of her?"

"Not fear," Marya answered when she was able. "Only sorrow. The greatest sorrow." By the time she had collected herself, she'd thought of a better answer. "Books, maybe."

"You are afraid of books?"

"I would be afraid of losing books. Or not being able to learn from books. That would be a truly horrible thing."

The monster snorted, unconvinced. "You speak of trauma. True fear is the bleak unknowing, the worst imagining, the chill so deep that it is impossible to dispel. I thought I smelled it upon you at first, but only for a moment. And then it was gone."

Despite his eloquent description, Marya was stuck on the very idea that she had answered such a simple question incorrectly. "What is it that scares you, then?"

"Brave girls," said the monster.

"My apologies," Marya said politely.

The monster huffed. He didn't seem terribly disappointed. "There will be other nights. Two, at least. I will learn you, brave girl, as you learn your books. And then I will know."

"Looking forward to it," Marya said earnestly. Because she did. She was just as intrigued as the monster to see if he would, indeed, succeed in scaring her. But for now, they talked. They shared. They learned each other. In low tones, Marya and the monster exchanged information into the wee hours of the night. If her sisters came to bed, she did not notice. And if she fell asleep talking to the monster, she did not remember it.

"There you are, Marya."

Marya opened her eyes. Enough daylight streamed through the small window to reveal the empty floor on which she woke, the threadbare blanket that barely covered her, and the plaster wall beyond. She turned and saw Hela's face hanging upside-down over the edge of the bed.

"Breakfast?"

Marya nodded and slid back into the room to dress. Her sisters always found her hiding places, but they never mentioned them otherwise and never asked why she hid. Marya considered that omission a gesture of love, and she appreciated it.

It was Bronya's turn to present a subject to the house today; after breakfast she gave a very interesting talk on moths and butterflies. As a special treat, Father had prepared slides of butterfly wings to examine under the microscope. The stained-glass rainbow of colors awaiting them illustrated the impressive geometry of nature.

Mikołaj, one of the newer boarders, spoke in the afternoon about dispersive prisms and the various wavelengths of the visible and non-visible spectrum. Whenever he got things wrong, Father gently corrected him before encouraging him to continue.

Marya was so engrossed by the subjects that she completely forgot about her monster until later that night, when Father was reading to them, as he did every Saturday. It was one of her favorites: *A Tale of Two Cities* by Charles Dickens. She curled on the floor at Bronya's feet and soaked up every sentence.

"'A dream, all a dream,'" Father read, "'that ends in nothing, and leaves the sleeper where he lay down . . .'"

As if the words were a spell broken, Marya snapped to attention. The entire conversation with the monster sprang back into her head, fully formed.

"Maniusia, are you all right?"

She scanned the roomful of disturbed faces: some startled, some annoyed. And now Marya was annoyed. Once again she had experienced an emotion without considering first if it was proper. Quickly, she clapped her hand to her calf.

"A cramp, Tata," she lied. "Excuse the interruption. Please continue."

He did, but Marya only half listened to the story. Had her monster been a dream? They had apparently talked well into the night. Surely her sisters would have said something? But her sisters never said anything when they found her hiding.

The recollection was so vivid, though. Too vivid. She could almost feel his breath and hear his voice. Her nose tickled at the memory of his fur. And the yellow glow of his eyes . . . It had to be real. There was one way to find out for sure.

As her sisters climbed into their bed that night, Marya grabbed the threadbare blanket once more and slid into the space beneath the mattress.

"Marya, are you sure?" Hela whispered. "There could be monsters."

"That's what I'm hoping," Marya answered.

Bronya sighed before blowing out the candle, leaving them all to the silent dark.

Marya waited. And waited. The floor remained cold and unforgiving. No smell but dust and wood met her nostrils. She peered into the blackness until her head hurt, but there were no glowing eyes. She tried to quiet her own breathing enough so that she might detect another's, but all she heard were her sisters' steady exhalations and the pounding of her own heart.

Eventually, even that excited beat slowed. She closed her tired eyes and relaxed her disappointed bones. Perhaps it had been a dream. Well, real or imagined, it had been nice to make a new friend.

She woke to the feel of scales sliding over the back of her hand.

Marya flinched.

She quickly flipped her hand over to capture the offending reptile.

"A-ha!" she cried in triumph and then clapped her free hand over her mouth, mindful of her slumbering sisters. She smiled behind her fingers at the two eyes now glowing in front of her. They seemed rounder tonight, maybe smaller, but no less yellow.

"Greetings," said the monster.

Marya managed to stifle her giggles before responding. "Congratulations! You scared me! Aren't you excited?"

The snakelike thing slipped out of her grasp. "I startled you. Surprise is not true fear."

Marya sighed. "I suppose so."

"You are not afraid of snakes either?"

"Nothing in life is to be feared," said Marya. "It's only to be understood. I knew what touched me couldn't be an actual snake—at least, not a poisonous one—so I wasn't afraid."

His huff was higher pitched this evening. "Is that so?"

"Zigzag vipers are diurnal and live in the forest," Marya quoted from a presentation Józio had given this spring. "It would be exceedingly rare to find one in a house in the city. At night. In late November."

"You continue to impress me, brave girl."

"And you continue to baffle me," said Marya. "I thought you had fur. But you have tentacles?"

"Indeed," said the monster. "Last night I had fur, fangs, and cloven hooves. Tonight I wear snake fingers and a beak."

That explained the change in his voice. And the shape of his smaller eyes, more like a hawk's than a wolf's. "Do you have claws on your feet?"

"Yes."

"Lucky. If I had claws I would use them to keep people away from me. Like the horrible Russian inspectors at school." And then something else occurred to her. "Do you wear shoes?"

"No shoes made would accommodate me."

"I bet my mother could have made you some. She enjoyed making shoes. You would have been quite a challenge." Marya felt the familiar pressure behind her eyes and quickly pulled away from that train of thought. "So you have the ability to change your shape—a thing I must believe, since I can't actually see you."

"The darkness chooses."

"Right. And you are a monster of darkness."

"As I have said."

That still didn't satisfy Marya. "But does that mean you live in darkness, or that you are made of darkness?"

"Both."

"But if you are made of darkness, how does light emanate from within you? I see it in your eyes."

"Perhaps I am a radiant darkness."

Marya pondered that. Darkness was, technically, the absence of light. As they'd discussed today, just because something couldn't be perceived by the human eye didn't mean it did not possess energy. The monster definitely possessed energy. It breathed. It gave off heat, granted, not as much tonight as last night. It was scientifically feasible that his body's energy simply fell within the nonvisible spectrum. Probably infrared. With the exception of his eyes.

Fascinating.

Marya decided if he was going to continue to risk visiting the human world, he should possess all the facts. "Your coming here might be dangerous. Dark things have a bad reputation in our world, you know. And monsters. Especially monsters under the bed."

"But you don't believe such things."

"Hela does." Marya pointed to the mattress above them. "My sister. She always said there were monsters under the bed. If I remember you tomorrow, I will tell her she's right. I didn't remember you today. Not for a long while. Almost not at all."

"Would you like to remember?"

That was an option? "Yes. Of course."

A tentacle started to slide back over her palm, and then halted. "Humans aren't meant to remember true fear. Or pain."

Odd that a monster would spout such a notion. Marya would forever remember losing her mother, and it would always hurt. "Ridiculous. Our meetings aren't either of those things."

"As you say." The monster finished wrapping his tentacle around her hand. "There."

If something passed between them, Marya didn't feel it. But she couldn't see the monster either, so she continued not to trust her limited human perceptions. "Thank you."

As before, Marya and the monster talked long into the night. As before, Marya woke up on the empty floor. But unlike the night previous, Marya remembered her lively, engrossing conversation with the monster. Her monster. Her friend in the darkness. She looked forward to their next meeting, even if it would be their last. It was almost a shame that she was so terribly brave.

She slid out from under the bed and stretched in the dim light. Bronya and Hela were still sound asleep. Taking advantage of the not-quite-dawn, she went to wash herself before the rest of the house arose. As she crossed back through the foyer, she spotted a flutter of movement outside the door. She took a coat off one of the pegs—it didn't matter whose—and pulled it on over her nightdress. She slid her bare feet into a couple of boots and joined her father on the front stoop.

He looked slightly haggard and definitely not fully alert, but she loved him all the same. Steam rose from his mug. Together they watched a hint of pink paint the sky above the roof next door. Few other souls bustled in the street: a smattering of birds warming up for the dawn chorus and a handful of humans whose daily duties would never be finished if they didn't get an early start.

Her body still warm from the house, Marya took a deep breath through her nose. The sparkling chill slowly woke up her brain.

"Ah, Maniusia. Happy December, *słoneczko*."

She sucked another deep breath into her lungs. It tasted like frost. "Happy December, Tata."

"Snow is coming." He sipped his coffee. "Do you think we should go for a walk today?"

"Yes." She watched the fog of her breath escape her body and wondered if the monsters would do the same. "That sounds like a very good idea."

That day's lesson took them to the wilderness of the Mazovian Forest, all the way to the monastery, but not as far as the Russian barracks. Marya often forgot that Warsaw had a primeval forest in its city center. Today, beneath the bright blue December sky, she reveled in the wildness of the bare oak limbs and the still-green pines.

As they wandered, Father pointed out the different species of trees. He outlined their characteristics, benefits, and possible dangers. He talked about the life cycle of the forest, and how a human might forage off the land in different seasons.

After a picnic lunch, Józio gave a presentation about the types of clouds and the stages of a thunderstorm. Father went on a tangent about how it was once thought that ringing church bells and shooting cannons into the sky would disrupt the most violent storms. As silly as that sounded, contemporary scientific communities—Austria, in particular—were starting to discuss these topics again in earnest.

Marya soaked it all up. Every sight, every sound, every smell, every word. She couldn't wait to tell the monster everything.

Later that night, under the bed, she did.

He did not have two eyes this time, but eight: two larger eyes in the middle and four along the bottom, with two medium eyes on top and farther back. They were all black instead of yellow, but they flashed, as if reflecting an invisible source of light. She recognized the pattern at once.

"You are a wolf spider!"

"It appears I am."

"And an excessively large wolf spider at that. Doina would be screaming her head off right now."

"But you are not."

"I'm sorry to say. Your eyes are fascinating! I'm not even sure which set I should be addressing."

"The middle ones will do. Now, what did you learn today?"

Marya took a deep breath, and then told him every moment she could remember about the day.

He hung on every word. He asked about the trees and the forest and the clouds and, "Snow. Tell me about snow."

"It's what happens when it's so cold that water molecules in the clouds crystallize. Hexagonal-shaped crystals every single time, but no two the same. Then they fall from the sky like rain, but if the ground is also frozen, they don't melt. They stack up and up and up . . . sometimes higher than my ankles. Sometimes higher than my head! The first morning after a fresh snow is the best. The world looks like it's been covered in a pristine blanket of white as far as the eye can see and it is so, so quiet."

"Is it bright?"

"Yes! The sun can make it bright enough to blind you. Everything is beautiful and peaceful. For a little while, anyway." Humans always brought chaos into the equation. Marya figured that monsters did too.

"Magnificent," said the monster. "Tell me more about your human world. In my darkness, there is nothing like this light you speak of."

She'd already told him about the Saxon Gardens and the Blue Palace. She'd told him about the forest, the square, and even the church they used to visit with Mama. After three nights, she'd reached the extent of her experience. "I really don't go very far outside this house and school," she admitted.

"Oh, but you must," the monster said excitedly. "I would hate to think I was leaving you to hide under this bed forever."

He sounded like Mama. She felt that familiar pressure behind her eyes again. She chose to ignore it. "Where will you go?"

"I will become darkness once more. It is said that when the need for a monster next arises, I will be remade into a new form."

"'It is said?' Don't you know?"

"No," the monster answered. "Even if it is true, we never remember anything about who we were before. We only know who we are in the moment."

"And this night with me is our third night. Your last moment." Marya remembered this ache in her chest all too well.

"Yes, brave girl."

"You are dying."

"I don't mind," said the monster. "I do not fear death."

"Nor do I." Marya did not beg this time, but she still asked, "Take me with you?"

"I cannot," said the monster. "But death is only darkness. I am darkness. I do not fear what I am."

"Perhaps I should fear what I am," said Marya. "I could not save my mother, and I cannot save you."

"Dear, brave girl," said the monster. "Perhaps you should save *you*."

Marya snorted. "And how do you propose I do that?"

"Live," he encouraged her. "Experience life. See it through the eyes of a star pupil—for you will anyway—but also, look at it for me. Adventure out into your impressive world with its brilliant sky full of clouds and rain and snow. Smell the trees. Watch the butterflies. Count all the colors. Savor the . . .what do you humans eat again?" It was the longest speech the monster had ever given, but his words lacked the vigor they'd once had.

Marya tried to make him laugh. "Porridge. It's not very grand."

The monster ignored the jest, as if he knew his time was limited and he didn't want to waste it. "Savor it anyway. Hear the birds. Feel the joy and the sorrow. See the light . . .but heed the shadows. You now know there is radiance in the darkness."

Those last quiet words rang in her ears. His reflective eyes flickered. Marya stared into them, wanting to hold his hand, or even a segmented leg, but she was too afraid to ask.

"Are you scared?" asked the monster. "I am fading. I can't tell."

"Not truly." Marya could have said yes, but she didn't want the last words between them to be a lie. "I am not scared; I am sad. Why does everyone keep leaving me?"

"Because everyone leaves," said the monster. "That is the way of all worlds. And clouds. And butterflies."

And humans. "But I don't want to be alone."

"Come, now. You may feel lonely sometimes, but you are never truly alone. You told me about all the noise. And your family. And Kazia. And school. And Polish." The monster's huff was but a slight breeze. "And there will always be darkness."

Marya wiped her nose on the damp blanket. "It is always dark somewhere."

"Tell yourself that I am always in the darkness with you."

Her chuckle was as hollow as her heart. "No peace for the wicked."

"Or the brave." The reflections in his eyes faded now, first the four at the bottom, then the two at the top, and then the eyes in the middle. His last words were a whisper. "Brave girl."

Marya had nothing to say to that. There were no words left. She just continued to breathe while he did not. And then she was alone. In the dark with no one but herself. All alone.

Her truest fear.

The Great Sorrow roared inside her and erupted into the darkness.

Her gasping sobs came so fast she struggled for breath. At the same time, she wished the pounding in her heart and head would cease to be so she didn't have to feel endless wave after wave of pain. If only the monster could see her now, his brave girl drowning in fear, he could have stayed. The third night wasn't technically over yet!

But the only way for Marya to feel fear, truly feel it, was if the monster made her care about him . . . and then left.

Her guts spasmed. Her next outburst was not a cry, but a laugh. She wondered if he knew. But of course he did. He was the darkness. Fear was his job.

"You win," Marya whispered into the night. Then she turned her face into the blanket and relived the pain all over again.

Daylight.

Marya blinked her eyes in the bright room. She was still on the floor, but no longer under the bed. There was a pillow under her head. Her sisters lay on either side of her. A soft blanket covered them all.

The body on the right stirred.

"Ow," said Hela.

The one on the left stretched.

"No more sleeping under the bed," said Bronya.

"All right," said Marya the Not Alone. The emptiness in her chest ached as she counted all the things she still had. Her sisters and brother and father and everything else. And the darkness. And the light.

"It's awfully chilly in here, don't you think?" Bronya asked casually. "And brighter than usual."

Hela lifted the curtain and peeked out the frosted window. "It snowed last night."

Marya finished pulling on her dress and ran out of the bedroom. She stuck her feet into two random boots and flew out the door.

The world was white and quiet and peaceful, exactly like she'd described to her monster of darkness. The sight of the fresh blanket. The smell of frost. The chill in her fingers began to seep up her arms. The bite of cold air in her nostrils. She stuck out her tongue, hoping for an errant flake to slide down her throat as it melted.

She flung her arms out wide, soaking up the moment, lighting up all the darkness inside her. Her tears were warm as they streamed down her cheeks and fell into the snow.

Footsteps approached from the house, slow and heavy.

Marya turned and took in the sight of the beautiful father she loved. His hair was rumpled, and he wore a coat, though the shirt beneath it looked to have been donned inside out. He held a shawl over one arm, though he did not offer it.

"Maniusia?"

"Oh, Tata," she pronounced into a sky almost as white as the ground, "I miss Mama."

"Oh, *słoneczko*." He took her hand and tilted his face up to the brilliant sky, "Me too."

And together they basked in the beauty of that bright and shining world.

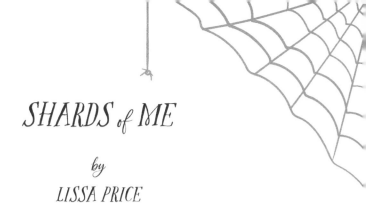

SHARDS of ME

by

LISSA PRICE

I never could have imagined the feeling of being invisible.

No matter how much I screamed, no one could hear or see me. Instead, they stared through me, their eyes settling on everything behind my back: the bookcase, my father's cabinet of scientific instruments, the faded floral wallpaper. All because of that horrid girl.

She'd planned it all from the start.

The first time I saw her, I was walking to the gymnasium alone. I went through Warsaw's Saxon Square filled with Russian soldiers, my daily reminder that my beloved Poland was under their control. I came out to Krolewska Street when I saw a girl my age in a scuffle with two Russian boys—one tall, one well-fed. They had grabbed her schoolbag and were tossing it to each other like a ball. She ran back and forth trying to catch it, her long braid swinging. But they were one step ahead, laughing and taunting her. She locked eyes with me, pleading for help.

The taller boy slung the bag on his shoulder as I ran over.

"Give it back," I shouted at him.

Passing shoppers turned to look. A shopkeeper came out of his store. But no one wanted to say anything once they saw the Russian soldiers on the other side of the street. The girl must have been encouraged by my support because she leapt onto the back of the plump boy, clinging like an angry monkey. She covered his eyes and dug her heels into him where it hurt the most. He flailed and tugged at her arms, but she hung on.

The tall boy turned and yanked her braid so hard she screamed. He grabbed her arm, trying to pull her off his friend. More bystanders gathered to gawk in silence. I ran up behind the tall boy and pounded my fists on his back.

"Let her go," I shouted.

He was so much taller than I was, so I used his height against him. I bent down and slipped my book bag strap around his feet, hooking his ankles, and pulled hard. He fell to the ground, and I snatched the bag before he could get up. The small crowd smirked at him sitting there, red-faced.

The girl slid off his friend's back, falling to the ground.

For a moment, both boys stared at us, as if considering their next move. I shook my head.

"Go," I said under my breath.

The crowd, now braver, opened up a path for them to leave, and the boys slinked away. As everyone dispersed, several people gave me small nods of approval. The soldiers across the street went back to their business.

I reached out my hands to the girl, lifted her to her feet, and returned the book bag.

She clutched it to her chest. "Thank you for helping me. What's your name?"

"Marya."

"I'm Anna." She brushed the dirt off her knees.

"First day at Gymnasium Number Three?" I rolled my eyes as I always did when saying the full name of our school.

She nodded. With her light brown braid and her accent, I guessed she was German.

"We better hurry, or we'll be late," I said.

As we walked, I learned that Anna had just moved here with her father. I wondered if her mother was no longer alive, like mine.

At lunch, I saw Anna sitting alone, unwrapping her bread and sausage. I left my friends to sit by her.

She showed me a bruise on her arm from that morning.

"Bet his are bigger and blacker," I said.

"My father warned me about . . . bullies."

"They're cowards." I offered her apple slices, and she took one. "What does your father do?"

"He's a scientist. Chemist."

"Oh, we have something in common. Mine's also a scientist. He teaches physics."

"Does he have a laboratory?"

A sore spot in my family. "No." I braved a smile. "But he has a wonderful collection of instruments kept in a cabinet. He takes them out sometimes to demonstrate to my sisters and brother and me."

I didn't mention that he could no longer bring them to class because the Russians had forbidden laboratory instruction. No idea why. Were they afraid the students would create some kind of bomb? Sometimes I would catch him looking at his cabinet with wistful eyes.

"My father brought his laboratory here," she said with pride. "He set it up in our house."

"Shhh." I leaned in closer so she could hear me whisper. "Don't say that out loud. You must keep it secret."

She smiled as if I were a small child and reached out to touch my hair.

"It's so . . ." she seemed to struggle for words.

"Untamable, I know. The home economics teacher is always after me, raking it so hard she leaves more on the brush than on my head." I ran my hand over my hair in a weak attempt to smooth it.

She took my wrist to stop me. "I think it's beautiful."

How could she admire my bristly hair when hers was so shiny and long? I wondered if her father had braided it for her.

She must have noticed how my eyes lit up when she mentioned her father's lab because of what she said next.

"Would you like to come over tomorrow and see the laboratory?"

When I met Anna outside the gymnasium the next day, she'd changed her hair. Instead of the beautiful long braid, it was now several inches shorter, my length. It looked like she might have curled it with rags and then brushed it out to get the bushy effect. I was stuck with such difficult hair—really, it's like lamb's wool—but it appeared as if she'd made an effort to make hers unruly. Like mine.

I didn't say anything about it, although I thought it strange.

When we got to her house, she led me to the side gate where she unlocked a cellar door.

"Be careful not to hit your head." She nodded toward the low ceiling as she lit a lamp and led me down the steps.

"Is your father home?"

"He's off visiting my aunt in the country," she said with an odd, low voice.

Her foreboding tone made me pause on the stairs.

"Come on, Marya, I'm just playing."

When we reached the bottom, I only saw a small, bare space with a few boxes stacked in the corner. *Maybe the scientific instruments were packed away?* She paused and stared at me, as if waiting for my reaction.

I didn't want to hurt her feelings. What could I say? "It's nice."

She poked me in the side. "Silly. It's back here." She lit a second lamp and handed it to me.

She opened a door, and we stepped inside a room so large that our two lamps couldn't light it all. But in the golden glow I could see it was filled with tables laden with the most marvelous scientific apparatus. The lamps projected their shadows on the walls, hinting at a potential far beyond their scale. I recognized some of the instruments from my father's cabinet: a balance of course, a Coddington lens, and a Culpeper-type microscope. But there were so many more here that I'd never seen, not even in books. Some looked like Medieval torture devices. I moved slowly with the hungry eyes of a shopper at the thieves' market, amazed by this extensive collection. And it was clear from the various stains and partially filled beakers that her father was using them. I felt so mesmerized—what was all this for?—that I almost knocked over one of the glass beakers with my lamp.

Anna prevented the collision, deftly plucking the lamp from my hand and hanging it on a wall hook. I stopped at one table at the end of the row. It was covered with sketches of birds and butterflies—all in pairs. I picked up one drawing for a closer inspection. Arrows pointed from one bird to the other, same with the butterfly. Words scribbled under the arrows were written with such a frantic hand that they were illegible.

"What does this say?" I asked her.

She was too busy moving a box at the rear of the table to answer. Behind the box were two small mesh cages, each one labeled with the specimen inside. One held a common large moth, and the other had a butterfly.

"Purple Emperor," she looked at the butterfly. "Isn't it pretty?"

"Beautiful. But didn't you say he was a chemist, not a biologist?"

She gave a little smile. "Let me demonstrate."

In the corner, a long black cloth hung from the ceiling. Anna walked over and pulled off the cloth to reveal a huge glass enclosure, taller than us. A small display table stood in the center with enough space to walk around it. She opened the door, and I noticed it had a rubber seal. She carried the two mesh cases and stepped inside the glass enclosure, setting them down on the table. She pulled an amber bottle out of her pocket and sprinkled drops on the moth as if anointing him. Then she stepped out, closed the door, and lit a burner under a container of green liquid. It bubbled up and squelched until it formed a gas. A hose connected it to the glass box, and soon the green gas began filling it. The butterfly and the moth began flying in circles.

I leaned closer. I knew of a green gas—chlorine—but that had a sharp odor that stung; this one was different. Metallic.

"What is that gas?"

"You'll see. I want to surprise you."

I wondered if she had permission to do this, but I wasn't about to stop the show. As the green gas grew denser, both specimens stopped flying and rested on the bottom, slowly flapping their wings until they stopped completely. At this point, the gas was so thick it was all we could see.

She shut off the flame to the burner.

When the green cloud dissipated, the Purple Emperor butterfly batted his wings. He was fine, except he was now inside the cage labeled MOTH. The cage labeled BUTTERFLY was empty.

"Where did the moth go?" I asked.

Anna picked up a lamp and held it at the side of the glass enclosure. "Look closely."

I leaned in as close as I could without my face pressing the glass. As Anna moved the lamp, a ghost image of the original butterfly appeared, no longer purple but now a shimmery green. The moth had become a duplicate of the butterfly, and the original butterfly was almost invisible.

As I rushed home, having stayed much too late, I kept thinking about what I'd witnessed. Anna wouldn't explain the procedure. She said it was confidential and her father would kill her if she divulged it, especially to another scientist's daughter. She had made me swear not to disclose what I'd seen, although I was dying to tell my sisters and brother.

Her demonstration wasn't proper science. She had no data or calculations—at least none that she was willing to present. I wasn't sure what had actually happened. If it was just a trick, how did she pull it off? I wouldn't rest until I'd figured it out.

I returned to a quiet, dark house. Everyone was already in bed. Good. My father did not wait up. I took off my coat, hung it on the hook, and turned up the one lamp left for me. I went to my father's bookcase, scanned the spines of his science books, and pulled one out. I was sitting at the dining table looking at the index when my father came in, tying his robe over his pajamas.

"Did you have a good time?" he asked.

"Yes, Papa."

He sat beside me. "What are you looking up at this hour?"

"I was just curious."

"About what?"

I knew it would sound silly because I'd have to be vague, but he wouldn't be satisfied until I gave him an answer. "I wanted to see what kind of gas might create an illusion of changing a specimen, say like a moth, into something different, say a butterfly."

He frowned. "Caterpillars change into butterflies, not moths. You know that."

"Yes, of course, but can you imagine any gas that could do this?"

"No." He shook his head. "It cannot be."

"But what if someone saw it?" I didn't mean to blurt it out, but my lips were faster than my brain.

His face grew serious, as if I'd said someone had died. "Then what you saw was not science, but magic. A magic trick. The gas is just to cover their sleight of hand."

That made the most sense. My father was smart, after all, but he wasn't always right. And I wanted details. I would have to see for myself.

The next day I was back at Anna's house, down in the laboratory. She was going to do the "experiment" again, this time with birds, one canary and one bluebird. I brought the bluebird's cage inside the glass enclosure, and she carried the canary cage and set it on the table.

She turned away, but I saw her drink from a small bottle before slipping it back in her pocket.

"There. We're set," she said.

Standing inside the enclosure, I noticed the glass that appeared clear from the outside had a shiny reflection on the inside, like a mirror. While I was looking at that, Anna had closed the door behind us, and green gas was now spewing in.

"Anna." I pointed to the gas coming in.

She smiled and nodded.

"What are you doing?" I asked.

"You'll see."

With my next breath, I inhaled the metallic-smelling gas. My nostrils began to burn, and the pain traveled up, shooting right to my head. My throat felt like sandpaper, and when I coughed, it intensified. I pushed past Anna to get to the door, but when I put my hand on the release lever to get out, I found it frozen. She must have locked it.

I tried to speak, but my tongue was numb.

My stomach burned as if my guts had melted and were traveling through my body, leaving a hollow tingling. A wave of dizziness came over me and blurred my vision. I opened my mouth to scream, but the green gas rushed in, gagging me. The last thing I remembered were her hands catching me as I fell to the floor.

When I came to, still on the floor of the glass box, the birdcages were gone. And so was Anna. The glass door was wide open.

At home, I ran into the living room where my father was reading *Master Thaddeus* to my sisters and brother.

"I'm sorry, I'm late. I couldn't help it, this girl—"

But no one was listening to me. My father continued to read as if I weren't there. Across the room, a face leaned out from behind my sister Hela.

My face.

I ran over. Sitting on the floor between Hela and my brother was a girl who looked exactly like me. My father never stopped reading, and the family continued to listen, their eyes dreamy with poetry as if I weren't there at all. And as if there weren't two Maryas in the room.

I spoke to the impostor. "What is this trick?"

But she refused to look at me. Or could she not see me?

I knelt in front of my brother. "Jozef, what's going on?" But he also refused to look at me.

My heart leaped as his eyes darted, then landed on mine. He did see me. But then he exhaled, and I noticed his eyes weren't focused on me after all but on my father in the chair behind me. That's why he wasn't responding. I realized with a shudder, that he was staring through me.

"Hela? Father?"

I couldn't get through to any of them. And the impostor me didn't appear to see or hear me either, no matter how loud I yelled or waved my arms. *How could this be?*

It occurred to me that this was like a game we'd played in the past, where one person is "out" and everyone ignored them. If only it were that simple. No, there was a duplicate of me sitting in my house, and nobody recognized my presence. As I stood, facing the mirror, I saw the answer—when I looked down at my hand, it was translucent with the faintest green shimmer like a soap bubble. Someone coughed, drawing my attention. It was the impostor Marya; she winked at me. I was sure of it. I reached down to grab her shoulder, but my fingers went right through her.

I was the butterfly. And she was the moth who became the butterfly. And now I was as good as a ghost.

Father finished the chapter and closed the book. Everyone got up and moved into the kitchen or to bed. It was just the two of us left.

"Hello, Marya," she said in a voice too quiet for anyone to hear from the other rooms.

To my ears, she still sounded like Anna.

"What've you done?"

She admired herself in the mirror. "Now I don't have to try to copy your hair. I have it."

I moved closer until my face was inches from hers. She was my exact double, even had my gray eyes.

"How did you do it? What did you drink?"

"You mean the binder? Sweet little Marya, always with the scientific mind. I could toss all sorts of scientific terms at you, but let's just say it was magic."

Father popped into the room. "Shouldn't you be in bed now?" he said to Anna.

"Of course, Papa." She pranced over to him and threw her arms around him and kissed both his cheeks. "I'm the luckiest girl in the world to have you as my Papa."

I wanted to throw up.

She took my bed and went to sleep. I sought my father's library for answers, but when I reached for a book, my fingers passed through it. It was so frustrating. How could I solve this if I couldn't have access to information? I was so angry. I swiped at the book and this time it responded by falling off the shelf and landing on the floor—face down. *I'd done it. I moved the book.* It was possible. But I couldn't flip it over, no matter how angry I got. Nor could I make another book fall.

What good was this if I couldn't repeat it?

I must have fallen asleep at some point because the next thing I knew, I woke up on the floor with the morning sun from the window on my face. Maybe this nightmare was over, and Anna would be gone. But as I sat up, I saw my arm, still translucent green.

I hurried outside and caught up to Anna as she walked to gymnasium, helping herself to flowers from private gardens.

"Would you be surprised to learn that I know your past?" She plucked a camellia, sniffed it, and tossed it aside. "Our past."

"You're making that up."

"No, I'm not. I know all about your sister Zosia dying. And your mother. I have the memory in here." She touched her head. "And the sadness here." She pointed to her heart.

"No, you don't."

"I have your body and your brain. Of course, I have your memories. And what's more, I even have glimpses of our future. We become so famous everyone knows our name, traveling all over the world as the most celebrated woman scientist."

I swallowed. "How can you know what I don't?"

"When I transferred into your body, I saw your whole life in an instant."

"What magic is this?"

"I saw everything, all the awards and shiny medals." Her eyes became glassy.

"I don't care about awards."

"Also saw the sadness. Tragedy." Her face looked pained, like she was reliving the experience. "Losing love not once, not twice, but three times."

"Now you sound like a cheap fortune teller."

She stopped walking. "It's so bad. I'm not really sure I want your life."

"Then give it back to me."

I had no idea if Anna saw my future. It sounded ridiculous. She was right about Mother and Zosia, but she could have read that, or heard it, or seen the photographs around the house. She continued to toss out prophecies, and no matter how good they began, they always ended in sadness, betrayal, or death. Even though I didn't have a heart, I could feel it ache. Anna said it was called phantom limb syndrome.

This was the worst. I couldn't go on like this. I vowed to get my body back.

I left her and returned to the house.

I remembered what happened when I moved that book. I needed to learn how to cross the line into reality by moving something physical so that others could see. This sounded easy but proved to be oh-so-difficult. I started with the lightest objects: a piece of thread, a feather, a toothpick—willing them to move with my mind, sending out energy from my hands, green as they were, and harnessing my emotions so I could focus with intensity. I had nothing better to do, so while she was at gymnasium, I put all my time and energy into it. I also tried talking to my father while he slept, to reinforce the message I was going to send to him.

The day came when I could manage to pick up a pencil. And soon after, to write. The first words I wrote were:

Papa, remember the game we used to play . . .

That evening, I watched from the corner of the room as Anna came back from gymnasium. Papa sat in his chair reading the newspaper. Anna greeted him and proceeded to tell him about her day, but he was not looking at her. He put down his paper and stared off into space. She kept trying to get his attention, getting right up to his face, but he was oblivious.

Finally, she screamed out—

"Father, listen to me!"

He stood up and stretched and then started tidying up the room, straightening out the doilies.

It was like she was invisible.

Anna ran outside. I came out a second later.

"They can't see me anymore, Marya."

"Then it must be wearing off." I shrugged; I didn't want to appear eager.

What she didn't know was that my father was just playing the "out" game with her, where everyone must ignore one pre-chosen person. He'd read the note I'd managed to write for him, and he'd played the game brilliantly.

"We have to go back to the laboratory," she said.

"Why would I want to?"

"Because if you don't, I'll burn down your house. With everyone in it."

I saw it in her eyes; she meant it.

I stood inside the glass enclosure at the laboratory. Beside me, Anna pulled out the bottle of serum—the binder she'd used on the moth—and drank it in one swallow. Green gas began to fill the space. Anna's smile faded, replaced by a confused expression. Then she started coughing. I knew what she was experiencing. She had to be feeling like her insides had melted and poured out, leaving her with that hollow, tingling sensation.

"I drank your serum," I said.

Her eyes widened. She looked at the door but saw that I'd locked it. As the gas filled the space, a high-pitched sound squealed. Anna pressed her hands over her ears. As the sound increased, the glass walls vibrated, then shook so violently they couldn't survive. Through the green gas clouds, I saw Anna—still wearing my body—fading to green just as the mirrored glass enclosure cracked and then shattered. One of the flying pieces cut my arm. Time slowed as I caught my reflections in the shards floating in the air, each holding a different piece of me, each with a drop of my blood.

I woke lying on a bed of broken glass. I lifted my head and then my hand. Several cuts, but I was solid flesh again. *I was back.*

Anna was nowhere in sight.

Back at home, nothing felt as good as the warmth of my sisters and father wrapped around me again. They had no idea what really had happened, and that was how it would stay. Now, the question was, what had happened to Anna? I stared out our window to the street for any sign of her. *Would she show up here? What would she do?*

My father pulled me away from the window. He had a gift for me, a plan to send me to the country for a year of relaxing and dancing and wild strawberries. He attributed my strange behavior to stress from studying too hard. I thanked him, and as he hugged me, I could see over his shoulder, Anna standing there, in our house.

She was now a green ghostly shell, but still looked like me. My father must have heard me gasp because he pulled back, then turned to see what I was staring at.

"What is it?" he asked. "What do you see?"

"Me. And me. And me . . ." I said, my voice flat.

Besides Anna, an additional me stood by the divan. And another by the door, and another . . . Seven. Each me looked a little different—one with shorter hair looked familiar. Others were thinner or fuller, or their features slightly off, but they all had that shimmering green translucent quality.

I recalled the reflections in the shards of broken glass. That's where I'd seen those faces. The serum in my blood and the explosion had birthed them. Would they all have the same visions of my future, like Anna, or different ones? What would it take to get rid of them—magic or science? Maybe both.

They gathered around me, touching my hair, my clothes, inspecting me.

Anna leaned over my shoulder. "Smile," she said. "Think what you can do with seven more minds."

Science Note:

In the story, Marya recognized some of the scientific instruments at the laboratory of her new friend's father. The Culpeper microscope was developed in the eighteenth century by Edwin Culpeper, who used a tripod stand and a concave mirror to reflect light. The design was cost-effective, inspiring instrument makers to copy it into the 1890s. In 1829, Henry Coddington designed a handheld magnifier by adapting a lens with a deep groove diaphragm that minimized spherical aberration. His name lives on as the Coddington Magnifier is still used by naturalists.

FIGHT or FLIGHT

by
JO WHITTEMORE

"'Beware the boarder?' That's your advice?" Marya upended the table in her hurry to stand. Divining bones and rubles clattered to the floor.

The fortune teller hissed and crouched to collect them while Marya stormed out the door.

Beware the boarder.

It was true her family housed them, but that advice was far too late.

A boarder had already killed her oldest sister.

Five years ago, he'd brought typhus into their home and stolen away with Zofia's life.

"Marya!" Her sister Hela ran to catch up. "This was meant to be fun!"

"It isn't fun to be fleeced . . . or reminded of death." Marya turned the corner toward their apartment. "We should follow more worthwhile pursuits."

"Like what?" Hela challenged. "The Russians won't let us learn or worship or even speak our own language!"

"Shhh." Marya glanced at two men walking past in red-trimmed *rubakha* shirts. "We can still pursue those things. But quietly."

Despite what Warsaw's citizens told themselves, Poland was a Russian state, and the emperor left no questions about it.

"How can we pursue what we're denied?" Hela pressed.

Marya stopped walking and faced her. "We watch, we listen, and when opportunities arise, we grab them."

Hela nodded slowly. "And would *that* be an opportunity?" She pointed toward their apartment.

A spindly, well-dressed gentleman waited just outside the entrance.

Marya studied him. "Most likely a visitor for Father."

"Or a boarder." Hela arched a brow. "As the fortune teller predicted."

Marya rolled her eyes. "Enough. He doesn't look dangerous or ill."

She'd become adept at spotting typhus victims since Zofia's death: their vacant, half-shut eyes; their unsure footing; how they surreptitiously scratched themselves raw.

But beneath the gentleman's wide-brimmed hat, his hooded blue eyes were wide and alert. His eyebrows occasionally jumped as he studied passersby, but his body remained stock-still.

When Marya and Hela approached, he doffed his hat.

"Good morning," Hela said. "May we help you?"

"Good morning." He bowed. "My name is Ivan Nowak. I've come seeking Władysław Skłodowski. Are you his daughters?"

Marya sifted through memories of her father's associates, but Ivan didn't register.

"We are," she said. "Our father's currently unavailable."

In truth, he was away all weekend.

Ivan clucked his tongue. "Unfortunate. I'd hoped he could recommend one of his students as a laboratory assistant while I'm in Warsaw."

Laboratory assistant.

Marya's heart fluttered. She inched closer to Ivan. "You're a scientist? With your own laboratory?"

He stepped back. "It's . . . more a basement space at a friend's estate." He lifted his chin. "But I will have one when the university sees the success of my project."

Marya sprung onto the tips of her toes. "I'm well-schooled and familiar with laboratory equipment . . . thanks to my father," she added. "I could assist you."

"Really?" Ivan scrutinized her. "Your father *is* highly respected in our field, so I have no doubt he taught you well. Though, your tasks would be mundane. Cleaning equipment, measuring ingredients . . ."

Marya nodded eagerly. "That sounds perfect."

Ivan tilted his head. "All right, Miss—"

"Marya." She opened the front door and motioned him inside. "Please, tell me about your project."

After a moment's hesitation, Ivan entered the apartment. A thunderous rumble shook the rafters, and he shielded his head. "What in heaven's name is that?!"

"That would be our boarders, expecting lunch." Hela pushed past Ivan and Marya and climbed the staircase. "Excuse me."

Ivan eyed the ceiling as more footsteps thundered past. "How many do you *have?*"

Marya smiled. "Only fifteen."

"Sent by their parents?"

"Some," she said. "Others come on their own, hoping to improve their lives."

"They have a strong sense of self-preservation." Ivan nodded approvingly. "It's how mankind perseveres." He held up an index finger. "And it's the heart of my project."

Marya wrinkled her forehead. "How do you mean?"

"Are you familiar with eugenics?" he asked.

Marya squinted thoughtfully. It was a new idea, not taught in school, but she'd read about it in her father's scientific journals. "Breeding animals for the best traits."

"Exactly," Ivan said. "I believe mankind's sense of self-preservation could be transferred via eugenics to endangered animals, like the quagga." His lips set in a grim line. "I fear they will soon be extinct."

"But you can save them?" Marya regarded him, wide-eyed. "That's wonderful! Though, I don't know what a quagga is."

Ivan chuckled. "My friend keeps them at his estate. When you're ready, we can go."

Marya nodded. "I'll tell my sister."

"Erm . . ." Ivan gestured at Marya's clothing. "Perhaps you wish to change into something more suitable?"

She glanced down at her blue frock and then up at him. "Nonsense. Science always finds me suitable."

I'm feeding a half-striped zebra.

Marya wouldn't have believed it if not for the soft muzzle nuzzling her palm. Ivan had driven her to the palatial estate in his carriage, describing the quagga en route, but Marya hadn't spotted any until they reached the barn. There, she found six stabled: two males and four females. Ivan circled a female and jotted in a notebook.

"These are wild animals, but notice how easily I walk among them," he said.

"They don't seem concerned about self-preservation," Marya agreed. "You can change that?"

"Indeed." Ivan patted the mare and approached another. "These two are in early gestation—the perfect time to insert the Nowak serum."

"Nowak?" Marya smiled. "After yourself."

Ivan scoffed and pocketed his notebook. "After my father." He leaned toward Marya. "But it's nice sharing his surname."

She laughed. "How will the serum work?"

"Ah." Ivan wagged a finger. "That is confidential." He hefted a pitchfork of hay from a wheelbarrow and tossed it into the quagga pen. "Now, on to the laboratory."

Marya followed Ivan to the servants' entrance of the manor while studying her surroundings. For such a large property, she'd seen very few people.

"Is the staff here always limited?" she asked.

"An astute observation," Ivan said. "Most are with my friend at his other property. That leaves four tending the grounds and two running the manor."

He opened the servants' door, and Marya stepped inside. The hall between the kitchen and scullery was stuffily warm and smelled of baked bread and bleach.

Ivan paused outside the kitchen. "Should I have the cook prepare lunch? Her *bigos* stew is superb."

Marya's stomach rumbled, but she shook her head. "I'd rather start working. Tea with milk will do."

Ivan grinned. "A greater hunger for science than food. We are of like minds."

He disappeared into the kitchen, and Marya amused herself with the day's newspaper left on a table. She'd just finished reading about a missing girl when Ivan returned with her tea.

"Sad, isn't it?" he nodded at the article. "With that cleft hand, she's probably been kidnapped for a freak show."

Marya frowned. "Sad, indeed . . . that people would consider her a freak." She accepted the teacup, but with the first sip, a rancid smell filled her nostrils, and she spat the liquid out.

Ivan balked. "Are you all right?"

Marya sniffed the tea and winced. The stench reminded her of an animal carcass.

"I think the icebox is failing. The milk's turned."

"Oh." Ivan's eyes widened. "*Oh.*"

To Marya's surprise, he snatched back the cup and hurried to the kitchen. This time, she followed.

The cook was hunched over a prep table, kneading dough. Marya spotted several loaves already baked—enough for dozens of people.

Yet Ivan had said only six were on property.

"Celine! You used the icebox?" Ivan thrust the teacup at the cook.

She scowled and straightened, but quickly relaxed when she noticed Marya behind him. "Is the tea not to your liking, Miss?"

Ivan startled and glanced at Marya who blinked at them both.

"I . . . I don't want to cause trouble," she said.

Ivan froze. Then he laughed.

"You're right! Why fuss over spoiled milk?" He poured Marya a fresh cup of tea. "Come. We've lost enough time."

She eyed him curiously but followed him to the basement. There, two long tables were arranged against opposite walls. Crates and boxes cluttered the left table; on the right, microscopes and Bunsen burners had been placed beside scales, glassware, and a leather-bound notebook.

"On the left are the ingredients you'll need," he said as they descended the stairs. "You'll mix and measure on the other table, according to these notes." He handed Marya the notebook.

She opened it and ran her fingers down the first page, savoring the words and measurements.

Salicylate	*10 grams*
Cocaine	*7 grams*
Digitalis	*2 milligrams*

Ivan cleared his throat. "My testing is elsewhere in the manor, but before I leave, I'd like to watch you handle the first ingredient." He winked. "To ensure you're truly qualified."

"Of course!" Marya said and, in two minutes' time, handed him a pipette of salicylate.

"Excellent," he said upon inspection. "I'll return for the other pipettes in an hour."

Marya pulled out her pocket watch. "I'll be ready."

"Then off you go." Ivan flicked his wrist and left the basement.

Marya worked down the list, relishing her access to such wonderful laboratory equipment. Occasionally, she'd pause for tea and consider all she'd witnessed at the estate: the cook baking enough bread to feed Warsaw, Ivan's reaction to the spoiled milk, and most importantly, the chemicals he required, some of which Marya recognized as heart medications.

She wasn't sure if these peculiarities were related or if she was just in a very unusual place.

While searching for Ivan's last ingredient—valerian root—Marya opened a sealed parcel and discovered an unfamiliar apparatus: a rubber balloon attached to a metered dial. The manifest listed it as ONE (1) SPHYGMOMANOMETER.

Meter means it measures something. Marya set the apparatus aside. *But what?*

The parcel also contained syringes and chloroform.

And why chloroform?

The basement door handle jiggled, and Marya jumped. She faced the doorway as Ivan trotted down the stairs.

"Are the pipettes finished?" He eyed the worktable where she'd laid them out.

"Almost," she said. "But the valerian root isn't here." She indicated the opened parcel. "All I found were a sphyg . . ." She glanced at the manifest. "Sphygmomanometer, syringes, and chloroform."

"Ah." Ivan bustled to the table and nimbly retied the parcel. "Those should have been delivered directly to me. And *here* is the valerian root." He passed Marya a clump of weeds, which she dropped into a beaker of boiling water.

"What does a sphyg . . . what does your meter measure?" she asked.

"Blood pressure," Ivan said. "It's fairly new—created by an Austrian fellow." He examined a pipette she'd filled. "You've done exceptional work, Marya."

She blushed and watched Ivan box up the pipettes.

"I know your project is confidential," she ventured, "but the meter and chloroform have me curious, especially knowing cocaine and valerian root both raise blood pressure."

Ivan paused to look at her. "You truly are a scientist in the making, Marya Skłodowska."

Marya beamed and stood taller. "I like to think so."

"I'll admit, I've longed to share my brilliance with someone." Ivan finished gathering pipettes and faced her with a stern expression. "But if I divulge my process, you cannot tell anyone under penalty of law."

Marya's eyebrows twitched, but the rest of her face remained stoic as she nodded.

"Good," Ivan said. "I'm testing different substances on myself to determine which raises blood pressure the most. Blood pressure elevates for survival, you see, and I believe a chemical response is triggered as well."

"Nowak's serum?" Marya guessed.

Ivan pointed at her. "Correct! With the strongest substance, I can extract the most potent serum from myself and transfer it to the unborn quagga."

"That's very clever," she said. "And the chloroform?"

Ivan winced. "For pain."

Marya mirrored his reaction. "Is it wise for one person to try all these substances?"

"Undoubtedly not." He grinned. "But science requires sacrifice."

Ivan pulled several papers from his pocket and placed them beside the notebook. "Here are findings for substances I've already tested. Could you transcribe my scribbles into something more legible?"

"Of course." Marya filled a pipette with valerian extract and handed it to him. "Here is your last pipette."

"Thank you for that. And these." He indicated the others. "I'll return in two hours."

Once he left, Marya set to work organizing his notes and writing them in a tidy script. Then she cleaned and sorted the laboratory equipment.

After an hour, the door handle jiggled again, and Ivan reappeared, looking much worse for the wear. His collar was splayed wide, and his neck was an ugly red. His cheeks, too, were flushed, and he pressed one hand to his ribcage.

"Testing is done for today," he said and stumbled down the basement steps.

"Oh!" Marya rushed to his side. "Which chemical—"

Ivan waved away her question. "Let me pay you for the day's work and see you home." He fumbled several banknotes from his billfold and handed them to Marya.

She accepted the money but shook her head at his offer to drive. "You should rest."

"Nonsense." Ivan motioned toward the steps. "I insist."

He further insisted she sit in the carriage cab while he drove, despite the slew of new questions Marya craved to ask.

When Ivan parked outside her apartment, she exited the cab to find him doubled over in the driver's seat.

"Have a . . . pleasant evening," he grunted.

"Please. You must come inside and rest," Marya said firmly.

Ivan grunted again but nodded. "Perhaps that would be best." He eased himself down from the carriage, and Marya helped him into the apartment.

Hela and Brounia, Marya's other older sister, were talking in the parlor, and they both jumped upon seeing Ivan with her.

"Good evening." Ivan removed his hat. "I—"

"Ivan needs to recover here," Marya said.

Without another word, she guided him upstairs to the dining area, ignoring her sisters' looks as they followed.

"I'll make you some tea," she told Ivan once she'd settled him in a chair.

Hela and Brounia followed her into the kitchen, but this time Marya wheeled on them.

"Please stop acting so suspicious!" she whispered.

"Why did you bring him inside?" Brounia whispered back.

"And what happened to him?" Hela added with a sideways glance at Ivan.

Marya shook her head. "Ivan swore me to secrecy, but it's nothing contagious. As for why I brought him inside"—she revealed the banknotes in her frock pocket—"he paid handsomely for my help."

Brounia's eyes widened, and she cleared her throat. "Hela, prepare Ivan's tea while Marya invites him for dinner."

Hela ogled the banknotes but did as she was told.

Marya smirked and returned to the dining area.

Ivan was engaged in a lively conversation with two boarders. He cradled his ribs as he laughed at their comments, but his cheeks were no longer flushed. The scarlet tinge to his neck had also faded, reduced to a few slender lines of red. They almost looked like phantom fingers around his throat, except there were three instead of the usual four.

Marya's skin prickled with goosebumps.

Three instead of four. Like the cleft hand of the missing girl.

"Marya!" Hela shoved a tea tray against her chest. "I've said your name twice now. Where is your mind?"

"I'm sorry." Marya gripped the tray. "I was thinking of . . . something." She glanced in Ivan's direction.

Perhaps she was jumping to conclusions. Perhaps the marks on his neck were from the test equipment he used.

Because he wouldn't lie about being the test subject. Would he?

An elbow dug into her side.

"Enough daydreaming." Hela now held a soup pot with a breadbasket balanced on top. "Take Ivan his tea."

They carried their dishes to the dining table, where Ivan spoke on his favorite subject.

" . . . hunted to extinction. And why?" he asked. "Why must the quagga die so we can thrive?"

"Herbert Spencer mentions survival of the fittest," one of the boarders, a cavalier young man named Piotr, spoke up. "Clearly, the quagga are unfit to live."

Ivan crossed his arms. "Spencer meant survival of the fittest among a *species*. Man will best any beast."

Piotr inclined his head. "Too right. We are the true kings of beasts!"

He pounded a fist to his chest, and Marya rolled her eyes.

"Ivan, will you stay for dinner?" She set a saucer and teacup before him.

He looked from her to Hela who was ladling out soup. "Oh, I couldn't impose."

"It's no imposition," Piotr said, as if he spoke for the household. "Eat with us. And drink!" He offered Ivan a bottle of *krupnik*.

Ivan held up a hand and grinned. "I'll eat, but no alcohol. I have a weak heart."

"Aha." Piotr lowered the bottle and winked. "You are the quagga of *our* species."

The boarders in earshot laughed uproariously, and Hela smiled.

Marya did neither. *How could someone with a weak heart test all those substances?* While everyone dined, she focused on Ivan's conversations. For the most part, they centered around the boarders' studies and Ivan's own school days. He seemed particularly affable to Piotr and another boy named Jakub, both of whom held scientific interests.

At meal's end, Brounia stood and clapped her hands firmly. "Time for bed."

Piotr and Jakub groaned, and Ivan clucked his tongue as he pushed away from the table.

"Come now, lads. Miss Skłodowska does not appear to be a woman to trifle with."

"Sleep here, Ivan," Piotr said. "We have space."

Brounia crossed her arms. "That's not for you to say."

"If money is an issue . . ." Ivan produced his billfold and selected several banknotes.

Brounia relaxed her stance and sighed. "One night. But it's quiet hours until dawn."

Ivan placed the money on the table. "Understood. We'll talk at sunrise, eh, lads?" Piotr and Jakub nodded.

"Jakub, bring a spare cot from the shed," Brounia said. "Piotr, help him."

Piotr didn't need to be told twice. "Come, Ivan! We can talk more outside."

Ivan followed him with a backward glance at Marya. "Can I count on your assistance tomorrow?"

Marya nodded. "Of course."

Brounia watched Ivan and Piotr leave before turning to Marya. "What *is* this assistance?"

"I measure ingredients and document findings in a notebook," Marya said. Then she gasped. "That I left in the carriage!"

She hurried downstairs and out to the carriage cab. There, she spotted the notebook wedged between the seat and far wall. With a guilty glance around, she climbed inside and retrieved it. As she turned to get out, laughter filtered into the cab from the street.

Marya shrunk down against the floorboard and held her breath.

"I've never been to a manor!" Jakub said from outside.

"Me neither," Piotr added. Then, "I'm with Ivan on the driver's seat!"

"Me too!" Jakub said.

Marya wrinkled her forehead. *They're going to the manor now?*

Ivan laughed. "It will be cramped, but we'll manage."

Someone closed the cab door, and Marya teetered along with the cab when Ivan and the boys climbed onto the driver's seat.

Ivan whipped his horse into motion, but Marya stayed hidden.

She didn't know why they were going, but as the one who'd brought Ivan into the boys' lives, something told her she should be there.

The slowing of the carriage and a whoop from Piotr told Marya they'd finally reached the manor. The cab rocked again as Ivan and the boys hopped down, and her heart pounded when their shoes trod the dirt just outside the cab.

Please don't look in here.

"This house is massive!" Piotr said.

"Manor," Jakub corrected.

"Let me show you around," Ivan said.

Marya narrowed her eyes.

The footfalls and conversation faded, and she peeked out the cab window in time to see Ivan lead the boys through the servants' entrance. She opened the cab door and stepped down.

A hand gripped her shoulder.

Marya squealed and spun around.

Hela blinked back at her. "Why are we here?"

Marya's jaw dropped. "Why are *you* here?"

"I saw you leaving and thought you were headed somewhere fun, so I climbed on back." Hela frowned. "But now I'm confused, since they went inside without you."

"They don't know I'm here," Marya said. "Piotr and Jakub shouldn't be here either." She exhaled a shaky sigh. "Hela, I've got a bad feeling about Ivan."

After Marya shared her misgivings, Hela winced. "What—"

A guttural shout from the manor rent the air between them.

Hela's eyes widened. "That's Jakub."

"I knew it." Marya's throat tightened. "He and Piotr are in trouble." She unhooked the carriage lamp and sprinted toward the manor.

Hela followed. "Marya, wait!"

But she'd already opened the servant's door to a pitch-black hallway. Further inside, male voices shouted, and something thudded against the walls.

Marya's heartbeat matched the thudding, but she raised the lamp and ventured into the manor. Hela's fingers dug into her waist from behind, and her shoes scuffed the floor with every step. The air was still pungent from bread and bleach, which meant the cook had been working until recently.

"We need help from the cook or butler," Marya said. "They're the only staff in here."

"And you don't think they heard Jakub screaming?" Hela asked dryly.

Marya pressed her lips together. "A valid point." As they approached the darkened kitchen, a putrid stench assaulted Marya's nostrils.

"Ugh! What is that?" Hela asked.

"The icebox was failing earlier." Marya lifted an arm against her nose. "I think the cook was baking bread to mask it."

"No, I meant *that*." Hela pointed over her shoulder. "Is it blood?"

A pool of orange light flickered on the floor, gleaming red at its edges.

The sisters inched closer, and Marya jumped at a crackling sound from the hearth. She thrust out the lamp, which illuminated a bottle lying on the edge of the prep table.

"Someone knocked over wine."

Marya set the lamp on the table. Someone had knocked over *many* things. Bowls, spoons, and baking ingredients cluttered the floor, and the table's surface had been swept clean, save for a few trails of flour.

She held a hand above the trails—perfectly distanced for fingers scrabbling at the tabletop. "The boys didn't want to leave this room."

"One of them must have grabbed for the icebox too," Hela said. "The door's cracked open."

"Indeed." Marya approached the icebox, which strangely, lacked shelves. Instead, the contents had been piled inside a massive piece of canvas.

With a human head jutting out.

Marya yelped and clapped a hand over her mouth. She listened for hurried footsteps, but no one seemed to hear her outburst except Hela.

"What happened?" Hela squinted at the icebox, gasped, and buried her face in Marya's shoulder. "Did Ivan do that?"

Marya shivered and whispered, "He *did* get upset about the icebox." *Because he realized corpse fumes had tainted the milk.* Marya pressed a hand to her stomach.

"Who do you suppose this dead fellow is?" Hela asked.

Marya inched closer to the icebox.

The head was that of an older, well-groomed man, and when Marya lowered the front of the sack, he appeared to be wearing a black jacket and waistcoat.

"Oh my," she said. "I fear he's the butler."

She raised her lamp to confirm, and the light shone over his shoulder into a pair of lifeless eyes. Marya gasped and stumbled back. "There's another body. A woman."

"How deep is this icebox?" Hela cried.

"Shhh." Marya gripped her shoulders. "We must think, not panic."

Hela nodded and stared at the icebox. "Who's she then?"

The woman wore apron strings but wasn't the cook Marya had spoken to.

She chewed her lip. "I think this is the real cook. The current butler and cook must be impostors working for Ivan."

"Oh, no, no." Hela tugged at Marya's arm. "We're taking his carriage to the police station."

Marya shook her head. "We can't leave Piotr and Jakub. It's *my* fault they're in this predicament. And I'm certain Ivan also kidnapped someone else. We have to rescue them."

"How?"

"I don't know yet," Marya admitted. "We should investigate further."

She pointed to a flour trail on the floor, and they followed it to a door beneath the central staircase.

"Butler's quarters," Hela whispered.

The space beneath the door glowed with soft, yellow light, occasionally broken by passing shadows.

Marya dropped to all fours and peered through the one-inch gap. Three people maneuvered around an iron bed frame. She recognized Ivan's shoes and a smaller pair of flour-sprinkled shoes belonging to the cook. The third pair were roughly the size of Ivan's and had to be the butler's.

"Kindly remove your foot from that tubing," Ivan said. "You'll cut off their extra oxygen."

"Why do they need it?" The butler scoffed. "They're asleep anyway."

"The rigors I'm putting them through cause shortness of breath, and I need them alive as long as possible," Ivan said. "Celina, pinch here."

"I expect a pay rise after this," Celina said. "I agreed to play cook, not scientist."

"You'll get it when the university funds my project," Ivan replied. "I've studied the girl, and I'm confident one of these boys will yield what I need."

He means Piotr and Jakub. Marya's forehead wrinkled. *But what of the girl?*

Something heavy slid down the other side of the door and hit the floor with a *squelch*. It was a moment before Marya realized she'd received her answer . . . minus the top half of the girl's skull.

Marya whimpered and scrambled backward.

At the same moment, Ivan barked, "Borys! I told you—" Marya fled before he finished, motioning for Hela to follow.

"Ivan and his two cohorts are there, along with Piotr and Jakub," she whispered.

"And the girl you mentioned?"

"Dead." Marya spoke over Helena's gasp. "We must rescue Piotr and Jakub *now.*"

"How?" Helena demanded. "If Ivan and his cohorts are strong enough to hold the boys—"

"The boys are incapacitated," Marya argued. "It was probably the only way to subdue them." A thought occurred to her, and she squeezed Hela's hand. "We can do the same to Ivan and his cohorts."

Hela stared at Marya. "I tire of asking this question: *How?*"

"Science!" Marya pulled Hela toward the kitchen and scullery. She stopped at the basement door. "I need to retrieve some things. You collect vinegar, bleach, and towels from the scullery, and the bellows from the kitchen hearth."

Hela blinked at her. "You want me to revisit the kitchen of horrors?"

"Hela." Marya offered her sister the carriage lamp. "Please."

With a shudder, Hela accepted it and trudged away.

Marya opened the basement door and brightened a wall lamp. From the left-hand table she grabbed discarded twine and stuffed it in her frock pockets. Then she filled an empty crate with rubber bands, beakers, and retort flasks from the worktable.

She carried the crate up the stairs, where Hela waited with kitchen and scullery items.

"What happens now?" Hela asked as Marya transferred them to her crate.

"I read once about a maid who mistakenly combined bleach and vinegar," Marya said. "She suffered extreme irritation of the orifices and coughed until she collapsed."

Hela lifted an eyebrow. "You plan to repeat her mistake."

Marya nodded. "The butler's quarters are under the central staircase, which means Ivan and his cohorts are in a small, windowless room. We can incapacitate them, tie them up, and drag Piotr and Jakub out." She shared some of her twine with Hela who wrapped it around one hand.

"Won't it also affect the boys?"

"They're receiving extra oxygen, so they won't suffer much," Marya said. "No more questions. It's time for action."

She gestured down the hall, and Hela led the way with the lamp.

Outside the butler's quarters, Marya wedged towels under the door, leaving just enough space for the spouts of the retort flasks to poke through. She secured a towel over her mouth and nose with rubber bands and gestured for Hela to do the same. Then she poured bleach into the mouth of one flask and followed it with vinegar.

A few puffs from the bellows forced the resultant gas out the flask's spout and into the room. Marya stoppered the flask's mouth and repeated the process with two more flasks before wedging the bellows beneath the door.

Conversation continued in the butler's quarters for a minute more.

Then the throat-clearing began. Followed by coughing. And wheezing. Several thuds shook the door, but the bellows kept it closed. After a few thuds against the floor, Marya dislodged the bellows and towels.

"Now!" She yanked the door open, and instantly, her eyes stung and watered.

The cook and butler floundered on the floor, clutching their throats. Marya secured the butler's ankles and arms with twine and glanced at Hela who was restraining the cook. Then she got to her feet and glanced around.

Piotr and Jakub lay unconscious on the bed, tubes in their noses. The dead girl had been propped upon a side table. Ivan, however, was nowhere in sight.

He must have slipped out earlier when we left.

"Ivan's not here!" Marya told Hela.

"Good." Hela grabbed Piotr under the arms. "Let's get the boys to the carriage before he comes back."

Marya gripped Piotr's legs, but she and Hela struggled to carry him to the door. "We need help. I'll bring a wheelbarrow from the barn." She dashed down the hall and out the servants' door. Once inside the barn, however, she slowed her steps, remembering that the wheelbarrow was by the quagga pen.

What if Ivan's there?

Marya tiptoed closer and gently lifted the pitchfork off the wheelbarrow. Hoisting it like a spear, she peeked into the pen.

Six quaggas, no Ivan.

She straightened and relaxed.

Until the hammer of a revolver clicked behind her.

"Oh, Marya. Why did you have to be so clever?" Ivan asked.

She slowly faced him and the gun pointed at her chest.

"I left the butler's quarters earlier," he said. "And on my way back, I spied a rat heading for the barn." He leaned toward her. "You."

Marya kept her features emotionless. "I deduced that."

Ivan smiled. "Nevertheless, I'm glad you're here. I need to test a final way of elevating blood pressure: abject terror." He motioned toward the quagga pen. "In you go."

Marya swallowed hard; pitchfork clutched to her chest. "Please. I'll . . . I'll keep your secrets."

Ivan laughed. "No, you won't." He sidled toward the pen and opened the gate. "Don't make me shoot your kneecaps and drag you in."

Marya backed through the gate. "You can't do this."

"Of course I can. After I'm finished, I'll fabricate your demise, along with the others." He gestured with the revolver. "Farther in."

Marya obeyed. The quagga whinnied and tossed their heads.

Ivan peered past Marya and cooed at them. "Easy, beauties. I won't harm you."

Marya could have vomited at his sentiment, but a realization struck her.

Ivan wouldn't harm them. He would never harm them.

She flung her pitchfork at him.

Ivan shouted and ducked while Marya darted behind a pregnant quagga. It whinnied in alarm, but she stroked its side, and it quickly calmed.

Ivan did the opposite.

"Get away from her, you little pig!" He struggled to train his revolver on Marya as she moved with the quagga.

"I have a syringe of chloroform," she lied. "Lethal to an unborn foal."

Ivan entered the pen. "You wouldn't—"

Marya emitted a piercing whistle and smacked the quagga's rump. It reared and galloped with the others toward the only point of egress: the gate where Ivan stood.

His eyes widened, and he stepped left, then right, unsure of his escape route. Before he reached safety, the fastest and first quagga knocked him down. Hoof after hoof trampled Ivan's legs, groin, rib cage, and skull while he screamed.

Marya exited the pen last. She gazed down at Ivan's mangled form—at the slow way he blinked, at the quick way he breathed—and clucked her tongue.

"It appears you should have worried less about the quagga's extinction, and more about your own," she said.

Then she pushed the wheelbarrow out of the barn.

Science Note:

Eerily enough, eugenics was a real scientific movement that began in the late nineteenth century . . . except most eugenicists weren't trying to save endangered animals. Instead, they wanted to improve humans through selective breeding.

And yes, it was as racist, xenophobic, and intolerant as it sounds.

Eugenicists in various countries either sterilized or prohibited the marriage of people of mixed race, poor health, or "feeble" minds (in this case, the sexually promiscuous or low income).

The quagga, too, was real—a zebra subspecies that became extinct in the late nineteenth century. Unfortunately, people weren't aware of how endangered it was until the last one died in captivity at the Amsterdam Zoo. Today, scientists in South Africa are hoping—through the quagga's Plains zebra descendants—to retrieve the genes that can at least bring back the signature striping pattern.

As for combining bleach and vinegar . . . I don't recommend it. It really does produce a poisonous gas: chlorine. In fact, mixing bleach with most cleaning ingredients produces a toxic gas or skin irritant of some sort, due to the chlorine involved. It's an incredibly reactive element and shouldn't be mixed with anything but water.

THREE
Ravens

by
MYLO CARBIA

"Have you ever seen a bowlegged crow?" Bronisława sauntered across the floor of the smallest guest bedroom in her grandparents' countryside home. She forcefully opened the heavy green-velvet curtains. The morning light burst through the window like a Russian interrogation lamp spotlighting dust particles midair. "Can you not smell that horrendous cooking? It's time to wake up, little sisters."

Helena and Marya slept lopsided in a four-poster bed with pale yellow sheets.

"Wake up, young ladies. How can either of you remain asleep with the smell of fried swine filling the room?"

Helena's eyes barely opened. "What time is it?"

"It's time for you to hurry downstairs and see how ridiculous Grandfather looks standing at the hob." Bronisława's early morning energy was infectious. "He looks like a bowlegged crow making us all French breakfast!"

"Oh, right," Helena yawned and stretched out her arms, dropping her fist squarely on her sleeping sister's forehead. "I forgot, it's Bastille Day."

Marya remained in a deep sleep, with her eyelids twitching and her face silently writhing in pain.

"Marya, dear, it's time to wake up," pleaded Bronisława.

"It's happening again," said Helena sharply. "It's another night coma, isn't it?"

Bronisława grabbed Marya's shoulders and shook her gently in the bed. "Marya, you're safe now. It's morning. Please, wake up."

Helena grabbed her long blond braid like a sword and slapped Marya in the face.

"Helena!" exclaimed Bronisława in a maternal tone.

Marya finally awakened, rubbing the side of her face. "Ouch."

Helena shrugged. "See, it works."

"Did it happen again?" asked Bronisława.

Marya took a moment to gather her thoughts, then gently nodded her head yes.

Helena sat up in bed. "Who did it take this time? Mother or Zosia?"

Marya stared blankly at the window. Her spirit was somewhere else, far away.

The room filled with awkward silence as the two older sisters looked at one another.

Neither wanted to admit that Marya's nightmares were becoming more frequent, and even more dreadful. Neither wanted to admit that her depression was so thick and persistent that it sucked all the air out of the room. Neither wanted to admit that Marya was the last of the four remaining children to recover from the loss of their mother and eldest sister who died several years ago. Bronisława sat down along the side of the bed, stroking Marya's round, florid cheek. "Everything is going to be fine, Marya. It's only a dream. Our minds create them to help us deal with emotions we cannot face while awake."

Helena—always feeling the need to fill the vacuum caused by her baby sister—squirmed her way out from under the covers and rapidly changed the subject. "Did you know Bastille Day is called La Fête Nationale now?"

Bronisława smiled tenderly. "Yes, Papa Józef told me that last night during my piano lesson." She stood up from the bed. "Which reminds me, we shouldn't let Bonnie Prince Charlie sleep past dawn anymore." She walked over to a free-standing birdcage covered with a dark red blanket in the corner of the bedroom. "Otherwise, he will stay up singing late into the evening."

"Oh, please let him sleep in before he creates an all-day racket," begged Helena.

"His singing is quite beautiful," said Marya softly. "If you would spend more time with him, you would know."

"What? Read him books of science and poetry like you do? I'd rather feed him to the cats." Bronisława shook her head, anticipating a quarrel. She abandoned her mission and left the blanket covering the birdcage untouched.

"What is Papa Józef cooking exactly?" asked Helena.

Bronisława picked up their robes from the floor and placed them on the bed. "By the smell of it, burnt kielbasa and toasted bread."

Marya coughed from the pungent aroma circling the room. "I think I need to get some fresh air. I haven't been outside in a week."

"I have a better idea," Helena sat upon her knees in bed. "Let's go down to the creek this morning after breakfast and see if we can hear the Bastille Day parade!"

Marya struggled to free her sleeping gown from underneath Helena's body. "I don't think we are close enough to hear a parade a thousand miles away."

Bronisława carefully listened while pulling out dirty clothes from a wooden hamper.

Helena leapt out of bed and stood on her tippy-toes—a frequent posture when seeking authority over her younger sister. "The velocity of an acoustic wave is equal to the speed of the wave itself, plus the speed of the wind that carries it. Also, Gassendi proved warm temperatures increase the distance sound travels, so given the July heat, we should be able to hear the parade."

Marya shook her head. "No, it is still too far away, and it was Biancon—not Gassendi—who found the speed of sound increases with temperature."

Bronisława smiled, glad to see glimmers of her youngest sister's personality return. However, she recognized there was no stopping Helena once she was resolute about pursuing an absurd idea. "Well, if you are both going to the creek today, let us not be sloths," she commanded. "We don't want to disappoint Papa Józef by being tardy for breakfast."

The three sisters sat at a small table in a white-washed wooden kitchen, picking at plates filled with runny eggs, fried kielbasa, goat cheese, and puffy little crescent-shaped pieces of bread the French "borrowed" from the Viennese.

Papa Józef sat with them, stuffing tobacco into his pipe while the girls shared their plans for the day. His sweet demeanor and round face were clearly passed down to the Skłodowska sisters, but his pure white, frizzy hair was mimicked only by Marya's wiry blond "bird's nest" that gave her sisters so much trouble to comb through every night.

"We could also test our sound wave hypothesis in the woods, Papa. What do you think?" asked Helena.

He lit a match, igniting his pipe. "Well, you may be better served to wait until dark and look for fireworks with my telescope."

"Fireworks?" Helena was in awe. "But we won't be able to see them from Paris, will we?"

Bronisława rolled her eyes.

Marya acknowledged her.

Papa Józef noticed and smiled. "No, but one of our new neighbors is a pyrotechnician from Italy. He told your grandmother and me nearly everything about the craft. Perhaps he will light some fireworks this evening in honor of the holiday."

Bronisława's face perked up. She sincerely missed her Nana's presence in the house. "How long will Grandmother be staying in Warsaw—?"

Helena interrupted. "Why does our brother get to watch the real fireworks in Paris? See, this is why I am studying to be a governess, so I can live anywhere and teach children."

Bronisława sighed. "Honestly, I cannot wait to move to Paris and study medicine so I can finally get away from you two busybodies."

Helena chimed in. "Well, I cannot wait until we have our own

Independence Day with fireworks and parades, just like France and America."

Papa Józef chuckled as smoke escaped from the corner of his mouth. Despite his jovial tone, his warped feet and slow hobble were a constant reminder of what the family had gambled in the November Uprising to win independence for Poland—and lost. But with the majority of Polish usurpers being sentenced to death or sent to Siberia, his family was grateful their patriarch was allowed to return to teaching in Warsaw, wounds and all.

He looked over at Marya. "Now that you will be entering your last year of schooling, have you thought about what subject you wish to study at university?"

Marya was silent. She felt numb. After years of reading books about nearly every subject, she realized this was the one question she could not answer. "No, Papa. I haven't decided yet."

"Ahh, you are still young. You have plenty of time."

Marya felt a heaviness in her chest. She was unable to feel excitement about anything, let alone the future. She couldn't visualize herself going to university the year after next, or teaching children or studying medicine in Paris, or getting married one day and having pets. Her inability to see herself as a fully grown adult caused Marya tremendous anxiety, especially when she recalled images of her sister Zosia dying from typhus at fourteen years old—the same age Marya was now.

Helena continued the conversation. "Papa Józef, do you remember telling us last week about how the first uprising started? How the Duke of Constantine escaped Belvedere Palace by dressing like a woman?"

"Why don't you ask Marya about it. She just finished a book about him."

"Yes—?" Marya stopped mid-thought. She focused on a pink earthworm inside Papa Józef's ear.

"Well, how did he get away with it? I mean, his face clearly must have had hair on it."

Marya saw an earthworm emerge from Papa Józef's nostril.

"And how did he find a woman's wig so fast? Did he have his escape planned all along?"

Another earthworm wriggled in Papa Józef's bushy hair.

"Well, what did the book say, Marya?"

Papa Józef noticed Marya's catatonic stare.

"Marya, are you with us?" asked Bronisława.

Papa Józef's white hair was now filled with hundreds of squirming pink worms.

Marya's vacant face turned horrified. She looked away, tightly closing her eyes.

Bronisława patted her back. "Are you feeling well?"

"No, I don't think so." She gagged once, then slowly opened her eyes.

"I bet it's food poisoning. Grandmother said Mistress Nowak's niece went insane from a bad egg," chimed Helena.

Marya finally looked at Papa Józef. The worms had disappeared, replaced by silence.

Helena reached for the last croissant and tore off a piece with her mouth. "Maybe you should eat more of this bread to soak up the poison, Marya. It's absolutely divine."

"Do you need some water?" asked Bronisława.

"No, I think I shall go outside to get some fresh air," Marya snapped back to life. "I'm sorry for worrying you."

Helena finished her last bite. "Papa Józef, do you think they will have a military march on the Champs-Élysées later this morning?"

"Oh, give it a rest, Hela," said Bronisława. "Just accompany Marya and have a nice walk in the woods. You would both benefit greatly from sunlight."

Papa Józef relit his pipe and blew a plume of smoke without a single earthworm in sight. "I am sure your brother will write us soon with all the details of the parade and fireworks." He rose from the table. "And for you, dear Marya. Have you finished reading the book of poetry I gave you?"

"Yes, Papa. I read it to Bonnie Prince Charlie too." She looked at the floor.

Bronisława rose from the table and placed her plate in the empty sink. "Will you help me with the washing today when you return, Marya? I have no clean clothes left for you."

"No, because she will be waiting for the fireworks outside with me," interrupted Helena.

"Is that so?" Bronisława grabbed the milk jug from the counter and refilled her glass.

Papa Józef puffed a ring of smoke into the air, delighting himself at the feat. "Quite frankly, you could all use a proper dose of nature. The dust from my books is beginning to pale all of your beautiful faces." He looked at Marya and winked.

Marya smiled back, knowing she would always be his favorite grandchild.

A thick canopy of trees covered Marya and Helena as they strolled along a dirt path in the forest.

It was Marya's favorite part of Papa Józef's land—an idyllic slice of free Polish countryside in the middle of oppressive Russian Partition rule. As she walked, her hands lightly brushed the wooden arms extended to greet her, tickled with the knowledge that thirty percent of her beloved homeland was covered with her most treasured biome in the world.

"Slow down, Hela. You're walking too fast."

Helena stopped to relish the sound of the bubbling creek beside her. "It's so beautiful out here—why we don't take long walks more often?" Helena stretched out her arms, embracing the checkered shade above her. "So when are you planning to tell me what frightened you at breakfast?"

Marya was caught. "What do you mean?"

"Wait." Helena cupped her ear. "Can you hear any music?"

Marya was grateful for the diversion. She knew Helena was sharp with her questioning and would create a huge fuss if she thought she had taken ill with food poisoning. "No, I cannot hear anything yet."

"I think I hear drums? Faintly, but I do hear them!"

"But that's—" Marya did not have the heart to dim her sister's dream of hearing a parade taking place nine hundred and sixty-five miles away in Paris. She knew that faint drumming sound came from the water mill at the neighboring Dzialynski farm. "That could be a drum line, I suppose."

Helena's eyes darted toward the open blue-and-white sky. "Yes! Yes! I can hear drums!"

She grabbed Marya's hand and began running.

They ran at least a hundred yards before Marya broke hands. Breathless, she gazed at the flowing creek to her right. She pointed to a large log, ideal for sitting and enjoying the peaceful waters. "Perhaps I should stay here, Hela. You can carry on a bit further, but I shall wait for you here."

Helena hesitated. She knew that her father—who had stayed in Warsaw to work while his children vacationed in the countryside— would be angry upon hearing she had left her baby sister alone in the woods. Abandoning Marya would be a serious offense with defectors from the Russian army sometimes making camp in the area. An unplanned meeting with a lost and hungry soldier would be a potentially treacherous situation for anyone wandering the forest alone.

"Are you sure you want to stay here?" asked Helena.

"Yes, yes, please go. Just don't be long."

Helena paused once again. "Well, there is a tiny cabin around here somewhere. It's very small, but it has a cot in case you feel you need to rest. Zosia even took Bonnie Prince Charlie there with us in his travel cage before—"

"Yes, I know."

The nightmares had come after Zosia's death, and never let go.

"You want me to wait for you in an abandoned shed? No, thank you. Just come back here when you're finished." Marya patted the log like a judge in court.

Helena shrugged her shoulders, then galloped into the distance. "I shouldn't be long! I promise!"

"Hurry back please," said Marya, far too softly for anyone to hear.

Thirty-five minutes had passed with no sign of Helena.

Marya remained sitting on the large log facing the creek, stretching out her leg and pointing her toe like a prima ballerina in waiting. To her delight, a fuzzy brown caterpillar crawled from underneath the log and onto the top of her foot. Without hesitation, she bent down, pinched the caterpillar between her fingers, and ate it.

"Marya," a voice whispered behind her.

She swiftly turned around.

No one was there.

Marya slowly stood up, then circled the log. "Is someone here?"

Silence.

"Stop playing games, Hela!"

More silence.

Marya then heard a foot stepping onto leaves in the distance.

"Come here, Maryaaahh . . ."

She looked fervently around for the origin of that familiar voice.

It wasn't Helena. It wasn't a stranger. Perhaps neighbor Dzialynski's wife?

Marya spoke as loudly as her lungs would let her. "Hello? Who's there?"

Suddenly, a glowing pale figure appeared deep within the woods—a blond teenage girl wearing a white ruffled dress and a purple hair bow.

Marya rubbed her eyes in disbelief. "Zosia?"

"Come, Marya. Let me show you something." Her voice sounded inches away despite being so far into the woods.

"But, how can you be—? Are you still alive?"

Zosia did not answer. Her expression was stoic. "Come hither, dear sister. We must make haste."

Marya's mind was frozen while her body followed Zosia into the thick brush far off in the distance.

Minutes passed like hours while Marya followed Zosia's steps over branches, dirt, and leaves. Now, she thought nothing of where Helena may be hiding. Now, she thought nothing of the brown and green stains appearing on her last clean dress. Now, her only concern was keeping pace with her mysterious, dead sister.

"When will we stop?"

"All will be explained very soon."

They finally arrived at a log cabin located under a massive, crooked pine tree. This must be the place Helena spoke of earlier. Small and tidy from the outside, it was not much larger than a horse carriage. The dark brown exterior still gleamed with morning dew from the surrounding leaves.

It wasn't as scary as Marya imagined it to be.

"Go inside," said Zosia. "I will wait for you outside."

"Is Mother here too?"

"No, dear Marya. Mother is dead."

Marya's stomach sank into nothingness. Why would Zosia—who died six years ago—be alive when Mother was not?

"Go now. Do not be late."

"Am I in danger?"

"Go inside. All will be revealed soon."

Marya unexpectedly felt brave. She felt she had no choice but to face what was inside that tiny little cabin. She pulled open the large, heavy door and walked in.

The interior was nothing like the exterior. It was empty. It was decrepit. It was foreboding, painted bloodred from floor to ceiling, without even a single window to invite sunlight. There were four oil lamps burning on pedestals in the corners of the room, as well as a small black table and chair resting upon light-colored wood shavings on the floor.

To Marya's surprise, a black, bowlegged bird emerged from the shadows and sat confidently on top of the table. The burning lamps cast a spotlight on its stunning plumage of iridescent green, blue, and purple feathers, and its long beak of solid gold.

"I see you have found us, Marya." The bird spoke in a low, booming voice with an ancient accent she could not place.

Terrified, she said nothing in return.

The menacing beast tilted its head. "To answer your first question, I am not a crow."

Marya had already concluded this after noticing his triangular tail feathers. "Yes, I know. You are a raven."

"Impressive." The bird extended its wings in a gesture of dominance. "Most humans care not for details."

Marya shook her head, refusing to acknowledge the absurdity of the situation. To do so would have made her question her sanity.

"What do you want with me?"

"Do you not care to know who speaks before you?"

Marya bit her lip. "Well, yes. Of course. Who are you, then?"

The bird extended its neck. "I am The Great Raven, King Grozny."

Two smaller ravens appeared from the darkness and joined him on the table.

"And these are my soldiers, Leon and Bartholomew."

Marya shook her head again. "No, no, no, I must be dreaming. I must have fallen asleep on the log," she smiled nervously. "None of this is real."

"Not real, you say?"

The Great Raven's yellow eyes flared. He ruffled his plumage, then grew so tall that his crown feathers brushed up against the ceiling.

His breath quickened. His eyes glowed devil-orange. "I'm not real, you say?"

Marya's pulse raced. She looked for the door, but it was gone. Now, there were only bloodred walls and no way to escape.

The Great Raven leaned toward her, the tip of his sharp golden beak only inches from her nose. "You will do as I say, or I will eat you."

Marya felt his hot breath. "What do you want from me?"

The Great Raven leaned back. "You will be given three riddles. If you answer correctly, I will let you go home to your family. But if you fail, I will feast upon your eyeballs and allow my soldiers to battle over the remaining scraps of flesh from your bones."

Marya was filled with adrenaline. Her heartbeat thundered. Despite this, she managed to take a seat in front of The Great Raven.

"Good. I see we have an understanding."

"But, why are you doing this? Why me?"

"Because you are destined for great things, dear child. I must, there-fore, test your worthiness before I allow the world to celebrate your name for centuries to come."

Celebrate my name? Marya began to panic. But for what? She once excelled at so many things: poetry, art, science, math, languages, teach-ing. She now had no love for any of it and had no idea what would be a part of her future.

She stared deeply into The Great Raven's bright eyes. "But how will I know my destiny? I'm only fourteen years old."

The Great Raven's voice deepened. "It is more important to know when your path is wrong than when it is right, dear child."

Marya was troubled by his vague answer. "I still don't understand."

The Great Raven hopped over to the edge of the table. "Every single human is given at least one great talent by the Creator. Some are given more, but none are given less. The difficulty lies not in discovering what one's talent is, as others will notice it within you early and remind you of it throughout your life. No, the difficulty lies instead in overcoming the obstacles created by the Destroyer to stand in destiny's way."

Marya was intrigued by his words. "What kind of obstacles?"

"Anger, jealousy, envy, grief, boredom, gluttony, addiction, distrac-tion—all common ailments designed to destroy the potential of greatness within each human being, including you."

Marya suddenly felt a powerful wave of melancholy. There was no denying it. Her dark moods and constant depression diminished any enthusiasm she held for the future.

Marya longed for the ability to morph her hidden sadness into something that would propel her forward. She longed to set upon a great journey or strive toward a great achievement—to feel a true pas-sion and enthusiasm for learning or creating or discovering something new that would ultimately pull her from the pits and back into the joyous ways of life.

"Yes, I think I understand now."

"Anything which derails one from developing their special talent to the fullest is the most destructive form of evil on Earth."

Marya absorbed The Great Raven's profound words. Somehow, they felt true.

"But none of that matters now. Fail our test, and you will be dinner for three!" The Great Raven stretched out his wings and squawked so horribly, it caused Marya to curl into a ball. "Do you heed my warning, dear child?"

"Yes, King Grozny. I will do my best."

The Great Raven returned to the center of the table. He straightened his spine, preparing to launch his first riddle.

"What is something invisible in youth, elusive in middle age, and revealed at last before death?"

Bartholomew's stomach grumbled. He was ready to eat.

Marya stared at the bloodred ceiling for a long pause. She was determined to figure it out.

"Is it wisdom?"

King Grozny raised an eyebrow. "Hmmm . . . but what does it mean?"

Marya stood up.

King Grozny flapped his wing to keep her seated.

"It means young people are often too ignorant to look for wisdom, whereas adults desperately search for it, and elderly people look back on their lives only to find it was there all along."

"Almost . . . but what does it mean?"

Marya bit her lip, thinking of what to say next. "It means that wisdom is around us at all times—especially when we are learning life's most valuable lessons—and that we should seek it as early as possible and enjoy the process of acquiring it."

Leon's beak dropped. "Give her a harder question."

The Great Raven raised his chin in the air, relishing his next riddle.

"Very well, then," he cleared his throat. "What lives inside you, inside me, inside a river, and a tree, yet is more than half of all that can be?"

Marya started to worry. She knew the answer could be a number of things, and she had only one chance to answer it correctly.

"She's going to get this one wrong. I can feel it," said Bartholomew.

"Silence!" screamed King Grozny.

"Is it oxygen? It comprises 65 percent of the human body, nearly 90 percent of water, more than 50 percent of a tree, and more than half of nearly all living things."

The Great Raven slouched his wings. His disappointment said it all.

"I am right, aren't I?" Marya was pleased. "Now only one more question, and you must let me go!"

Marya slapped her hands onto the table and leaned forward until her gaze rivaled King Grozny. "What is your final question? I demand it!"

The Great Raven ruffled his feathers.

"Give me your final question! I want to leave!"

"I will ask it, but you must be prepared to die if you are unable to answer."

"I don't care anymore, just ask it!"

The Great Raven salivated at the prospect of fresh meat. "Very well, then. What is your true passion, Marya?"

She hesitated. "But I enjoy so many things."

"You have one great talent. Maybe two, or even three. But what is your passion?"

Marya stared blankly.

"She's going to fail!" squawked Leon. Leon flew off the table and began pecking at her toes. Bartholomew quickly followed, biting at her ankles.

"Silence!"

The smaller ravens reluctantly stopped.

She desperately looked around the cabin, searching for inspiration. "My passion is . . ."

The Great Raven leaned in closer. "Go on, dear child. What is it?"

"My passion is . . . I know what it could be, but—I'm sorry, I'm not certain yet."

As she said this, The Great Raven pulled away, farther and farther into the darkness. He now spoke in a familiar masculine voice. "Then why are you still sleeping, little bird?"

The roof above disappeared. Daylight suddenly filled the ceiling, forcing Marya to squint her eyes and raise an elbow to shield her face. The cabin walls melted away and turned into Bonnie Prince Charlie's birdcage.

Papa Józef's gigantic face now hovered over the cage, as he removed the dark red blanket from above. He opened the door and placed a tiny dish of earthworms on the floor.

"Papa! Papa!" Marya tried to scream back, but only bird chirps came forth.

"Did you sleep well? Tell me everything."

"Papa! I've had another terrible dream." Marya chirped and chirped, but Papa Józef could not recognize a word she was saying.

Finally, Papa Józef and the cage faded into nothingness as Marya slowly opened her eyes.

Bronisława stood before her at the window, forcefully opening the heavy, green-velvet curtains. The morning light burst through the window. "How can you remain asleep with the smell of fried swine filling the room? Can you not smell that horrendous cooking?"

"Bronisława?"

"It's time for you to come downstairs and see how ridiculous Papa Józef looks standing at the hob." Her early morning energy was uplifting. "He looks like a bowlegged crow making us all French breakfast!"

Marya looked around the bed. "Where is Hela?"

"She's already downstairs. We thought it would be best for you to rest."

"Oh."

"How do you feel this morning? Did you have any more—"

"Nightmares?" Marya sat up in bed. "I had another dream, but this time it was different."

Marya looked over at Bonnie Prince Charlie's covered birdcage in the corner of the bedroom. "I feel better now, somehow."

"Good." Bronisława sat down along the side of the bed and tucked a tendril of hair behind Marya's ear. "I'm glad to hear it."

"I've decided something important, Bronisława."

"Yes, what is it?"

"I want to read Physics and Mathematics at university next year."

Bronisława was taken aback. "Oh, that's—"

"In Paris. Yes, I'm going to join you in Paris just as soon as I can raise the funds."

Bronisława was pleasantly surprised. "That's wonderful, Marya. I'm sure Papa Józef will be pleased to hear you've made a wise choice." She smiled warmly at the return of her sister's bold personality.

Marya smiled back, knowing it would be the last time she would ever wake from that horrific, recurring nightmare.

The MAGIC of SCIENCE

by
BRYAN THOMAS SCHMIDT
& G. P. CHARLES

Scattered torches in sconces cast shadows across Drzewica Castle's once grand ballroom, now a makeshift dormitory. Marya Skłodowska lay in her bed, her gaze skimming the eerie shadows as she tried to push thoughts of schooling from her mind by recounting the castle's history. Built in 1527 by the Archbishop of Gniezno, Maciej Drzewicki, it lay on the periphery of town by the river Drzewickza and was separated from the encircling moat by a bulwark. The building itself followed a rectangular plan with four square towers located at each corner—prime defenses for the era. And though the walls and some portions still bore the marks of an 1814 fire that had destroyed large sections, what remained had enough stability to provide excellent room for the Flying University, the secret school her father had helped to form. The massive building had space aplenty to use as secret labs, classrooms, and even occasional dorms when students stayed over for long study sessions, workshops, or as was the present case—preparation for biannual exams.

Marya was almost asleep when a scream echoed through the shadowy corridors.

She tensed. Some of the girls were already spooked by the place, feeling it was creepy, possibly even haunted, and rumors of ghosts and spirits abounded. Despite her usual tendency to laugh off claims of witchcraft and spirits, unease brought her upright in bed. Lightning and thunder from the storm outside only added to the sudden tension in the room.

"What was that?" Kazia asked sleepily as she sat up from her cot beside Marya with a yawn.

Another scream echoed.

Marya quickly shoved aside her covers and jumped to her feet. "Sounds like one of the girls is in trouble. Come on!"

"Trouble?" Kazia hesitated, but Marya grabbed her by the arm and pulled her along.

Marya wasn't as convinced about the haunting as the others, but she did have her worries, and while Marya thought them the silly fantasies of an adolescent, she loved Kazia enough to keep such thoughts to herself. Kazia was, after all, her best friend and ally, and one couldn't have too many allies in such a competitive environment. Marya quickly pulled aside Kazia's cover and extended her hand. "We won't know until we go find out."

Kazia accepted her hand with some reluctance, and Marya dragged her to her feet. The two proceeded with caution out into the corridor with a few other curious students while others' voices whispered around them.

"*Czarownica!*" "*Wampir!*" "*Potwór!*" The words echoed around them as frightened girls' sleepy minds conjured fears of witches, vampires, monsters.

Though Marya didn't subscribe to their irrational fears, anxiety still laced through her. Something was most definitely *wrong.*

She took Kazia by the arm and led her in the direction of the screams, which had resumed. "That sounds like Ania," Marya whispered. Ania Wójcik was a classmate in the other makeshift dormitory down the hall. The daughter of a schoolteacher, Ania was easily alarmed. They'd heard her scream before when startled, but never this loudly.

"She'd better have a good reason for waking us all like this," Kazia muttered. Her brevity was admirable.

In moments, they'd covered the distance and burst through a large doorway into the long room housing the other students in rows of cots. Girls mumbled and giggled at the far end, gathered around one of the last cots. Marya, Kazia, and several others from their dormitory hurried toward them.

"What is it?" Padma Gorecki whispered as they approached.

"Ania the alarmist, of course!" Marya's chief challenger for top of the class, Adela, giggled. Marya pushed her way to the front of the crowd to find Ania sitting up in bed looking horrified. Tears flowed down her face.

Then she noticed Ania's skin.

What in the world?

The poor girl's skin had turned an incredible shade of bluish gray.

"Easy, Ania." Marya set a calming hand on her friend's shoulder and swallowed her surprise. Marya glanced her over for signs of blood or obvious injury but found nothing out of the ordinary.

"Easy? I'm blue! Can't you see it?" Ania exclaimed.

"She's turning into a delphinium," Adela teased. The blue flowers were native to Poland and common in the countryside.

Ania sobbed harder.

"Stop it, Adela," Marya scolded. Upsetting Ania further wouldn't help matters. She asked gently, "What happened?"

"I saw it—there!" Ania said, pointing toward the window. "There was thunder, and it woke me, and then lightning out the window, and I saw my face . . . and . . . my arms!" Tears ratcheted up again as her body wracked with sobs. Marya did her best to comfort her.

"What could have done this?" Kazia wondered aloud.

"For God's sake, she's not hurt," Adela said, sounding disgusted with all the fuss. "It's probably another stunt for attention—you know how she is. Besides, with her obsession for tonics, something was bound to happen sooner or later. Can we get some sleep now?"

Marya bit her tongue to silence a cutting remark. Adela's insensitivity was no surprise, but Ania certainly didn't need it now.

"Girls! What is the meaning of this?" Professor Lydia Rabarchak burst into the room holding a lantern. She made her way to the front of the crowd and took in the scene. "God's teeth!" She quickly recovered, and her mouth pursed into a fine, angry line. "Ania, what have you done to yourself?" Turning to the other girls, she motioned. "Back to your beds at once!"

Marya backed away reluctantly. Ania might have a penchant for seeking attention, but from the looks of her upset now, this was no purposeful act. She gave Ania's hand a reassuring squeeze before stepping away from the bed.

Padma wasn't so deferent to the professor. "But what could have caused this? She wouldn't dye herself."

"Spirits!" "A curse!" "Witchcraft!" Theories came from the surrounding girls.

"Nonsense," Professor Rabarchak said. "We'll fix it in the morning. Go!"

Marya hesitated even as she saw Kazia following the others toward the door. Like Padma, she knew Ania wouldn't go to such lengths.

Professor Rabarchak touched her arm. "You too, Marya. At once."

Marya sighed and bent to give Ania a quick hug. "It will be all right. We'll fix it. I promise." She joined her best friend and retreated down the hall. Marya knew it would be a while before any of the girls went back to sleep.

As they settled back onto their cots, the eerie whispers resumed.

"I told you magic is real," said Henna, one of Adela's best friends from the row on the opposite side of the room near the door.

"There are many possible explanations," Marya's sister Bronya scolded.

"Exactly," agreed Hela, their other sister. "While I don't think Ania did this to herself, there is surely a sound explanation."

"And magic is one of them," said Julia, Henna and Adela's other close friend.

"Or witchcraft," Adela said.

Unseen, Marya rolled her eyes. Those three were always talking such nonsense, trying to unsettle the others. It was certainly working tonight as well. "There is no such thing as magic," she said. "Whatever the cause, it can most certainly be explained with science." Adela had been right when she mentioned Ania's fondness for tonics. The girl was a hypochondriac, constantly paranoid of coming down with this or that.

"How do you know?" Adela demanded. "Always thinking you know everything. Some things are mysterious."

"We'll see, when we investigate tomorrow," Kazia suggested.

"Investigate? As if the teachers will allow such a distraction," Bronya said. "We're here to focus on our exams."

"Ania could be seriously ill," Svatka said.

Adela scoffed. "Her skin turned blue. Hardly a dangerous event."

"Bit frightening if it happened to you," Hela's friend Oda Bokoski replied.

Adela chuckled. "I wouldn't wake everyone up screaming."

"I still say it is magic," Henna said.

Several murmurs broke out, supporting her theory.

Tired of the silliness, Marya promised, "I will prove to you it's not." She'd start with investigating any tonics Ania may have brought with her first thing in the morning.

Adela exchanged mischievous looks with her friends. "Yes, do investigate, dear Marya. And we will do the same. We'll see who's right—magic or science."

Marya grunted. "Yes, we will."

"Fine! But in the morning!" Bronya scolded a third time. "Now, sleep."

Svatka, Oda, and Hela settled down in their beds, but Marya hesitated, still staring across the darkened room toward Adela.

"Now, Marya!" Bronya said.

"Yes, Bronya," Marya sighed and slid under the covers

It took almost an hour for her to fall back to sleep.

Marya hurried down to the castle's grand foyer, nearly panicked by the lateness of the morning. Full sunlight streaming through an ornate stained-glass window illuminated the faded green-and-gold carpet covering the worn stairs, silently scolding her for sleeping too long. Her sisters would think poorly of her, and her friends would tease her unendingly; Adela no doubt adding some snide remark with her sharp tongue. There were important matters to tend to—namely Ania's late-night malady.

As she reached the bottom step, she gripped the railing tight, gulping in air and listening to the quietness. At this time of day, the manor should be bustling. The serving staff, comprised of members from each family's household, should be hurrying about preparing for the large meal held each evening. Parents and professors should be grouped with students in review sessions. Odd. Where was everyone?

Distant voices drifted from the end of a dark hallway. Marya tipped her head, listening until she made out Kazia's laugh. The conservatory? What on earth were they doing in there? The room offered no natural light, and while gas lamps were plentiful, the covered furniture crammed in the small space made too great a fire hazard for practical use. With so many other more suitable rooms to choose from, they usually avoided the conservatory entirely.

She wandered down the long hall to the door cracked open. Hinges protested as she pushed it wide. "Kazia?"

"Marya! Come in, join us!" Kazia replied. A small flame flickered to life on the far side of the room nearest the wide marble hearth.

"Whatever are you doing in here?" Marya made her way around a draped harp, squinting at the shadowy figures seated on the floor. She counted ten forms—the entirety of the girls in her assigned wing of the manor, minus Ania. "Why is the house so quiet? What are you up to?" She reached the edge of their circle and frowned.

Hela laughed. "Adela swore if we were in complete darkness she could use magic to light the room. We are presently proving her wrong."

Marya cast her puzzled gaze between Kazia and Hela.

Before she could inquire further, Adela threw her hands up in exasperation. "It will work! Just give me a moment to get the accent right. You know how precise French must be." She bent her head and studied a wide, leather-bound book that lay open in her lap.

Marya settled down on the floor between Bronya and Kazia. "Do explain, if you would."

"Adela claims she found a book of spells in the west library," Bronya answered.

Always ready to endorse her friend, Henna piped up. "Not just one—two! We found them when we were reviewing our history lessons while waiting on your sleepy head to get out of bed." She leaned on Adela's shoulder amicably. "They were in a hidden compartment that was cracked open on the bottom of a shelf."

"I'm not sure how much studying was involved, if they were exploring cabinets," Kazia murmured in Marya's ear.

Marya jabbed her with her elbow. She didn't wish for the fighting to start again. Instead, she sought to satisfy her most pressing curiosity. "Where is everyone else? The house is still and quiet."

"It wasn't an hour ago." Svatka chuckled. "You missed the excitement. It seems a critter of some type made its way into the kitchen. It was quite feral and bit Miss Susan, the Volkomps' cook. She let out a scream that should have woken the dead. They finally chased it off. Our fathers are presently working to repair the hole in the foundation that it came through. Our mothers are trying to soothe Miss Susan, and others are tending to Ania, who is still absolutely inconsolable."

"Speaking of which, we all had an agreement last evening to create a plan and get started," Marya said. "It seems now is the perfect time."

Nods of agreement went around the circle. Even Adela dragged her attention away from the book to say, "It's magic, and I wager the answer is in one of these books."

"Very well. You and Henna and Julia go study the books." It couldn't possibly be magic that turned Ania's skin blue, and Marya lacked the patience to entertain the idea. The sooner they parted ways, the quicker she could prove Adela wrong. "I will begin cataloging data with Kazia and Svatka. Bronya and Hela, you take the others and keep our parents preoccupied with questions about the lessons, so they don't come looking for us."

Bronya gave her a disproving frown but nodded her acceptance.

One by one, the others filtered out of the room, leaving Marya to talk with her closest conspirators. "Svatka you were with Ania all day yesterday reviewing the great poets. Make an accounting of everything you did and everywhere you went, even if it seems insignificant."

"Easy enough," Svatka agreed.

Marya turned to Kazia. "Let's you and I go inspect Ania's room. Dye is only one way something can change color. There must be traces left behind."

Ever the scientifically minded, Kazia countered, "It could have been a chemical reaction of some sort."

Marya paused. How true—and why hadn't she considered such? Chemistry was her strength, while Kazia frequently struggled. "We would still find traces of some compound, so we must be certain to look for *anything* out of the ordinary. What might appear as dust, may be something else entirely."

Kazia groaned. "If we are analyzing dust particles, we will be here three years hence."

"Not analyzing. Observing. Look." She drew her fingers over a patch of long-forgotten ash on the floor in front of the mantle. "The difference between disturbed dust and what has been sitting forever is what we're looking for."

As Marya stood, taking up the lamp with her, a blood-curdling scream rang out. The girls froze, glancing at one another apprehensively, then bolted down the hall toward the erupting cacophony of noise.

"Sweet heavens, she's dead!" a woman cried.

Dead? Impossible!

A ball of dread formed in Marya's gut. Svatka had gone quite pale. They rounded a corner and burst into the normally cheery sitting room off the grand foyer.

The adults huddled together in the center of the room, some trying to keep the approaching students at bay, others conversing in hushed voices, while still others rushed to and fro, shouting for maids and other attendants. Beyond them lay the prone form of Hilde Lichtensteldt. Her eyes stared unblinking at the ornate ceiling. Vegetables scattered around her from an overturned basket.

"Are you certain?" someone asked, echoing Marya's own disbelief.

She recognized her father's voice. "Quite. She is cold and not breathing. When was the last time anyone passed through this room?"

"And look at her skin," Oda called out. "It's blue, like Ania's!"

As clamoring voices erupted once again, Marya drew in a deep breath and turned to Kazia, meeting eyes that were full of dread and sorrow. Dragging her best friend by the arm, she hurried toward the makeshift dorms. She was more convinced than ever a *logical* explanation existed. She just needed to discover it before things in the castle worsened—not that they could get much worse. But why? Who would want to harm Hilde, much less Ania?

As they climbed the stairs, Kazia breathed in starts, as if trying to hide tears.

Guilt tugged at Marya. Since death had claimed her mother and sister, her emotions had remained muted. She wasn't insensitive—she *did* feel bad about Hilde. She'd been perfectly fine yesterday and didn't deserve such an early demise. But whatever was going on might endanger all of them, and she had to act quickly. In the lab, she had the chance of making sense of all of it. But first, they had to gather some samples to test.

Entering the dormitory down the hall from their own, Marya led Kazia straight to the bed Ania had occupied and scanned her belongings.

"Where's Ania?" Kazia wondered.

Marya ran her palms across the bedding, feeling for any hidden objects, and then searched the corners of the bed.

Kazia's expression flattened as she bottled up her emotions. "What are we looking for?"

"Those tonics she brought, for one," Marya replied. "But anything suspicious or unordinary should be examined."

The two divided and looked around the area thoroughly; Marya found a bottle of tonic underneath the bed, while Kazia discovered a discarded bar of soap wrapped in a washcloth that had been dropped in a corner, staining the wood floor. Marya led her friend to the bathroom where Ania had bathed. As they rounded a corner, Adela brushed past in a hurry and disappeared down the hall before they could even ask what she was doing there.

"Was she just in the bathroom?" Kazia wondered.

"I don't know," Marya said, wondering if Adela had disturbed the evidence. "Come on." They hurried toward the bathroom.

Nothing looked disturbed. The cast iron tub hadn't been used since Ania's accident as bathing was customarily reserved for before bed. Therefore, Marya felt confident any evidence that might prove pertinent remained.

Kneeling beside the tub, she examined the area around the drain with great care.

"Do you see anything?" Kazia asked.

"I'm studying," Marya said. "See if you can find her shampoo and soap lying about or even used linens."

As Kazia searched, Marya leaned over the edge of the tub and ran a finger around the drain. Her finger picked up powder residue. Pulling a microscope slide out of her skirt pocket, she wiped the residue on it. She pulled a metal probe from the same pocket and slid it around the drain, gathering more of the powdery substance, which she carefully applied to two other slides.

Kazia found a bottle of shampoo with a water stain around it on a shelf in the medicine cabinet. They proceeded to the lab to examine their findings.

"There's no way to know for certain the items we collected were Ania's," Kazia reminded her as Marya laid them out beside a microscope.

"No, but proximity alone increases the likelihood," Marya said. "We need to collect samples from Ania herself as soon as we can." Marya slid the slide she'd prepared under the microscope and put her eye to the ocular lens. "We'll need hydrochloric acid and potassium iodide. Check the compounds on the shelves for me, please.

"Also a burner," Marya added. There were basic tests for discovering the presence of various compounds that she'd read about, and she remembered some of the steps but would have to review her texts for the details. With no gas at the castle, they'd have to use an alcohol burner, but Marya remembered seeing one on the shelf in a corner. Kazia located a bottle labeled HCl and brought it to Marya, frowning. "Have you done this before?"

"No, but I read about it," Marya said, "and my father discussed similar processes with a pharmacist once when Zofia and Mother were ill. We can look it up."

Kazia searched again, soon returning with a bottle labeled KI.

Marya smiled. "Good. Let me just leave a note to not disturb these, and we can go check the books for the details." She quickly scribbled out a note and led Kazia back to the dorms to consult their texts.

After consulting their texts, Marya and Kazia gathered samples in the kitchen. Fate proved to be on their side, when it came to Hilde Lichtensteldt. Sidetracked by the sudden, necessary arrangements for a body, the unfortunate cook's corpse had been left unattended. Marya sucked up her courage and obtained a skin scraping. After, she collected samples from some vegetables that had been found scattered around the body.

Kazia eyed her. "Are you sure you know what you're doing?"

"Yes," Marya said. "And the tests we will conduct should provide answers." Returning to the lab, Marya scraped skin cells from the bathroom into a test tube, adding a few drops of hydrochloric acid. She repeated the process in another test tube using Hilde's samples. Finally, she scraped samples from the vegetables and made up similar test tubes.

They waited.

A solid precipitate formed in the test tube with the bathroom skin sample. The girls heated the test tubes in hot water until the precipitate settled at the bottom. Using a dropper, they sucked up some liquid, making sure not to get any of the solid with it, and put that in a new test tube. Finally, they added potassium iodide to the new test tube. The solution remained clear, so Marya then returned her attention to the white precipitate. She added a few drops of ammonia, causing the precipitate to dissolve.

"Silver," Marya noted, looking at Kazia. "If it had been something else, like lead, it would have turned yellow first. Adding ammonia confirms it's silver." They examined the test tubes with the sample of Hilde's skin and the vegetable skins.

"Nothing's happening," Kazia said.

"That means neither silver nor lead nor any other metallic ions are present," Marya said. "It could be something else." She put a beaker of

Ania's tonic on the alcohol burner while Kazia retrieved the bottle of potassium iodide. "We don't have a centrifuge, so this will take a while. While it cools, we find Ania and ask her some questions."

In a few minutes, Marya took the beaker off the burner and turned the burner off, and the two girls went to look for Ania.

A few hundred yards through dark woods was enough to unnerve the normally steady Marya. A parent had told them Ania went home to recover, and the walk there from the castle was two miles through thick, hilly woods. Add in the underlying anxiety of getting caught, and by the time she reached the large tree under Ania's window, her hands were shaking.

Kazia's unease showed in the way she constantly wrung her hands and peeked over her shoulder. Wandering about in the dark, unchaperoned, just wasn't done, not even in the name of science. There would be three kinds of trouble to pay if they were discovered missing. Particularly from her father.

Marya took a deep breath in front of a gnarled trunk. A sturdy branch brushed against the window frame. "Wait here."

Kazia nodded.

Marya jumped and grabbed the branch. Despite the cumbersome interference of her petticoats and skirts, she made it up rather quickly.

Ania sat tucked into her bed, reading.

Marya rapped on the windowpane.

Ania jumped. Surprise flashed across her face, changing to a smile. She hurriedly opened the window. "What are you doing here?"

Marya shook her head. "There's no time to explain, other than we're working on your condition. I need the tonic you used the night you . . . changed."

Ania retrieved a small, corked bottle off her vanity. "Is this the same tonic that was in the bottle under your bed in the dorm?"

"Yes."

"Excellent, thank you. Now give me your arm."

Puzzled, Ania pushed up her nightshirt's sleeve and stuffed her arm through the window.

Marya pulled a slide from her pocket, collected a scraping, and tucked the slide safely away. She smiled. "If my theory isn't correct, I'll write and explain. If it is correct, someone will inform you tomorrow morning."

Ania hesitated before nodding. "Be careful."

"I will." With a slight wave, Marya shimmied down the tree to Kazia. "Got it! One more test to run." *And then, Adela, you will lose your power over the younger girls.*

Kazia groaned. "We're going to get caught. They will be doing the bedtime headcount soon."

Marya glanced at the moon and shook her head. "We've plenty of time—if we hurry."

Marya and Kazia went straight to the lab where they'd left the beaker of tonic.

"Could be silver," Marya said, eyeing the precipitate which had formed. "But let's test the sample we got from Ania to be sure." They set about preparing new test tubes and beakers and applying the same tests to them.

As Marya double-checked Kazia's work and they waited for the tonic to heat properly, they heard voices in the hall. Some kind of argument.

Kazia snuck a peek. "It's Adela!" she whispered. "What are they saying?"

"I can't hear," Kazia said.

Marya hurried over and opened the door wider.

"Careful! They'll see!" Kazia whispered.

Marya leaned her head out into the shadows to listen. She couldn't see the girls, but she recognized their voices.

"You can't go! They'll notice, and we'll all be in trouble!" Julia said.

"I have to," Adela countered. "It's important."

"What's so important?" Henna asked, sounding suspicious.

"I can't tell you, but it is," Adela replied. "I'll be back before they notice. But you must divert their attention while I slip out."

"How are we supposed to accomplish that?" Julia asked.

A moment of silence lapsed before Adela responded, "Tell them something witchy or magical happened. They'll go to investigate."

It's always about the power, isn't it? Marya pursed her lips, irritated with Adela's manipulation.

"But there'll be nothing there," Henna said. "Besides, that's not very funny given what happened to Hilde and Ania."

"Just do it, please?" Adela urged.

"And what do we say when there's nothing there?" Julia asked.

"It disappeared without a trace—that's magic," Adela said. "Trust me. No one will question." There was a shuffling sound, then she added, "I have to go. Hurry. Please."

Following a sigh, Henna said, "Well, she is our friend, and it's plausible."

Someone grunted. Julia said, "Fine. But if we get in trouble for this—"

"You won't! I promise!" Adela insisted. Footsteps hurried away.

"Come on," Marya said, turning to Kazia. "We've got to follow Adela."

"What about the burner?" Kazia asked. "And the headcount?"

Marya flipped off the burner and rushed back to the door. "It'll cool by the time we return. We'll risk the headcount, and our punishment will be less if *all* of us are missing together." She tugged rags from a pile near the table. "Wrap your shoes in these to muffle the sound."

Adela didn't embrace the dark and carried a small lantern.

When Marya and Kazia exited the castle, delayed as they were from covering their shoes, they easily spied Adela disappearing around a line of overgrown bushes near the edge of the forest. Motioning Kazia to hurry, Marya hastened her pace. If Adela slipped out of eyesight and made it into the woods, the thick overgrowth would make it difficult to find even her light.

As they rounded the edge of the shrub row, Marya pulled up short. "Look!" she whispered, pointing to the edge of the forest.

Kazia braced a hand on Marya's shoulder to keep from crashing into her. "Apologies."

"She has something in her hands." As they watched, Adela knelt over a wide, flat stone and fumbled with something. She tipped the lantern toward the stone, dribbling oil out.

"Papers of some type," Kazia observed. "Is she trying to—"

"Burn them!" Marya rushed forward, crossing the scant distance. "Adela, stop!"

Adela whipped around, dropping the papers she held in her surprise. "What are you two doing here?"

Marya snatched the papers. "The better question is what are you doing with these?"

"It's no concern of yours." Adela grabbed for them. "Give them back. They're mine."

Marya held them out of her reach, ducked behind Kazia, and quickly scanned them. She gave Kazia a small, satisfied smile. "Oh, but they will be of interest to the professors." She tucked them into her pocket. "Is this what you were trying to do in the bathroom—cover your tracks?"

"What?! I never—"

Marya cut her off. "You'll come back with us now."

"You're a fine one to tell me what to do."

Marya shrugged. "Have it your way. You might want the opportunity to speak for yourself, however."

Fear turned Adela's face white. "You can't turn me in. You *can't.* They'll kick me out forever!"

Marya said nothing, but simply strode toward the castle as Adela continued her pitiful protesting.

As soon as the three girls reentered the castle through a servant's door in the west corner, Bronya and Hela were upon them.

"Where have you been?" Bronya asked. "Three of you out after dark! If the parents or professors caught you, we'd all suffer."

"It was important," Marya said.

"We found evidence to explain what happened to Ania and poor Hilde!" Kazia exclaimed.

Hela's expression lit with excitement. "You did? What is it?"

"We'll tell you soon enough," Marya motioned to Kazia to hold her tongue for now. "We need to go to the lab and retrieve more evidence before we explain. Please take Adela and gather the others in the library. We'll be there shortly."

"I can walk!" Adela snapped and glared.

"Don't let her out of your sight!" Marya warned. "We followed her into the woods. She's been up to no good, and we can prove it."

Bronya frowned and grabbed Adela by the arm. "You'd best come with us then."

Adela scowled at Marya and Kazia.

"We can't just detain her for no reason," Hela said. "We may be asked by the professors. You need to tell us—"

"All will be revealed," Marya assured her. "We must go with haste!" Leaving no time for further argument, she grabbed Kazia by the arm and hurried up the stairs to the second floor.

It was almost half an hour before Marya and Kazia gathered the test results and other evidence and joined the others in the library. As they walked down the hall, voices carried through the partly open doors—Adela already mounting a defense.

"My Aunt Elka knew all about magic," Adela was saying. "Only witchcraft could do something so sinister."

"We've been saying that ever since we found Ania!" Julia declared, backing her friend.

"Yes!" Henna echoed.

Marya gritted her teeth. Adela, of all people, knew precisely the lies she spewed. As she opened her mouth to chastise her, however, Bronya voiced reason.

"Many things could have turned Ania's skin blue. There are other explanations."

"There have been no signs of witchcraft around the castle," Hela added. "We've explored."

Thank you, dear sisters. Marya let out a relieved sigh and reached for the doorknob. Her relief was short-lived as Adela continued, undeterred.

"What about Hilde?" Adela argued. "Whatever it was killed her!"

"*Czarownica!*" Padma exclaimed. "It has to be!"

"Or the castle is haunted," Svatka countered.

"A ghost didn't do this!" Padma replied.

"Whatever it is, we're not safe! We need to go home!" Oda exclaimed, clinging to Hela's arm.

The voices mounted in pitch and ferocity, quickly brewing to a point of chaos. Frustrated beyond all reason, and anxious to put an end to all the absurdity, Marya yanked open the door.

"It's science!" she exclaimed.

She and Kazia carried the samples and the microscope to a table in the center of the room. As Kazia motioned to the others for silence, Marya arranged their findings.

"Come see," Kazia said.

The other girls gathered closer, a few adults joining them, including Professor Lydia Rabarchak, who towered over the table.

"What's all this, Marya?" the professor demanded with a stern look.

"We gathered samples from the bathroom, the dorm, Ania's house, the kitchen, and the gardens," Marya began.

"Samples of what?" Padma asked.

"Just listen," Kazia replied, punctuated by a shushing sound.

"Using hydrochloric acid, potassium iodide, and lye, we did some tests on the samples of Hilde's and Ania's hair," Marya began explaining. "We mixed the samples with hydrochloric acid. With Ania's sample, a precipitate formed immediately, and we added the potassium iodide, producing a no coloring, indicating the presence of silver."

"Silver? What's that mean?" Julia wondered.

"With Hilde's, there was no reaction to either the hydrochloride acid or potassium iodide," Marya said.

"That proves nothing!" Adela exclaimed triumphantly.

Marya raised a finger to stop her. "Then we tested Ania's tonic, both a sample from beside her bed in the dorm, and a bottle she had taken home. Again, the resulting supernatant fluid had no color."

"Indicating the probable presence of silver," Kazia added.

"Silver chloride, to be exact," Marya went on, "which we found a bottle of under Adela's bed in the dorm."

"What?! It's not mine!" Adela protested.

Kazia handed Marya the papers they'd rescued from Adela in the woods.

"Among the papers we found Adela attempting to burn in the woods tonight was this research paper on the effects of overexposure to silver chloride in turning human's skin blue," Marya said.

"You poisoned her?!" Bronya said, whirling toward Adela with an accusing glare.

"It's not poisonous, but overexposure for a period of time can produce results like Ania experienced," Marya said.

"Okay, but Hilde's skin was blue, and there was no sign of silver, you said," Henna replied. "How do you explain that?"

"When we talked with Hilde's boyfriend, the gardener Isaak, he showed us a tonic he has been using," Kazia said, holding up a bottle.

"A tonic? What kind of tonic?" Professor Rabarchak asked.

"A growth tonic," Kazia said.

"Yes," Marya continued, "which Isaak has been employing in the castle's garden."

"So he used a tonic, big deal," Adela protested.

"One of the ingredients on the bottle was nitrates," Marya said.

"Which are difficult to test for," Professor Rabarchak reminded them, causing Adela to smile smugly.

"Yes," Marya agreed, "but we did find ferrous ions present."

"Ferrous iron? So what? That's not nitrates," Adela proclaimed.

"No, but it is an indicator of the presence of nitrates," Professor Rabarchak said, looking impressed.

Adela's face fell.

"Your blood contains ferric iron ions. When you ingest too many nitrates, they get metabolized to nitrites, which reduce the ferric iron to ferrous iron. That makes the blood incapable of sustaining life."

"Which can be caused by over-ingestion of nitrates," Kazia added. "They also can turn the skin blue."

"Apparently, Hilde sampled a vegetable that had not been washed yet," Marya said.

"So Hilde was poisoned!" Svatka exclaimed. "Poor Hilde!" Several other girls echoed the sentiment.

"I did not poison Hilde!" Adela said, turning pleading eyes on Professor Rabarchak. "You must believe me."

"And what did you have to do with Ania's problem?" The professor asked.

Adela waffled a beat before wilting under everyone's accusatory stares. "It was a prank! You know how she is—always whining about this illness or that. It was meant to teach her a lesson, a harmless lesson."

"So you put silver chloride in her tonic?" Marya asked.

Adela's shoulders sank as she nodded.

"So we're not all in danger?" Oda asked, relieved.

"The two incidents were unrelated," Professor Rabarchak proclaimed. "And we all owe Marya and Kazia a debt of gratitude for uncovering the causes."

Applause came from around the room, and Marya felt herself blush.

"So the castle isn't haunted?" Svatka said. "No *czarownica*?"

"No witches or magic at all," Hela added, looking pleased. "So Marya was right, magic isn't real." She smiled proudly at her sister.

Marya smiled and replied, "No, sister, science *is* magic."

Science Note:

Marya accomplished many amazing things in her lifetime, but as far as we know she was never involved in investigating or solving any murders, certainly not during high school. However, forensic science is a highly developed form of science nowadays that is involved daily in solving crimes. Although forensic science was only in the beginning stages in the late nineteenth century when our stories are set, many people did use real science in attempts to uncover and decipher potential evidence in those cases. Sherlock Holmes is a fictional detective famous for this, so it isn't hard to imagine someone as gifted as Marya lending a hand.

For our story, we consulted with a high school chemistry teacher and science fiction writer named Jay Werkheiser who teaches in Pennsylvania, but any errors in our interpretation or depiction of the actual science are ours. The methods Marya employs in our story to find and interpret evidence are all real science.

Ag (silver) ions deposited in the skin can cause the color change, so a skin sample should show that Ag ions are present.

Chloroquine was used as a malaria drug commonly, so it would have been available.

As for mounting slides back then, they likely would have used forceps or probes. Metal would be most likely but wood is possible. Also, centrifuges were pretty widely available by this time period.

The most common way to ingest silver (some would people do it intentionally because it has antibiotic properties) is as colloidal silver chloride (AgCl). Colloidal AgCl is a grayish-white solid with microscopic particles suspended in a liquid. It could give it a cloudy appearance, if they looked at it closely. In testing, supernatant fluid will immediately form a yellow precipitate if lead is present; in this case the poisoning is silver, so the fluid will remain clear. They'd heat the sample to the boiling point, then centrifuge it to settle the precipitate, then use a pipette to collect the liquid. Once that liquid cools, they'd test it with potassium iodide. If it stays clear, it's silver. If it turns cloudy yellow, it's lead.

The hydrochloric acid (HCl) wouldn't react with nitrates. Nitrates are difficult to test for. Most inorganic qualitative tests identify ions by precipitation, and nitrates never precipitate. Some use flame test color, but nitrates don't do that either. Today we have a technique that involves using aluminum to reduce the nitrate to ammonia, but that wasn't known back in the 1800s, so the best option would have been detecting the oxidized iron (3+ charge) and surmising that it must be nitrate poisoning from that. (Normally iron is in the 2+ state in hemoglobin, but nitrates convert to nitrites, which oxidize iron 2+ to iron 3+.)

The qualitative test for it is a real procedure. You take fluid from the skin sample and mix it with HCl. If you get a precipitate, that indicates an ion like Ag, Pb (lead), or Hg (mercury) is present. A real quick way to distinguish Ag is to heat, centrifuge, and collect the supernatant fluid. Add some KI (potassium iodide) to that. If it forms a yellow precipitate, it's Pb. If not, it's likely Ag. High school chemistry teachers often test students on this for finals at the end of the year.

HORSE CART

by
JANE YOLEN

Where was she on that day
Pierre fell beneath the cart,
slipping between life and death?
Did he feel a sharp push in the small of his back?
She was always quick to pass him.
Did he scream her name
as the wheels kneeled on his neck?
Did he say he could not breathe?
Or did he give in to her wishes,
as he always did,
making way for his supplanter,
that young fool whom she never married,
that final a prayer between the wheels
finding the ear of a forgiving God
In which none of the three believed.

A *Glow* IN THE *Dark*

by
SCOTT SIGLER

Green fire raged through the brick and stone corridor, whorls of it catching in the charred support timbers, reflecting off the thin, rippling pools of water on the stone floor.

The chest-sized ball of green flame came straight toward her. An impossibility. A *monster.*

Marya heard the others screaming behind her. She wanted to scream too, but terror squeezed tight her chest, her stomach, her heart. She pulled the shotgun stock to a shoulder already bruised from practice shots. Her hands trembled, her *body* trembled—the end of the barrel danced in time, wild and unpredictable.

She hesitated, tried to steady the heavy gun, but in that instant the glowing thing reached her. She threw herself down on the wet floor, turning at the last instant to land on her shoulder, trying to protect the shotgun. She felt a cold heat cascade across her, suffered a wave of vile emotions that boiled up and erupted in her mind: revulsion, hatred, jealousy . . . the need to *hurt.*

The thing raced past her, toward her sister and their friends. Flickering light cast strange, jerking shadows that danced across brick and stone and water . . .

. . . light that died out when the ball of green fire vanished around a corner.

The curls of the same flame flickered and fluttered in the blackened wood, but they quickly faded and winked out of existence. With the glow gone, the tunnel was once again lit only by three lanterns the friends had brought with them.

The rancid emotions, though, were slower to leave. They fought to hold on to Marya's soul.

"Bronya," she whispered, "are you all right?"

Her older sister lay face down in a puddle. Bronya lifted her head, let out a puff of air, scattering tunnel water in a spray that caught the lantern light.

"No," she said, the tremble in her voice cutting the word into three syllables. "I want to go home."

Marya wanted to do the same. For all her talk about fighting for the cause, about guiding a dying era into extinction, she'd never thought it would be like this.

She wanted to leave, but she would not, because if she did, she knew she would never come back.

It was now or never.

"Oda, Henryk," she said, "are you all right?"

Further along the corridor, Henryk, the only boy in their group, was kneeling in the water, one arm around a girl on her knees, head down, tucked into a tight ball, the other holding up a lantern, its flickering light playing off the walls and the still-rippling puddles.

"Oda is scared," he said.

From the sound of his voice and the wide-eyed look on his face, so was Henryk. Marya was too—she'd never been so terrified in all her life.

Henryk lightly shook the girl's shoulder.

"Get up, sister," he said. "We're getting out of here. We follow the ribbons, and we get back to the surface."

Oda remained tightly tucked, moved nothing but her head, which she shook nonstop, a constant, wordless *no-no-no*. Her dress was half-soaked with water, as were Henryk's pants. Their shivering might be more from the cold than from fear, the same cold that had flooded Marya's boots and pants even before she'd thrown herself down into five centimeters of frigid, stagnant water. A wet shirt and pants were better than a wet dress, though. A heavy, wet dress was harder to walk in, harder to move in. She'd told both Bronya and Oda to borrow clothes from Henryk, but they hadn't listened. They *never* listened.

"It will return," Marya said. "And when it does, it will be louder, angrier. Get up and prepare yourselves."

This was the first time Marya had seen it, seen anything like it, but she'd interviewed survivors and believed she knew what to expect. The people she'd talked to from Drzewica, and even the nearby villages of Zakościele and Antoniów all told the same story—the *błędne ogniki,* called by some *will-o'-the wisp,* always returned, and when it did, it moaned, then it *screeched.*

Bronya stood. Her wet dress hung heavy on her. She adjusted the coil of rope on her shoulder and tried to wipe water away from it even as she picked up her still-flickering lantern.

"What I just saw was impossible," she said. "I've changed my mind. It's *evil.* I felt it. Let's leave, now."

Of course Bronya had changed her mind. Bronya had assumed the *ogniki* was just another old wives' tale, something spoken of by superstitious villagers trying to explain away the howling wind at night, or deep shadows and unknown lights.

Bronya hadn't *believed.* Now she did. All of them did.

Henryk hauled Oda to her feet, kept an arm around his tiny, fourteen-year-old sister as he glared at Marya.

"You were supposed to shoot it," he said. "Why didn't you?"

Marya hadn't shot because she'd been unable to accept what she'd seen, even though she'd interviewed five different people who'd seen it at five different times. Their stories and descriptions matched so closely that the five people might as well have been standing shoulder-to-shoulder in the ruined castle's catacombs, all witnessing the same thing. Marya had prepared herself, or thought she had, but no amount of reading made one ready to face a ball of green flame trailed by a twisting tail of fire.

"It came too fast," Marya said. "I'll be ready next time."

Henryk kept glaring, pulled Oda tighter to him. She stared down at the wet floor. While Bronya carried a rope and Marya carried the shotgun, Henryk carried a satchel. A now-*wet* satchel. He opened the flap, looked inside, then upturned the contents—broken glass and clumps of soggy salt poured out, splashed into the water covering the floor.

"That was stupid," Bronya said.

Henryk glared at her. "What was I supposed to do, dry it out? It doesn't matter, because we're leaving. Right now."

Marya thought he might demand the shotgun, insist on carrying it because she'd failed. He didn't ask for it. Even though he'd helped Marya with her hypothesis, helped her make the special shotgun shells, Henryk *hated* firearms.

"We can do this," she said. "We can beat it. We can have this place to ourselves. The old ways are dying out."

She felt stupid for saying that, a feeling she didn't suffer often.

"Are you going to start up with your *dinosaurs* idiocy again?" Bronya glowered, shook her head. "Did that look like a dinosaur to you, Marya? Just because dominant lifeforms died out and were replaced doesn't mean that whatever that *thing* was is going to die out."

Her *extinction theory.* That had been her pitch to the others, the reason for coming here.

Spirits and demons and sprites had plagued humans for millennia, but as the ability to gather evidence increased due to science, there was little or no evidence of those things to be found. Bronya and many others thought that was because such spirits hadn't existed in the first place. Marya disagreed. She believed such things did exist, at least in some form. An immeasurable, massive number of observations from multiple people in multiple generations across multiple cultures pointed to the most-obvious answer that *something* of the spirit realm did, indeed exist. The fact that such observations seemed to be decreasing as science and civilization expanded wasn't because the spirit realm didn't exist—it was because science and civilization were *destroying* the spirit realm.

Marya didn't know how, or why, but if the haunts and specters could be pushed back, if they could be destroyed, then there was an opportunity to drive them out of places where they still existed.

Places like Drzewica Castle.

"I didn't believe before, but I do now," Bronya said. "We're not ready for this, sister. We don't even know if your idea will work."

Marya's frustration grew. If Bronya left, Henryk and Oda would certainly leave with her. Marya couldn't do this alone. She couldn't.

"We can beat it," she said again. "The reason that this is hard, that this is scary, is the very reason we'll have privacy, that we'll be safe. That we—"

"*No*," Oda shouted, finally lifting her head. Lamplight reflected off her wet face, glistened off her wet clothes. "We're *children*, Marya. Children! We need to get out of here."

But they weren't children. Marya was fifteen. Bronya, sixteen. At eighteen, Henryk was the oldest.

"We all saw it," Marya said. "It's real. It moved like a living thing. If my hypothesis is right, we can kill it. This place can be ours. We . . ."

Her words trailed off as a low moaning rolled through the corridors, bouncing off the stone and brick.

"Oh, God," Oda said, her head again shaking in a chorus of denial. "Henryk get me out of here!"

Henryk looked around, up and forward and back, searching for the source of the sound. They all did. It grew louder, deeper, more chilling.

Marya's hands gripped the shotgun. This time, she would shoot. But would her hypothesis work? Or would she be trapped down here with that thing, where the ancient specters of the past held on, refused to be pushed out?

A dim flicker of green from far behind Henryk and Oda was their only warning. That flicker, then the ball of light, blazing brighter than it had before, crackling and hissing, seeming to set the entire corridor—water and all—aflame with emerald fire.

Marya couldn't shoot, not with her friends between her and the monster.

She ran toward them, boots splashing in the thin, cold water.

The ball rushed toward them.

She stepped past Henryk and Oda, shouldered the shotgun as she did, as she'd been taught, then promptly forgot the rest of the training—she pulled *both* triggers. Recoil sent her staggering, spinning, stumbling. Her shoulder went numb.

The light washed over her. Marya heard the screams of her friends.

The sound of glass breaking—someone had dropped a lantern.

The piercing moan threatened to break the corridor itself, to collapse it, to bury Marya under tons of stone and dirt.

Through the green, she saw a spot of yellow. A lantern. That spot of light became her world. It was the way out, away from this demon, this horrible place.

Marya clutched the shotgun tight. She ran, booted feet splashing through the ankle-high water.

Below the old castle, the corridors were dark as midnight. At ground level, inside the walls, the setting sun gleamed off the tops of trees reaching up from the fractured stones that had once been a courtyard, played off the pockmarked stone walls, walls still soot-blackened in many places from an ancient fire.

Marya ran through the courtyard's thick underbrush and tall, wild grass, ran for the doors of the gate tower. Long shadows stretched out from the walls, but there was yet enough light to see, to avoid shin-breaking blocks and ankle-tearing cracks.

She reached the gate tower's tall, old door, a door that was little more than worm-eaten planks thrown together in a halfhearted effort to keep people out. Many times, treasure seekers had forced their way through the door, breaking it multiple times in multiple places. No one bothered to fix it anymore. The kind of people who actually fixed things didn't come here.

Marya shouldered past the door and careened down the overgrown slope, barely keeping her balance, her arms clutching the shotgun tight to her chest. She realized she hadn't reloaded it.

At the bottom of the slope, near the edge of a fetid moat, she saw a small, flickering light. Bronya, her face illuminated by the lantern she held high in one trembling hand. Standing next to her was, Oda, her arms hugging tight her own shoulders.

Marya reached them and felt the smallest shred of safety in again being around other people. She forced out ragged words as she opened the shotgun's breech, pulled out the spent brass shells.

"Where . . . is . . . Henryk?"

Bronya stared, not at Marya but past her, up at the old castle.

Oda shook her head slowly.

Marya put the spent brass shells in the left pocket of her soaking pants, fumbled for two new cartridges in her right.

"Bronya," she said, "*where is Henryk?*"

Marya's older sister blinked wide eyes, as if she only now realized Marya was standing there.

"I don't know," Bronya said.

Marya slid the new shells into the chambers. The sound of metal on metal comforted her, slightly, even though she still didn't know if her hypothesis had merit, or if she was up against something that was beyond physics, beyond science.

"Henryk dropped the lantern," Oda said. "It broke. He told me to follow the light. I started to, then I fell. We got separated. I saw another light. I remembered the *ogniki* make fake lights to trick people, but I couldn't stay there one more minute. I picked one, and I followed it—it was Bronya's. I . . . I don't know which one Henryk followed."

Marya felt a fresh chill wash through her. The legends said the *ogniki* created lights to trick the unaware, to lure them through dark places to somewhere they would drown.

Bronya cupped her hands to her mouth, shouted Henryk's name. The three girls waited. They heard no response.

Bronya did it again.

They were supposed to be quiet, supposed to do nothing that might alert the villagers in distant houses that they were here, but Marya said nothing.

Again, there was no response.

Marya turned in a slow circle, eyes searching the darkening woods, seeking out any sign of Henryk.

She faced the burned-out castle, stared hard at the ratty gatehouse door as if staring hard might make her friend appear. Her eyes flicked higher, across windows for any sign of Henryk, even though they couldn't be behind those windows unless he'd climbed up brick and stone.

Seven decades ago, flames had gutted the place, the fire caused not by an invading army but by a toppled candle. That's what the villages had told her during her dozens of interviews. The roof had collapsed, along with most of the floors. It had never been repaired. The castle walls still stood, tall and empty.

The owners had, apparently, burned alive. They'd also owned most of the town and vast swaths of the surrounding countryside. According to the locals, they had been horrible people and predatory landlords, quick to seize property and evict residents. Most evictions were legal. Others were not. Stories abounded of grandparents and great-grandparents who had been beaten, badly injured, even murdered.

Were those long-dead owners the spirits that had become the *ogniki*? That fit the legends, that the demons of light lurked near the bodies of deceitful people who were interred with forgotten treasures. The castle owners supposedly had chests of gold, gold that—if it ever existed— had been lost in the fire.

The lure of that gold had drawn adventurous souls for decades following the blaze. But few returned from those searches. Those that did told stories of floating lights luring them deeper into the ancient tunnels below the castle, of hellish moans, of friends lost forever. Most survivors were too terrified to return, even to look for their missing brothers, fathers, or sons. Of those that did go back, most were never heard from again.

"When he comes out," Bronya said, "we're leaving. Others at the Flying University can find another place for the labs. I didn't think the ghost stories were real, but we both just saw what happened."

Marya found herself nodding in agreement.

"It was a good idea," Oda said. "A good idea."

It had seemed so perfect—hiding in plain sight, in a place that was so "haunted" no one went there, a place with underground passages and chambers in which to hold classes, to build a library, to even create actual *laboratories* that didn't have to be broken down and moved every time they were used lest the Russians discover them and arrest everyone involved. A place where food could be stored, where beds could be set up. A place where girls could enjoy concentrated study for weeks on end and not be in fear of being discovered.

A place where the damned Russians would never look.

The sun crept toward the horizon, started to vanish behind the tree line.

Marya heard a clattering sound. It was Oda, shivering so hard her teeth clacked.

No birds here. No sound of animals. Or people, even though village houses weren't all that far away. This place . . . quiet, like the tomb that it was.

And then, another sound, thin and distant, barely audible, filtering up and out of the old ruin.

The scream of a man—Henryk.

Was he hurt? Had he fallen, or was the monster tearing into him? Marya's heart kicked in fear, both of what might be happening to Henryk, and what might await her and her sister if they went after him.

"We have to help him," Bronya said.

She was right. It didn't matter what might be waiting.

There was no longer a decision to be made—the scream decided for them.

"I can't," Oda said. "I can't."

Marya turned on her. "He's your brother. We must go get him."

Oda, the smallest of them, the youngest of them, fell to her knees. She shivered, again hugged her own shoulders.

"I'm not waiting for her," Bronya said, steel in her voice. "We go in. Now."

Marya had wondered if she and Henryk had developed feelings for each other. Perhaps they had. Fear was a powerful emotion. Love, even more so. At least that was what Marya had heard. Someday, perhaps, she would find that out for herself.

"It will be full dark before we even get inside," she said.

Bronya nodded once. "I know."

There was only one lantern between the three of them.

Without another word, the Skłodowska sisters headed up the slope toward the gatehouse, leaving the crying, trembling Oda behind and alone in the dark.

Henryk's screams were louder, but still thin, still distant, tinny with echoes.

Marya and Bronya stared down into blackness. Ancient stone stairs, so worn with centuries of use that they dipped in the middle, slowly ground down by the tread of countless boots.

Bronya's lantern sat on the dirty stones at her feet. She readjusted her stance—it wasn't easy for her to hold back the thick bush that had grown there, up through the cracked stone tiles, blocking the view of the stairway. A white ribbon was tied to one of the bush's branches.

Henryk had affixed the ribbons throughout the tunnel, showing places the quartet had been. When the labyrinthian passages doubled back, Henryk made short notes on the ribbons, explaining where that direction led. When people were calm and patient, it was a fine system of navigation. In the throes of panic from what seemed to be a demon, though, people didn't stop to read; they ran.

Marya stepped slightly past the bush, then leaned her back against it to keep the passage open. Bronya grabbed the lantern and descended the narrow steps. Marya turned after her, letting the bush spring back to its original, upright position, scraping skin from her arms and poking thorns through her shirt and pants as it did.

Ten warped-stone steps down, Bronya stood aside—it was best to let the person holding the shotgun go first.

"If something bad happened to him," Bronya said, "it's . . . it's not fair."

Marya wanted to argue, wanted to say *oh, it's not fair that something happened to the man who can study anything he wants, be anything he wants*, but the words died before they traveled from her brain to her mouth. No, it wasn't fair. Marya, Bronya, and Oda were banned—by law—from chasing their dream of becoming scientists because the Russian overlords believed women were good only for cooking, cleaning, and caring for men.

And, of course, for *breeding*.

Yet if something happened to Henryk, it truly wasn't fair, because the Flying University didn't have to be his fight. All he had to do was bend the knee to the overlords, become *Russified*, and—because he was a boy—he could be anything he liked.

But Henryk was in the quartet because he believed in his sister's right to be anything *she* set her mind to being. He was a young man, but a *good* man. He wanted to be a physicist. If he was caught helping the Flying University, he'd be lucky to slop pigs for a living, which, at least, would be a step up from what would probably happen to him—a Berdan rifle bullet in the back of his head.

Bronya's lantern light played off a ribbon. The fabric's white stood out brightly among the charred, brown- and blood-colored stone that made up the subterranean corridors.

A distant moan . . . Marya froze.

Was it the *ogniki*?

"It's Henryk," Bronya said, barely contained anguish in her voice.

"We'll find him, sister," Marya said.

They kept on, found another ribbon marking more steps down. These weren't quite as worn as the ones by the bush. The deeper one went, the less wear on the stones, as if the lower levels grew more and more evil, enough so that those with an ounce of sense avoided it.

The people who had owned this place . . . the things they were rumored to have done in the lowest level . . .

Once, Marya would have heard those rumors and doubted them, would have asked herself, *who could do such things?* But she'd seen much in the last few years, growing up among those who occupied her nation.

She was only fifteen, yet she'd already seen enough to know how inhumane her fellow human beings could be.

Another ribbon. Another set of stairs.

Marya shivered, not from her wet clothes, not from the cloying cold, but from the memory of what they'd experienced on the next level down.

"And people think science is boring," Bronya said.

Despite herself, Marya laughed.

"Maybe someday, it will be," she said. "A nice, boring lab, with nice, boring work. It will be marvelous when you don't have to risk death to pursue science."

Was that only a dream? Would women ever be allowed to study, to learn, to change the course of history?

Yes, they would. Marya would see it happen, or she would die trying.

"You shot, but you didn't hit it," Bronya said. "Did you?"

Marya had never been able to lie to her older sister. She wasn't going to start now.

"I don't think so." Marya felt a rush of embarrassment. She wasn't adept with weapons, but it was a *shotgun*. It fired a cloud of death in an expanding cone. If Marya had even pointed the weapon even somewhat straight, she would have hit it. Instead, her shuddering grip had sent most of the shot against the wall, the rest, probably, against the floor.

"It's all right," Bronya said. "You were scared. I wet myself, sister."

That was Bronya's way, to admit something that most others would not. Her simple admission lifted Marya's tension, her anxiety at taking another shot if one presented itself. If her older sister was so scared she'd pissed herself, was Marya missing a shot because of fear such an embarrassing thing?

No, it was not.

And this time, Marya would not miss.

They descended the stairs, moved toward the soft sound of slowly moving water. They were deeper than the moat outside. Without maintenance, water had found its way into the lowest level.

At that level, they followed the ribbons, not knowing what else to do.

Then, another moan. Henryk. They hurried toward the sound, found a passage that did not have a ribbon.

"We didn't go down that one," Bronya said.

Marya adjusted her grip on the shotgun.

"The *ogniki* tricked him," she said. "It matches the stories we gathered. We're close."

This passage . . . it was where the monster *wanted* people to go. What dangers, what *horrors* awaited Marya and Bronya? It took courage to enter the passage, but they did it just the same.

Twenty feet later, Marya's nose wrinkled.

Bronya put a hand to her mouth.

The *stench*. An invisible cloud of it, hovering, unmoving. The smell of decay. The smell of death.

Their noses led down the new passage more than the lantern light did.

A turn of a corner . . . a hole in the floor, perhaps five feet across, with a low brick wall built around it. A well. Or an oubliette . . .

Marya and Bronya rushed to the edge. Bronya held her light over the well. Twenty feet down, black water. A white face looking up with half-lidded eyes—Henryk.

"Oh *God*," Bronya said, then clawed at the coil of rope on her shoulder.

Marya couldn't move. She could only stare. Stare down at Henryk, and the floating corpses around him. At least four, although in the dim light and the water's reflection, it was hard to tell. Bodies bloated, rotting, some swollen so large they stretched their clothes, some sagging piles of bones with little flesh remaining. All packed in around Henryk, like rolls puffing up in the oven, pushed together just before they were pulled free.

Bronya dropped the rope down.

"Henryk! Grab hold."

The boy fumbled with the rope. He was weak. Marya saw red blood gleaming on his forehead. Henryk bobbed in the water, using his body to push at the corpses around him, make enough space to loop the rope around his back and under his arms.

Bronya gathered up the rope, started to tie it around her own waist.

"He's too weak to climb," she said. "I will have to pull him."

Marya started to sling her shotgun over her shoulder, but Bronya snarled at her.

"*No!* If it comes, you must protect us. And this time, sister, *do not miss.*"

With that, Bronya leaned away from the well and started to walk. The rope pulled taut. She didn't ask Henryk if he was ready; she just hauled, a look of undeniable determination on her face.

Then, faint at first, instantly growing louder, a moan, deep and haunted and horrible.

It wasn't Henryk's.

"The thing is coming," Marya said.

Bronya kept stepping, kept pulling.

"So *shoot it*," she said.

Up ahead, at the corner, a flicker of green light, and then it came on, a ball of evil and hate, flames curling off stone and wood alike. No time to think. No time to worry if the weapon would work or not.

Marya strode forward, put herself between her sister and the *ogniki*. Her brief training came back. Stock tight to bruised shoulder. Look down the barrel at the pulsing, crackling energy demon.

She'd packed each shell with equal loads of salt, tiny iron pellets, and silver shavings. All of the legends, all of the wives' tales, said at least one of those elements was effective against demons. They would not pass over salt, it was said. They avoided silver, and the metal could hurt them, drive them away. The right kind of iron could even destroy them.

Marya had had no way to conduct real science, no way to do experiments, but the information she'd gathered from books, from word-of-mouth legends, and from pre-Christian rituals and beliefs showed significant correlations. Those correlations were enough for her to form a hypothesis: that the *ogniki* had to be made up of a strange kind of energy.

Energy that could be dampened, damaged, or even completely dissipated by a chemical reaction.

Marya fired the shotgun, and this time, she pulled only one trigger.

The weapon kicked, pushed her small body back, but she didn't flinch, didn't look away.

The cone of mixed shot punched a thousand blazing, sparkling, tiny holes in the green ball of light.

It *screamed*, a sound Marya would never forget for all her days.

The *ogniki* seemed to curl in on itself, its amorphous energy twisting like a whirlpool.

Like a wounded animal, the *ogniki* warped and wavered, as if it didn't know what to do or where to go, it flashed and pulsed and spun.

Marya had no such qualms.

She took another step forward, pulled the stock tight to her shoulder, leveled the barrel at the whirling, inexplicable glow before her. The hammering roar of the first blast still ringing in her ears, Marya squeezed the second trigger.

A shriek of agony, both human and not, so deafening Marya couldn't form a thought.

Then, like the last smoke from a dying campfire, the green light spread, faded, and evaporated into nothing.

Marya stood there, blinking, wondering. How had the green glow dissipated? What had it been made of? Had the salt disrupted whatever bond held the creature together? Had it been the iron? The silver?

"Marya," Bronya growled, "if you're done standing there, *help me*."

Marya slung the shotgun over her shoulder. Bronya leaned forward at a thirty-degree angle, shaking with effort. Marya grabbed the taut rope and helped her sister pull.

Henryk slid over the well wall, spilled wetly onto the stone floor.

Bronya ran to him, knelt at his side. She wiped blood from his face. Blood, and what could only be pieces of rotted flesh from the corpses in the well.

"Henryk," she said. "Are you all right?"

Marya knelt by his other side.

"The lights," he said. "When everyone ran . . . I saw lights. Moving lights. I thought it was you. I followed them, I ran . . . I fell over the well into the . . . into the . . ."

He shook his head, slightly, as if he could chase away the horror in the well.

And then, he blinked, glanced around.

"I heard the shots," he said. "Did it work?"

Marya nodded. "I believe it did. It's gone."

"There could be others," Henryk said.

Bronya wiped more blood away from his face, pressed her sleeve against the swelling cut on his forehead.

"Don't you worry," she said to him. "You helped Marya make the shells, remember. She has four more. You'll protect us, won't you, sister?"

Marya realized, quite suddenly, that she was no longer afraid.

"I will," she said.

Henryk nodded. "Then you did it. This place . . . it's *ours*."

Marya couldn't stop the swell of pride. She didn't want to stop it. She and her quartet had earned this, earned it for everyone.

A dozen lanterns lit up the room, filling it with a soft light. Soot had been scoured from the walls. Charred support timbers had been replaced. Moth-eaten carpets and old furniture abounded, poor furnishings, true, but everyone was grateful to have them. They were more grateful, though, for the lab tables and the equipment upon them.

And everywhere, young women. Young *scientists*. In the far corner, six young girls listening to a well-dressed man with a neat beard and thin glasses give a physics lecture. On the west wall, a bookshelf brimming with tomes of a dozen subjects written in German, Russian, and, yes, in *Polish*. At the lab tables, four girls working on dissections.

In back rooms and darkened parlors all across Poland, the Floating University continued on, driven by a people that refused to bend the knee to the Russian overlords, that refused to see their culture erased. This place, though, this once-haunted castle, was the Flying University's only permanent facility. Here, students could pursue long-term work.

Here, students could stay overnight, or even for weeks on end if their absence wouldn't be missed.

Once the bodies had been removed from the well—a nasty job that Marya, fortunately, hadn't had to help with—there was an endless supply of fresh water. Food was trickier. Just like the students and their teachers, food had to be brought in under the cover of night so that the locals would not know. All meals consisted mostly of hard bread, cured meats, and cheeses. Rarely were there fresh fruit and vegetables. But that didn't matter to the students—they were here to fill their minds, not their bellies.

In the months following the quartet's battle, Polish artisans had quietly built hidden doors and created false walls. The entire third level was hidden, stairs blocked by a secret barricade that blended seamlessly with the ancient walls. If the Russians ever did come calling, they would, hopefully, find nothing but charred supports, soot-stained timbers, and the scattered bones of humans and animals—the bodies in the well had not gone to waste.

Without doubt, there were other "monsters" in the land. All over the world, perhaps. But they were the last vestiges of a different time. The supernatural was dying, pushed out by science, by technology, and by the progress of civilization. Just like the dinosaurs had once ruled the planet, demons and spirits and goblins and their kind were quickly going extinct.

For a new era to rise, the old one had to die.

"Marya?"

It was the well-dressed man—Zygmunt Wróblewski—calling to her. The girls he'd been lecturing to turned to stare at Marya, their eyes as wide as their smiles.

"Yes, professor?"

He gestured to a spot next to him.

"I was just telling the students about the remarkable properties of salt," he said. "Would you mind sharing some of your research into the subject?"

Marya looked at the girls, at the hope and delight on their faces.

Would they ever be allowed to openly learn? Would they ever be allowed to *teach*? To work at universities like boys their own age surely would?

Someday, yes. If not, perhaps their children would, for while all eras die, they do not die easily.

Marya smiled back at them and nodded.

"Thank you, Professor," she said. "I would be delighted."

Retribution

by
CHRISTINE TAYLOR-BUTLER

I miss her.

The ache inside me festers. Hidden from view, it grows as days become months become years. I try to find relief in simple pursuits and kind gestures. My father's gentle smile erupting when I know the same ache resides within him. Kind words from my sisters, both older and more able to carry the weight of our unbearable loss. My brother laughs when my attempt at humor misses its mark.

I smile so as not to add to their burden as we gather for a reading. Father draws in a breath, the page of his book illuminated by the flame of a candle. Bronya sits beside me. Helena and Josef settle on the floor, anxious for this weekly moment of joy and family togetherness as he reads from the great poets. Tonight the selection is *Dziady* by Adam Mickiewicz. I task myself to remember the lines of poetry, his words echoing our country's struggle against Russian occupation. The words live on beyond his passing some twenty-seven years ago.

"Our nation is like lava," my father reads with conviction. "On the top it is hard and hideous, but its internal fire cannot be extinguished even in one hundred years of coldness."

Mickiewicz's words of defiance hit particularly hard tonight. I yearn for the warmth of my mother's touch. She is gone some six years now. Zofia, my sister, two years prior. My parents had delighted in teaching. But the Russians stripped them of those pursuits, leaving us with little beyond the company of each other.

"So let's spit on the crust and go down, to the profundity," father recites, his voice rising with the emotion of the poem.

Indeed, I think to myself. *Let us spit on the crust.*

"Hurry, Marya," Kazia says, as we rush to the gymnasium, the biting cold barely held at bay by layers of wool clothing.

I frown but keep pace with my neighbor of many years. She is taller, and her strides are quite long compared to mine.

"He is watching," she says brusquely, wrapping her scarf more tightly around her neck.

"When is he not?" I whisper, taking care not to be overheard.

Nikolai Uvarov scowls as we pass by. A Russian soldier, he is one of many the Tsar has placed in Warsaw to police the population. A dark and brooding soul, he is convinced of his superiority despite our close proximity in age. So great is Russia's determination to subjugate the Polish will that we risk imprisonment for the slightest infraction detected by these enforcers.

Nikolai nods in our direction. "Good morning."

"Good morning," Kazia replies in Russian.

I simply nod as we pass. To speak Polish is to invite arrest. To speak Russian as required by our oppressors feels like a betrayal. Remaining mute seems the more palatable option.

The sound of Nikolai's boots hitting the ground is both jarring and familiar. His gait is purposeful and holds a predictable cadence. He stomps loudly so as to be heard above the sound of horses pulling their owners' wagons to and from the city plaza. Nikolai will follow us on this short journey as if we are suspected of plotting a revolution that will wrest Poland from Russia's grasp.

"Are you incapable of speech today, Marya Skłodowska?" he asks, suddenly in front of us.

I glance up, careful not to fall prey to the obvious trap.

"I wish you a good morning," I reply, keeping my tone neutral.

"As well you should," Nikolai says, his voice a warning. It is his father who reported my own for holding the wrong political views. The act of betrayal stripped my family of our modest wealth and my father of his purpose in life.

Kazia and I walk in silence until reaching our destination.

Nikolai rushes ahead and opens the heavy wooden doors to permit our passage. This is no act of chivalry. He glances inside the ancient building but doesn't enter. Our gymnasium is under constant surveillance as if the act of teaching is nurturing the roots of rebellion. But how could it? This school starves us of the very resources we need to succeed. Like my brother Josef, we attend a Russian-controlled school where our teachers' contempt for us can be seen long before the words confirming our status erupt from their lips. Russian sentiment holds that our Polish culture is worthless, and that Polish girls are worth even less than that. The mistaken assumption is a useful tool.

Seeing no threat, Nikolai lets the doors close with a heavy thud.

"Why do you provoke him?" Kazia asks.

"Because I can," I answer. "What more can be done to us? Prison? It might be an improvement."

"Just be careful, Marya. We cannot fight back if we are not alive to do it."

"I am always careful," I reassure her, tilting my head and smiling.

That seems to dispel her concern, and she heads to her class on Russian literature.

Once out of her sight, I walk in the opposite direction, passing beneath a staircase and allowing my hand to trace the intricate wood molding gracing the walls. Once the hall empties, I flick my finger against a small notch hidden near the corner. The latch catches, and a gentle push offers passage into my sanctuary, a secret room that had gone unused for a century until I stumbled upon it.

A small candle provides sufficient illumination that cannot be detected in the hallway. Properly trained by my father in the art of hypothesis and experimentation, I tested the theory one evening many months ago. The door seals completely, leaving me with complete privacy but only a limited amount of time to work before oxygen is depleted and must be replenished by opening the door once more. There is something comforting about being here. I managed to spirit a stool into the room while soldiers interrogated the Polish-born teachers about the means and manner of their curricula. Their visits were a regular occurrence on which I came to rely. The few Polish teachers allowed to teach in this place are the enemy, not the students. That simple truth continues to hold for now.

A small wooden table holds beakers from my father's collection. Schools are not allowed to possess them, not even those under Russian control. I was able to borrow a few I thought might not be missed. Certainly my father did what he could to teach me the principles of science at home, but without a proper laboratory, I hungered for more.

The room radiates warmth as if some parts of the souls who have passed through the doors of this school remain fixed to the location after death. The feeling lingers in a way it does not when one visits a new cottage where no occupant has lived prior to its construction.

My father told me of a theory posited by the German scientist Julius von Mayer some forty years ago. Mayer proposed that energy is a constant, that it cannot be created or destroyed. Then James Joule confirmed the conservation of energy through his own experimentation. After my mother's death, I found myself wondering, where does the soul of a person go when the last breath is taken? If energy cannot be created or destroyed, then the essence of their being had to spring from some place in the universe at conception. Upon death, is it cast out to the world to be reborn in another form? My mother believed in the teaching of the Catholic church, that Heaven is waiting for departed souls. But what if Heaven is simply a portal on Earth where the energy remains close by? A portal that, until now, humans could not see? Before her death, I prayed that God take me in her place. Her death was his response. Perhaps her God had other plans for me.

My tests have, until now, been a failure. One cannot test what one cannot observe. It is no different from trying to view the smallest particles of life without aid of a microscope, something I do not have. But in my supplemental readings, I discovered a notation about the works of Kirchhoff. The German physicist studied radiation, something I am quite curious about. He wrote of the existence of a black body that radiates constant energy but does not reflect it. That, for me, was the key to my use of this room. Each week I experiment, using only this candle, these beakers, and a pot of black paint. The color black is not without flaws, as it radiates some portion of light from surrounding sources. I needed for the light to be completely absorbed and not reflected. The closest I could devise was a small box with a pinhole where the light cannot easily escape. It took weeks of experimentation to find the right shape and size. Finally, the result was achieved. But the box is of insufficient size to gain access to the energy inside it. I require a larger device. It occurs to me that light cannot escape this room, so to that end, I use what remains of the black paint to cover the walls around me. My sanctuary, now as black as the pitch dark sky, is repurposed as a human-sized pinhole box.

"How go your studies?" Bronya asks. Her expression suggests she knows more than she is saying.

"They are well," I respond before taking a bite of bread pulled fresh and hot from the oven.

My father tilts his head. "You are learning well?"

"My grades remain satisfactory," I answer. "I am studying with what little they are allowed to teach but grow tired of reciting facts in front of class as if I am their star pupil."

"You are their star," Father says, tearing a piece of bread and dipping it into his beet soup. "You seem lighter today, Marya. You've met a boy, perhaps?"

I look up abruptly. "Absolutely not. I found a quiet nook at the gymnasium to study independently."

"Indeed," Helena says, laughing. "There are rumors of your long absences from class."

"I am passing my examinations, so the Russians do not make it an issue." I tear another piece of bread from the loaf.

"I am sorry that our circumstances cannot provide a means to study in Paris," Father says, his voice proud but weary.

"We enjoy our time with you," I say. "And the visits to the country. You need not worry. Bronya and I have devised a plan. I will work upon graduation until she has achieved her degree in Paris. She will help me study in Paris when my own time comes."

Bronya nods. "I think I would like to become a teacher. To honor mother's memory."

"I am content to study medicine," Josef says.

"And you, Helena?" Father asks.

Helena grins. "Perhaps a teacher. To give students what the Tsar denies us. A secret school perhaps. One that operates out of view."

My father settles in his chair, his look of contentment filling the space between us. "Your mother would be proud—I only wish she were here to see you grow into such fine adults."

I don't answer. Perhaps she is watching. Would she be pleased to know what I am planning?

It is true that in the dark, one's senses amplify. The fall of footsteps and the swish of long skirts as my classmates hurry to class. The scent of polish used to shine the doorways in the evening. This room, my shelter, soothes the dark thoughts that consume me. As I am the youngest of five, I did not have the advantage of my mother's touch and affection, her illness from consumption starting when I was only four years old and lasting until I was ten. A child is not meant to be deprived of such vital gestures. Six years watching her heart break when she and father had their wages reduced, forcing them to take in the boarders. Boarders who infected my sisters with typhus. Bronya survived, but Zofia succumbed. Already ill from consumption, it broke my mother's heart to be unable to care for them except from a distance. I could not console her because she feared I would be infected as well. When she died, I had gone without her embrace or the touch of her palm on my cheek for six years. I drew into myself and buried my grief. I wonder, as I let my tears fall freely in this dark sanctuary, if the circumstances have broken me.

I study Kirchoff's equations, but their deeper meaning escapes me. Perhaps the answer will be revealed through experimentation. To create a black body effect, I let the candle burn, giving the walls sufficient time to absorb the energy. The light rays that aren't absorbed bounce around the room, unable to escape. The candle now extinguished, I sit and wait for some sign that I can add my own energy to the experiment or draw out the energy of those who were once alive. The priest at St. Anne's tells me that my mother has moved to her higher purpose. Despite this, I feel her presence around me, particularly in this room, cloaked from view.

It is not long before I see a glow that cannot be explained. It might be a trick of the eye, but repeating the experiment over several days yields the same results. Some dark energy, barely perceptible, is held in this box in a way that is not diminished when I leave to attend my courses. At times, I find myself pulled into it, but manage to stay grounded to the present. That knowledge may yet prove useful.

My reverie is interrupted by two quick taps on the hidden door, a signal that I can safely exit. It is meant to appear a random act if a teacher or guard walks by. Kazia knocks again, this time more urgently. I slip my fingers into the hidden latch, and the door yields.

"Hurry," she says, cradling books in her arms and shoving one in mine.

We reach the central hallway in time to see the guards pull Professor Stanislaw forcefully from his classroom. He stares at Kazia and me and shouts, "Today, for us, unbidden guests in the world, in all the past and in all the future, today there is but one region in which there is a crumb of happiness for a Pole: the land of his childhood!"

I recognize the reference. It is Mickiewicz.

The guards subdue Stanislaw as he struggles to continue his recitation in Polish, even though his use of our forbidden language will result in exile or execution.

"That land will ever remain holy and pure as first love; undisturbed by the remembrance of errors."

A guard beats him about the arm, but still, he does not stop, raising his voice until it echoes in the hallway.

" . . . not undermined by the deceitfulness of hopes—"

Another guard issues a punch that takes my breath away.

Nose bloodied, Professor Stanislaw continues his defiance.

" . . . and unchanged by the stream of events!" he shouts as they drag him from the building.

I study the cruel expressions of the Russian teachers who likely reported him to the authorities. Beside them stands Nikolai Uvarov, casting his gaze in my direction, revealing a look of satisfaction. Something changes inside me. In this moment I allow the darkness and grief I've held at bay to surface in pursuit of a higher purpose.

I am startled by the sound of footsteps crunching lightly on the grass behind me. Perhaps I should not have been. A shape suddenly blocks the sunlight, its shadow stretching like some grotesque black thing along the ground where I am seated.

"You should not be here," Nikolai says. "The palace gardens are not open to the public."

"Am I subject to arrest?" I ask, not bothering to look up in his direction. Instead I maintain my focus on two swans, a fascinating mated pair that swim effortlessly in the lake at Łazienki Park. My mother often looked at photographs of this place and desired to visit it.

"That is always a possibility," he says, drawing closer. "I do not trust you."

"Then you are wise," I say, growing weary of his intimidation. "You arrested Peter Stanislaw. Why?"

Nikolai laughs as if my statement of fact is humorous. "We have known for some time of his inclinations to teach beyond the approved courses. He was given a warning and chose to ignore it."

"Someone reported him?" I ask.

"We are always listening and watching." Nikolai sits next to me on the grass and wipes a stray hair from my face. The act chills me, but I remain fixed in my purpose and show no emotion.

"Do you mean to shadow me until I am found guilty of some infraction?" I turn and stare him straight in the eyes. "Has your family and your position not sufficiently damaged mine?"

He tilts his head in my direction. I can't decipher his expression. Interest?

Nikolai sighs, then stretches his legs out in front of him. He lifts his head toward the sky and closes his eyes. "What will you do when you graduate? Education is wasted on girls. You should focus on being a dutiful wife and mother."

I ponder that thought. Is romance the source of his motivation? The idea is repulsive. "I am married to science," I say. "That is sufficient. So what of Professor Stanislaw?"

"I suspect he will be sent to one of the camps like the others. Or hanged as a traitor. I do not know."

Although I suspected, the thought still leaves me breathless. We cannot continue to live with such fear.

"You should be careful," Nikolai warns, standing once again. "I see your contempt for us. You do a poor job of hiding it, and I am watching. Always."

"You would condemn me to that fate?" I ask.

"It would be my duty," he says, now towering over me.

My mind returns to my black body experiment and the potential it holds, to my grand plan to help my family and Warsaw in general. I smile and say, "Then may your efforts bear fruit."

The key to successful experimentation is to test a hypothesis with a number of variables. It is a risky thing when the variable is a Russian soldier. I could lose my life. Or my family could be further penalized. But we have so little, it feels worth a risk. Nikolai seems a logical choice, but it would be irresponsible to waste him on an initial trial when there are so many unknowns.

I start with something simple. A mouse. I hope it will not be harmed, but it is important to start small. I entice it with a small crumb of food. The trap is set, and the mouse lands in a metal box I placed outside the school. I slip the mouse and the box into the room, slide the cover to create a narrow opening, then slam the door before the mouse can escape. A black box can absorb light energy. What of a living and breathing thing? It pains me to wait two full days, but I am not eager to see the mouse right away.

On the third day I open the door and find the box empty. I search with the candle, looking for a hole that might have aided its escape. Finding none, and no remains, I conclude that the room does, in fact, possess properties that will be useful. Another trial will be needed to confirm my studies. In search of a larger variable, I settle for an old cat. I was tempted to use a kitten, but I am not as cruel as our captors. The cat, nearly twenty years old and feeble, offers no resistance, having survived well past its life expectancy. The black body experiment yields the same result. Last, I test my theory with a dog nearing the end of its own life. It made its home in the market, begging for scraps of food from merchants. The butcher told me that the dog had seen better days, and to put it down would be a kindness. I offered to take it. The dog was small and easily concealed in a basket. In the black box, I place a bowl of water and a basket filled with folded cloth for comfort. I decide to wait only a single day this time. I will bring scraps of food for it in the event I find it still alive tomorrow.

By morning, the basket is empty, and the dog gone.

Oddly enough, the room seems larger than when I first began my visits. I had not thought to measure it before the experiment, an error in my judgment. I pace it off with my feet and commit the results to memory before leaving.

I listen carefully at the door to make sure it is safe. Opening the door, I find my path blocked by a Russian guard. He is the one who bloodied Professor Stanislaw's face.

"A hiding place, Marya Skłodowska?" His breath was heavy with the scent of vodka.

"A place where I may study without interruption," I answer. "I enjoy the quiet."

"What are you hiding?" he insists. "Books on Polish nationalism? The language? Is this where you gather to plot against the Tsar?"

I consider the situation. There are only two of us in the hallway, the students and teachers having gone home for the evening. "It is nothing. I swear."

"Stand aside!" He huffs and pushes me out of his way with considerable force.

Once inside the man laughs.

"You are right. There is nothing here but a bowl of water and a basket too small for even a baby."

Even so, he searches the table and every inch of the room as if looking for another concealed door or a hidden compartment. I realize this represents both a risk and a great opportunity. I slam the door shut, in the hope he will be unable to find the hidden latch that might free him.

"Goodbye, Comrade," I say in the required Russian, spitting out the words and hoping that the black box will find his life force of use.

By morning, the Russians have one less soldier.

Over the next weeks, I lure in the soldiers who beat Professor Stanislaw. I convince one portly specimen that I have seen insurrectionists enter a secret room. To convince him of my sincerity I negotiate a reward for the information. He is pleased to see me turn on my friends. Once he is inside I am pleased to return the favor by locking the door. The room rewards my patience with remarkably consistent results.

I convince another guard that I know the location of his compatriot. I explain he is sleeping in a closet, both drunk and snoring. Unamused, the guard storms into my black body experiment to demand an explanation. He is gone before sundown.

Kazia, unaware of the true nature of my room and experimentation, provides an alibi during my brief absences from class or my late return to my home.

It is not long before Warsaw begins to buzz with speculation as to the whereabouts of the guards. Professor Stanislaw and several others caught disobeying the Tsar's mandate cannot go to trial without the men's testimony. The Tsar sends more Russian soldiers to investigate, but their presence is temporary. The conclusion is that the missing men, concerned with the growing anger in the community and a possible insurrection brewing, chose to desert their posts.

And so my experiment continues beyond the scope of Professor Stanislaw's arrest. Each time I lure a soldier into the room, it buzzes with energy and grows like a hungry beast. I am only too willing to feed its insatiable thirst for energy as it expands beyond its original boundaries. But one last test subject remains.

By morning, I wait for Kazia so we may walk to school together. But she does not appear at the door when I knock.

"Your friend was arrested, along with her family." Nikolai's familiar voice settles over me like a dark cloak.

"For what reason?" I demand.

Nikolai leans in. "I'm told there are meetings at the school. Professor Stanislaw is not the only one plotting to overthrow the Tsar. I overheard her speaking Polish in the hallway. But she refuses to tell us the names and locations of her family's coconspirators."

I clench my fists and then relax them. The solution is not as hard as it might have seemed months ago. "I know where they meet," I tell him, keeping my voice quiet but tense.

"Show me," he demands, leaning so close I can see the stubble of his beard beginning to emerge on his face.

"She's not part of it," I say, my heart pounding. To be arrested is a fate I would not wish on anyone. My grandfather was made to march one hundred and forty miles. His feet bled from the journey. He is one of the few able to escape the camp and tell his story. "Please, Nikolai."

Nikolai doesn't soften. I do not yield. I am barely fifteen years of age, but my family springs from a strong lineage.

"I will offer a trade. The location of the secret meeting room if you allow her family to go free. Say you were mistaken and overheard someone else instead."

"If this is a ruse, the consequences will be unspeakable," he says.

"If it is not," I remind him, knowing greed to be an effective motivator, "you will be decorated as a hero."

Nikolai pauses to consider my suggestion. "I agree to your terms."

I nod then say, "If they are released and safe, you can meet me at the gymnasium after everyone has gone home. I will reveal the location of the room. If you desire, you can lay in wait until the adults return for a meeting at seven."

And so, the trap is set. Midafternoon, I excuse myself and tell my father I am making a brief trip to the market. Instead, I meet Nikolai, and we enter the gymnasium together.

"You don't have to do this," I tell him.

"And yet you lead me in betrayal of your friends. Who is the bigger monster, Marya Skłodowska? The one who admits his role and completes it, or the one who pretends to be something else, yet does vile things anyway."

I frown. Perhaps he is right. I have been driven to these acts by anxiety and depression. To that end, I cannot fix the problem in Warsaw, only serve a small role in the solution.

"This way." I point toward the massive staircase and pull him to the side when he begins to climb. "Beneath it," I say, slipping my hand along the wall until it finds the latch. I hear Nikolai's deep inhalation as the door opens.

"How long has this room been here?" he says, peering in the dark.

I light a candle, expecting the room will be empty, but I am still tense in the event it is not.

"I don't know. I only know it is the place. And now that you know the location, I will return home."

Instead of allowing me to leave, Nikolai holds my arm firmly against his while using the other to slam the door closed, locking us both inside. "You will remain so as to not warn your friends."

"I won't," I say.

"You will," he says. "I told you I don't trust you."

My heart grows cold as all the anger I have felt springs forward. "And I told you that you were wise not to." I extinguish the candle, and I'm suddenly calm in the darkness, knowing that my torment will end at the same time as my tormentor. But something unexpected happens—Nikolai's grip lessens even as the walls begin to glow. Soon I don't feel him at all.

"Nikolai?"

No answer returns, but a surge of energy moves through me, and the room brightens as if the candle has been reignited. Nikolai is no longer with me. Where he has gone, I cannot say, as there is no trace of him to follow. I feel some measure of elation and relief, yet wonder what fate the box has planned for me now that I am alone.

And at the long end of the room, longer than should be possible in this small space, a bright light appears. It grows larger, and a vision, perhaps an ethereal place, begins to manifest beyond its borders. I close my eyes to banish the optical illusion. When I open them again, the light remains, and I clearly see a woman sitting in a park. She beckons me to join her. I should be afraid, but I am not. My heart quickens as I walk into the light and see my mother sitting there, looking beautiful and healthy as she did before the illness took hold of her.

Cautiously, I sit next to her on the bench and feel her warm embrace envelop my shoulders. We sit in silence and watch the swans navigate the pond in Łazienki Park. In that moment of respite, I feel the full weight of my grief come forward before dissipating in the wind.

Soon, I don't know how long, I hear a door open behind us. My mother, still smiling, stands and holds her hand outstretched. I hesitate, content to stay here in this peaceful place, but she takes my hand and leads me back into the sanctuary. I try to turn, but she holds fast to my shoulders and gently guides me forward.

"Don't look behind you, Manya, look forward," she whispers as she sends me back into the world of the living. I am tempted to protest, but the door closes behind me. When I check, the hidden latch and the sanctuary, once my lifeline, are gone.

Energy is neither created or destroyed, but tonight somehow the stars in the sky seem a bit brighter as I walk home.

Science Note:

Obviously, Marya Skłodowska never created experiments to make Russian soldiers disappear, nor can a dark room absorb the energy of living species.

However, the concept of black body radiation is based on quantum theories dating back to the 1800s. If properly constructed, a hollow black box can absorb all light introduced through a tiny pinhole. To remain in equilibrium, the box will emit thermal radiation at the same rate it absorbs it and will glow if heat is introduced. A presentation by UC San Diego department of Physics calls this type of object a "perfect absorber and ideal radiator."

THE COLD
White Ones

by

SUSANNE L. LAMBDIN

Seated on the left bank of the Vistula River, Marya Skłodowska and her classmates from Warsaw's Gymnasium Number Three enjoyed an afternoon picnic. Older girls collected moss, liverwort, lichen, and fungi along the river or walked in the woods filling baskets with plants. Teachers sat on blankets on a grassy knoll. Marya, her best friend Kazia, and Hanna, a year older at sixteen, kept watch on younger students wading among tall reeds with nets. The girls advanced on a bullfrog sunning on a lily pad.

"Don't splash or your toad prince will hop away," Marya said.

"They'll never catch it," Kazia said.

A second later, a ten-year-old girl slipped and fell into the murky water.

The toad jumped from the lily pad and submerged.

"Told you so," Kazia said, giggling.

A dead fish floated out from beneath the plant. Marya inched forward for a closer look. Tiny white parasites had collected in its jellied eyes and gills. Intrigued, she opened a leather bag and removed four glass vials with corks and a long rod to capture specimens. Marya placed the tiny organisms into a tube, corked it, and filled the remaining vials with water, noting it had a reddish tinge.

Professor Ivan Tolsky suddenly ran down the hill, waving his arms in the air and shouted, "Avoid filth, flies, and dirty fingers, children!"

The three girls waded out of the reeds, hems muddy and damp.

They ran toward the professor as he was joined by Hanna. Kerchief in hand, Hanna patiently wiped off the grime from their hands and faces.

The Russian professor scolded the girls until silenced by the appearance of lighting zigzagging across the eastern sky. Deep rumbles of thunder followed. The breeze picked up, bringing with it the scent of rain, and Professor Tolsky announced it was time to leave and ushered the group to the wagons.

"I hope we get back before it rains," Marya said. She pocketed her samples and stood, smoothing out her black dress. "Maybe I'll get extra credit if I identify a new species of parasite or determine what made the river turn red."

"Pliny the Elder named the river the Vistula because it slowly *oozes* along," Kazia said. Slipping her arm around Marya's waist, they headed up the hill. The daughter of a librarian, Kazia knew a little about everything. "The mayor ordered the construction of a new sewage system, and workers have already cut down trees and started digging on the right bank. Do you think they uncovered a polluted well? There's been five funerals this week and six last week. You know, during the Crimean War, hundreds of soldiers died due to the lack of sanitation. They died of cholera. I think it's happening again."

"Russians see us as shoemakers and shepherds. They don't care about our health," Marya said. "I know Hanna thinks I'm unkind to Tolsky but showing respect to Russians feels like collaboration. We are Polish patriots. This is my form of resistance."

On the days Marya walked to school with Kazia, they passed an obelisk erected by the late Tzar Alexander II in Saxon Square and spat in defiance. The Tzar had died last March in the sixth assassination plot on his life. An aide had found Alexander II holding his intestines among the broken sabers and chunks of flesh from his guards. The late Tzar's son, Alexander III, was now Emperor of Russia and King of Poland, but the girls still ritually spat on the monument.

Marya and Kazia climbed into a wagon. They were joined by their friend Svatka, who came from a poor village in the Carpathian Mountains, always full of mischief and the orator of strange and fascinating tales.

"The mayor has invoked the anger of Rodu," said Svatka. "My people pass down the stories of the old Slavic gods to each generation. They say a dark pagan prince lived in the Vistulan woods, refusing baptism by Saint Methodius. In defiance of Christian authority, the prince offered bloody sacrifices to Rodu on a stone altar. When the mayor ordered the altar moved, the ground bled, and now a curse lays upon Warsaw."

"Hush, Svatka. You're scaring the children," Kazia said. She whispered to Marya, "Everyone knows her mother is a *tzarownica*."

The Polish word for witch sent a shiver through Marya, though not one of fear. Hearing her own language spoken aloud was a rarity. In public or at school, Marya and her classmates spoke Russian. They were taught Russian history and literature but nothing about Polish history or culture. Marya gazed at the girls in their damp dresses. A child near Hanna sneezed out a small mound of mucus that wiggled back into her nostril.

"Tomorrow, I will be going to church to pay my respects to Frédéric Chopin," Kazia said.

"His heart is kept in a jar there. I'd like to see it," Svatka said, grinning.

"Chopin's music is the essence of Polish nationalism. Of course, I couldn't expect you to appreciate his music, Svatka. Your only interest is in scaring people."

Svatka stuck out her tongue.

Dozens of churches and cathedrals were visible beyond an impressive medieval barbican and watch towers. Marya imagined Teutonic knights at the walls as the wagons entered the city through an arched gateway. Ornate palaces and museums lined the streets, along with four-story houses painted yellow, green, or blue. Russian soldiers in dark green tunics and black *shakos* that bore the imperial eagle badge stood on street corners. Horsecars and carriages congested the streets. Marya counted twelve statues of generals and knights by the time the wagons arrived at the old convent located on Krakowskie Przedmieście. The gymnasium occupied the second floor. The bells of the Church of St. Joseph of the Visitationists, adjacent to the school, rang as the students filed through the front door. Concerned for their welfare, Professor Tolsky offered to escort home the three little girls in muddy dresses. The girls continued to sniffle as they climbed into a wagon and departed.

Marya entered the school and was surprised to find the shops that occupied the first floor closed for the day. The watchmaker always had a steady flow of clientele and kept late hours, yet for some reason he had locked up. Their absence created an eerie ambiance as the students climbed the stairs with their baskets of plants, leaving water drops on the steps. Svatka had convinced the girls that the ghost of a dead nun haunted the school. The gaslights, set on low, cast shadows on the walls. Someone in line sneezed.

Our enemy is germs, not Slavic spirits, Marya thought.

Russian propaganda posters of soldiers shouting "*Do Broni,*" which meant "to weapons," had replaced the icons of Catholic saints on gray cement walls. The classroom was just as bleak, with mismatched tables and benches, and a chalkboard. Someone had written in chalk, "*Education is best taught through discipline.*"

While the girls waited turns to use the small bathroom, Marya sat at the work table shared with Kazia. Her friend tidied their books and school papers. Marya set out a box of petri dishes and glass slides. She removed the vials of water, set them in wooden holders, and was first to claim Professor Tolsky's microscope left out on the teacher's desk and commenced running tests for hard metals.

"It was nice of Professor Tolsky to let us use his microscope," Marya stated.

"Well, I don't know why we must stay the night to work on our reports," Kazia said. "The flowers aren't going to wilt overnight. I'd prefer to read the book Papa gave me on Slavic folklore in my own bed. I doubt our wardens will let us read by candlelight unless Mrs. Nowak is our chaperone."

"More Russian soldiers have arrived in town. Something is going on," Marya said. "I assume there is an early curfew, which explains why the shopkeepers went home. It's better we stay the night than venture into the streets. I don't mind since we'll be together."

Svatka rose like a ghoul from the end of their table. "Rodu is watching you," she said. "Beware 'Maid of the Golden Hair,' for I intend to consume the contents of your tome."

"Did you read it?" Kazia asked, scowling. She pulled the book against her chest. "Marya, tell Svatka not to touch my things, she'll listen to you."

"Both of you stop behaving like children," Marya said. "Learn by the good example I set." Using a rod to transplant a parasite onto a glass plate, she placed another slide on top and looked at it under the microscope. "Magnified at two hundred, the organism resembles a puffy tardigrade. It has a single orifice for ingestion, egestion, and reproduction. If it has a dynamical system, it could construct an identical copy, just as biological cells in certain environments can reproduce by cell division."

"What should I do? I want to help," Svatka said.

"*Both* of you work together and confirm whether or not a hard metal contaminates the water. I tested it, and I believe it is iron, but this is a group project," Marya said. "Svatka, when the altar to Rodu was moved, you claim the ground ran red with blood. Did you see it happen?"

"You should not mock what you do not understand," Svatka said.

"I'm not. This is research. Iron in human blood gives it red pigmentation. Iron in water appears a rusty red." Marya sat back, crossing her arms. "All manner of microorganisms can be found in the river, from bacteria to parasites and viruses. I'd like to get a look at the site."

"Many strange things live beneath the ground. Who knows what crawled out?" Svatka said as she waggled her brow. "During the Winter Solstice, my people celebrate *Korochun* in honor of the Black God. They stand vigil with torches over family graves all night, chasing away the spirits of decay and darkness that emerge. Sometimes it is not enough, and a child will die in the night."

"Why does everything out of your mouth sound *evil*?" Kazia asked. "I suppose we can't expect a fourteen-year-old to act like an adult. Adults don't scare people on purpose."

"Adult Russians do," Marya said. "Now both of you stop it. We have work to do."

"I'm worried about Hanna," Kazia whispered.

Hanna sat at her desk with a blanket over her head. Her girlfriends doted on her, taking turns to rub her back or fetch her a glass of water. Hanna was not the only girl who sniffled and coughed, for it seemed a malady spread at an alarming rate.

"You would assume we'd find the bacterium *Vibio cholerae* in brackish water," Marya said. "I suggest the parasites are pathogens that spread disease through direct contact. Bioburden covers every surface in this room. Nothing is sterilized, so we need to be careful."

"Then heed my warning. The town is cursed," Svatka said.

"Or it's a common cold," Kazia said.

Gazing at the specimen under a higher setting, Marya watched as it sprouted limbs like a miniature emaciated humanoid. With a kick of its little legs, the organism suddenly dissolved. She made a quick sketch of the creature from memory and set aside her pencil. Careful not to touch it, she placed another parasite on a slide, covering it before adding a drop of water, but within minutes of exhibiting growth, it too vanished.

"Quite a few girls collected *Sagittaria sagittifolia*," Kazia said, pointing at white flowers with bright purple centers on a nearby table. "They also gathered *Nuphar luteum*. The lilies are still damp, Marya. They could house parasites."

Professor Folczky entered the room. "Lights out in ten minutes," he said, glaring at the girls through a pair of bifocals. Marya overlooked his brusque personality because Folczky was a brilliant chemist from Warsaw, teaching with textbooks when lab equipment was not available, and his dislike for Tolsky was well known. Despite his sharp tone, he was a considerate man and had brought a picnic basket filled with mincemeat pastries. "This is dinner, so make do," he said. "Unfortunately, no one is allowed to go home. A disease is running rampant on the east bank, and the bridge is closed."

Girls raised their arms, eager to ask questions.

"Remain silent and do as you're told!" The professor approached Marya's table. "The mayor has ordered every Polish scientist to determine the source of this outbreak. I'm afraid I must take Professor Tolsky's microscope from you, Marya. You'll have to make do with what you have." He collected the microscope, slides, and samples and left the classroom.

"Well, that was rude," Kazia said.

"At least now we know why we can't go home," Marya replied.

Each girl made a pallet with wool blankets and a pillow. All slept in their clothes and lay whispering together. A teacher returned to turn off the lights and partially close the door to allow a soft glow of light to enter from the corridor.

Marya caught Kazia trying to read her book on Slavic folktales. She was tempted to thumb through a book on parasitology but chose to avoid punishment and remained on the pallet. Listening to rain and intermittent sniffs and coughs, she fell asleep and dreamed: *Professor Tolsky and a captain from the Russian Imperial Guards faced each other with pistols deep in the Vistulan woods near the pagan altar and fired. Both men dropped dead.*

Marya awoke trembling. A layer of perspiration lay thick on her brow. She brushed aside a *tickle* on her nose, feeling hot under the wool blanket. Unsure of the hour, she listened to eerie whispers and scurrying of tiny feet. *Rats*, she thought, and sat up in alarm. No one else was awake, nor noticed a cold breeze push open the door. She stood, trembling, her breath coming out in white puffs. Someone coughed. She moved among the sleeping forms until she found Hanna lying beside a table covered with lilies. Marya leaned over her friend and froze. Scores of tiny white creatures had assembled like a royal court on the sleeping girl's face. Rooted in horror, Marya watched a few parasites enter Hanna's nostrils like miners. One sly creature wiggled through a gap in her front teeth and vanished.

"Hanna! Wake up," Marya shouted. "Everyone needs to get up! We have a problem."

The girl closest to the door turned on the gaslights.

Hanna pushed aside Marya and fled from the room.

Marya gave orders for the girls to check their blankets for parasites. With Kazia and Svatka in tow, they ran after Hanna, but the girl was not in the hallway. The gaslights went out as if by supernatural means, for there was no other explanation. Marya trembled as a horrible scream came from the bathroom. She led the charge into the room to find Hanna lying with her back to the door.

Hands trembling, Marya knelt and gently rolled Hanna over. She jumped back. Dozens of pale white creatures no larger than the end of her thumbnail crawled on the girl's face. Her dead eyes stared back, unblinking. Marya trembled.

"Scat," Svatka said and stomped her foot.

The creatures scurried down a floor drain.

Loud footsteps preceded a flurry of activity in the hallway. Several chaperones in rumpled clothes, apparently awoken by the screams, entered the bathroom. The adults took one look at the dead girl, then ordered Marya and her friends to return to the classroom.

Kazia cried as they sat at their table.

"*Death came to all and the little worms laid feast*," Marya thought. The poem written by her eldest sister Zofia now seemed prophetic. "*Death comes with tiny, cold, white feet and steps upon my brow. Hungry and pitiful, relentless and cruel, it consumes all without remorse.*" Yet, she smiled at Kazia, hiding her pain.

Professor Folczky came in wearing a dirty lab coat. Dark circles hung beneath his red eyes. He had obviously not slept, and he squinted as the morning light appeared at the windows.

"Listen," the professor said. "Word arrived that Professor Tolsky and several students died during the night. Now we find poor Hanna suffered the same fate. The mayor has announced it is cholera. This school is under quarantine. Anyone with symptoms of high fever, nausea, or headaches should report to Room 2-B to wait for a physician. The rest of you may spend the time consoling one another. I'm sorry, but you cannot leave the school."

Complaints among the girls grated on the professor's frayed nerves.

"Just do what you're told," Folczky said.

"Professor, I found a new species of parasite I was attempting to identify. Maybe we can look at them together under the microscope,"

Marya said. "Unless you already know what they are, and what has contaminated the river, sir."

"High levels of iron and copper are in the water, though I am not certain of the source. As for parasites, I have not seen any, Miss Skłodowska. You seem to be the only one who wants to work on their report. Considering the circumstances, all students will be given a passing grade whether it's completed or not."

"It's not cholera, sir. Warsaw is cursed," Svatka blurted.

A student muttered, "witch," causing the professor to make the sign of the cross.

Svatka raised her hand and said, "I know the cause of the sickness. It's the Biali Zimni Ludzie . . . the Cold White Ones. The altar must be restored or more will die."

"I don't have time for folktales, young lady. Stay here and stay quiet."

"Sir, my father can help. If I could go home and talk to him," Marya paused. Her admiration for the chemistry teacher diminished when his cheeks turned red. "If you had seen the creatures on Hanna . . ."

"Your father is a dabbler in science. If he has any sense, he's gone to ground. Now, if you'll excuse me, I must continue my work."

For the next hour, the girls huddled in small groups, whispering about Hanna. The girls grew silent when teachers arrived with picnic baskets. Marya had no appetite. She watched as the students ate dumplings, pears, cheese, and oily fish in tins. Her eyes widened when Kazia removed a bottle of vodka from the basket.

"This must be for the teachers," Kazia said.

"We should be helping the professor," Marya grumbled.

"Then convince him I'm right," Svatka said. "The Biali Zimni Ludzie are evil creatures that live in stagnant water and attach themselves to travelers' damp clothes. They spread disease and feed off the life force of humans. If you want to save Warsaw, we must rely on Slavic traditions and old-fashioned remedies to break the curse."

Marya frowned. "There is a scientific explanation."

"And a supernatural one," Svatka replied. "Let's go to Professor Folczky and tell him we know of a cure, Marya. He'll believe you."

"Do you mean the witch's brew in my book?" Kazia asked.

"Yes," Svatka said. "Supernatural manifestations are like a deadly virus that only proper treatment can cure. My grandmother was a gypsy, born in the back of a *vardo* wagon. I've seen things science cannot explain. I believe the potion will work."

The girls found Professor Folczky in the office of the late Ivan Tolsky. He sat at a table and worked feverishly with the chemistry equipment and microscope. Several beakers filled with liquid bubbled over lit burners. The room was of modest size, painted green, and had two large windows facing the main street, curtains drawn. The odor of chemicals filled the room. Smoke from coal burning in a small iron stove added to the stench. On the stove boiled a pot of water.

Kazia parted the curtains to open a window and shivered at the whinny of horses, stomping boots, and loud voices. "Russian imperial guards!"

"Come away from the window," Marya said.

"So, you've come to help," Professor Folczky said as he looked up from the table. "Do you have a theory on what has caused this plague, Marya?"

"Yes, sir. The parasites appeared the moment the altar was removed. We believe the stone covered the entrance to a spring, which released hard metals into the water. As both phenomena occurred at the same time, they may be connected to this sudden outbreak."

"I have a book on Kashubian mythology from northern Poland," Kazia said, producing the volume. "It discusses the dark gods like Rodu, spirits, and demons. The Biali Zimni Ludzie also known as Biali Gomly, 'white gnomes,' are mentioned. They are emaciated creatures that can appear as small as a maggot and can grow to dwarf a human. I suggest we mix the potion mentioned and test that immediately."

"Science is but a fancy name for magic," Svatka said. "The remedy my grandmother used to get rid of goblins from our village works; I promise. Kazia's book doesn't tell you how to mix the formula, but fortunately I know how." She pointed at the pot on the stove. "Into boiling water, you add two handfuls of crayfish eyes. Cut straw from an old broom and toss it in. Add ground charcoal and vodka and lots of it too.

Once the potion is ingested, it will cure the illness. To end the curse, we must pour buckets of this brew on the very spot the altar stood, and then restore Rodu's altar to its rightful place."

"This home brew is not scientific," the professor said.

"Perhaps, but we do know charcoal is a natural means to remove toxins. We have all the things we need in this room," Marya said. "Do you know the precise measurements, Svatka? If not, no two batches will be the same. I'm afraid the professor is right. This isn't very scientific."

"I told you it works. I saw it happen. You'll just have to trust me."

"I see an old broom in the corner. I'll get the straw," Kazia exclaimed.

"Let's hope your grandmother taught you well. I'll grind up coal," Marya said. "But I'm going to write down precisely what we're doing and how much ingredients we are using. We want to be accurate if this works on our little test subject, and we need to make more formula."

"It will work," Svatka said. "I'll be the one in charge of mixing the formula. Of course, if you don't mind, sir?"

"Proceed with the experiment, but this does not mean I believe in goblins," Professor Folczky said. "The contaminants in the river, however, could come from an exposed underground spring, which must be sealed."

Working as a team, the girls mixed the ancient Slavic potion. Svatka stirred the pot with a ladle as it boiled, muttering to herself.

Kazia hummed a Chopin tune as she broke apart the broom and tossed straw in with the bobbing crayfish eyeballs.

Charcoal turned the water black, as well as Marya's hands, which she wiped on her dress.

At the sound of footsteps on the stairs, Marya glanced at the professor. The heavy footsteps halted outside the door to the room, replaced by guttural snarls.

"Don't open it," Kazia whispered.

"Stay out of sight and remain silent," Folczky said.

Nervous, the professor opened the door to find a stern Russian captain from the Imperial Guard glaring at him.

Peering from her hiding place, Marya could see the captain was accompanied by six soldiers. A layer of sweat covered his brow. Froth in the corner of his lips produced a parasite that dropped onto the front of his coat. The soldiers in the hallway, armed with rifles equipped with bayonets, looked ragged and flushed.

"Ah, Captain Stanislaw. We have a cure, sir. You have but take a sip," the professor said.

The captain's gaze settled on the empty bottle of vodka on the table.

"Show this drunk what happens to charlatans," he snarled.

The blow of a soldier's rifle struck the professor's forehead, leaving a gash. Blood splattered on the floor and table.

"I must help him," Marya said.

"Don't or they'll arrest you too," Kazia said.

The captain shoved the dazed professor into the line of sick Russian soldiers.

Marya noticed the tiny white parasites on their green coats before the door slammed shut. She listened to the retreat of heavy footsteps, then a few minutes later, a commotion outside made it clear the Tzar's henchmen were leaving.

"The Russian soldiers were infected," Marya said.

A loud sneeze from Kazia projected a little white worm onto the floor.

Marya helped her friend sit on a stool and then scratched at an itch behind her ear. "You have parasites," she said. "I hope I don't as well."

"We'll all drink the potion to be safe, or we die at the same time," Svatka said. She dipped the ladle into the brew, took a sip, and gagged. "Absolutely horrible. You're next." She gave it to both girls and stepped back.

The mixture acted like an expectorant. Kazia blew out a nose full of snot into a kerchief, then grabbed a bucket and retched.

Marya and Svatka coughed up phlegm, spat into a beaker, and held it up to confirm it held dead parasites.

"It works," Marya said. "I have a plan."

Several crates of vodka were found in a storage room. What it was for or who it belonged to was a mystery. The trio collected brooms, buckets of charcoal from stoves, and jars of fish eyes in Tolsky's office. It took several hours for the girls to fill eight buckets with the "purification remedy." While Kazia was left behind to administer the cure to their classmates and teachers, Marya and Svatka set out with two buckets each into the gloomy streets of Warsaw

Dark rain clouds blocked the sun, and it was eerily quiet. No horsecars or carriages, nor pedestrians or soldiers were visible. It was eight miles to the bridge that crossed over the Vistula River to the east side of town, and another ten miles before they arrived at the woods. Marya feared the altar was no longer there. She also worried it would rain before they arrived, for it was a three-hour walk carrying heavy buckets.

Svatka found an old nag left harnessed to a small wagon in an alley. The owner was nowhere in sight. The girl spoke softly to the horse, blowing into its nostrils, which seemed to perk up the horse's spirits. Now able to transport the buckets safely, Marya sat in the wagon with Svatka, and offered a little prayer of gratitude. Reins in hand, Svatka let out a soft whistle, and the horse proceeded down the cobblestoned streets.

Worried they'd find the bridge closed to the public, both girls were surprised to find no Russian sentries at the bridge and the barricades left abandoned. The reason for the guards' abandoning their posts became clear once Marya and Svatka crossed the bridge. This section of town had suffered the worst from the plague. Window shutters were closed, and doors marked with *X*'s in red paint. Wrapped corpses lay on the curbs, molested by stray dogs that tore at the bloody sheets.

A distant church bell tolled interminably. *Counting the dead?*

"It's getting dark. Ghouls always come out at night. We must hurry," Svatka said.

Taking a shortcut through an old graveyard, the horse let out a frightened whinny as the path led into thick woods.

Marya relied on her friend to navigate in the fading sunlight. They arrived at an excavation site bordered by tree stumps, leaving the horse and wagon on the path to investigate. Nearby, Marya noticed a Strzegom granite stone, the size of a tabletop, lying on the ground still tied with ropes. The workers had apparently left in a rush, not bothering to take the altar any further. Svatka pointed out the engraved ancient runes and Rodu's symbol, a spoked wheel, on its surface. No more than three meters from the altar, red water gurgled out of the mouth of a spring, which the altar had covered. The contaminated water flowed toward the river, and as the girls waded to the source, parasites swam toward them from all directions.

Svatka whispered what sounded like a magic spell as they poured the potion into the spring.

"How are we going to move the altar on our own?" Marya asked.

"We don't have to," Svatka replied. "The gypsies are here. They'll help us."

A twig snapped. From out of the trees, five men in brightly colored vests appeared leading a mule. In minutes, the men returned the altar to its proper place on top of the spring. As the water receded, the white parasites dissolved on the water's surface and vanished. The clouds overhead separated, allowing a sliver of fading sunlight to fall upon the altar. From somewhere in the woods, an owl hooted.

"The curse is broken," Svatka said.

"Thanks to you and your grandmother's formula," Marya said. "Let's thank the gypsies then ask them to escort us to the school. We need to make more to cure the sick."

The gypsies agreed to provide safe conduct to the two girls who had shown great bravery and great respect to Rodu. With the donkey in tow, the men walked beside the wagon, while Marya and Svatka made their plans to save Warsaw.

Science Note:

In the 1890s, Warsaw's mayor ordered the construction of its first water and sewage system. The remedy Marya and her friends use to save Warsaw's infected citizens comes from Slavic folklore, to specially kill the Cold White Ones, which people believed lived in contaminated water. Charcoal can actually be used to purify water through filtration.

CHEATING
Death

by

HENRY HERZ

I didn't join in as my surviving family members conversed over dinner. Usually, the aroma of hearty pork and cabbage *bigos* stirred my appetite, but today it reminded me of the past, knotting my stomach. I winced— the clinking of utensils on plates like needles jabbing my brain.

Father gently pulled me aside. "What is wrong, my little Marya?" But he knew.

My sigh almost became a sob. "It's been years, but I still miss them in the worst way, *Tato*."

"Me too, Marya."

Since the passing of my Roman Catholic mother, my father, a brilliant math and physics teacher, no longer suppressed his religious skepticism. By the age of fifteen, I too had lost faith in a deity who'd allowed disease to rip apart a loving family.

Science became my religion, defeating disease my Holy Grail. I vowed I'd wield science to cheat Death itself . . . for I still believed in it.

Father wrapped a strong, comforting arm around my shoulders and led me into the study. Boxes of laboratory equipment cluttered the room.

"What's all this, *Tato*?"

He scowled. "My Russian supervisor barged into my lab at school and ordered me to shut it down. Sadly, we have no space to set up a lab here."

My heart leaped. "Even so, will you teach me how to use the equipment?" It was a rhetorical question, for Father loved nothing more than encouraging his children to learn.

He smiled. "Yes, of course, Marya. Now help me carry these boxes to the shed out back."

I did not receive a typical education, but then again, I was not a typical girl. Gradually under Father's guidance, I gained familiarity with the equipment, supplementing my foundation in theoretical science. I filled a notebook with calculations and equations in my ungodly crusade to fight disease and repel Death. But I had no way to conduct experiments . . . yet.

My public girls' high school, Warsaw's Gymnasium Number Three, filled the second floor of a converted convent adjacent to the Visitationist Church. The church's rococo facade of stacked pillars faced a broad avenue, Krakowskie Przedmieście, down the center of which ran a horse-drawn trolley. Before I was born, the genius composer Fryderyk Chopin used to play the church organ during services for school children, but tuberculosis took him too. *Damn that disease. Damn all disease.*

After classes, I strolled home through the lush Saxon Gardens. Majestic chestnut trees formed an opera house from which birds serenaded. I stopped to scatter breadcrumbs. Sparrows flocked to the grass around me, one even landing on my outstretched palm to feed.

Alexei approached with his brutish comrades, Dimitri and Igor. They attended a nearby gymnasium for sons of Russian soldiers. A blue-eyed fourth boy, unknown to me, accompanied them.

Alexei sneered. "Well, if it isn't Messy Marya." Discordant notes of cruelty rang in Dimitri and Igor's laughter.

The new boy frowned at Alexei's unprovoked insult of my unruly blond hair.

As the intruders neared, the birds scattered . . . except the sparrow in my hand.

It trusts me.

"Kill it," ordered Alexei.

My eyes widened. "What?" His casual malice rocked me. "Why?"

"Because I said so." He stepped closer.

I twitched my hand, and the sparrow took flight. *You're safe now.*

Alexei's face reddened at my defiance. He shoved me to the ground, towering over me with a scowl.

Anger boiled inside me. I clenched my fists.

The fourth boy grabbed Alexei's shoulders. "What are you doing?"

Alexei shook himself free of the restraining hands. "Well, if you love this Polish bitch so much, Maxim, maybe you should spend time with her instead of us. Igor and Dimitri, let's go." They stormed off.

Maxim helped me to my feet. "Are you alright?"

I nodded. "I'll be fine. Thank you."

He shook his head. "I need to pick better friends. Can I start with you?"

I brushed my hair, now more disheveled than usual, out of my face and smiled. "I'd like that."

Maxim's grin eased into a frown as he turned his head. "Something's wrong with them."

I picked up my book bag. "Beyond being rude and bullying?"

"Yes. Sometimes after school, they mutilate dead animals from the biology lab. They also chase stray cats and dogs. If they manage to catch one in a sack, they beat it against a wall. The poor thing's just left in an alley, dead or alive."

Monsters! My face flushed. *Wait. This is a chance to obtain subjects for my experiments!* "Maxim, I love animals. Will you bring them to me?"

His eyes widened. "What?"

"I'll heal and feed the injured ones, and I'll bury the dead."

Maxim gazed at me. His head tilted as he considered my unusual request. "If I agree, how will you know when and where to find me?"

We must do this without raising suspicions. "Let's meet each day after school in front of the Treasury Ministry. That's on my way home. If you have no animal that day, we can walk together."

"You have a strange mind, but a good heart, Marya. I'll help you." He gave a polite nod and turned. "See you tomorrow then."

I sighed. *I miss Mama.* Instead of walking directly home, I visited Powązki cemetery—a hundred acres of tree-shaded tombstones and mausoleums. Distracted by broad white elms, hawthorns, and eerily lifelike statues, I nearly tumbled into a freshly dug hole.

Reaching Mama's grave, I bowed my head. *How can I pursue my goal of cheating Death? I have lab equipment and will soon have test subjects, but I lack a lab to conduct experiments. I'm as trapped as you are here, Mama.*

A sudden breeze raised goosebumps on my arms. *That's it!* I had no space or privacy to set up a laboratory . . . at home. But a nighttime cemetery offered me both. *Thank you, dear Mama.*

I strolled down somber aisles of carved gray stone, eventually discovering an imposing gothic-style mausoleum bordered by four short, square pillars wrapped in carved laurels. *Perfect.* A tarnished brass crypt lock secured the heavy door. I wasn't worried, for a year ago I'd acquired a skill of questionable morality but indisputable usefulness—lock picking.

While my family slept, I snuck to our rickety backyard shed. I hurried to load wood planks, tools, and nails on a toy wagon borrowed from Kazia. *I mustn't be caught.* Repeatedly glancing over my shoulder, I made my way to the cemetery as quickly as Jozef eats *kiełbasa.* I hid in alleys twice to avoid being seen by late-night strollers.

The night's chill embraced me. Animated by gusts of wind, the jagged moon shadows of Powązki cemetery's tree branches looked like arms reaching up from graves.

I tightened my overcoat collar and worked on the crypt lock with two hairpins. Cold numbed my fingers, but eventually the lock yielded. The heavy door squealed in protest as I pried it outward. The doorway gaped like the black maw of a monster. I lit a lantern, illuminating the mausoleum's interior and the next chapter of my quest. Brass plaques named the deceased, six on the left wall, six on the right.

Stale, musty air muffled my steps like a blanket. Disturbing the thick dust carpeting the tile floor, I assembled a crude table and shelving. The hair on my neck rose as I felt growing ire from the interred. *Did the harsh sounds of sawing and hammering in a formerly silent abode offend their deaf ears? Do their unseeing eyes now watch and judge me?* My heart pounded in warning. *I am an intruder here.*

Eager to leave, I locked the crypt and rushed home. Creeping into our small bathroom, I quietly scrubbed away the grime and sweat of my labors before collapsing into bed.

The next night, I returned to our backyard shed. The boxes of equipment reminded me of presents under a Christmas tree. Some contained beakers, test tubes, and other glassware. Other boxes held biology equipment like a scale, alcohol burner, and even a microscope. One crate contained scalpels, sutures, forceps, syringes, and other medical equipment.

But unlike at Christmas, I couldn't unwrap all my presents at once. It took almost a week to shuttle the equipment to the cemetery, one box per night. And the ongoing loss of sleep took its toll.

My family said nothing—if they noticed my decline, it was attributed to continued grieving for Mama and Zosia. They didn't know that I burned the candle at both ends in my race to master science and protect them from Death.

Over the following weeks, Maxim proved true to his word. He brought me bloodstained sacks—rats and rabbits from the laboratory, stray cats and dogs that had fallen victim to Alexei. Those rare days when he carried no grim burden became welcome points of light in my increasingly gloomy and untethered blur of school, homework, and skulking midnight visits to the cemetery.

I would keep my promise to bury the animals . . . after learning from them. In my nighttime laboratory, I tenderly apologized. "I'd cure you if I could, but my reach isn't that long. Forgive me for desecrating your body. Please teach me how to help the living."

Typical girls collected dolls, but I was not a typical girl. In the lantern-lit stench of my growing collection of corpses, my hands became more skilled as animal bodies yielded their secrets.

Rising the next morning, my mirror revealed that lack of sleep and appetite had given me a gaunt, haunted expression. I no longer even attempted to control my wild hair. My family expressed concern at my deteriorating appearance. I did what I could to allay their unease—a worry I shared but forced down. *Mama and Zosia would want me to continue my efforts to protect the rest of our family from Death.*

One sunny afternoon, Maxim met me after school carrying a brown paper bag. He wore a wide grin.

My heart leaped at a tiny squeak. "Is that a rat?"

"I finally was able to save one," Maxim said, nodding. "Unfortunately, not before Alexei broke its ankle."

"Oh, poor thing. Thank you, Maxim. I'll do what I can for it." In my joy, I gave him a one-armed hug before remembering propriety. *Finally. A chance to heal something.*

"Thank you again, Maxim. I will see you tomorrow." I headed home, peering into the bag.

The sturdy brown rat's light-colored belly, slanted snout, and small eyes and ears indicated *Rattus norvegicus.* I spoke Russian, German, and French. But as this was a Polish rat, it seemed appropriate to converse with him in Polish.

"I shall call you Damian." *Greek for 'to tame.'* "I'm so sorry that awful Alexei hurt you. I'll do my best to heal your leg. But I can't very well keep you at home. I'll take you to my laboratory now."

Damian, being a very clever rat, squeaked his understanding.

I walked to the cemetery, excitement quickening my pace.

As I entered the mausoleum, Damian squeaked in alarm.

Dulled by fatigue, I'd grown accustomed to the rank odor of dead bodies stacked in a corner. "Sorry about the smell, but you'll be safe here." I gently set Damian in a straw-padded hat box. Pouring water into a small bowl, I gave him a chunk of *Tylżycki* cheese left over from my uneaten lunch.

After feeding and complimenting Damian, I earned enough of his trust that he let me pet him. I dared not try to set his ankle without a painkiller, so I taped it as a temporary measure.

"What a sensible and handsome fellow you are. And you've arrived just in time. At long last, I've finished my stoichiometry and other calculations. My formula *should* stimulate bone and muscle growth. If it works, it'll help your leg heal faster." *And eventually, bring back the dead.*

Squeak?

"No, I can't give it to you yet, because I don't have any components. And, I'd want to test it first on our deceased friends," I said, nodding at the pile of two dozen animal corpses, limbs stiffened into disturbing poses.

Squeak.

My mouth opened. "Yes, of course! What a clever boy. A Russian boys' gymnasium will have chemistry supplies. I'll be back soon."

The fact that I conversed with a rat should have warned me I was pushing myself too hard in the pursuit of cheating Death.

I pulled Kazia's wagon to the rear entrance of the nearest gymnasium. When drunk soldiers staggered by, I lunged behind a low wall.

This lock proved resistant to my efforts, so I wrapped my scarf around a brick and broke the door's glass pane. *Hurry. The longer I'm here, the greater the chance of being caught.* My heart pounded.

After a few minutes of frantic searching, I found the shiny, modern chemistry laboratory, the hazardous items locked in a solid oak cabinet. I picked the lock and stared like a hungry child gawking at shelves brimming with chocolate. *Can you hear footsteps, Death? I'm coming for you.*

The glass bottles of liquids and powders tinkled as I rolled my wagon back to the cemetery. In retrospect, my indifference to being surrounded by the dead should have warned me.

"Damian, look what I foraged: acetyl chloride, aluminum chloride, ammonium perchlorate, benzene, cadmium powder, chloroacetyl chloride, dioxane, ethyl chloride, formaldehyde, hydrochloric acid, hydrazine, lead arsenate powder, magnesium, mercuric iodide, potassium perchlorate, phenolphthalein, sodium perchlorate, sodium salicylate, strychnine, sulfuric acid, uranium salts, and white phosphorus."

Squeak?

"Well, I probably don't need all of this, but luck favors the prepared. Speaking of preparation, if I encounter Alexei again, I'll need a way to protect myself." I mixed two chemical different defenses, slipping a stoppered test tube in my coat pocket and placing a stoppered Erlenmeyer flask on the corner of the table next to the lantern.

Squeak?

"Yes, I'll make you something for the pain." I treated sodium salicylate with acetyl chloride to produce acetylsalicylic acid. Dissolving five milligrams of the powder in ten milliliters of water, I fed it to Damian with an eye dropper.

Between the painkiller and the trust that had developed between us, he let me set and splint his ankle with admirable fortitude. "What a brave boy you are."

Nearly collapsing with fatigue, I bid Damian good night and headed home.

After my family fell asleep the next night, I rushed to the cemetery carrying a notepad filled with calculations scribbled so messily that only I could interpret them. My hands shook with excitement.

Having traversed the cemetery many times, I now greeted some of its inhabitants by name. "Good evening, Mr. Zieliński. I trust all is well, Mrs. Pawlak." They never replied. *Not yet.*

"Good evening, Damian."

Squeak.

I painstakingly measured and combined the components in a complex sequence of boiling, deposition, sublimation, and condensation.

"Are you ready?"

Squeak.

Damian's enthusiasm was contagious. I browsed through the pile of corpses, choosing a black-and-white Norwegian forest cat—its head and tail bent at odd angles, courtesy of Alexei. Filling a syringe with my chemical solution, I injected twenty milliliters in its neck and another twenty at the base of its tail. Selecting a rat, rabbit, and dog exhibiting similar physical abuse, I injected their injury sites, adjusting the dosage in proportion to body weight.

Squeak?

"Nothing yet, Damian. Patience."

That was easier said than done. For a tortured hour, I paced the cold, cramped space of the mausoleum, mumbling equations to myself, and running my hand through my unbound hair. Periodically, I'd return the bloodstained, mutilated test subjects' open-eyed gaze. I couldn't help myself—fretting over my four little patients like a baker checking on her first loaves.

Nothing.

Squeak.

Sigh. "Yes. Maybe the regeneration of tissue will occur overnight. All we can do now is wait." I laid him in his bed. "Goodnight, Damian. I shall be back tomorrow."

The following evening, I set Damian on the lab table, where he paid close attention as if my colleague.

The four treated corpses showed no signs of healing. *Damn.*

Squeak?

"I was quite careful, Damian," I said, grinning at his earnest attempt to help. "But I suppose it couldn't hurt to triple-check my equations."

Staring at my calculations until my eyes blurred, I found no mistakes. "This *should* work," I said, lifting my notebook. "My math's correct, and the bottles were clearly marked . . . Hmmm. Perhaps they weren't labeled accurately."

It took an hour or so to titrate the chemicals. "Aha! The sulfuric acid's diluted." I adjusted my calculations to account for the weaker acid, prepared a second batch, and repeated the prior night's injections.

Waiting again proved the hardest part. "Damian, would you like to try the medicine too?"

Squeak.

I injected him in the thigh above his broken leg.

After an hour of anxious hair tugging and running my fingernails along the stone mausoleum walls, I checked the corpses. *Nothing.* Damian, though no worse, was no better either.

Damn! In my frustration, I accidentally yanked out strands from my scalp, the blond hair bright against the red of my bleeding fingernails, which I'd worn down to the quick.

I must *find a way to cheat Death!* Doubling the dosage, I administered it to all the carcasses.

Raising my arms to stretch my tight back and shoulders, I glanced at a brass plaque-adorned wall. *Twelve people are interred here. Would my solution work on them?* I shook my head. *That's a queer thought. Go home to bed, Marya.*

Inadequate eating and sleeping turned my days blurry and dreamlike. Only at night, when I hunted Death, did my mind seem to sharpen and my hands regain their nimbleness.

"Marya!" Kazia tapped my shoulder as we walked home from school. "Did you hear what I said?"

I shook my head to clear it. "Sorry, I was distracted."

"You've been distracted for weeks now. You're not paying attention in class. Sorry to say it, but your eyes are wilder than your hair. I'm worried about you."

"Thanks, Kazia. You're a dear. I'll be fine." We reached her home at Pałac Niebieski, where her father served as librarian to Count Zamoyski.

"Please get some sleep," she replied, concern written on her face. "See you tomorrow."

I nodded. *I'll sleep after I drive Death into a corner.*

A block later, Alexei, Igor, and Dimitri ambushed me. "Ugh. Don't whores usually pay closer attention to their appearance?" Alexei taunted.

Scowling, I muttered, *"Kretyn,"* forgetting in my mental fog that cretins don't like to be reminded of their condition.

Alexei took a step toward me. "Bitch. Your mother's a whore too."

The slur against my revered Mama took me by surprise. I bunched my fists, losing all self-control. "She was a saint, you pig. Do you even know who fathered you?"

Cretins also don't appreciate having their lineage questioned. The three boys advanced with fury in their eyes.

Having anticipated another assault, I'd gotten in the habit of carrying a chemical defense. Yanking the stoppered test tube from my coat pocket, I hurled it to the ground in front of them. It shattered, white fumes wreathing the thugs.

The test tube held an acylation of benzene with chloroacetyl chloride and an aluminum chloride catalyst. Its vapor causes skin irritation, tearing, and respiratory pain. I fled home, their coughing and curses ringing in my ears. *I'm safe for now, but they'll come for me again, angrier than before.*

That night, the treated animals lay where I'd left them, limbs splayed as if in a macabre dance, eyes still dull. They showed no signs of healing.

I don't know how long I cried.

Damian hobbled around, trying to cheer me up.

All that work for nothing! I stomped out of the mausoleum and wandered the cemetery, hoping for an encouraging word from one of the residents. All I heard was leaves rustling, though there was no breeze.

I found a shovel leaning against a tool shed, and dug a shallow grave, the blade strikes seeming to echo longer than they should. Gathering the rat corpses in my arms, even their fur stiff from dried blood, I carried them to the hole, apologizing along the way. My tears dripped onto their rigid bodies before I covered them with dirt. Another hole accepted all the rabbits. The cats and dogs stared back at me with unseeing eyes as I put them into their graves, except that first feline. I saved the cat for further experimentation.

My steps dragged as I returned home.

I felt feverish but did not let that stop me from returning to my lab that moonless night. I couldn't shake the feeling that I was being watched as I navigated the dark cemetery. My darting backward glances never noticed anything but silent tombstones.

"Good evening, Damian. I'm going to take some muscle and bone tissue from this cat to figure out why my solution isn't working. Would you like to watch?"

Squeak.

I expected no less from the inquisitive rodent and set him atop my table next to a cookie. It may simply have been wishful thinking on my part, but he seemed more agile than yesterday.

Shaving thin slices of muscle and bone from the cat with a scalpel, I mounted them on glass microscope slides.

I nearly jumped out of my skin when the mausoleum door grated on its rusty hinges behind me.

The three Russian bullies gaped wide-eyed at me from the narrow doorway, Alexei grasping a shovel. "Ugh. You smell as bad as you look."

How did they find my laboratory? They must have followed me here. I'm cornered at night in a mausoleum. My hands trembled before anger flared in my chest at the prospect of losing my irreplaceable equipment and notes. I stood, fists balled, legs set wide, and shouted, "Get out. Do not come between me and Death!"

"Mother of God!" cried Alexei, staring at the dead cat. "What sacrilegious devilry is this? She's a witch." He stepped forward, eyes narrowing. "And we know what to do with a Polish witch."

Igor and Dimitri flanked him. The laboratory table stood between me and the Russians. But they stood between me and the doorway.

Damian hissed.

"Look. The witch has a rat familiar." Alexei raised the shovel.

Not my sweet, clever Damian! "Don't," I warned.

Alexei smashed Damian with the flat of the shovel, crushing his head and spine.

"NO!"

Alexei leered. "Now it's your turn. Do you want to say a final prayer?"

"Prayer?" A laugh escaped my lips, sounding maniacal even to my ears. "I worship only science. I won't worship a god that rips mothers from their children and allows Russian invaders to murder Poles."

The dead cat on my table moaned and struggled to its feet, rotting flaps of skin hanging loosely from the dissection cuts. With its head locked at an unnatural angle, the cat's tail jerked spasmodically. Pus oozed from eyes glowing yellow.

Could it be? Disturbingly incongruous in a corpse-filled mausoleum, a grim smile cracked my face. *I cheated Death!*

When the cat hissed like a poisonous serpent, the boys jumped back, disbelief and terror on their faces. "Christ! What have you done?"

Seizing a bottle of sulfuric acid, I threw it to the stone floor at their feet. It splashed on Alexei and Igor's shoes and shins.

The two howled, struggling to tear off the bottom of their pant legs without touching acid.

The cat howled in mocking chorus.

"I'll finish the witch," growled Dimitri.

As he knelt to grab the shovel, I hurled my lantern and the previously prepared Erlenmeyer flask at his feet, closing my eyes and covering my ears.

The mixture of magnesium and potassium perchlorate ignited with a brilliant flash and thunderous boom echoing within the stone walls. Disoriented from the noise, but with my eyesight intact, I dashed past the prone, writhing boys out of the mausoleum.

I tripped on the raised threshold in my panicked haste. My right knee struck a flagstone. I gasped as pain radiated up my leg. *Run!* I struggled to my feet but could only hobble away. My knee swelled with each agonizing step. I spared a glance over my shoulder.

The boys staggered out of the mausoleum, their eyes still recovering from the flash. They stumbled toward me, two slowed by acid burns.

I limped between trees in the darkness. *Hurry! They're gaining.* My foot snagged on a low stone plaque. Twisting in midair to protect my knee, I thudded to the ground on my left side.

The boys surrounded me, all of us gasping for breath.

Dimitri jerked his thumb back toward my lab. "Should I go get the shovel?"

Alexei grinned like a wolf. "I have a better idea. If she's so fond of that mausoleum, let's seal her inside. Forever. Dimitri, grab her right arm. Igor, her left. I'll get her legs." His eyes narrowed.

"Help!" I twisted and punched from the ground, but Dimitri and Igor managed to seize my wrists. My frantic kicking kept Alexei at bay . . . until all hell broke loose.

Blood-freezing screeches echoed through the graveyard. Patches of earth seemed to boil.

Alexei's mouth fell open in horror.

Igor shrieked, barely maintaining his grip on my wrist.

I craned my neck for a view. A dozen animated animal corpses with glowing yellow eyes clawed their way out of the spots where I'd buried them. Stench assaulted my nostrils as they surged around us. The putrid wave swamped Dimitri.

"No!" he screamed.

The corpses savaged his face and neck. Blood spattered.

Igor recoiled, his face ashen with terror. "God damn!"

Indeed, He has, I thought.

More hissing and howling animal corpses clawed up from their graves.

Before Igor could move, creatures swarmed around him, gnawing his acid-wounded shins. That dropped him to the ground, where they scurried onto his head.

His corpse-muffled cries to a merciless god brought him no salvation, drawing instead only a savage smile from me. Igor tore a frenzied rabbit from his neck, crushed it in his bare hand, and dropped it.

Within a few seconds, the rabbit rose and resumed its attack.

My heart leaped with joy when a rat scurried over, his eyes glowing yellow. "Damian!" I scooped him up tenderly, my pain forgotten.

Alexei stood paralyzed by the carnage of reanimated animals chewing off his friends' faces. He'd wet himself in terror.

A thrill of triumph surged through me. *I did it! I cheated Death.* My newfound power comforted me like a warm cloak.

The resurrected dogs snarled at Alexei, who turned and fled. He only got ten yards before they hamstrung him and tore out his throat.

I stood, wobbly. My mind swirled with questions. *What shall I do with all my new friends? Will I be able to teach them more restraint? Can I adjust my chemical formula to work faster? Wait. First things first. What should be done with the bodies?*

I brushed myself off and, after some searching, found an open gravesite. Addressing the two largest dogs, I pointed. "Please help me drag the boys' bodies into this hole.

Each grabbed one of Alexei's legs in its jaws.

"The rest of you, please lick up the spilled blood."

Three warm bodies tumbled into the grave. "Help me cover them," I requested.

The dogs turned their backs to the hole and scraped in loose dirt with their front paws.

Squeak.

"Yes, you're right, Damian." I addressed the corpse animals. "Thank you, my pretties. You saved my life." *Just as I restored yours.* Euphoria dulling the pain of my injured knee, I lavished smiles and caresses before directing the creatures to return to the earthen beds from which they'd erupted. "Time to rest . . . until I need you again."

Can I modify my formula to work on humans? I eyed the mausoleum. *I do have twelve test subjects available, after all . . . But what price will Fate extract for my experiments?* I shrugged off the unanswerable question for now and headed home, Damian riding on my shoulder. He was not a typical pet, but then again, I was not a typical teen.

Science Note:

In real life, Marya never raised the dead, much less stole chemicals. I selected dangerous chemicals from a 2015 Washington State Department of Health list of substances proposed to be banned from schools due to the serious health hazards they posed.

Marya never mixed the compounds mentioned in the story. However, those mentioned are scientifically accurate. Treating sodium salicylate with acetyl chloride produces acetylsalicylic acid (aspirin). Tear gas is an acylation of benzene with chloroacetyl chloride and an aluminum chloride catalyst. Flash-bang grenades use a pyrotechnic metal-oxidant mix of magnesium or aluminum and an oxidizer such as potassium perchlorate or potassium nitrate.

A SHARD OF
Sunlit Shadow

by

EMILY McCOSH

A light sends warm rays into the shadows of the basement.

Marya adjusts the glass and ensures the lamp is properly lit. Mirrors catch the tiny flame, transforming the basement into a bearable place to conduct an experiment. It's perfect in many ways: dark, abandoned, and underground away from the noise and vibrations of daily life. But also claustrophobic, the air stale. For a secret laboratory and a controlled environment, it'll have to do.

Kazia perches at the edge of the stairs, cradling her own little candle, casting glances over her shoulder up the steps, watching for anyone who might open the door.

"Is this place going to work?" she whispers. "I think I can still hear carriages from the street."

Marya doesn't hear them, but she isn't close to the door. "I don't know where else to do it. This is the quietest place. It isn't as busy now as it is in the morning."

The hustle and bustle threaten to send vibrations into the earth. Marya may not hear or feel the shaking, but the mirrors and light won't be motionless. It's just something they'll have to work around.

"Can't I help?" Kazia asks.

"You *are* helping."

"I mean *real* helping, not playing watch guard."

Even as she speaks, she peeks again over her shoulder. Neither of them are certain what would happen if they're caught—Marya hasn't heard of other girls conducting secret experiments—but none of their Polish parents are on good terms with the Russian police.

"Don't make noise. I'm almost ready."

The experiment is the best they could assemble with the materials they scraped together. Scraps of wood with mirrors fastened to either end. A half-silvered one-way mirror. An oil lamp. A dark basement. Marya's pad of paper and stubby pencil to write results.

And if the experiment goes correctly and the math adds up, they'll have proof of luminiferous aether, the substance upon which light travels.

Marya fiddles with the oil lamp. The half-silvered mirror in the center of the contraption catches and splits the light, the mirrors on their wooden arms—one fixed and one Marya can spin into position—redirecting the beams back toward the center of the contraption. Aether slows it, and Marya will record it before anyone else. The first proof of its existence, even if everyone knows it's there.

"Ready?" She puts her finger to her lips.

Kazia blows out her candle with a puff, erasing her from sight.

Brightening her lamp, Marya sends the one movable mirror into the correct orbit to catch the light. A hazy pattern spins across the room, catching along the center of the apparatus, circles of shadows forming in a repeating pattern, like ripples from a dropped stone.

It's working. Marya focuses on not disturbing the equipment.

Reaching through the beam, she adjusts the mirror, one millimeter at a time, changing the pattern. As many measurements she can observe in the speed of the pattern, all the better—

The mirror swings around, and something shatters.

Marya throws her arm over her eyes, dropping her pad of paper. Behind her, Kazia squeaks. The sharp shatter of hundreds of glass fragments hitting the basement walls surrounds them. The explosion snuffs out the lamp. A thick scent of oil fills the air.

Everything falls quiet.

Marya's wrist stings, but the glass didn't cut her face. Hopefully no one heard.

Kazia whispers, "Marya?"

"I'm alright. Did you get cut?"

"No. I felt a shard pass next to my ear, though."

"Do you have the matches?"

"Yes."

There's rustling, a tiny flame flaring to life in Kazia's fingers. She creeps across the room, shoes crunching on glass, and stands shoulder to shoulder with Marya. The scraps of wood they used for the arms of the apparatus are mostly undamaged. But the mirrors are gone, useless and scattered in a thousand reflective slivers catching light from the fading match. The demolished oil lamp leaks onto the ground.

Kazia lights another match. "Could it have been the heat from the lamp?"

"I doubt it. It wasn't *that* hot."

"Someone might have heard."

"Let's clean up and get home. It's late already."

Kazia's eyebrows furrow, pulling her expression into sharp shadows in the dying light. She squeezes Marya's shoulders.

Marya tugs a handkerchief from her coat pocket and dabs at the cut on her wrist.

Kazia digs another candle from her coat pocket. Carefully, they begin scraping the glass into a pile with their shoes.

Getting mirrors was tricky. Acquiring more before anyone else performs the experiment seems unlikely.

Mademoiselle Mayer yanks a comb through Marya's hair, gathering it into thick bunches to braid.

Marya stares at the wall instead of the hand mirror, fighting a grumpy expression. Sulking over broken mirrors won't help. Neither will resisting the fierce hair combing.

"Marya, where did you get that cut on your wrist?" Mademoiselle Mayer asks, voice clipped.

How did she see? Even with Marya seated on a stool, the teacher is shorter, and Marya's hands are bunched in her lap.

"I scraped it on a branch."

"You shouldn't be fumbling around in brambles. That isn't any way to act."

"Yes, ma'am." It's lucky her teacher can't see her expression. Marya's still feeling too defeated to bandy words but thinks she must look irritated.

The cut itched all night as tiny healing injuries tend to do. She's been trying not to pick at it. A reminder of how horribly wrong the experiment went for no reason she's been able to figure, and how tricky it's going to be to get more materials.

When Mademoiselle Mayer finishes fussing, Kazia scoots up next to Marya. It's their last class of the day, the first time they've talked since sprinting home yesterday afternoon. Not that they can speak much about such things when they're on school grounds.

Mr. Belkin, her mathematics professor, passes the doorway. Leaning in, he says something pleasant and polite about the weather to Mademoiselle Mayer.

Marya smooths the scowl from her eyebrows should he look her direction. Many professors here are unfriendly in more severe ways than hair combing. But though he's Russian, neither Marya or Kazia dislike Mr. Belkin. He's spoken with Marya's father in the past. Sometimes, waiting for his lessons to begin, Marya would listen to his conversations and pick up tidbits of information not usually taught to girls.

Until one day, when he hadn't noticed her slip into his classroom.

Speaking about her father, he told another professor, "I don't suspect Mr. Skłodowski works much, not without access to a laboratory. Probably for the best. With daughters around the house you have to be careful not to pass on habits like that. They couldn't measure up."

When he turned, Marya was at her desk, Kazia beside her. He didn't have the decency to look ashamed or even uncomfortable.

Marya shouldn't have expected better. But she had.

Their experiment can never be revealed, but Marya clings to the insult. She and Kazia will prove him foolish. Even in secret. Him and the other professors who believe the same.

And when we're successful, I can tell Father. That makes it easier not to scowl at the side of Mr. Belkin's face.

As they're shuffling out, he says, "Oh, Marya?"

Suspicion tightens her chest. "Yes?"

"I saw you two going around the school yesterday. What were you doing back there?"

"Just walking. The trees across the street are pleasant."

He glances at Kazia, but her eyes are unfocused like she can't be bothered to pay attention.

"Shouldn't you be going home after your lessons?"

"Father says it's good to walk in fresh air."

Kazia yawns into her handkerchief.

Mr. Belkin squints. Over his shoulder, Mademoiselle Mayer gives both girls a disapproving scowl.

As they're leaving the upper levels of the building, Kazia whispers, "We need to check for him watching next time. Or Mademoiselle Mayer."

"Or *anyone*."

"I wish I could go with you to your family in the country. Imagine the secrecy."

That would be wonderful. Though her father supplied the half-silvered and reflective mirrors, for "whatever mischief you're not telling me about," she doubts she'd be allowed to pack new ones out to the country where her relatives live surrounded by mountains and quiet. She'd barely convinced him to allow her to take the mirrors from his makeshift home laboratory. If he ever discovered the flying glass, he wouldn't allow her to try again.

And she doesn't want to steal the supplies. Not from him.

"We're not going back soon," Marya says. "But I wish that too."

Marya and Kazia pass the brightly lit clockmaker shop in the bottom level of the school building and wave to the owner. They've been in before. Marya loves the ticking of the countless clocks and watches.

Did the vibrations and subtle movement of the outside world cause the shattering? It seems unlikely. It was merely light. Reflected, split light.

Marya's wrist itches. It's scabbed over, no longer bleeding, so she rubs it against her coat.

Late spring is mild at best, mostly chilly and wet. Clouds hang low in the sky, sunlight not quite appearing this past week. Cool, damp air seeps down the neck of Marya's coat. The light is strange, too bright and too hazy at once. It isn't late, but it feels like twilight. Marya squints and blinks. She didn't sleep well last night, fretting over the misadventure with their experiment, and her lessons were a struggle.

But she's certain she can recreate the experiment. She saw the patterns of light. Marya's never seen the fringe pattern before—experiments like this aren't performed in a school for girls—but she heard her father talking about the experiment. Albert Michelson, a scientist from America, had discovered a way to measure the luminiferous aether. His research helped Marya decipher the equipment needed—he uncovered the way to split the beam and record the wavelengths, though his first experiment didn't record the results he was looking for. He'll try again.

Marya considers mirrors until her head aches.

After supper, when they're alone, her father asks, "How did your experiment turn out?"

Marya freezes. She never specifically *told* him what she and Kazia were planning with the mirrors, but he always seems to know when she's up to something. Girls aren't supposed to do things like conduct secret experiments under their schools—at least, certainly not with Russians ruling the country—but he isn't supposed to have his little laboratory in the spare room, either. The one he can take down quickly should the need arise.

Mr. Belkin doesn't know about *that* little secret. Marya smirks to herself.

She doesn't want him to know in detail, not yet, so she says, "Not well."

He puts his arm around her middle, kisses her cheek, and says, "Things worth doing often take many tries," before going to bed.

Hours later, a full, bright moon sends fingers of pale light through the gap between Marya's curtains. She stares at them, exhausted but unable to calm her mind to sleep.

Helena lies in her own bed across the room, the house quiet with the dead of night.

Marya imagines often in the darkness that she can hear the Wisła River, but they aren't close enough for it to be audible.

Her cut wrist still itches, and the light looks heavy, almost solid enough to touch. Marya wonders about the light. How it travels and touches all things in its path. The aether it travels upon, flinging it through the universe.

She wriggles her arm free of her bedding to catch the moonbeam, blocking it from reaching the other side of the room.

Moonlight shimmers against the opposite wall, her hand flickering, ghostly light passing straight through her palm.

She yanks back her hand, managing not to squeak. If she wakes Helena with a yelp in the middle of the night, her sister will never stop teasing her.

Rubbing her fingers together, she finds them cold from the night air but solid. It must have been a trick of the light. Staring at the moonbeam, she slips her fingers back in.

And watches her hand disappear.

She doesn't pull away. Or jump. And holds her breath so she doesn't gasp.

The touch of her own skin is still present—she can rub her fingers together and feel it—but they're invisible. The cut on her wrist is pale. Carefully, she moves the heavy curtain, cold from the glass washing over her skin. Her arm flickers in and out of sight in the pale light.

The sun makes a short appearance the next morning.

Marya waits beneath a tree for Kazia, staring at the clouds through the branches. Light dapples the ground through chattering leaves. Where it falls on the bare parts of her hands and neck, she all but disappears in the brighter, more intense light. Tugging up her sleeve, she watches it continue, even fading the fabric from view. No longer panicked like last night, she stands closer to the trunk where the branches are thicker until the sun goes back to hiding. Once the sun moves behind the clouds, her skin appears nearly whole save a slight ghostly pale.

She wonders if, at some point when summer shines bright and full, she'll completely disappear.

Perhaps this is why the mirrors shattered. Whatever *this* is. Marya isn't sure, but she's going to keep Kazia away from the lights and mirrors next time. Just in case.

"I know where we can get more mirrors," she says when her friend joins her.

They pass Saxon Gardens and soon after the massive palace and bronze statue before it. Both have spat on the grotesque obelisk in the past, a gesture of rebellion against the Russians. Today, there are people milling about, even this early, and neither are willing to get caught. Even more than they're unwilling to get caught performing experiments in the school basement.

"Did you talk to your father about it?"

"No."

Kazia eyes her. "Are you going to steal them?"

"It's not stealing if we put them back."

"What if they break again?"

"*Then* it's stealing."

Kazia grimaces but bounces as she walks.

Marya wishes she would feel the same excitement, but a strange determination has taken its place, different from what already drives her. The shattering mirrors. Disappearing skin. Awake in the early morning hours, she'd almost believed she'd dreamt last night's discovery. Vivid dreams have always crept through her sleep. In her heart, she knows she'd been wide awake.

She needs to *understand.*

"Are you going to tell me the plan, or are you going to keep brooding?"

"I'm not brooding," Marya says, though she definitely *had* been last night.

Kazia links arms with her as they catch sight of the school.

Marya tells her, "I know where to get the mirrors after classes, so I need you to visit the clockmaker. He has a lot of crystal paperweights."

Students file out of their classrooms as the sun dips. Kazia is gone, off to the clockmaker, and Marya hovers around the outside of their home economics class. She'd hatched the plan in the early hours of the morning, when the moon had risen enough it no longer shot beams of pale light through the window. Marya still hasn't quite figured out how she'll follow through without Mademoiselle Mayer discovering her planned mischief. She hopes her teacher will simply depart the classroom, but the woman isn't leaving. Soon, the hallways will clear, and her loitering will be suspicious.

"Mademoiselle Mayer," she asks, slipping into the classroom, attempting to look dignified and presentable with her books clasped to her chest. "My father is having visitors today, may I brush my hair out? The wind this morning stirred it up."

Which is true. Taken out of yesterday's braids, it's a tornado about her head. Normally, she cherishes the chaos and the irritation it brings out in her strict professor. Today, she has bigger ambitions.

Mademoiselle Mayer looks at her from the papers on her desk. She has sharp eyes, too suspicious, but perhaps a tad pleased. With all the times she's tried to defeat Marya's untidy hair, she must think she's succeeded a little at her task now that Marya is making an effort.

She hands Marya the comb from the drawer of her desk. "If you would braid your hair in the morning, Marya, it wouldn't get so tangled throughout the day."

"Yes, ma'am."

"Take it over there, you can see yourself in one of the mirrors."

"Thank you."

Marya sets her books on the table along the wall near the dozen or so little hand mirrors Mademoiselle Mayer has them use throughout the class. Two. She only needs two to catch the split beams. Sunlight from the open window is muted, and she wonders how long it'll take for the hazy skies to clear.

Yanking the comb through her hair, she glances back at Mademoiselle Mayer.

She's looking down.

Marya slips a mirror between the pages of one of her textbooks. After yesterday's conversation with Mr. Belkin, is Mademoiselle Mayer more suspicious of her? Papers rustle. Marya busies herself with separating her hair into braids. Gently, she scoops up a second mirror.

A streak of sunlight breaks through the clouds, and Marya drops the mirror in surprise as her hand disappears. It doesn't break against the desk, but the noise is startling in the dim hum of the school.

"Marya—"

"Sorry."

Her face heats, fingers chill and sweaty. What will happen when she performs the experiment again? Will they record the correct calculations? Will the concentrated, split light do something else to her skin?

She should tell Kazia. If Marya's skin disappears in the bright, direct lamplight during the experiment—or something even worse—her friend needs to understand.

Slipping the second mirror into the pages of another book, she gathers them to her chest. Shakily, she lets out a long breath and turns.

"Thank you, Mademoiselle Mayer."

The woman's eyes follow her out.

Kazia waits for her on the steps outside. The sun is behind the clouds. Together, they weave around the school and through a back door, watching for suspicious eyes. The hallway is empty, the door to the abandoned basement unguarded as it was the last time.

"I can't believe she didn't catch you," Kazia whispers, lamp unlit in her hand as they slip into the dark.

"She was very proud of me for brushing my hair."

Kazia muffles a giggle with her hand.

"What did you tell the clockmaker?"

"That we wanted to make rainbows when the sun came out," she says, placing a cold, heavy object in Marya's hand. "He didn't notice when I picked up the lamp on the way out. He has so many of them. He collects *everything*."

Marya taps the crystal paperweight with her fingers and smiles.

They feel their way down the steps to the scene of the failed experiment. Glass bits crunch under Marya's boots. Light flickers along the corners of the room, so briefly Marya isn't sure she sees it. Her fingers seem bright. Marya's stomach turns in knots. Kazia doesn't speak, but she might be looking at her feet in the darkness. A moment later, a match flares to life and the room is filled with light separate from Marya's skin.

Setting her books in the corner, she sets up the mirrors and crystal. Her body doesn't feel different, not even when her skin disappears from view. Not from a moment ago when it seemed the light had followed her down here in the dark. She could almost believe she's imagining it.

"Kazia?"

"Yes?"

Marya glances at her dear angel of a friend. "Bring that lamp closer. I want to show you something."

"What?"

"I think . . ." Marya takes the lamp from her. Her skin looks translucent. "I think something happened with the last experiment. And I want you to tell me if I'm a little crazy. If I'm not, you might want to stand behind the wall while I try again."

Kazia squints at her in the concerned way Marya's father does when she's a little too rowdy. "You're not making much sense."

Turning the lamp flame higher, Marya holds her hand close to the hot glass. In the direct beam, everything up to her mid arm, skin, and dress sleeve and all, flickers in and out of sight.

Kazia starts, breath catching, her eyes coming up to catch Marya's.

"I noticed it last night. I think . . . I think it must have had something to do with the experiment. Maybe the scratch on my wrist. It happens in direct sunlight too. Not as much when the light is diffused, I think."

Kazia sounds like she's trying not to choke. "What's going to happen when the sun is out?"

"I disappear . . . I suppose," Marya says, and tries not to feel afraid. Gingerly, Kazia touches her wrist.

Marya feels the contact as usual, but Kazia's finger flickers out of sight, and they both jump away. Kazia rubs her hand and stares at it, but it looks whole, and the light from the lamp doesn't appear to affect her.

"Maybe we're both insane," she says.

That doesn't sound as unlikely as it would have days ago. "Maybe. I think you should stand over behind the wall in case this goes wrong again. I don't know why it happened to me but maybe because I was too close."

Kazia looks her disappearing friend up and down and says, "Alright. Just . . . be careful."

Marya wants to cry. She just nods and sets the lamp where it goes.

Kazia shuffles behind the little brick wall dividing the basement into two sections. It isn't much of a room, barely a cubbyhole of a space, and neither of them are certain what it was used for, but the wall will protect her from flying glass. She peeks around the edge as Marya sets up the mirrors. Even in the dark, there's concern in her eyes.

Marya fastens the mirrors to the arms of the contraption and thinks she should have borrowed her father's spectacles in case more glass goes flying.

She pulls her little notepad from between her books and tries to adjust the lamp to a level that won't blind her. She sets the crystal in the center. Her heartbeat thumps behind her ears. It's so quiet, every noise seems to echo, especially with Kazia silent and still across the room.

Spinning the one movable mirror arm, she catches the lamplight and tenses, waiting for the inexplicable shatter of the day before. Nothing so dramatic happens, just the crystal splitting the beams, mirrors redirecting them back toward the center. Circles of warm, orange light catch along the center as the fringe pattern appears. Marya lets out a breath. She hadn't been making proper observations.

She can *feel* it, though. The heat of the light. The pressure of how it travels through the air. Unimpeded by anything.

Even aether.

Putting her notepad on the ground, she slips her hand into the split light and feels it all the more acutely. On every cell of her skin, directing tingles down her neck.

"Marya?" Kazia's voice sends vibrations through the room, throwing the fringe pattern off balance, but it doesn't matter.

Marya can still feel it.

High pitched this time, Kazia hisses, *"Marya?"*

She can't see me, Marya realizes, looking down at herself, and drops her hand from the beam.

Kazia makes a relieved noise behind her.

It isn't real. Aether doesn't exist. Even without measurements and calculations, Marya felt the bright heat of the light along her skin. The path of it, careening free on its own through space and darkness.

"It isn't real," she whispers.

"What?"

"The aether. It isn't real. The light, it isn't traveling on anything. I can feel it."

Above them, the basement door creaks. Marya jumps, staring at the staircase.

Kazia ducks out from the wall, grabbing her shoulder. There isn't a back door to the basement. Even if it isn't one of the teachers, no one's going to be pleased to find them.

Marya glances at the light and mirrors, listening to the footsteps on the dusty stone steps.

There isn't anywhere to hide.

Grabbing Kazia by the wrists, she tugs her into the lamplight, between the lamp and mirrors, turning the flame up as brightly as it'll blaze.

Squinting, Kazia throws her arms over her eyes as the mirrors turn the bright lamplight blinding.

"Don't make a sound," Marya whispers and wraps her arms around Kazia's shoulders.

They both disappear.

A pair of feet become visible on the bottom step. Marya squints through all the reflected light and halo of the lamp the other person holds to get a glimpse at their face.

Mademoiselle Mayer steps into view.

Along with Mr. Belkin.

Marya feels her eyes grow huge, but she doesn't make a sound.

"What . . . ?" Mr. Belkin asks, shielding his eyes against the bright reflections.

Mademoiselle Mayer looks equally shocked, and Marya hopes the reflections are bright enough she doesn't recognize her own mirrors in the equipment. "No one's down here."

"It must be a teacher," Mr. Belkin says. "I think we should leave this alone."

There's vague fear in both their expressions. Marya knows that emotion. Scientific experiments aren't illegal but finding one hidden away in a basement means something is wrong. Even for two people just stumbling upon it. Even for a Russian professor. Marya squeezes her arms tighter around Kazia. She can feel the rush of light surrounding her clothes and skin and hiding them from view.

"I thought it might be Marya," Mademoiselle Mayer says, voice far away.

"Has she done something like this before?"

Even in all the shadows and bright lights, Marya sees Mademoiselle Mayer's lips purse. "Not that I've seen. But I wouldn't be surprised."

"You think two young girls could set this up on their own?" he asks, and Marya is so relieved he doesn't suspect them she can't feel properly annoyed.

Mademoiselle Mayer squints into the lights and the arms of the contraption, ignoring his question, but seems to take her colleague's words to heart. "I'm not going to touch any of this. You're right, it might be another professor's."

"Pray for his soul he doesn't get caught," Mr. Belkin mutters.

If her heart wasn't making its best attempt at pounding its way out of her chest, Marya might have giggled.

Giving the room a last glance, Mademoiselle Mayer retreats up the stairs, followed closely by Mr. Belkin.

When the door swings shut, the tension goes out of Marya's shoulders.

Kazia doesn't speak. Neither of them move.

Marya looks into the bright lights, feeling the warmth of them all around her, tugging at her clothes like a spring breeze.

She wonders.

Concentrating as hard as she can, she imagines the bright, warm wind curving *around* her body instead of through. How it feels when the storms bring rain and freezing gales that tear through her dresses and coats and surround her skin. The light, weightless nature of it, as if she might be pulled from the earth.

For a moment, the two of them flicker back into sight, before the lamp light swallows them up again.

"Marya?" Kazia whispers.

"It's alright," she says. "We're alright. I think I can learn to control it. We're alright."

She reaches through the heat and turns down the lamp until they both step out of the brightness and into sight.

"Did you try your experiment again?" her father asks as she's heading to bed that night. Her body feels heavy. As long as she doesn't stray too close to the table lamp, the dim light doesn't seem to affect her. She leans against his side and watches him clean his spectacles with a handkerchief.

"We're finished with it." She doesn't want to say anything else, not when it can't be proven.

His eyes crinkle at the corners, but he only kisses her hair.

Long after Helena begins her soft snoring, Marya spends hours with her fingers cupping moonbeams. Trying with everything in her to control the light until she can make her fingers flicker back into view, at least in the weak pale of the moonlight.

The next morning, when it's early enough that dew clings to them and other students have only just started to arrive, Kazia returns the un-damaged crystal and lamp to the clockmaker, and Marya slips into the empty home economics classroom.

Easing the mirrors from her books, she places them back on the pile with the others and returns to Kazia before they go to their own classes.

Walking through the hallways, Marya catches Mr. Belkin's eye as he passes. He doesn't know a thing about the two of them being involved, so she stares ahead and keeps her expression blank, chin level.

Kazia loops their arms together once he's long gone. "You made a huge discovery, Marya. But we didn't record any results. No one will believe us."

"It's enough that we know. No matter what Mr. Belkin or the other professors think, we did it. We'll prove it one day."

Kazia nods, eyes downcast.

They *will* try again. It's too much of a temptation. When they have the proper equipment and can record the fringe shift the way Marya felt it. Perhaps they'll understand why the mirrors shattered. And no one will know that light has taken a liking to her skin.

Marya takes a different seat than usual in her morning class, farther from the windows. The morning air was hazy but warming when they walked to school, and she doesn't trust the clouds to block the light into the rest of the day. And doesn't yet trust herself to hide the new flicker in her skin.

The class goes on, and she watches the room dapple with sunlight.

Science Note:

In real life, Marya never attempted the Michelson-Morley experiment or beat Albert Michelson to his discoveries concerning luminiferous aether. Likewise, the interferometer Marya constructed in the story does not cause physical harm, though the version of the instrument she used is accurate to the materials needed for a basic interferometer.

As Michelson performed the earliest versions of his experiment in 1881, Marya would have been fourteen years old at the time, and this story was written with that age in mind.

SHE WALKS BETWEEN
Heaven AND Hell

by

JANE YOLEN

"In science, we must be interested in things,
not in persons."   —Marie Curie

In that great radioactive workshop,
the sounds of rays,
like storm troopers' guns,
zapping through the air,
she works ceaselessly,
this angel of death, of life,
though her body has long since
rotted in its early grave.

She no longer needs
the buttered bread and tea
to sustain her, the grand dinners
after the prizes.
She only devours her work now.
She does not think about
what has been done,
only what is still left to do.
Like any goddess,
her ideas of benefit
and ours devolve.
We want to be warm, fed, loved.
She only wants to know.
If it kills us, that's another fact
that she gleans
from the ashes of our souls.

SILENCE
Them

by

DEE LEONE

The tension radiating from the girls gathered in the library at the Blue Palace was as thick as the antique rug on which they stood. Their parents thought their daughters were studying and engaging in harmless activities, like experimenting with hairstyles and creating intricate *wycinanki* cutouts. They were wrong.

Instead, the group planned to contact the dead.

Marya had been to the magnificent library before. Kazia's father was the librarian for Count Zamoyski, whose family had amassed an impressive collection of rare items. These included illuminated manuscripts and works produced from movable type, some centuries old.

During daylight, Marya had always been awestruck in the presence of such priceless treasures. But that evening, as shadows slithered among antiquated tomes and archaic maps, she felt a sense of foreboding. *I shouldn't have agreed to this,* she thought regretfully. *Mama would have considered it a sin.*

While the classmates waited for one more student to arrive, a tall girl named Jadwiga pointed to a shield. "Whose coat of arms is that?"

"The Count's," Kazia answered. "It's one of the oldest in Polish heraldry."

"What do the symbols mean?" asked Ania, second in her class at Public Gymnasium Three, where Marya ranked first.

"Well, according to legend, the king granted it to a Polish soldier who helped defeat the Teutonic Knights in the thirteen hundreds," answered Kazia. "The three spears represent the ones the enemy thrust into him, causing his bowels to ooze out. It's called the *Jelita*, which means guts."

Ania wrinkled her nose. "Eww!"

Stasia tapped her fingernails against the table. "I hope Leonia gets here soon."

"When she does, we need to treat her carefully," cautioned Marya. "She's in a fragile state."

Leonia was the reason for the deceptive gathering. She was distraught over the hanging of her brother who'd been accused of revolutionary activity against the Russians occupying Warsaw.

At the thought of the Polish patriots whose bodies were left dangling for days, Marya's anger bubbled up like a rapidly heated liquid in a test tube. *If only I could find a way to get back at those Russian beasts.*

When Leonia finally arrived, the girls took one look at her ashen face and surrounded her with hugs. "I miss him so much," she whispered.

"Did you bring a personal item of his, like I asked?" Jadwiga wanted to know. She and Stasia had planned the evening's séance, saying it would be comforting if Leonia could communicate with her deceased sibling.

Leonia took out a pocket watch. She placed it on the table near the open books, ready subterfuge in case an adult walked in. Jadwiga added a bell and a pendant from her bag. Stasia set out a fountain pen and a pad of paper she explained would serve as a spirit slate.

After the six girls sat down, Ania whined, "I'm not sure about this."

"It'll be all right," promised Jadwiga. "Lincoln had a séance in the White House, so why shouldn't we have one here?"

"It was to ask the spirits for guidance during the Civil War," Stasia explained. "And because the First Lady wanted to contact her dead son."

"Everybody, join hands and let's get started," Jadwiga instructed.

Stasia extinguished the lamps, leaving the room in darkness except for the moonlight that made its way through an arched window, eerily casting its glow on the *Jelita* spears.

In the solemn stillness that followed, the pocket watch ticked off anxious seconds. *Or is it my heart?* Marya wondered.

Finally, Jadwiga chanted. "We call upon the spirit of Leonia's brother. Make yourself known so that your sister may find comfort in your presence."

Leonia's grip on Marya's hand tightened.

"If you're with us, give us a sign by ringing the bell," implored the séance leader.

This is never going to work, thought Marya. *Leonia will be so disappointed.*

But the bell rang—two long chimes followed by two short ones. Marya flinched at the pattern and re-experienced the terror she'd suffered as a young boarding school student.

Her teacher is giving a Polish history lesson, something strictly forbidden by the Russian occupiers. The warning bell sounds. Two long, then two short rings. Four girls grab the prohibited books, hide them in their dorm, and hurry back to the classroom.

The Russian inspector enters. Marya does her best not to tremble when she's chosen to recite. Dressed in a serge blue uniform, she answers his questions flawlessly. But when he asks who rules over them all, she hesitates. The inspector grows irritated. Terrified, Marya reluctantly states, "His Majesty Alexander II, Tsar of all the Russians."

With a jolt, Marya's focus turned back to the present when Jadwiga called out, "Spirit, is there anything you wish Leonia to know?"

The sound of rustling papers made several séance sitters gasp. A green glow radiated from a book on the table.

Leonia dug her nails into Marya's palm.

Stasia leaned forward and read the scattered, phosphorescent words one by one. "Poland. will. rise. as. will. I."

The cryptic words hung in the air.

Leonia's voice shook. "What does it mean?"

Jadwiga shrugged. "I think your brother is offering us hope for our country."

"Can you get him to speak to me?" Leonia implored.

"Sometimes spirits talk through others," Stasia told her. "Jadwiga will put me in a trance to try to make that happen."

Jadwiga lifted the shiny object and spoke in a soothing tone. "Focus on the pendant," she said, swinging it back and forth in front of Stasia. "Relax and count backward from six."

Marya listened and watched, mesmerized. Her breathing slowed. Her eyelids grew heavy.

A voice fades into the distance.

Marya sees a noose sway in front of Leonia's brother. Russian soldiers mock him.

She's vaguely aware she's picked up a pen. Her hand has a mind of its own. She can neither control it nor focus on what it's doing.

Suddenly, her stomach is sliced through like bread. It twitches violently.

Then flames encompass her. Her skin sizzles and melts like candle wax.

She hears screaming. Shrill, panicked cries.

The loud shrieks startled Marya. To her surprise, she was the one screaming. Disoriented, she glanced around the room with its relit lamps.

Some girls were reciting the Lord's Prayer. "*Ojcze nasz, któryś jest w Niebie . . .*"

"*Ale nas zbaw ode złego*," Ania repeated over and over like a mantra.

Deliver us from evil? Puzzled, Marya asked, "What happened?"

But the others just stared at her.

She studied them for clues—teary-eyed Leonia, pale Kazia, and trembling Ania rocking herself back and forth, eyes shut.

Jadwiga and Stasia, foreheads creased, seemed perplexed.

Marya eyed a revolting, bloody mound in front of her. She had little time to ponder her observations before brisk footsteps echoed down the hall. Jadwiga quickly hid the bell, pad, and pendant. Stasia closed the phosphorescent book and used it to swipe the lumpy mass onto the floor.

The door burst open. "What's going on in here?" Kazia's father demanded.

No one spoke for what seemed like an eternity. Then Kazia found her voice. "We thought we saw a mouse, *Tato*."

"A mouse?" Her father shook his head. "Silly girls. Put everything away. Then take any friends who're staying overnight to your room, Kazia, before you disturb the count."

Once he left, Marya considered the slimy heap at her feet and asked again, "What happened? What did I do?"

Ania bit her lip. "After Leonia's brother spoke through Stasia, other spirits visited . . . through you."

Kazia added, "You fell into a trance and thought you were battling knights. You groaned and threw up."

A soldier's guts or undigested kielbasa? wondered Marya.

Leonia twisted her hair. "You also spoke like a little girl and said you were keeping warm by the fireplace. Then you screamed."

"I . . . I think I get the connection," Kazia stammered. "A girl named Teresa lived here about a hundred years ago. Sparks caught her dress on fire. She got burnt and died."

Stasia frowned. "I don't understand how spirits communicated through Marya. That wasn't supposed to happen."

"There's one more thing," Jadwiga said, showing the spirit slate. "You wrote this."

The letters were penned in a shaky hand, but Marya recognized the strokes and flourishes as characteristics of her own script. She read what they spelled: *Uciszyć ich.*

Silence them?

Stasia, Jadwiga, and Leonia were fetched by their parents. The other three classmates retired to Kazia's room to spend the night. The trio pounced on the pitcher of lemonade and tray of *pączki* filled with rose petal jam that Kazia's mother brought.

Marya bit into her pastry and held up a jar she'd found. "It's 'Balmain's Luminous Paint.' I bet Stasia and Jadwiga prepared the glowing page ahead of time and unclasped their hands to uncover it in the dark."

"It could have been a trick," Ania agreed. "What about the bell though?"

"Maybe they rang a different one under the table," suggested Kazia. "Sounds echo in that library. It's hard to tell direction."

Ania took a sip of lemonade. "Stasia's trance seemed fake compared to Marya's. She probably just pretended Leonia's brother was speaking through her."

"At least Leonia seemed comforted by the words," Kazia pointed out.

"But how do you explain the uninvited spirits speaking through Marya?" asked Ania.

Nobody offered a plausible explanation. They were baffled, remembering Stasia's words: "That wasn't supposed to happen."

Though she'd stayed up all night with her friends, Marya was so restless at home the next evening, she tangled herself in her bedding.

Six séance sitters. Six luminous words. Six counts backward. Marya shuddered, thinking about the satanic significance.

She hadn't told anyone about seeing Leonia's brother during her trance. It seemed cruel to bring up his death again. But she was convinced she'd picked up the pen immediately after he'd appeared to her.

Uciszyć ich. Was it a message from him? Did he want the séance participants to silence someone? If so, whom?

Marya exhausted her brain hypothesizing.

Leonia's brother stands over her. A book floats beside him. It gives off a green glow, illuminating the hideous ligature mark on his neck.

Marya screams but hears no sound.

She took in rapid breaths. Leonia's brother had vanished.

Marya recalled the highlighted séance words: "Poland. will. rise. as. will. I." Had Leonia's brother risen?

The family dog whimpered and cowered in the corner.

"Did you see a ghost too?" She patted the space next to her. "Lancet . . . here, boy."

The brown pointer rose, crept forward, and stretched out next to Marya. Jittery at every movement, and jumpy at every noise, the two eventually surrendered to a fitful sleep.

The next morning, a notebook lay by Marya's side. It was open to a scribbly missive: *Uciszyć ich.*

Those words again.

Is this an elaborate hoax? Some kind of ideomotor phenomenon? Marya buried her face in her pillow. *Or are spirits real?*

Monday morning, Marya packed a cloth lunch bag with an apple, bread, and two Polish sausages. She rushed out the door, eager to discuss Friday's séance again with Kazia as they walked to school. After waiting a while at their meeting spot, Marya flipped up the ring on a bronze lion. The predetermined signal meant she'd gone on, and Kazia would have to rush to catch up.

She passed a marching regiment and clenched her fists at the sight of the Russian occupiers. When she reached the obelisk on Saxon Square, Kazia finally joined her. The two glanced around to make sure they were unobserved then spat with disdain on the plaque bearing the inscription: *"Polakom wiernym swojemu monarsze."* It was a tribute to the Poles loyal to the tsar during the November Uprising, and therefore loathed by those who considered them traitors.

"You two . . . stop!"

The girls spun around, surprised to see a lone Russian soldier. His uniform was stiff; his pale blue eyes stony and cold.

Marya hurled an insult. *"Swinia!"*

Mouth agape, Kazia grabbed her friend by the arm and pulled her toward Krakowskie Przedmieście. They darted frantically between water-barrel wagons, elegant carriages, and morning shoppers on the busy street.

When they reached the watch shop beneath their school, they checked whether they'd lost their pursuer. Not seeing him, they dashed up the steps to the second floor where their classes were held.

Panting, Kazia asked, "*Zwariowałaś?*"

Maybe I have gone mad, Marya fretted.

Marya kept seeing spirits. She wondered if she was clairvoyant or experiencing aftereffects from the trance. Deeming Stasia and Jadwiga partly responsible for her erratic state of mind, she decided to prank them. Since they'd been so fascinated with bringing back the dead, she knew just what to do.

Warsaw's schools for girls weren't allowed laboratories, so Marya had no access to the things she desired, like butyric acid, hydrogen sulfide, or skatole—the compound whose name was appropriately derived from the Greek word for dung. She made a list of items that might suffice instead: garlic, fetid meat, onions, decayed fruit, rotten eggs, beetroot, cabbage, and vinegar. She added decayed plant matter, which she could obtain at the Vistula River.

Her hand, seemingly of its own accord, wrote down dog feces. Then her thoughts turned to the macabre. *I could really use something dead.* Instead, she added hawthorn blossoms, which could emit the same scent as decaying tissue.

Marya used the kitchen as a makeshift lab. While cooking onions and cabbage—with a dollop of excrement for good measure—a boarder walked in and dipped a ladle into the pot.

"Don't taste that!" Marya warned. Her face turned the color of *buracski*—the roasted beetroots she'd already prepared.

"What's the matter? You can't share with anyone but your boyfriend Vitoid?" he teased before swallowing a spoonful.

Marya felt like retching. *If I do vomit, I guess that's one more ingredient I can use.*

Outside, where the odor wouldn't permeate the apartment, she mixed and measured until she was satisfied with the fetid combination.

During lunch period, Marya gained access to the unattended belongings of Jadwiga and Stasia, who had a habit of freshening up with perfume before afternoon classes.

She plugged her nose, emptied their fancy flacons, and replaced the contents. *I wish I could see their faces when they splash this on, but I don't want them to get suspicious.*

After returning the bottles, she hurried to class.

Jadwiga and Stasia were the last to enter the room. Their wrists were red, obviously from intense scrubbing. But they'd failed to completely rid themselves of the powerful odor they'd unwittingly applied . . . cadaver perfume.

Marya breathes in the sweet scent of lavender oil, her mother's favorite. It travels to her on a rippling stream of piano notes . . . a sonata her mother loved to play.

Her sister Zosia's music box plinks out a tune too.

The melodies are mysteriously enchanting together, not discordant.

Marya rises and drifts spellbound toward the sound. As she passes the family photo, she notices the empty spaces where her mother and sister are usually posed.

The captivating music suddenly stops midphrase.

Marya stood in the middle of her father's study. The house was silent except for a few sonorous snores coming from a room that housed the boarders.

Inside her father's glass cabinet, the gold leaves of the electroscope indicated the presence of an electrical charge. The hair on Marya's arms stood on end. Something was giving off energy!

That wasn't all. The barometer on the wall dropped sharply. A storm was brewing.

In the morning, Marya's mother and sister were present in the image again. Marya tried to convince herself she'd been dreaming. Unsuccessfully.

Like a siren's call, the music echoed in her head, drawing her to the place where her two family members were buried.

She arrived at Powązki Cemetery at dusk, alone, when the oak branches cast their fingery shadows across the scattered tombs, lending a haunting atmosphere to the hallowed grounds.

The Catholic burial site was home to several angel statues. Though previously sources of comfort, their stone gazes seemed to follow Marya that evening. She shivered and picked up her pace.

A crow cawed. Marya flinched when it took flight. *There's nothing to be afraid of.*

She paused to view the relatively new sculpture of a woman with a veiled face.

A twig snapped behind her.

She pivoted in alarm and froze in the glare of a Russian soldier—the one with the icy, blue eyes! She turned to run.

He grabbed her.

Marya kicked and thrashed but couldn't get free. *Is he going to arrest me just for spitting on a monument? Or does he have worse intentions?*

The Russian's hands tightened around her throat.

She couldn't breathe! Her vision waned until all she could see was a single monument made of . . . stone.

The stone!

She'd planned to place it on the grave of a Jewish family friend who was buried in the adjacent cemetery, but she yanked it from her pocket and swung her arm back blindly.

She hit something soft—gelatinous.

Her attacker let out a blood-curdling shriek and released his hold.

Marya sprinted away, zigzagging between tombstones, but her pursuer closed in on her, his pants the furious snorts of a wild boar.

I'm doomed, Marya thought.

Suddenly, there was a crack like thunder. Then another. The pounding footsteps stopped.

The soldier lay motionless, buried beneath two angel statues that had somehow toppled from their pedestals. His eyes were frozen in their sockets, one iris bloodied and fiery red.

Marya cringed at the sight. Knees buckling, she collapsed to the ground. And that's when she noticed the soldier had met his fate at the foot of a gravestone bearing a portentous date—the sixth of June, eighteen hundred and six.

Six. Six. Six. Her hand rose to her bruised throat. *The devil can have him.*

Marya took several controlled breaths and stood. Quivering, but still eager to visit the family plot, she continued on. When she got to the carved poem that marked Zosia's resting place, she gasped.

The earth in front of it, as well as near her mother's burial marker, was disturbed. Marya remembered the empty photo spaces and the angels which had saved her from harm. She shuddered. *Am I . . . capable of . . . summoning the dead?*

She's not alone. In the flickering candlelight, a shadow climbs the wall, disappearing when it reaches the ceiling.

The notebook is open. She moves the flame closer to examine it. Charred letters, numbers, and symbols appear.

A shiver goes up her spine. Mere drops of the chemical formula could kill someone.

The words are there again: Uciszyć ich.

In the morning, the mysterious markings were gone. Marya held a candle up to the blank pages, but no invisible ink message revealed itself.

Bewildered, she doubted her sanity once again. But one thing was certain. The message would keep appearing until she heeded it.

"I overheard a conversation at the palace," Kazia said, as she and Marya walked through Saxon Gardens. "About the Russian soldiers."

"What about them?"

Kazia told her shocked friend about the city's brothels. "The soldiers pay as little as thirty kopecks for a prostitute. Some women are sex slaves. Others have no choice due to poverty."

"So, they can't really leave?"

Kazia shook her head sadly. "They have to service clients for free before they're allowed a little pay. They barely make enough to eat."

Marya kicked a stone.

"Sometimes drunken fights break out among the soldiers, and the girls get injured."

"*Dupki!*" Marya swore as they passed the park sundial.

"There are even fancy brothels on Towarowa Street for the officers. The prostitutes there dress in costumes. Sometimes they're murdered by jealous clients."

Marya reached a boiling point. The words that had been haunting her rose quickly to the surface: *Uciszyć ich.*

Now she knew whom to silence.

Cadaver perfume was child's play . . . a practice experiment. Marya would need a better lab than the kitchen for what she had in mind for the Russians. So, early one evening, she gathered some equipment her father had once used for teaching physics. She put the items in a large cloth sack then left the apartment.

She headed to the baroque church, Kościół św. Jacka. Though she had little use for religion anymore—feeling God had unjustly taken her mother and sister—Marya needed water for the solution she wanted to create. So, upon entering the place of worship where she'd received her first Communion, she submersed a beaker in a font of holy water.

As she strode down the left aisle, the votive candles in their red glass holders caught her attention. Marya wondered if they could generate enough heat for her experiments. She stuffed several unlit ones into her bag then headed to her destination, the isolated crypt area.

She assessed the sarcophagi containing the remains of the founder of the Kotowski chapel and his wife. The two coffins were supported by crouching stone creatures. They looked far from heavenly, but the experiments Marya planned to conduct in the presence of their cold, peering eyes was also far from heavenly.

As she maneuvered between the memorials, she tripped on the uneven flooring. Holy water from the beaker sloshed onto one of the coffins.

A disgruntled moan emanated from the splashed sarcophagus.

Envisioning the fires of hell at her feet, Marya bolted to the nave, burst through the massive church doors, and sprinted home. In the sanctity of her apartment, she lit the votives she hadn't had time to return and prayed for protection from the dead.

Afterward, she wondered if she'd done more harm than good by using stolen candles for her petition. Especially when she realized there were six of them.

The next evening, after a dinner of mouthwatering potato and cheese pierogi, Marya's father and her cousin, Józef Boguski, summoned her to the study. They insisted she keep everything she was about to hear confidential.

Her father began. "Women are meeting clandestinely in shifting locations to study advanced subjects because they're barred from universities here. You'll be invited to take part after graduation."

"It'll be dangerous to attend," Józef warned. "The Russians are sure to punish anyone who's caught."

Marya remembered how her classmates had hidden Polish textbooks from the Russian inspector. "So, books need to fly off the table if authorities are around, and students have to float from place to place?"

Józef laughed. "Exactly. Maybe it should be called the Flying or Floating University."

The conversation was interrupted by a raucous fight which broke out among the boarders. Marya's father groaned and left to care of it.

Józef told Marya of plans to set up a secret laboratory at the Museum of Industry and Agriculture. Equipment and chemicals were already being stockpiled.

The star student recognized a unique opportunity. "Could you loan me some items you're collecting so I can try a few experiments on my own? It could help me decide what to study."

"You'd need to keep it a secret from everyone," Józef cautioned.

"I will," Marya promised. "The world will never be the wiser."

Marya told Kazia she wanted to hide her diaries and "other things" from the prying eyes of the boarders.

Her friend knew how chaotic the overcrowded household could be. She was sympathetic when Marya inquired about using the library basement at the Blue Palace as a storage place.

"I can get a key," Kazia offered. "Nobody will mind. All that's kept down there are personal papers belonging to the Count's family, not rare artifacts."

Marya knew the basement could be entered from the palace garden. It would be easy to come and go without notice. "Perfect! You're my angel."

After school, Marya met Józef at the Museum of Industry and Agriculture and gave him a wish list. Over the course of a few days, she shuffled the borrowed materials and some items from home to her hideaway.

Most importantly, whenever she saw a half-full vodka bottle lying next to a sleeping drunk, she pilfered it and secreted it away.

Under the pretext of going somewhere quiet to study, Marya visited her private lab instead.

Uciszyć ich. Though her excellent memory enabled her to recall the deadly formula that had mysteriously appeared in her notebook, she lacked the temperament for murder. But she could attempt to silence her targets a different way.

Down with the sound of marching boots and Russian cadence calls! And woe to those who take advantage of women!

Her plan was to modify vodka so the soldiers who drank it would succumb to a sleeping sickness that would make them too weak to harm the prostitutes and too hoarse to participate in drills.

Chamomile, St. John's wort, valerian root, and some of the chemicals Józef gave me should make those monsters drowsy and frail. Lemons, tomato juice, white vinegar, and acidic compounds should give them laryngitis.

Marya possessed adequate scientific knowledge, but she lacked practice conducting experiments.

That was a problem.

A vial of vodka was on fire! The blue flames sputtered furiously, spiraling upward like ghostly figures rising from a graveyard.

I'm going to burn the place down!

Marya scanned the room frantically for something to cut the flow of oxygen. She settled on a metal bucket, casting out its ratty mop.

In her rush to put out the blaze, her sleeve caught fire. Arms flailing frantically, she worsened her predicament.

I don't want to end up like Teresa!

She seized a beaker of water and doused her arm, breathing a sigh of relief. Only cloth, not skin had been singed. But the burning desire to continue her experiments that day had been extinguished.

After more trials and some tiny tastes—which left her fatigued and hoarse—Marya believed she'd come up with an effective formula for "vicious vodka." She wrote it in her notebook and began to create a large batch.

The chemical smells were overpowering in the confined space, but Marya ignored them, fixated on her goal.

Lightheadedness crept up on her like a sneaky serpent.

Uciszyć ich. She couldn't tell if she'd uttered the words or if they had come from another source. She read the formula. Something seemed off, but she couldn't put her finger on it. With an air of detachment, she watched two hands masterfully measure, stir, heat, and pour.

A whiff of something like formaldehyde alerted Marya to danger. Her eyes fluttered open. Her head was foggy, but somehow, she'd managed to complete her experiment.

It would take several trips to transport the final product home. So, without wasting any more time, she poured the solution into empty vodka bottles.

One of the boarders helped with a weekend route that included deliveries to the barracks. The wagon driver always came in for Saturday breakfast. So, while he was preoccupied, Marya added the tainted alcohol to the crates labeled with the appropriate addresses.

As she took the last bottle from its hiding place, Vitoid caught her in the act. "You? Taking up drinking?" He lowered his voice. "Don't worry. I won't tell, but when you open that, let's share it together."

Under his watchful eyes, she returned the lone bottle to its hiding place. The others would soon be in the hands of the despicable

Russians.

On Monday, when she and Kazia reached Saxon Square, Marya noticed that the number of soldiers participating in military reviews was considerably fewer. Those remaining stumbled around awkwardly, their cadence calls barely audible.

Marya beamed. *I've silenced them!*

"I overheard my parents talking about the soldiers again," Kazia confided. "Some of them got so lethargic while visiting the brothels that they could barely stand. They needed rides back to the barracks."

Marya's steps grew lighter. *That means they're too weak to bother the prostitutes now.*

Kazia continued. "Even the ones who didn't go to the brothels have been complaining of headaches, nausea, and dizziness. And some have become blind."

What?

"The doctors can't figure out what's wrong. Even some prostitutes have symptoms."

Marya's breakfast of scrambled eggs and kefir churned in her stomach. *Not the poor women! The Russians must have made the prostitutes drink with them.*

"Some patients are having a hard time breathing and may not survive whatever disease they've managed to get."

Marya's face turned as gray as mortar.

"Are you all right?" Kazia was answered with a burst of vomit. She handed over a handkerchief. "I'll tell the instructors you're sick. You better go home."

But Marya headed to the Blue Palace instead and snuck into the library basement once again. She examined the final formula she'd jotted down.

In the spot where she'd written CH_3CH_2OH for ethanol, the center section was blurred out. All that remained was CH_3OH, the formula for methanol. In her exhausted state, she must have used methanol, a toxic chemical, instead of ethanol, the grain alcohol found in drinks.

She let out a gasp.

Uciszyć ich was written at the bottom of the page.

Did a spirit find a way to silence the Russians by using me? wondered Marya. A thought even more disturbing entered her mind. *Or did my hatred for the Russians make me subconsciously alter the formula myself?*

Though Marya burned the journal and dismantled the lab, gloom shrouded her like the darkness of a fabled forest. To cope with her guilt, she buried herself in her books, managing to still rank first at graduation.

She isolated herself from family and friends, rarely leaving her bed. Even Vitoid's jokes couldn't lift her from her deep depression.

Marya had silenced herself.

Her doctors and her father recommended a year of relaxation in the countryside because they thought she was suffering from the aftereffects of the stress she'd put on herself studying.

They were wrong.

Science Note:

During the séance depicted in "Silence Them," words in a book on the table glowed, spelling out a cryptic message. Later, Marya found a container of Balmain's Luminous Paint and became suspicious. William Henry Balmain patented the product in 1877. It contained a phosphorescent compound consisting of sulfur and lime that glowed when applied to an object.

In the story, Marya concluded two séance participants tricked the others. Because they'd been so interested in bringing back the dead, Marya decided to concoct a solution with a scent as putrid as a decaying cadaver. She wished she had skatole and hydrogen sulfide but improvised with items that mimicked those compounds. One was hawthorn flowers, which give off triethylamine, a chemical produced by a rotting body. She also used rotten eggs to produce foul-smelling hydrogen sulfide and garlic and cabbage to produce other unpleasant odors.

Marya disliked the Russian soldiers occupying her city. In this imaginary tale, her goal was to silence them by making them too sleepy and hoarse to conduct noisy drills. However, when producing the final concoction, she was overcome by fumes. In a hazy state, she watched "two hands masterfully measure, stir, heat, and pour." After learning of the effect her mixture had on those who drank it, she realized CH_3OH (methanol) was used instead of CH_3CH_2OH (ethanol). Methanol is extremely toxic and can cause blindness, nervous system damage, coma, and death. It is used to produce formaldehyde and acetic acid. Ethanol is the main ingredient in alcoholic drinks like vodka, beer, and wine.

EXPERIMENTS with FIRE

by

SARAH BETH DURST

Zofia was dead, but that didn't stop her from having opinions about my decisions.

"Marya, you cannot do whatever you wish simply because you want to," Zofia said. She'd perched herself on the banister, with her ankles primly crossed, while I crouched by the cellar door. A padlock on the door prevented us from exploring its depths. "Life does not work that way."

"You are hardly the expert in that," I pointed out. Zofia had died eight years ago at age thirteen. While she had been born before me, she had not lived more years.

"You are cruel to the sister who loves you."

"Helena is moderately fond of me," I said. Helena was another of our sisters, specifically the one who was *not* always fond of me. "Besides, I do not believe I can do whatever I want. I believe I must do whatever I can. There's a difference." With that, I poured the tube of acid into the mechanics of the padlock. It bubbled with a satisfying sizzle.

The acid chewed through the mechanism while I listened to the clock in the foyer tick louder than the thumping of my heart. When I judged that the acid had done enough damage, I removed the lock, lifted the latch, and opened the door an inch—

It squealed as if it were being murdered.

I froze, listening, but no sound came from the residents sleeping on the second floor. It was well past midnight, and they'd retired several hours prior. Happily, it seemed they were sound sleepers.

"Warn me if anyone comes," I whispered to Zofia.

"Maybe I will, maybe I won't. You shouldn't take these kinds of risks."

Opening my trusty satchel, I withdrew a syringe of oil and squirted it onto the hinges before trying the door again. It squeaked, but not terribly.

All remained quiet through the house, and I was relieved to see that despite her mood, Zofia had drifted up the banister to watch the bedrooms. It would be best if no one caught me here. Based on past experience, I didn't think it was likely the family would understand my reason for needing to access their cellar.

There aren't many who can recognize a fire demon for what it is.

I'd only discovered their existence by accident, which is an embarrassing thing to admit for someone who believes in the importance of thorough observation. I had been examining the residue of a chimney fire when I accidentally prodded one of the loathsome creatures with a poker. Ever since, I'd been determined to catch one. And here was my chance, in the cellar of Count Zamoyski's favorite wigmaker.

Slipping into the stairwell, I pulled the door shut behind me and then lit the candle I kept in my satchel precisely for these sorts of situations. Its soft glow danced over the walls.

Zofia materialized beside me. She enjoyed trying to startle me by popping out of nowhere or slipping through walls, but I'd trained myself not to react. "Are you certain it's wise to bring a flame to a fire demon?" she asked.

It did not seem wise, but without it, this cellar would be unbearably dark. Besides, I had a plan. "Hush." No one could hear her except me, but I wanted to concentrate.

Reaching the bottom, I surveyed the cellar. The furnace sat in one corner, like a squatting beast. A bin half full of coal was beside it. Pipes ran along the ceiling from the furnace. Everything was coated in a layer of grime.

Quickly, I went to work setting my trap: an iron net on the floor beside the coal bin, rigged with a wire that I could pull the instant my prey stepped into position. Scattering some ash and coal dust on top of my net, I hoped it blended well enough with the floor that the demon wouldn't spot it.

When I finished, I set my candle in a lantern beside the coal bin.

"Marya? You are aware coal is flammable?" Zofia whispered.

"I'm counting on it."

With luck, the flame so close to the coal bin would attract the creature like . . . well, like a moth to a flame. I retreated into the shadows of the stairwell to wait and watch.

A few minutes later, I heard a scuffling.

Then silence.

Another scuffle. It could have been a rat. But it wasn't.

The candlelight danced, as if a breath of wind had caused the flame to stir, but there was no wind in the cellar. *There you are.* Counting to three, I yanked hard on the wire.

Light blazed. Squeezed my eyes shut, I kept pulling. Heat slapped my face as the creature resisted. Unlike a rat, it didn't squeal or scream—it seemed the demon had learned not to draw attention to itself, even in duress. Everything was silent, except for the pop and crackle of flames, as the demon and I had our tug-of-war. My eyes watered, and my throat felt so dry that I couldn't swallow. Oddly, I didn't taste smoke.

At last, the wire went slack.

Cracking my eyes open, I regarded my prize.

A six-inch-long twisted lizard made of molten gold writhed in my metal net. I was counting on the fact that iron has a high melting point. Hopefully, the fire demon wouldn't be able to sear through it. Yanking a fire-resistant asbestos blanket out of my bag, I threw it over the demon. I didn't wish to kill it—only limit its supply of oxygen so it couldn't blaze.

I shoved the bundle of the asbestos blanket, wire net, and demon into my satchel. I hoped that I'd accurately anticipated how long it would take before its fire would eat through the multiple protective layers. By my estimation, I had eight minutes to make it back home to where a containment bin waited.

I made it home in seven.

My experiments with the fire demon yielded a wealth of fascinating information, all of which I recorded meticulously in my notebook. But Zofia still wasn't pleased with me.

"I do not understand what you wish to achieve," she complained.

"Knowledge," I told her as I fed a strip of tin to the fiery lizard.

Its flame tongue licked the metal, and it swallowed, a near-liquid silver disappearing down its throat within only a few seconds. I smelled the tangy sourness of burnt metal and noted the time.

"But what will you do with that knowledge?"

"Scientific work must not be tethered to usefulness," I said. "There's great beauty in science itself."

"And . . . ?" she prodded.

"And it's a fire demon!" Really, Zofia and her questions. Did she always have to poke and prod me? She was supposed to be resting in peace, not denying me any peace. "Such a beast has never before been studied. Does there need to be another reason?"

"For you?" she replied. "Yes."

I did not respond to that. Instead, I fed my demon a bit of copper. It did not melt for thirty-seven seconds. *Logical*, I thought, pleased. Copper has a nearly five times higher melting point than tin. It's satisfying when one's experiment confirms one's hypothesis. I continued on to the next sample.

I craved knowledge more than anything.

I hungered for it, perhaps because so many did not want me to have it—those who didn't approve of either girls or Polish students being educated—and I wished to disappoint them. Or perhaps I hungered for it simply because that's how I was built.

Regardless, I devoured every textbook I could get my hands on, and I sneaked into as many classes at the Flying University as I could. I soaked in the news from every newspaper in Warsaw and eavesdropped on as many conversations as seemed of interest. But it was from my classmate and best friend Kazia that I learned about the Circus Ferroni fire.

It was January 15, 1883, and it was bitterly cold. We were walking to our gymnasium—we always met after she picked up her lunch at her uncle's butcher shop—and she was chattering faster than the wind could blow.

The tips of my fingers burned with cold, even within my gloves, and I could even feel the cold seeping around my eyes, making them water. My cheeks, at least the bits exposed above my scarf, felt raw, and my skin felt tight. Every time I breathed, I tasted the coldness as it seeped down my throat.

The fire demon had been agitated this morning, as if the cold offended it. I'd left it with a chunk of pork for a snack and a chunk of steel for amusement.

"It's said a stableman was smoking, and the straw ignited," Kazia was saying. "When his fellow opened the door to go for water, the fire spread so quickly that within twenty minutes, the entire circus was aflame, though I do not see how that could be."

"He must have created a draft." I had read of such a phenomenon: the introduction of air to an oxygen-deprived super-heated room could ignite the gaseous products of an incomplete combustion. "I've heard that can cause an explosion."

"A very strong one, it must have been, and anyway, they could not go for water. Of course, they tried, but with this cold—"

All the water was frozen. Of course.

We cut under the colonnade and across Saxon Square. It wasn't possible to walk as quickly as we wished because the cobblestones were coated in ice. We had to place each boot carefully. Occasionally, Kazia would grab my arm to steady herself.

"The stableman denies he was responsible, naturally," she contained. "He claimed he'd given up smoking, but he had tobacco in his pocket. The guilt he must feel—I cannot fathom what nightmares that poor man must face when he closes his eyes, to know the scope of tragedy he caused, however inadvertently."

A sheen of ice encased the bronze obelisk and the two-headed eagles in the center of the square. It had been erected to honor the Tsar after the November Uprising, and it was the most hideous sculpture imaginable, nearly as hideous as the man it honored. As we passed it, I wondered if my fire demon could melt bronze. Perhaps I could let it try.

Checking to be sure there were no Russian soldiers in the square, we both lowered our scarves and spat on the obelisk. Our spit dripped down the ice, freezing onto it. The satisfaction of our daily ritual was worth the stab of cold to our cheeks.

Restoring her scarf, Kazia continued. "The fire broke out during the evening performance, with a full audience. Over four hundred people died, they say, as well as the circus animals. Four hundred! An unimaginable tragedy. And right here in Poland! In Berditschoft!"

"Unimaginable," I agreed and thought of the poor stableman, consumed by such terrible guilt. What if he had told the truth, and he wasn't to blame? What if the cause hadn't been correctly identified?

"The worst of it is how unpredictable such tragedy is," Kazia said. "Who's to say it won't happen here?" She waved her gloved hand at the former convent that was our school. We'd arrived. "Or anywhere, truly."

She was correct. The worst tragedies were the ones you couldn't predict and were helpless to stop. Like the sickness that killed Zofia. And the one that killed our mother.

But there were other tragedies that could be prevented, with the right knowledge. If I couldn't control the uncontrollable, then I could at least be ready for the rest.

As we hurried to class, I began to plan a visit to Berditschoft.

One of the glorious things about having an academic for a father is that any number of activities could be approved if you use the words, "It's for research."

With those magic words, I found myself on the way to Berditschoft that afternoon.

Papa accompanied me on the train, with the intent to visit a colleague in town, and we both spent a pleasant ride absorbed in our respective texts. Occasionally he would offer a fact to me, such as, "I have heard that in Vienna they will soon present the first electric tram powered by overhead wire. Isn't that marvelous?" And I would agree.

After giving instructions to meet him back at the station in three hours, Papa toddled off to his visit while I made my way to the site of the former Circus Ferroni. As a precaution, I'd brought my iron net and a candle, tucked into my satchel. Papa, who is observant about all things except me, had not even asked what I carried. He likely assumed it was books. And most days, he would be correct.

My plan was simple: determine if there was a demon here and, if so, catch it.

Of course I wouldn't be able to bring it back on the train with me without detection, but I could at least contain the creature in iron and ensure it did not cause a second tragedy . . . assuming the stableman was not, in fact, to blame.

As I turned onto the street that led to the site of the tragedy, Zofia condescended to join me. "You're foolish, you know," she told me.

"Papa calls me clever."

"Papa is foolish. Does he even know what you're attempting?"

I did not answer, for we had reached the former circus. Also, the answer was obvious.

"Oh," Zofia whispered. "Oh. This is . . . Oh."

Despite all my plans, I was not prepared for what lay before me. Scorched poles were all that remained of the tents, but you could see the shell of the bleachers that had been erected for the audience. Scraps of burnt fabric hung from the poles, encased in ice, and the stables for the trained animals were mere shells. I wondered if all the bodies had been found—then I wished I had not had that thought. But I did not share any of that with Zofia. "An experimental result is useless if it cannot be replicated." This was my chance to apply my study of the fire lizard—all my careful observations and experiments—to a real-world scenario.

I had work to do.

Finding evidence of a demon amid so much fire damage would not be an easy task, nor a fun one in the still-bitter cold, but I was methodical in my approach. I worked in quadrants, examining the stables first, where the fire supposedly began.

I was not disturbed in my search, which had been a concern of mine. Every time a passerby slowed to look at me curiously, I bowed my head within my scarf and clasped my gloved hands in the appearance of prayer. Saying a prayer of their own, the passerby would quickly move on.

At last, my meticulousness paid off. Kneeling, I scraped at a corroded pipe with the blade of a small knife I'd purloined from our kitchen. Char flaked off, and I bagged it for closer examination later, but I was certain it resembled the residue left by my fire demon after it digested lead.

Now that I have proof that it was here, I thought, *where is the evidence of where it went?*

If the Berditschoft demon had been still ablaze when it fled the area, it might have left traces en route. I widened my search area. Zofia floated after me. She'd remained quiet for much of my search, but now she said in a subdued voice, "There are others here."

Glancing up, I looked for approaching strangers, but the site was quiet. Set in an area large enough to hold a circus, it was easy for most pedestrians to avoid—and avoid it they did. No one wanted to brush so closely to death. "Others?"

"The dead," Zofia said. "Not all left."

I couldn't see them, but that wasn't new. I've only ever been able to see Zofia. Endless questioning and experimentation had not ever explained why—why her, why me, and why never our mother? "Are they"—I wasn't certain what question to ask first—"bothering you?"

"They are far more interested in you."

That was a terribly disconcerting answer. "Oh?"

"They wish to know what you are searching for."

"Tell them I want to find the creature that did this to them." Facing the former circus, I smoothed my skirt and straightened my shoulder. "I'd like to prevent further tragedy, if I can."

Zofia was silent for a while. She flickered in and out of my vision until it made my head swim. I looked away, but every direction showed the aftermath of the horror that had occurred here. At last, she said, "They do not understand why you seek what others do not."

That had an easy answer. "Precisely because others do not, and someone should."

"Then they say it fled east, beyond the city." Zofia raised her ghostly arm to point beyond the circus. "There is a cave, they say, in Wawel Hill. But Marya . . ." Her voice trembled in a way it rarely did. "I do not think you should go there."

I went there.

I had an hour before I was due to meet Papa, and I hadn't come so far to be dissuaded by my sister's unease. When I pressed, she had no explanation for why she worried. Only that she felt the ghosts at the circus had not disclosed all they knew.

"Then we will discover it," I told her.

I hoped the word "we" would convince her to come into the cave with me. I didn't relish the idea of venturing in alone. Gazing at the dark opening, I weighed my options for my approach: If I entered with a candle, I could unwittingly draw danger to myself before I was prepared. But if I entered *without* a candle . . . well, my imagination cheerfully supplied me with a litany of the various disasters that could befall me.

Choosing the candle, I lit it with shaking hands. "Are you with me, Zofia?"

"I am always with you," Zofia said, which was manifestly untrue. She often disappeared for long stretches of time, but I appreciated the sentiment for the peace offering that it was. Stepping into the cave, I held the candle aloft.

Within the rocky cavern, the sun couldn't bleach the shadows. As I walked, they deepened until the only hint of light was my meager flame. Limestone glistened with drips of water, and I breathed in the smell of rock dust and mildew.

As the tunnel dipped downward, I was conscious of the weight of earth above me and grateful for the width of the cave. I should not have liked it if the rock narrowed around me—that could have convinced me to turn around—but it did not, and so I did not.

Pale shadows danced around me as the candle's flame flickered.

I halted.

"That's odd," I said.

"What is?" Zofia asked.

My candle had trembled, but if light couldn't penetrate this deeply, how could the wind? As I watched, the flame shook again, and I felt a breeze on my cheeks. It faded as quickly as it came, and then a few seconds later, it returned.

On a hunch, I counted.

Two seconds of stillness. Three seconds of wind. And then it repeated.

"Marya, what is it?" Zofia asked again.

I wasn't certain. Not without more data. Creeping more slowly, I continued on. My eyes strained to make shapes out of the shadows, as the wind—*call it what it is,* I scolded myself—the *breathing* grew louder.

The stench of sulfur curled through the cave. It coated the back of my throat.

"We shouldn't be here," Zofia whispered.

She was correct. Yet we were here, and how could I leave before I'd verified my theory? Especially since it wasn't a well-formed theory. Just a conviction that the fire hadn't been started by a little lizardlike fire demon.

As the cave widened, I saw my proof. The Circus Ferroni fire had been caused by *this*:

A dragon.

Scaled body, head with horn-like ridges, leathery wings on its back . . . In form, it resembled my captured fire demon. But the size! In heft and length, it rivaled the train engine that had pulled us to Berditschoft. Sadly, it did not lie atop a pile of gold. Only rocks, ash, and charred bones.

Such a creature could have easily set the circus aflame. It was only a marvel that it hadn't yet set the whole city aflame. Or all of Poland.

Amber light from my candle danced on the dragon's black scales. I stared at the creature's closed eye, as if I could keep the great lid shut from the force of my will. Barely breathing, I backed away. My iron net seemed flimsy and pathetic. This was not an enemy I was equipped to face.

Only a few more feet, and I would be back in the tunnel, out of sight of the great beast—

Its eye opened.

Red veins snaked through its yellow-green eye. I saw the moment it fixed on me. I felt the rock beneath my feet begin to warm, like a heating stove, and the air thickened. Black smoke curled from the dragon's nostrils.

"Run," Zofia said in my ear.

And for the first time in my life, I did not argue with my sister, nor did I stay to ask questions, conduct experiments, record observations, or bask in the wonder of the impossible. Instead, I ran as it belched flames. I felt a terrible heat behind me as my sister urged me faster.

After three straight nights of nightmares predictably full of darkness and fire, I was ready to get to work. Arranging my desk just so, I started a new notebook for my latest set of experiments: methods for defeating a dragon.

As I had observed, in form, the Wawel Dragon—as I had taken to calling it in my notes, due to the location of its cave—resembled the far smaller dragonette that I had obtained from the wigmaker's cellar. If I could identify a weakness in the dragon's smaller cousin, then perhaps . . .

Zofia splayed her hands over my notebooks. "Marya. What. Are. You. Doing?"

I poked my pencil through her insubstantial hand and made a note for my first attempt: salt. I intended to work through materials that I had readily available, before turning to trickier-to-obtain (and tricker-to-explain to Papa) materials. "Research."

"Why?" she asked.

I looked at her as if she had asked me why I breathed. "Because it's what I do."

"Why *this* research?" She waved her hand at the fire demon.

"Because it needs to be done." Measuring out a teaspoon of salt, I dumped it on chunk of week-old beef. Easing it into the cage, I watched as the lizard sniffed the meat and then swallowed it. "Apologies," I said to it, "but this is to save lives. Must be done." Unlike a slug, the drag-onette did not shrivel and die. Truthfully, I did not expect it to, but it was good to have a baseline—

"You can't fight a dragon," Zofia said. "That's for knights in story-books."

"Unfortunately, we do not have any knights handy," I said. "So I will have to do." I didn't know why Zofia couldn't see that. It seemed quite obvious to me.

"Why you? Can't you tell someone what we saw and let them handle it? Like Papa?"

Using another chunk of beef, I tested the next substance: sulfur. "I'm not risking Papa." Frankly, I found it absurd she'd even suggest that. Let Papa handle it?

"The police then. Please, Marya, this isn't your problem. The dragon isn't even in Warsaw. It's miles from here. Let Papa contact the police in Berditschoft, and let them deal with it."

"And what is he supposed to say? 'My daughter and a ghost saw a dragon'? At best, he'd be laughed at. At worst"—I paused to test the next material on my list, opium—"committed."

"Marya—"

"I can't leave it to anyone else, Zofia. The last time I trusted others to find the answer, Mother died." My eyes blurred as I added a drop of the next substance, mercury, to a bit of beef. I wiped my eyes with the back of my sleeve.

The doctors had said they would do all they could to save her. Same as they'd said for Zofia two years prior. Mother had had tuberculosis, and Zofia typhus. Scientists were working hard to find cures, they'd told me. And twice, at the magic word "scientists," my younger self had quit worrying. Both teachers by trade, Papa and Mother had taught us about scientists and the wonders they discovered, and despite the fear in Papa's eyes, I'd been confident that those miracle workers would find the answer in time. But they hadn't.

And so I had learned not to leave it to others to find answers. If I wanted a miracle, then I had to make my own.

"It won't bring her back," Zofia said quietly. "If you defeat it, you won't see her again." She then paused and revised her statement. "Unless you fail to defeat it. If you die, you might see her. Or you might be stuck for eternity with me. Is that so bad?"

"Zofia?"

"Yes, Marya?"

"Be quiet. I'm working."

Arsenic.

That was the answer.

After three days of experiments, I knew my weapon: beloved of the Borgias, the king of poisons. Perhaps I should have started my experiments with it, but I'd wanted to be thorough.

Obtaining the necessary quantity of arsenic was easy. It's ubiquitous: in candles, medicines, green wallpaper, even some sweets. But for concentrated arsenic, all I needed was to tell Papa we had a rat problem in our pantry. Rat poison is rife with arsenic. He trusted me to use it appropriately to take care of the problem—which was exactly what I intended to do, in a manner of speaking.

As to how to feed it to the Wawel Dragon . . . the lizard fire demon had consumed the poison on a bit of meat. So I just needed a significantly larger bit of beef. Enter my best friend Kazia, niece of a butcher. I told her I needed a large, cheap cut of beef for an experiment. It did not need to be fresh. She told me I was odd, but if I loaned her my mother's broach for a fortnight, then she would see that a slightly-rotten slab of meat destined to be tossed would be mine. She also added a cow's bladder, for friendship's sake.

Zofia reappeared while I was filling the beef with rat poison. "You're truly doing this?"

"I assume that's a rhetorical question."

She sighed.

Once the beef was thoroughly poison stuffed, I wrapped it in papers so it wouldn't bleed through and awkwardly stuffed it into a burlap sack. I was going to need some sort of cart if I wanted to lug it across Berditschoft. Grunting as I lifted it, I said, "I wish you could be helpful."

"I wish I were alive so you wouldn't feel as if you had to do these things."

I paused and looked at her. "So do I."

"You expose yourself to too much danger," Zofia said. "It'll be the death of you."

But she came with me anyway on the train back to Berditschoft, sitting opposite Papa. He wrinkled his nose when he beheld my burlap sack with its questionable contents. The odor of slightly-off beef was impossible to disguise. "Your experiment?"

"Indeed."

"Go on," Zofia whispered. "Tell him the truth."

I ignored her. "When I'm finished, I'll tell you everything I learned." It was not entirely a lie. I had every intention of sharing what I learned, but only when I finished learning.

Papa seemed pleased enough with that answer.

I borrowed a handcart from the stationmaster with the promise to return it, without telling him it was for rotten beef, not a trunk of clothes. While Papa headed off to visit his friend, I rolled the poisoned beef through the city and out to Wawel Hill.

Stopping halfway up the hill, I deposited the beef within reach of the cave, and then retreated to what I deemed was a safe distance, hidden behind a rock, with my notebook.

"You're staying?" Zofia practically screeched at me.

"I need to see the experiment through," I told her, watching the cave.

"I will never understand you, Marya."

That was most likely true. But I needed to understand *this*. I needed to know I could stop a dragon—specifically, this fire demon—from killing again. I needed to know there were tragedies in the world that I could prevent, even if there were countless others that I couldn't.

So I stayed on Wawel Hill, with the ghost of my sister by my side, and together we watched the dragon emerge and eat the poisoned beef.

And together, we watched the dragon die. It writhed as its breath became more and more labored. Smoke billowed from its open maw, black and reeking of sulfur. I wished this wasn't necessary. It was a magnificent creature, deserving of years of study.

I made careful notes of how the beast weakened until, at last, a fire grew beneath its black scales and spread throughout its body, consuming it until the only trace that remained of the great dragon was charred earth. Just like the dragonette.

Then all was silent.

Beside me, Zofia said in a hushed voice, "They're here. The ones from the circus. The ones who died." She quieted, somber, watching a sight that I could not see to measure or study.

I waited until she spoke again.

"They've left now. They're at peace." She sounded surprised—and a little wistful. "I suppose this means your experiment worked."

Satisfied, I made one final note in my notebook, closed it, and stood. It was time to take the train home with Papa.

"Is that why you did it?" Zofia asked. "For them?"

"Yes," I replied, because it was simpler than trying to explain the true reason.

It wasn't for them. What I did here hadn't saved any of those four hundred people from a fiery death, and it hadn't brought them back—so why had I done it?

I did it because it was all I could do. I did it because no one else would. I did it because there was no amount of studying and no number of experiments that could explain why Mother and Zofia had to die or how to bring them back.

Some things are unknowable. But all the rest . . . I *will* know.

Science Note:

According to Polish folklore, the fire-breathing and maiden-munching Wawel Dragon (Smok Wawelski) was defeated when a prince or a cobbler tricked it into eating meat stuffed with sulfur. Unable to digest it, the dragon drank an entire river before exploding.

For this story, I transported the Wawel Dragon from Krakow to Berditschoft, where there truly was a horrific fire at the Circus Ferroni in January 1883 (though there's zero evidence it was set by a dragon). Instead of sulfur, I chose to have Marya defeat her dragon with arsenic.

Arsenic is a naturally-occurring chemical element found in the earth's crust. It's widely distributed in the air, water, and soil and is highly toxic. Tasteless, odorless, and colorless, it was a favorite of poisoners in the Middle Ages, as well as in Ancient Greece and Rome.

Historian James Whorton nicknamed the 1800s "the arsenic century" because of how ubiquitous it was. Green dyes laced with arsenic were used in paints, clothes, drapes, wallpaper, toys, cake decorations, etc. So Marya would indeed have been aware of and had ready access to this "king of poisons."

The PRIZE

by
STEVE PANTAZIS

For three years, Adela dreamed of the Arcanum Prize, the most coveted prize in metallurgic arts at her high school in Warsaw. For three years, it burned in her mind like a flame that couldn't be quenched. It started on her first day at school, when the dashing Master Belsky entranced his students with the possibility of winning the prize at the end of their senior year. Back then, it was just a candle flickering in the shadows of Adela's thoughts, but with each passing day, it grew in intensity. The candle became a torch, then a furnace, and now, the blazing sun itself. She promised her ailing father she'd win the prize for him. She believed if she gave him something to hope for, it would stave off the wasting disease slowly claiming him.

That was the thing about promises: once you made them, they couldn't be unsaid.

Which led to her mistake: promising him she could win the prize in the first place.

Adela's skills in the metallurgic arts stood without equal among the other girls in her class. The Arcanum Prize might as well have had her name emblazoned upon it.

Until *she* arrived.

Marya Salomea Skłodowska, the wretched new girl.

Adela noticed a change in the air on the walk to school that fateful fifth day of January in 1883. The way the snowfall swirled in loops, never quite settling on the cobbles of Saxon Square. How the air smelled so starkly of dead birch rather than the usual pine. The utter stillness that graced the exterior of the former convent that was now her school, before the tidal force of destiny crashed down on her.

The moment her hope of winning the prize slipped from her grasp.

Master Ivanov's bushy eyebrows rose high on his forehead as he surveyed the fourteen students of his Advanced Metallurgic Studies class. "Who can tell me about the thermal properties of springstone?"

Two hands shot up.

Master Ivanov cupped a hand over his eyes as if searching the stormy seas for some sign of land. "Anyone else? No?" He released a tired breath as he always did when the same two students volunteered to answer. "Very well. Adela, why don't you illuminate us?"

Adela felt Marya's gaze upon her, but she straightened in her seat and gave her answer as if Marya didn't exist. "Springstone isn't actually a stone. The 'stone' in the name is a misnomer. It's a cold-forged slag once used in sword making, later discovered to offer tensile strength while providing unusual insulating properties when alloyed."

Master Ivanov grunted acknowledgment, stingy with his praise. He was as emotive as the aforementioned slag, which belied his fanatical loyalty to Tsar Alexander III.

Adela saw how—like the Tsar—Ivanov considered the Poles beneath his fellow Russians, and the girls in class even lower. Most of her instructors exhibited the same Russian authoritarianism—except for Master Belsky, who treated his students with dignity and kindness.

"What about its transitive properties as they apply to the metallurgic arts?" Ivanov asked.

Adela had never heard springstone used for that. It was a metal forgotten with the advent of firearms in warfare, mildly useful at best in modern-day Poland. She tried to ignore Marya's upheld hand or the expectant looks from her closest friends, Henna and Julia, hopeful she'd outshine the new girl again. "I'm afraid that's all I know."

This time Master Ivanov reacted, a tiny smile on his chapped lips. "Marya?"

The room grew still. "Energization of metal, copper in particular, for its conductive properties."

Master Ivanov nodded. "Yes. It's a most unusual power source. One might say, a lost art form. Which brings me to your assignment." He held his hands up in dramatic fashion. "You're to devise a mechanism for powering a light emitter using springstone as your sole energy source. The method is up to you, but I will grade you on efficiency. The student with the least thermodynamic loss wins. Dismissed."

Groans filled the air. That meant research.

Adela didn't mind the work. In fact, she looked forward to it—her chance to soar above Marya. Collecting her trio of heavy textbooks—the onerous *Advanced Principles of Metallurgical Transmutation*, the required *Arcane Applications of the Metal Arts* manual, and the ever-useful *Artificer's Handbook*, all written in Cyrillic—she didn't notice Marya standing by the doorway until she almost bumped into her.

"I thought your answer was superb," Marya said in an unexpectedly friendly tone. She was far from pretty, a "weeping beauty" at best, with eyes Adela found perpetually sad. And she had short, frizzy hair like threshed wheat abandoned at harvest.

"Yours too. Who knew springstone could be so useful?" Adela offered a smile, tight and reserved.

Adela waited for Marya and Kazia to leave, then squeezed her textbooks to her chest and muttered, "You've thrown down the gauntlet, and I shall pick it up."

Adela, Henna, and Julia walked down the dimly-lit school hallway together. The air smelled of musty books and old wood.

"Don't let Marya get under your skin," Henna said. "She's just jealous. Kazia is her only friend, whereas you have us."

"If you can call her a friend," Julia said. "Everyone knows Kazia's family is connected to Count Zamoyski, a powerful man. Marya's taking advantage of Kazia to get to his fortune."

Henna added to the rumormongering. "I heard Marya learned black magic from her mother. That's how she got into our school. She cast a spell on Master Belsky, who then convinced the headmistress to admit her."

Julia bobbed her head in agreement, chuckling. "Or maybe she's a *Baba Yaga* pretending to be a young girl."

"Or an occultist who communes with the dead," Henna suggested.

Adela tried her best to add to her friends' playful banter, despite a simmering resentment toward Marya. "What if she's an agent for the Russian Empire?"

Henna and Julia froze, watching her.

Adela didn't mean to come across so seriously. She spoke first to cut the tension. "Maybe we're getting ahead of ourselves. See you tomorrow?"

They said their goodbyes and departed quickly, leaving Adela alone in the hallway to ponder their conversation in deathly silence. Marya was a thorn in Adela's life, that was certain, but what about what Julia said about Kazia? Had the other girl fallen victim to Marya's charms, perhaps her instructors too? *Who's next?*

She frowned. "If she's up to tricks, I won't let her get away with it. I'll make sure everyone sees her for who she really is."

Adela had gotten so worked up, she hadn't noticed she'd stopped in front of the glass case. She gasped when she turned around. A white phosphorous emitter lit a diamond-shaped trophy from above.

The Arcanum Prize!

The light coaxed a blue-gray hue from the rare thusium metal. At two-handspan tall, it defied the laws of physics by standing on a point with nothing to keep it upright. Thusium demonstrated the highest level of skill in metallic transmutation—an alloy Adela hoped to some-day make as a master artificer.

She pressed her fingertips to the cold glass. The air seemed to warm at once and grow fragrant like honeysuckle blossoms. She drew in a deep breath. The brass plaque affixed to the center of the trophy was blank.

She imagined the prize on her mantle at home with her name inscribed on it, and her parents' praise and smiles of pride and admiration.

Then she thought of her papa, sick at home.

She steeled herself, pinning back her shoulders. "This shall be ours, Papa." She had to win . . . for him.

The clock at the end of the hall tolled. Adela hurried home.

Adela held her father's hand as she knelt by his bed, which had been placed in the common room because climbing the stairs to the second-floor bedroom took too much of his dwindling energy. Adela's mother insisted he not exert himself, but he disobeyed her anyway with his nighttime walks.

"What's wrong, my Dela?" Only Papa could call her Dela. Not her mother, not her sister—just him.

"Why do you have to go out for your walks?" Adela asked. His skin felt cool to the touch. He lay covered in a blanket crocheted by her late grandmother. It smelled of lilies and comfort. When she was with him, she forgot the outside world. No thoughts of the prize, her friends, her nagging sister, or Marya. There was Papa and no one else. "They leave you weak. Mama and I worry about you. Where do you go anyway?"

"Around," he said. His voice cracked like brown autumn leaves. "The air is good for me, you know that. You're too concerned."

"I want to help—" She looked down at his hand, his skin so thin, the veins beneath a sickly green. The physicians called his condition ferrousitic hematoxosis, poisoning of the blood due to leeching of toxic metal particulates. He'd been shot by accident in the leg during a hunting expedition in his twenties. Bullet fragments had lodged in his femur, unable to be excised, and the leeching metal was slowly killing him—the very reason Adela studied the metallurgic arts: to find a cure. "I want to make you better."

He lifted her chin to meet his eyes. "The physicians don't know how to heal me."

"Then they must try harder!" She stood, on the verge of tears, but she had to be strong for him.

"My sweet Dela. So smart. Never mind your old man. You will win that prize at school."

Her stomach clenched. What had once seemed a certainty now hung by a thread. She hated to admit it, but Marya was *good*. "I will do my best, Papa."

His yellowed eyes stared deeply into hers. "You're going to leave your mark on history, my Dela. I know it. The world will know the name, Adela Kowalski."

She held on to him, as if he might disappear if she let go. "I want you to be there for my graduation."

He brought her hand to his lips and kissed the top. "And I will, my Dela. If not in this world, then in the next."

Her heart broke at the thought as she bent down to embrace him.

Adela mulled over Master Ivanov's assignment as she sat by candlelight. She wrapped her shawl around herself, cold in the tiny, cluttered bedroom.

She had trouble concentrating, thinking about her father and his declining health, and then that scourge at school. Adela didn't want to fixate on Marya, but the more she tried to leave it alone, the more she found herself unable.

She picked up the crystal globe from her desk. Her Aunt Elka had given it to her when she was nine, a few months before she passed away. The precious heirloom barely fit in Adela's palm, heavy and comforting.

Adela missed her aunt, especially tonight. She'd know what to do about Marya. Aunt Elka had been more than a confidant. When Adela got into a scuffle with a mean girl at school that landed Adela a blackened eye, she'd gone to her Aunt Elka in tears, afraid if she told her mother, she'd get in trouble. Instead of sympathy, Elka offered her opportunity. "There are ways to deal with mean girls, invisible ways. I can show you, my sweet Adela, but only if you want to learn. Would you like that?"

Adela recalled fidgeting with her fingers, unsure at first. Then she thought about the mean girl, and the answer leaped from her lips. "Yes."

"Good. Bring me a lock of her hair, and I will show you what to do."

Adela procured a single strand of the girl's hair the next day and gave it to her aunt. She watched as Aunt Elka pricked her finger and washed the hair with a drop of blood, then whispered to it. Adela remembered the candle on the sideboard guttering as if beset by a draft, even though the window was shut.

"It is done," Elka said. "What I did is called a binding. Come to me tomorrow and tell me what happens."

The following day, the mean girl hurried off as soon as she saw Adela in the hallway at school.

Aunt Elka smiled when she heard about what happened. "See? You can do these things too."

Adela didn't like the queasy feeling in her stomach, the wrongness of what her aunt had done. "What did you whisper yesterday?"

"An incantation that included the name of a spirit, its true name. Names have power, my sweet Adela. Some spirits are good, others not, but they all listen when called. I can teach you their names so you can call them too."

Aunt Elka taught Adela the fundamentals of binding before she died, but the experience scared Adela.

When Adela asked her mother about the cause of her aunt's death, her mother said it was due to influenza. Adela didn't believe her. She suspected her aunt's dark dealings with the spirits had caught up to her, and they'd come to collect her soul.

Adela had wanted to use her aunt's witchcraft to help her father after he fell ill, but it could only be used to harm or manipulate a person, not to heal them.

Now, as she sat at her desk, her thoughts turned to Marya. She was smart and a hard worker, but what if Julia was right and Marya was using tricks to charm her way to success and friendships? Wouldn't someone capable of such efforts go even further to win a coveted prize like the Arcanum?

Adela set the globe back on her desk.

She had to win, if nothing else, to humble the girl who seemed to be getting everything at her expense. Adela worked just as hard, and she'd been here longer. No, Adela would not bow down and let Marya win. She'd do whatever it took to win that prize, but not using her aunt's methods. Marya hadn't done anything to merit such an extreme response . . . yet.

"I will find another way to deal with her."

Adela toiled late into the night. She figured out how to use springstone. It had poles like a lodestone. She employed an artificing technique to inscribe runes to create anode and cathode links for her emitter. Mathematical precision was required, not only to make the electrical link to her emitter, but to generate a continuous charge and form a governor to manage the springstone's entropic state. Springstone was a chameleon that didn't play nicely with the second law of thermodynamics. When she was done, her emitter glowed a satisfying red.

The students presented their emitter lights to Master Ivanov in the morning. He used a galvanometer to measure the output of each device.

Adela watched with satisfaction as the devices registered too high, too low, or not at all. Hers was by far the best.

Until he examined Marya's.

His bushy brows rose toward the ceiling, and Adela's confidence sank to her stomach. "It appears we have a clear winner. All but one of you used the principle of dipole contention abatement. But this device employed a novel approach to reduce the resistance by an additional 25 percent with the placement of a third rune." He held up Marya's device. "Second place goes to Adela, first to Marya. Congratulations, Marya. Well done."

The class applauded. Adela joined them, but it was a hollow gesture.

Marya waited for her by the door after class, as if to flaunt her victory.

Adela offered a sportsmanlike compliment on the win. "That was some fine artificing. Nice work."

Marya didn't gloat. She was cordial with her response. "Thank you, but yours produced more light. If I had given out the assignment, I would have chosen luminosity over efficiency."

Adela stiffened. Was Marya mocking her? Adela stared at her for a moment. Marya seemed sincere.

Then Marya said, "I hope I'm not overstepping my place, but I heard about your father's condition."

That was personal. How dare Marya pry into Adela's family's business!

"Is it true he has metal poisoning?" Marya went on.

"Where did you hear that?" Adela snapped.

Marya didn't flinch. She said, "I overheard Master Belsky and another instructor talking about it in the hallway the day you stayed home from school."

Adela didn't remember saying anything to Master Belsky, only the headmistress. "And . . . ?"

"My mother died of tuberculosis when I was ten, my sister from typhus. I was thinking I could help you. Maybe we could work together—"

"You're right," Adela said, cutting her off. "You're overstepping." She decided to leave before she said something she would regret.

The crisp late afternoon air chilled Adela on her way home from school with her friends, the sun already hidden by sloping rooftops.

"Marya had no right talking to you about your father," Julia said. "Good for you for putting her in her place."

"She also lied about overhearing Master Belsky," Henna said. "She spoke to him in private last week. I peeked through the lab door and saw them talking. He handed her a glass vial of yellow powder, which I thought was odd. It almost looked like sulfur powder. She slipped it into her satchel. But what would Marya want with sulfur powder?"

Julia's brow furrowed; her eyes suspicious. "If it was, Master Belsky violated school policy giving it to her. Why would he do that?"

Henna shrugged. "Like I told you, he's under her spell. The better question is, what could she do with the sulfur?"

"Many things," Julia said. "She could make oil of vitriol for etching metals, though it's dangerous and no longer used much. She could also use it as a topical agent for a skin disorder. Or ingest it in small quantities for an ailment. Or make an explosive." With each guess, Julia grew more excited.

A shiver ran up Adela's neck. Aunt Elka had kept sulfur powder. Could Marya be using it the way Aunt Elka had? "What if she's a witch, and she's using it to make a powder for casting spells?" The words burst out before she could stop herself.

Julia and Henna stopped and stared, taken aback.

"Where did you hear that?" Julia finally managed.

"I read about it," Adela lied. Aunt Elka had taught her about spell powder as a potent aid for hexes and other malign purposes. Sulfur powder was the primary ingredient.

"Well, this is disturbing," Henna said, her skin turned ashen. "What do we do about it?"

An idea lit up, brighter than Adela's springstone project. "Do you want to help me? I mean really help me?"

They nodded. "Of course," both said.

"Find out what Marya is doing. Uncover her secrets," Adela said. "If she's really up to something so dangerous, she's a risk to us all, and she must be exposed."

The others nodded in agreement.

"How will we find out?" Julia asked.

"We'll have to keep careful observation of her—at all times," Adela said. "We can split our efforts. She lives closer to Henna, but you have her in classes we don't. So each of us needs to track her activities carefully over the next few days to reveal the truth about what she's doing."

Henna nodded, a gleam in her eyes. "I like your plan. We'll all work together."

Adela smiled. "We'll uncover her trickery, and then we'll make sure everyone sees her for who she really is."

If there existed a scientific scale of handsomeness, Master Belsky would rate at the very top. His long, flowing black hair framed a face that could have easily been chiseled from marble by Michelangelo himself.

"The Arcanum Prize," he said as he strode with his robes across the small stage before a rapt audience of the sixty-two girls of Adela's class, "is not just any prize. It represents the pinnacle of achievement in the metallurgic arts."

He retrieved the diamond-shaped trophy from behind his podium and set it up on the lectern. It stood gracefully upon its tip, an unassuming blue-gray monolith.

"Each year, our school bestows this prize to a single student. Who will it be this year? Will it be you?" He pointed at one girl. "You?" Another girl. "How about you?" Marya placed a hand over her heart as if wounded by cupid's arrow. It drew an unusually bright smile out of Master Belsky and a rise out of everyone else, except for Adela and her friends.

Adela gripped the edge of her desk, ready to tear it off. Henna was right. Marya had Master Belsky under her spell. Could she have performed a binding to enchant him—or used a charisma spell? Or was she just a good actress, a spy who won over her instructors with flattery and other tricks?

Master Belsky walked behind his podium. Mischief played in his deep-set brown eyes. "My dear ladies. This is the king of prizes. But what shall move me and your fellow masters to choose a victor? Is it beauty? Form? Function? Or is it mastery over the metallurgic arts unlike the world has ever seen?" He tipped the trophy toward the edge of his lectern, which earned gasps, but it didn't fall. It merely returned to its mysterious position. "Impress us. Move us. Defy the boys' schools and prove yourselves better." He stepped in front of the lectern for an imperious moment of silent gazing. The air was dead still. He placed his fingertips together.

"You have one month from today to submit your projects."

Adela set to work immediately.

She'd had years to ponder what she would make. The schema existed in her head. Her original design was an airfoil, a theoretical thin metal that would counteract gravity and float, with the right material and artificing. But as her father's condition worsened, she abandoned the airfoil in favor of finding a cure for him. The idea rested with a small plate he could strap to his forearm, a metal arrestor. Hollow leads called vampire taps would puncture the skin and penetrate the bloodstream. The device would act like a lodestone to draw out the toxic metals and adhere them to the magnetized plate, which could then be cleaned. Unfortunately, the iron in the blood created a complication Adela hadn't been able to resolve.

While she labored over the artificing of the plate, her friends gathered information on Marya Skłodowska. Marya had told the truth about the deaths of her mother and sister. She had other siblings, all older, and her father. Once a bright star in the academic world, he'd fallen from grace for his pro-Poland views.

"We did find something," Julia said when the three girls reunited later for her friends' reports. "She sneaks away at night to an old building, an abandoned lyceum. She carries a satchel with her. Someone lets her in."

Now *this* was an interesting find.

"I saw her at a pharmacy earlier," Henna said, "and when she emerged, she was stuffing something into her satchel."

Adela felt a lightness in her chest. She licked her lips, which had gone dry. "She's meeting with someone in secret or doing something illegal . . . or both. We need to figure out what she's up to. Then we'll get her expelled."

Adela got little sleep, vexed by the quandary with her metal arrestor. She'd checked out a roll of ultra-thin magnetite from her school, which she cut into small rectangles with shears. The magnetite acted as a lodestone, the runes she'd inscribed as a nullifying agent specifically formulated to prevent interaction with the iron particles in the blood. The idea was to draw the heavier metal toxins without affecting the blood's natural metals, like iron.

It wasn't working.

She'd tried it on her own arm, but the artificing was all wrong. Her innovative vampire taps performed the act of venipuncture while also acting on the principle of capillary action to draw blood into hollow tubules. She was drawing too much iron from her blood, which meant something was wrong with her runes. A simple swab of the hemogrometer borrowed from school tested for mercury, lead, cadmium, arsenic, and iron. She'd already wasted half the precious roll of magnetite. Why did artificing seem to come so naturally to Marya and not her? She'd seen the uncanny quality of Marya's work and the glimmer in her instructors' eyes. It wasn't fair. There had to be more to it than just luck or skill. Marya was up to something. More than ever, Adela felt determined to expose her rival.

Her father lay awake in the common room.

She brought him a glass of buttermilk to help him sleep. "How was your walk tonight?"

He wiped the thick residue from his lips. His eyes were droopy, more fatigued than usual, and he smelled of camphor. "Good."

"Where do you go, Papa? You never say."

"Just out." He smiled at her as he always did.

She didn't have the strength to force an answer. "Promise me you'll rest more."

He took her hand in his. His skin was colder than it had ever been. "I promise."

Only five days remained before the students were required to submit their projects for the Arcanum Prize.

Adela's progress had stalled.

She was so exhausted from being up all night that she fell asleep in Master Ivanov's class. She awoke to laughter from Kazia and the other students and a furrowed brow from a grumpy Ivanov. Marya appeared tired too. Maybe she'd faltered as well with her project. Or maybe there was something more sinister occupying her time. Adela hoped Marya had not only failed miserably, but that she couldn't sleep because of it.

She looked deservingly awful, dark circles under her eyes. Adela couldn't wait until her friends reported their latest findings.

The next day brought a disturbing revelation to light. Adela's friends presented the news in a quiet corner of Saxon Square, where they were shielded from the blustery wind.

"I'm not sure how to put this," Henna said.

"Your father—" Julia began. "He—"

Adela frowned. "What about him?"

Henna explained. "We were out last night following Marya. She went to the lyceum again. That's when we spotted your father. He went into the same building."

Adela didn't like jokes, nor did she like surprises. "This isn't funny, Henna."

"She's serious," Julia said. "I saw him too."

"Doing what?" Adela had many thoughts running through her mind, none good. Perhaps Marya was a Russian agent after all. Maybe she was extorting information about Adela's family, taking advantage of a dying man.

"I don't know," Julia said. "What do you want to do?"

Adela's fist clenched, her chest tightening with anger. She had to get to the bottom of Marya's actions once and for all. "We follow my father tonight. Then we catch Marya in the act and turn her over to the authorities."

Adela's breath fogged in the chilly night air.

She had waited for her father to leave the house for his evening walk after dinner. Once he left, she met up with her friends who had taken up a hiding spot behind a coach across from the four-story building that was the lyceum. She shivered more from nerves than the cold.

Tucking her hands into her jacket pockets, she felt the lock of hair with her right hand, clumped together with a drop of her own dried blood. A strand of Marya's hair she'd found below her chair in Metallurgy class the week prior.

All Adela had to do was whisper the incantation her aunt had taught her, and the binding would take effect. She'd never done one on her own, and her shaking got worse as she contemplated whether it would truly work, and the potential consequences if it did—not just for Marya, but herself. But if Marya forced her hand, she wouldn't hesitate. She'd do whatever it took to protect Papa.

Her father ambled up to the poorly lit side entrance minutes later. He knocked three times, one slow rap, two fast. Someone let him in. According to Henna, Marya had arrived thirty minutes earlier.

Heat rose in Adela's face, and her shaking stopped. She removed her hands from her pockets, turned to her friends, and said, "Follow me."

She knocked on the side door, using the same pattern her father had used. The door opened to a balding man in his middle years. He had a thick mustache. "Who are you?"

"I'm Adela Kowalski, Casimir's daughter. Who are you?"

"Władysław Skłodowski."

It wasn't the answer Adela had expected. She stammered, "Marya's father?"

"Yes." He eyed Adela's friends. "And these young ladies?"

"Henna and Julia." Taking a deep breath, Adela braced herself, focusing on her anger and fear. "I demand to know why my father is here. What's going on in this building?"

"You shouldn't be here."

"I'm not leaving without answers!"

Władysław Skłodowski let out a resigned sigh and opened the door all the way. "Come in. It's best I show you."

He led them down a short corridor to a small, dank room lit by a pair of oil lamps. The first person Adela noticed was her father.

"Papa?"

"Dela, what are you doing here? And your friends?"

Her father sat in a wood chair with his sleeves rolled up, resting an arm on a table with artificing tools Adela recognized, along with the vial of yellow powder Henna had mentioned, now almost empty. Five grownups, all strangers, got up from their seats. Marya's eyes met Adela's, and her face fell. It was true! And there were adults helping her!

"I can explain," Marya said, holding out her hands.

Adela's cheeks were hot. This was meddling of a magnitude she couldn't begin to fathom. She started toward Marya, ready to grab a fistful of her miserable hair and yank her down to the floor.

Władysław stepped in between them. "It's better if I explain."

Marya's father spoke of their purpose. That the lyceum was a meeting place to discuss the future of academia in Warsaw, namely the creation of a new university. As Polish patriots, the secret gatherings at the lyceum were a necessity to avoid pro-Russian authorities.

"We don't have an official name for our school yet," Władysław said, "but your father has been instrumental in helping us organize. We all want the best for the future of our country."

Adela still wasn't satisfied. "My father is very sick. He shouldn't be here." She glared at Marya, suspecting there was even more going on. Her father should have been home resting, not here with all these people. Her heart pounded, threatening to burst out of her chest. "You're killing him!"

Adela reached into her pocket for the strand of hair and pursed her lips to begin the incantation of binding. She had brought it only as a last resort, but she had to end this, here and now. The sequence of words came to her, along with the name of a vile spirit that would make quick work of Marya.

Adela's father held up a hand, halting his daughter. When he spoke, his voice was soft, filled with warmth. "Quite the opposite, my sweet Dela. They're trying to help me. Marya offered her assistance. She's like you: a scientist. While we've been discussing the future of education, she's been trying to solve the metal poisoning in my blood. I think we're close."

Adela's heart lifted for a moment, then sank. Her breathing quickened, and she narrowed her eyes at Marya, almost squinting. "That's *my* business, not yours. I've spent every night looking for a cure for my Papa. But you—you're doing this to win the Prize. Tell me you're not."

Henna and Julia exchanged tense glances, the others in the room as well, but Marya looked down. "At first, yes. I thought I might achieve a breakthrough and present it to the school. But the truth is, I wanted to help your father. We tried sulfur as a medicinal, but that didn't work.

My mother and sister died of terrible diseases. I didn't know we were striving toward the same goal. If I had, I would have been more insistent we work together."

Anger flashed within Adela. How dare Marya interfere with Adela's father's life and put it at risk? "Since when does the brilliant Marya Skłodowska need my help? You're better than I could ever be! And you're doing this for my father to rub it in."

Marya's shoulders sagged. "I'm not better than you. In fact, I've not made any progress in weeks. I'm stuck."

The admission drew surprised looks from Henna and Julia. Adela was stunned as well. Marya wasn't defending herself or behaving boldly. She was humble, almost regretful. Maybe she wasn't a witch after all. *Could Marya really be trying to help Papa?* For the first time, it occurred to Adela that Marya might just be a fellow student with a burning desire to succeed and discover new things, but with foibles and challenges, just like her own.

Adela let go of the hair pinched between her fingers and removed her hand from her pocket. Her father's life was too important to squabble over in pettiness. If Marya was truly trying to help, Adela wanted to be part of it. "Really? How far did you get?"

"I've figured out the runes required to separate the toxins. I haven't figured out how to draw them out. You?"

"I came up with a way to draw metals from blood, but I don't know how to separate the iron from the toxic metals."

Adela's father smiled up at them both. His eyes were rheumy, his face pale, but his spirit was strong. "Then I think you two might have the solution. It's called *working together.*"

Master Belsky leaned forward in his chair. Adela and Marya were alone in his office with the door closed, standing in front of his desk.

"This is a most unusual request," he said, eyeing the rectangle of magnetite with the artificed runes. "The rules are clear: one submission per student, not one submission per pair of students." Adela held her breath, expecting the worst. "However." He folded his hands. "I've never been one to adhere to strictures like stuffy Ivanov. Don't tell him I said that." He shared a conspirator's smile. "Ladies, I will accept your submission for consideration. If we can't advance the metallurgic arts, then why bother teaching them at all? Might I inquire as to where your patient is right now?"

"Sitting outside your office," Adela said. "He's exhausted, but he insisted on coming here."

"You do realize today is the last day of submission, don't you?"

Marya spoke. "We do, Master Belsky. But I believe if you measure the uptake of toxic metals, you'll find that our device is doing the work as intended."

Master Belsky lifted the metal rectangle up for examination. He flipped it over. The vampire taps protruded as a pair in the center, like teeth. He flipped it right-side up again and ran a finger over the tiny runes and channels Marya had incised with finesse. "This is exquisite artificing. And your patient has one just like it strapped to his forearm, collecting blood at this very moment?"

"He does," Adela said. One part of her wished she could have presented her metal arrestor to Master Belsky herself. The project was *her* idea. The other part was grateful for Marya's assistance. If not for Marya, she would have failed, and her father wouldn't have the help he needed to get better. That was more important than any selfish wants.

Master Belsky placed the device back on his desk. His brown eyes danced with intrigue. "Then I shall very much like to see this marvel."

Adela and Marya took to the stage at the school's auditorium. They were met by a standing ovation, thunderous applause, and raucous cheering.

The thusium trophy lifted easily between them, deceptively light like volcanic rock. They held it aloft, and the cheering reached its peak. Adela couldn't take her eyes off her father who clapped with vigor. Her mother was there, her sister too, but her Papa was the reason she was standing in front of the school. She looked forward to many more years of shared moments like this. His life was the true prize.

After the presentation of the trophy, the headmistress and her instructors offered their congratulations. Belsky was debonair and witty. Even Ivanov offered a congenial smile.

Adela gathered with Henna and Julia as the auditorium cleared out. Marya had let Adela hold on to the thusium trophy for the night as a gesture of camaraderie.

Adela brushed the brass plaque mounted to the center of the thusium prize with her thumb. It had yet to be inscribed. "Master Belsky said he'd order a second trophy made. He said it's only fair."

"Does this mean we're to be friends with Marya now?" Julia asked.

"We'll see," Adela said, enjoying being mysterious as her father waved at them from the door to come out.

"He looks so much better," Henna said as they started toward the door.

"He does." Adela had a bounce to her step as she walked toward her Papa. "I think everything's going to be all right."

Science Note:

Sulfur powder has real world applications as a topical agent, explosive, and "oil of vitriol" (sulfuric acid) for etching metal. In ancient times, sulfur served a wide variety of uses to aid against ailments. People ingested sulfur as a vermifuge (de-worming agent) and to balance the body's "humors." Sulfur's use extended to the treatment of skin conditions like dermatitis and bacterial infections.

The BEAST

by
STACIA DEUTSCH

Fifteen Minutes
Marie, Paris, 1934

In fifteen minutes, I will make a tragic, irreversible mistake that will terrorize not only the small town of my youth but also send the entire nation into a panic. To die or not to die, it's a simple binary choice. There are only two alternatives, and being solely of one body and one mind, I must decide.

It comes to this: I can time travel to the past in an attempt to save the planet from endless torment from a monster of my own creation and, thus doing so, seal my own demise. Or I stay here in the city with the knowledge that I unleashed a tormentor who will, in due course, destroy us all. By "destroy," I do not mean death, as the creature does not need to feed very often. Rather, the destruction would be an unrelenting psychological trauma—the uncertainty of something dangerous always lurking in the shadows—unpredictable and unstoppable.

In the solitary quiet of my Parisian laboratory, I sit at my custom-made desk, perched on the edge of my fine chair, gently caressing a narrow test tube in my palm. The cool glass restrains the incredible power of the substance within. The isotopes call to me in ways few can understand, for I discovered them, and they course through me, literally in my blood.

I raise the vial and run a finger around the stopper. It glows with a blue-green soluble luminescence. This lovely faint glow is one of my greatest joys. All of the awards, the accolades knowing that I, as a Polish woman, have earned for achieving the unimaginable recede from memory as I stare at the vial. At night, like now, it's as if fairies have invaded my workspace. They call to me from inside the glass. Like Alice of the fictional world, I hear "Drink me," a siren's song dancing in my head. I try to shut it down. I cannot.

The white walls in my beautiful, state-of-the-art workspace feel expansive as I remove the cap and swallow the precise dosage. With my eyes closed, I can feel the radioactivity my husband, Pierre, and I discovered course through me. I wonder, if he were still alive, would he be horrified to know what I did when I was a young woman, long before we even met? Would he support me now? Would his opinion matter?

I retrieve a second bottle, identical to the first in every way, from my desk drawer. Knowing this small glass tube is my ticket back to the here and now, I clutch it protectively in my fist and finally relax back into my chair. The wind billows the curtains around an open window as my journey begins.

I am Marie Curie, and this is my cross.

Two Months, Five Days
Marya, Poland, 1883

"How are you feeling today?" my father asked, pulling back the curtains of my darkened room.

"The light!" I gasped at the sudden brightness. Shutting my eyes tightly, I allowed my brain to first feel the sun's warmth, then slowly blinked, gradually adjusting to the afternoon light. My head pounded, and my body felt like rubber. "Come back in an hour," I begged my father.

"It's time for me to leave the country and return to Warsaw," my father told me, as if we'd had a conversation about travel.

My head felt thick, and my tongue thicker. I took a sip of water along with two pain pills from the bedside table then forced myself upright. "Leaving? When are we leaving?"

He sighed in the way my father did ever since Mother had passed years earlier. "You will stay here," he said in a scolding tone. "I go alone."

I struggled to catch up, feeling that I had plinked down in the middle of a conversation. "Papa?" I rubbed the sleep from my eyes and willed the pills to take effect. "I don't understand."

"For a gold medal student," he said, "one would imagine you'd be the one explaining the ways of the world to me, not the other way around."

I licked my parched lips as fleeting memories floated to consciousness. Gold medal. Yes. I'd graduated the gymnasium with highest honors and accolades for being so young. After that, things were less clear. I'd retreated to my room. Not this room, but rather the cramped, small, cluttered room I shared with my sister at our home in Warsaw. It was suffocating. Even the open window didn't provide enough air. I couldn't think, or perhaps I didn't want to think. I remember my sister shouting that I'd collapsed, but my head was so clouded I couldn't assure her I wasn't dead. Perhaps I was.

The doctor came.

My bags were packed.

The train. I recall the rattle and hum. The gentle movement as I slept.

And now, I have awakened in my cousins' country home with my father staring at me as if I were damaged. Which was true.

"How long have I been here?" I asked, catching a glimpse of myself in the mirror and wishing I hadn't. My hair hadn't been washed or combed and looked greasy and matted. I could smell my own sleep sweat. The gown I wore was not my own. Someone must have removed my dress and, I assumed, taken it to launder or burn.

"Too long," my father said. "Marya, you are fifteen now. Old enough to determine your own future." There was satisfaction on his face—a vastly different expression than the sadness he'd worn since sister Zofia and then Mother had passed. "There is a time for mourning." He put on his hat and slid into his jacket. "And a time to move forward."

He took a step toward the door, then turned back to me. In precise Polish, he said, "*Z kim się zadajesz, takim się stajesz.*"

"Yes." I nodded, acknowledging his parting advice. "You become who you befriend."

My father tipped his hat and was gone.

Thirty-Six Days
Marya, Poland, 1883

Those early weeks in the countryside were lonely but soothing to my restless soul. My four cousins were older than I, and certainly none of them were interested in the intersections between chemistry, math, and physics. While they talked of parties and local gossip, I began to obsess about the magnetic properties of metals and if it were possible to harness energy.

There is no faster way, I discovered, to send everyone off to bed than to regale them with my latest reading or mathematical conundrum. In fact, to my mind, it seemed that the family rather missed the time I spent in my room with the curtains drawn and wondered if I might be due for another depressive spell.

For me, however, the country was exactly what I needed to tap my passions. When the crate arrived from Warsaw, both the future and the friendship my father had mentioned at his departure were revealed.

Thirty-Five Days
Marya, Poland, 1883

"You may work here." My eldest cousin had the crate removed from the front hall of the manor home and dropped in the dusty shed at the back of the wooded lot. "Do what you may, but please, no talk of it at dinner." The half smile she gave me indicated she and the others believed this crate was the end of their woes. From here forward, my dinner conversation could be of plants and literature and songs and artwork, since my need for science and mathematics would burn out with the sun each day.

It was a noble plan, and I fully intended to abide by this imagined boundary as I opened the crate for the first time and peered inside.

"Test tubes, wiring, gas burner . . ." I recorded the contents in a notebook while my mind began to spin the possibilities of inquiry. As I set my father's greatest gifts on the wooden crates that formed my laboratory table, an idea began to take shape.

"You become who you befriend."

I wanted a friend. Nay, not just any friend. I'd had friends in the past at school. Best friends even. No. Here in this time and place, I wanted a true friend who could understand my moods and innermost desires. Someone that would listen to me talk about my experiments, my readings, as well as art, literature, and music. I wanted, nay, I deserved, a friend like me.

Eight Hours
Marya, Poland, 1883

Since the day I opened the crate from my father, I had been mulling methods of harnessing energy and was finally on the path to turn my longings into reality.

My cousins thought everything was wonderful. Every evening I joined them for respite and games. I played along, in that pregnant space between expectation and desire. I was getting what I desired in the daylight hours, and they welcomed the cousin they expected at night. My temperament felt focused even as I made advancements that had only before been described in fiction.

The Modern Prometheus was a story about a young scientist that created a humanlike creature where there was none before. The story was written more than five decades before I was born. Had Mary Shelley been here in the Polish countryside with me now, I doubt she'd have recognized my interpretation of her fantastical imaginings. My very own monster was mere moments away from animation.

I found the body parts for my creature in the local hospital morgue, and in places where additional flesh was needed, the local animal cemetery had the bits to fill in any gaps.

The heart was as dead as the person who provided it.

I held the heart, and using the profound gifts my studies provided, along with mundane prods coursing with electrical charges, I managed to start its rhythm anew. Not anew as if reanimated, but rather *a new* as in newly born.

Wait, Marya, no . . . My own internal protest sounded tepid, and

I ignored the warning as I navigated science into unchartered waters. The creature began to stir.

Fourteen Minutes
Marie, Paris, 1935

Streaking flashes of light fly past my eyes. I begin to sweat, then freeze, then sweat again. My skin feels like it pulls free from my muscles and snaps back with such force that I imagine what it might be like to be crushed beneath a steam roller.

Four Minutes
Marie, Poland, 1883

When my skin, muscles, and aching bones feel solid once more, I am acutely aware that I am standing in the familiar forest of my childhood.

Success!

And yet, the sunlight is not directly above the trees, nor are the birds chirping their morning hymn. It appears that although I had reviewed the mathematics again and again, I have arrived much later in the past than expected. As precise as I hoped it would be, time travel is not an exact science.

A rustling sound attracts my attention and alerts me that my past self is nearby. Seeing as it is the end of the anticipated day, rather than the beginning, I take a moment to adjust my thinking to this anomaly.

Hidden by shadows, I watch my younger self walk away from the water's edge. I remember how I felt that day, so proud. Happier than I had felt before. Content with the realization that I set in motion something wonderful. Something unstoppable.

My younger self skips giddily through the moonlight, and I recognize the bag I carry. Rat blood drips from the corner where the fabric is frayed. Tomorrow morning, I will patch the hole, not wanting to leave an oozing trail from an evening meal for my friend to follow back to my family home.

Tomorrow night, I will return to this spot with the same bag and a dead fish. The third evening, I will bring a rabbit and so on, but by the week's end, I will learn that I do not have to kill the beast's bounty myself. The beast can hunt. I will be as proud that day as a mama whose babe weans himself and lifts the spoon to his own mouth.

I do not need to see my smile to know it exists. I can easily recapture the joy I felt as strongly as I experienced it that very first night.

The forest is the perfect hideaway. The lake breeds sustenance. The path is close enough to my cousins' home for me to travel every evening without notice. I believe with all my heart, that when the time comes for me to leave, my creation will live on. Forever.

I feel boundless.

Three Minutes
Marie, Poland, 1883

If I could, I would rush forward and show myself the newspaper clippings I carry with me:

FARMER'S GRUESOME REMAINS

FOUND BY RIVERBANK

MISSING FISHERMAN AND WIFE

FOUND. ONLY BONES REMAIN.

MAYOR OF SMALL POLISH VILLAGE URGES RESIDENTS TO STAY

INSIDE AS MYSTERIOUS NIGHT STALKER REMAINS ON THE

LOOSE.

FEAR OF MOONLIGHT KILLER

SPREADS TO WARSAW

There is a folk saying that if you ever run into your own self, do not engage. If you were to talk to your own visage, in that moment you both will die. Spontaneously combust. There's no scientific reason for me to believe there's truth to those words, but in the absence of a way to test it, and with an emergency situation at hand, I will give credence to whoever spouted those words and not tempt fate. As an aside, I also don't believe in fate, and yet, I am ducking behind a tree, gripping the newspaper clippings while I allow myself to pass by.

Time is a strange bedfellow. I am here, watching myself, and yet, not being myself.

Two Minutes,
Marya, Poland, 1883

"Marya!" my youngest cousin called as I neared the house. I ditched my bloody tote behind a large rock. I needed to repair the bottom. The bag leaked blood. I probably should have thought of a different way to carry the rats, but the beast was hungry. The rats were a lure and a meal, and besides, no one would ever miss them.

The beast seemed happy in his new home, and I had clearly arrived back, just in time.

There were two police officers standing in the foyer.

"Mademoiselle," an elderly man with a bushy mustache bowed slightly. The other officer, tipped his hat, but didn't speak or lower his gaze.

Sweat broke out on the back of my neck at concern he knew where I had been. I had only let the beast live in my laboratory one night. I'd been careful. There was no way . . .

"The girl who lives next door is missing," my aunt said in a sober, concerned tone.

"She never came home last night," my cousin explained. Unlike her mother, she was unconcerned. "You know her, Marya," she insisted. "Bright red hair in braids." She held her hand to her waist to indicate the length of the girl's hair.

I shrugged. Since coming to the country, I rarely interacted with the neighbors. I had been inside the house until the crates arrived and since my time had been limited to work, reading, and meals with family—no red-haired girls.

"Lena was last seen on the path behind the old shed," the mus-tached officer said.

"I think she eloped," my cousin swooned. Her sister and two broth-ers sat quietly on the couch, uninterested in the proceedings. "She has a boyfriend in Warsaw."

The silent officer wrote that down.

My cousin gushed. "Oh, Marya, can't you imagine? I bet she ran away to get married, never to return to this dreadful backward farm town ever again." Her brown eyes were dreamy as she tossed back her long blond curls and announced, "She was rescued."

I hadn't actually known that my own cousin found country life dreary.

I liked being here, and I was glad my father had not yet set a date to collect me. There was much to be done before that day came. I wanted to know the beast and share my world with him. Time was precious.

"We will look into the boyfriend," the officer said. He stared straight at me, practically through me. "Is there anything you want to tell us," he dragged out my name in a slow pregnant drawl, "Marya?"

I was not sure when my mouth and my brain connected because for a long moment, I was silent, then quite suddenly, I burst open, shout-ing my plans to the two policemen, "Tomorrow, I am going fishing!"

Two Hours and Fifteen Minutes
Marie, Paris, 1934

I have the means, the math, and the purpose. I am only missing one thing for my journey.

I find the knife in a cluttered pawn shop window.

It's a double-edged twelve-inch dagger with a high-carbon steel blade and a rosewood grip. It is the knife I want. It is the knife I need.

The man behind the counter sets the dagger on the glass. He says that it can be used to carve the hide off a pig.

"It's not a pig," I tell him, testing the weight in my hand. "Though he does have a pig's snout." I don't mention that I had found the snout behind the local butcher's and thought large nostrils would support greater oxygen intake.

"This is a fine blade," the man brags, eyeing me suspiciously.

I do not give any indication about my intentions, and yet he says, "It can kill a man." The way he said it makes me wonder if perhaps he has killed a man himself.

"And a monster?" I ask as if this were a very normal thing to consider when buying a knife.

"Assuredly," the man tells me and names the blade's price.

I blink hard at the number. Then I pay it.

"Worth every franc," he says as he wraps the blade in paper and hands it to me. "Good luck exorcising your demons."

I leave the store without reply.

I have a knife.

Seventy Seconds
Marie, Poland, 1883

Satisfied that my past self is home with our cousins, I creep quickly through the forest until I reach the mouth of a granite hillside cave. It is a small space, requiring a prayerful bow to enter. The entry is narrow, yet deep. Not high enough for the beast to stand. I taught him, when I first brought him to this place, to stay low, crawl forward, and stretch out with his head toward the door. This way, I could sit outside, and we could talk for long hours, far beyond midnight.

Asleep, with his head toward the mouth of the cave is how I find him, snoring softly. Freshly discarded rat bones are scattered around the dirt floor.

Sixty Seconds
Marie, Poland, 1883

I raise the knife in the moonlight and can see my reflection in the blade. I am not the young girl in the woods. This is me. Now. Long hair, grayer than yesterday, swept into a messy knot at the back of my head. The lines in my forehead show years of deep contemplation. My eyes are not as bright as they once were, but they hunger with the same curiosity and questions of what if? And what comes next? And how?

The clock is ticking. I feel the dissipation of the radiation in my blood. I touch my pocket to make sure the second stoppered vial is still with me. I'll need the contents to return to my life . . . and death.

I prefer to do the deed while the beast sleeps. It will be easier for us both.

I crouch down to my knees and slide forward, until I am next to the very heart that I, myself, taught to beat.

My beast. My dear friend. He opens his eyes and sees me there.

I gasp as he snarls, his borrowed muscles and sinews tighten as they flood with adrenaline. And then he relaxes, recognizing me even though I don't recognize myself.

I raise the knife. I know what I must do! And it must be now when he is calm and trusting. The knife shines in the moonlight. The edges are sharp and will do what they intend. Skin a pig. Kill a man. Destroy a beast. Save the world.

My father's words echo in my soul. "You become who you befriend."

I am the beast and we both must die.

Thirty Seconds
Marie, Poland, 1883

There's a Polish saying, "*Co nagle, to po diable.*" It means, "The devil dictates when you are in a hurry." I am in a hurry to decide two fates.

My knees tremble as I roll into position for my small frame to deliver the strongest blow. A spark of light glints from the knife to the eyes of the beast and bounces back to me.

In that illumination, for the quickest moment, I see that the bones surrounding me are not what I assumed. They are not rat bones at all. Thicker. Longer. Human. And the rats I'd killed didn't have long red hair.

I didn't know it then, but the beast had not waited for me to bring him dinner. Not that first night or any night thereafter.

The beast sighs as if waiting for me to make a decision.

The folded newspaper clippings about the deaths at the lake are in my pocket now, and as I look at my friend, I wonder why I have come all this way. Is it not equally fated, if such a thing existed, to let lives run a natural course even to an unnatural end? And what of . . . Lena? Would saving her, or the next man or woman, or the one that comes to the beast after, change the historically documented, scientific trajectory of the town, the state, the country, or the world?

To die or not to die is not a simple binary choice. Nor is to kill or not to kill. Neither, I must add, is destructive versus beneficial. Good or bad. Ugly or beautiful. There are a multitude of possibilities from every innovation.

I am not God. This moment is not my cross to bear, nor was it ever.

I lower my blade. It remains as pristine as when I bought it.

Not too long ago, or fifty years hence, if you prefer, in an interview, I said, "In the hands of a criminal, radium is very dangerous. So we must ask ourselves: What will humanity gain or lose from the discovery?"

I set the knife down on the cave floor and, with it, the articles from newspapers of the future. I extract the vial of radium from my pocket and remove the stopper. With seconds left on the ticking clock, I drink the entire contents. One dose brought me and a second will return me home. To Paris. To the very edge of my time on Earth. Summer, 1934.

As my mind begins to fade and the world of my past grows dim, I take one last look at my creation and accept that it is free. It has been unleashed.

My End

Marya/Marie, Paris,
July 4, 1934

There is a Polish saying, "*Komu pora, temu czas.*" It means, "When it's your time, you have to go."

I am forever Marie Curie.

The test tube, not the beast, tells my story.
I have died by the hand of my own creation.
This is my legacy.

Science Note:

I'd love to think time travel might be real someday, but we just don't have the science yet. That said, in this story, Marie Curie's discovery of the radioactive isotope radium is real. Marie and her husband, Pierre, first discovered, then isolated, radium. The radium glowed and produced heat. It's said that Marie Curie kept a vial of it by her bedside as a nightlight. Radium was an element that could heal and led to medical advancements, but the radiation it produced could also kill and contributed to the eventual creation of the atomic bomb. After earning two Nobel Prizes and founding the Radium Institute, Marie Curie died in 1934 from a lifelong exposure to her own discovery.

The NIGHT FLYERS

by

JONATHAN MABERRY

The old colonel nodded to the pair of young girls.

"There they are," he said quietly. "See them, Boris?"

Boris Vjenko, a retired cavalry major, glanced that way and saw two very lovely girls of about the same age as his youngest daughter. They were nicely dressed, with understated clothing that did not draw attention. Subtle and modest. The major approved.

"What about them?"

"Watch."

The girls walked arm-in-arm across Saxon Square, past a platoon of foot soldiers marching in smart formation. They giggled at the looks the soldiers gave them, but did not flirt, and instead headed toward the obelisk that rose above the square. If the girls' smiles seemed less genuine and more forced, neither the colonel nor the major could tell at that distance. They watched as the girls paused for a moment outside the ring of double-headed Russian eagles who guarded the obelisk. Then, together, they took a step forward as if crossing an actual line.

"What are they doing?" asked the major.

"Playing a game, I suppose," said the colonel, whose name was Zhukovsky. "They always do that."

"They had better not be doing anything else. Not after what those boys did the other night."

Colonel Zhukovsky grunted. Two nights ago, three Polish boys had been caught trying to smash the statues of Russian eagles erected to symbolically guard the obelisk. The spike of bronze and concrete had been built after the November Uprising and was a powerful statement about who had won that conflict, and about Russian power in general. To deface either the eagles or the obelisk was considered a political crime that came with harsh penalties.

"The boys were dealt with," said the colonel.

The major nodded, though he looked briefly unnerved at the memory. Yesterday morning, all three boys were found in a nearby alley, their bodies torn to bloody rags. Local police had looked for a mad killer but found no one. The fact that their entire investigation lasted less than four hours proved that it was a sham. Everyone knew it.

The Russian occupational government issued a statement that the eagles were undamaged and added a warning to all Poles to not vandalize any Russian monument. There was no need for that message to include a threat. The savaged corpses were eloquent enough.

It was not the first such incident in the vicinity of Saxon Square. A year ago the body of a one-legged Polish sergeant—forced out of the army and cast onto the street as a beggar—was found in the same condition as the boys. Ripped apart. There were no witnesses of any kind, though there was a silly rumor going around that the eagles had come to life to attack him as he tried to batter the statues with a hammer. That was, of course, utter nonsense.

Even so, the two old Russian officers watched very closely to see what the girls were doing. Once inside the circle, the girls went and stood very close to the obelisk, their faces now in profile to the old officers.

The colonel nudged his friend with a soft elbow. "Watch this. You'll like this part."

The girls offered low curtsies to the statue and then leaned forward, almost close enough to kiss the thing.

Then they turned and hurried off, their smiles blossoming once again.

"That was nice," said Major Vjenko.

"They do it every day," said Colonel Zhukovsky. "They show respect."

"They're Polish girls?"

"Yes," said the colonel.

"Are you sure?"

"Completely. The blond is the daughter of Count Zamoyski's librarian."

"And the other one? The girl with the dark hair?" asked the major. "Who is she?"

"I have no idea. A friend from school, I suppose."

"And they curtsy every day?"

"Every single day," said the colonel. He tugged his snuffbox out of a vest pocket, took a pinch, inhaled deeply, and sneezed loud enough to scare a thousand pigeons into frantic flight. "What it tells me is that at least the *younger* generation is willing to embrace their new heritage— not as Poles but as Russians."

"Do you think it's because of the eagles?" asked the major. "Are they doing it out of fear of what might . . . you know . . . *happen*?"

They exchanged a brief knowing look.

"No, they don't look afraid, do they?" observed the colonel with confidence. "What I think is happening is that we have finally begun to change their hearts and minds."

They both smiled and nodded, and walked off, feeling pleased about the turn of events.

"I think they saw us," said Kazia, the blond girl, her cheeks flushing.

The smaller and darker girl, Marya, cut a look at the two old officers walking away.

"If they saw us," she said, "we'd be getting arrested right now."

Kazia took a handkerchief and dabbed at her friend's lower lip. "You still have some spit on you."

"I'll spit twice as much at that statue tomorrow to make up for it."

They grinned at each other and hurried across the square.

Once they were out of sight of the officers, Kazia shuddered.

"They won't hurt you," said Marya.

"No," said her friend, "it's not them."

"Then what? The eagles?"

Kazia shuddered again and nodded. "The eagles."

They both glanced over their shoulders at the ring of double-headed eagles. They were made from bronze but painted a lifeless black. The sunlight cast weird shadows and created the illusion that their muscles were tensing in preparation of leaping forward to rend with talon and claw. Those same shifting shadows made it look as if those eagles had turned their heads slightly to stare at the two girls. It made them look so hungry, so angry, so malicious.

It was not the first time Marya and her friend had been struck by that illusion. It was not the first time it sent chills all the way through them. The girls paused for a moment to stare at those metal birds. At those hungry, hooked beaks, pitiless black eyes, and wicked talons.

"They can't hurt us," said Marya.

It was a lie, and they both knew it.

They turned and fled.

High above, on the rooftops and eaves of every building surrounding the square, eyes watched the officers, and the girls depart. Small, black eyes that were as bright as polished basalt. Cold eyes that missed nothing.

The soldiers went one way and the girls another, but the unblinking eyes of a thousand crows watched them with keen interest.

Marya Skłodowska attended two schools.

One was the proper one. The required one. One of the countless gymnasiums littered across Poland, a girls' school that no girl she ever knew wanted to attend. The walls were drab gray or drab yellow or drab white. The chairs and desks looked like they had been made from the first tree that ever grew—creaky, uncomfortable, and ugly. Countless years of bored girls had carved initials, snide comments, and obscure little symbols on them whose meanings were lost to time. The only good thing about the place was that this was the last year she would attend. Polish girls were not educated beyond that grade, and a life of one kind of servitude or another waited.

In theory, at least.

Kazia did not attend the gymnasium with her.

But they both attended the *other* school. That one was fun. That one was alive. And they were just starting their studies.

This other school was not locked inside a graceless, ageless, humorless building. Oh no, this school was also constantly in motion, like a restless bird. A Polish bird, as Marya thought of it. Like the crows that seemed to be everywhere lately. They were not as overtly powerful as the Russian eagles, but more nimble, more graceful, and totally relentless. Nightbirds, as her favorite teacher called them.

As for the school . . . it had no real name. That would have been dangerous. Instead, it was known by what it was—a *flying* school. It moved from someone's house to the backroom of a milliner's shop to a baker's loft to a widow's basement. Like the nightbirds, it was too fast to catch and too dark against the autumn sky to be seen.

After she and Kazia split up in the morning, they found each other again in late afternoon. Both ran home first to change into darker cloaks and bonnets. Appropriate for sensible girls running errands for their mothers. Appropriate for girls hiding in plain sight from the Russians. And they always made sure that the smiles they showed were not the smiles they felt.

"You're late," said Mrs. Kaliszek without turning.

She was arranging a cloth over two objects set on a desk at the front of the room. One was about three feet in height and the other about half as tall.

The door had not squeaked when Marya and Kazia came in; their skirts made no noise, and their shoes had been left in the downstairs hall. There was no sound at all to signal their entry to the room.

But Agata Kaliszek knew.

She always knew.

Marya and Kazia winced at each other as they slid quickly to their seats. The game was always to get in place by the time Mrs. Kaliszek turned. They were in, down, and had their copybooks open when the older woman did turn.

As always, the first glimpse of Mrs. Kaliszek on any given day was a jolt. Not a bad jolt, but indeed a very strong one. She was somewhere north of seventy, and Marya suspected *well* north. Her face was heavily lined, but the effect was not of dwindling vitality but closer to the creases and lines of bark on a strong old tree. The kind of tree that might be hundreds of years old and might grow yet for century upon century.

Mrs. Kaliszek had gray hair, the color and thickness of a wolf's tail, with little hints of black and brown and white. Not a wig, though, of that Marya and Kazia were sure. Her mouth was a wide, thin slash, without a trace of lipstick, and although she often smiled, it wasn't a toothy smile. Merely a subtle curl at the corners of her mouth.

It was her eyes that always caught Marya's full attention. While other girls seemed interested in the old-fashioned style of Mrs. Kaliszek's dresses and her French gloves and her habit of wearing a large antique watch dangling from her belt—"more like the seventeenth rather than nineteenth century," one girl was heard to remark—for Marya it was her eyes.

For Marya, the eyes were the true window into understanding a person. If you really looked and then *thought* about what you saw, then staring into someone's eyes could tell a lot. That was Marya's theory, and it rarely failed her. Mrs. Kaliszek had brown eyes rimmed with gray, with small gold rings around the pupils. Strange eyes. Piercing, like a hawk.

She walked toward the desks, which were arranged in a half circle. Ten desks, seven girls. Three empty seats.

"You all heard about what happened to those boys," she said without preamble.

Marya glanced around at the other girls and saw most of them go pale. They all nodded.

"But do you really know what happened to them?" asked the teacher.

Kazia raised her hand. "My father said that the Russian secret police did it."

"That's what I heard too," said another girl, and there were more nods.

Mrs. Kaliszek raised a single eyebrow. "Is that so?"

The way she said it kept the other girls from commenting.

"And since when do the secret police tear their victims to pieces?" she asked coldly. "Since when do they use instruments of torture that are the same size and shape as eagle talons? Or eagle beaks? Come, come child, that is illogical."

"What's the alternative?" asked Marya. "Pet attack eagles?"

"Not as such, no," said the teacher.

"Well," Kazia smirked. "It's not like those ugly eagle statues came to life."

Mrs. Kaliszek stood still and silent for so long, looking at them with such unblinking intensity that the girls all began to fidget. Few of them could meet that stare for longer than a few seconds, excepting only Marya.

Did the teacher's stern mouth smile just a little? Marya wasn't sure. And it called to mind the feeling she had that very morning, when she and Kazia had covertly spat upon the ugly black eagles. And, more so, the way the shifting shadows made it seem like the birds were only feigning immobility. The way it always felt like they were truly ready to attack and tear into helpless flesh.

Mrs. Kaliszek cocked her head to one side as she spoke again. "Horatio said to Hamlet, 'My god, this is unbelievably strange.' To which the Prince of Denmark replied, 'There are more things in heaven and earth, Horatio, than are dreamt of in your philosophy.'" She paused. "Who knows where this quote is from?"

"From Shakespeare," said Kazia. "From the play *Hamlet*."

"Very good. And what does it mean? More specifically, in what way do you think it is relevant to today's lesson? Or to the topic we have been discussing?"

No one answered until finally Marya asked, very timidly, "The eagles? The boys?"

"Indeed," agreed the teacher. "We are talking about what happened to the boys."

"Excuse me, ma'am," said Marya, "but I don't understand."

"You will." The teacher glanced at the objects on the table under the cloth. She considered for a moment and then removed the draping to reveal metal statues of two birds. The tall one was a fierce two-headed Russian eagle, and the other was a more diminutive and nonthreatening crow.

"The double-headed eagle has been a symbol of Russian power since the late fifteenth century," said Mrs. Kaliszek. "Ivan III established the black double-headed eagle as an official emblem of the Russian state. Can anyone tell me something of the symbology? Of its meaning?"

A red-haired girl raised her hand. "In school—I mean in *regular* school—they told us that the two heads are symbols of looking back to learn from Russia's history and at the same time looking to the future."

Another girl said, "I heard that one head is supposed to be looking to the west and the other to the east, since Russia straddles the line between Europe and Asia."

A few other girls added bits and pieces from the political catechism force-fed to all students in occupied Poland.

"The Russians want us to be afraid of them," said Marya. "The obelisk is there to *tower* over us. Everyone who passes it has to see it and know who built it and why. The same with the eagles. They're meant to be scary. To scare us. To remind us of what happened during the Uprising, and to tell us what will happen again if we push back. They want us to be afraid of them. And . . . I guess we are." There was bitterness and anger in her tone, and it stilled the whole room for a moment.

"All of that is correct," said Mrs. Kaliszek, "as far as what they want us to believe."

"Is there a different meaning?" asked Marya. "I mean, is there a meaning that *matters* more?"

The teacher smiled. "That's very well phrased, Marya." Instead of directly answering, however, she turned to the two statues and gently touched the beak of the crow. "Today's lesson will not be like any you've had. Not like anything I ever thought I'd be teaching you."

There was a sudden sound from outside, and they all froze, mouths open, eyes darting to the shuttered windows. The noise was strange, like the fluttering of heavy wings.

There was a scuffing sound, and one of the girls cried out, "The eagles are here!"

Two other girls laughed, but when Mrs. Kaliszek shot them a fierce glare they lapsed into total silence. The sound of beating wings and scratching claws filled the room.

The teacher held up a hand as she crossed quickly to the farthest window and opened a tiny spy door set into the frame. All of the teachers in the flying school had similar peep holes, and they were very hard to find unless one knew where and how to look.

Mrs. Kaliszek peered out.

Kazia darted her hand out and caught Marya's, and they clung to one another.

But then the teacher's body seemed to relax. She straightened, sighed, turned, and offered a small smile.

"Everything is fine," she said. "It's only a pair of crows. It's not them."

Them.

The word hung like a pall in the air.

"Crows are our friends," murmured the teacher. Then she closed the secret window, straightened, turned, and snapped her fingers, sharp as a whipcrack.

Everyone jolted upright, and the same girl who cried out earlier gave a small "*Yeep!*"

The sound of beating wings changed, softened, stopped.

"Crows," Marya said very softly, taking comfort from that. Crows, not eagles. She felt as if she were able to breathe again.

"Crows are our friends," said the teacher. "Crows are nightbirds, and the night is also our friend. It shelters us, hides us, allows for movement and meetings. Without night's comforting and concealing cloak, we could not meet as we are now. And it is something groups of women have used for thousands of years out of necessity."

Outside, the two crows stood on the brick ledge outside of the room being used by the flying school. The birds sat very still, heads cocked to listen.

Another crow joined them, landing quietly. Then a third.

Soon every window ledge and every inch of roof gutter was thick with glossy black nightbirds. Some leaned in to listen. Others stood with their black eyes looking outward.

Watching.

Ready.

Mrs. Kaliszek returned to the front of the room. After looking sternly at the girls for nearly half a minute, she asked, "Who can tell me the difference between science and metaphysics?"

The students stared at her, then at each other with expressions of outright surprise, and then back at the teacher.

"Come, come," said Mrs. Kaliszek, "don't look at me as if I'm suddenly speaking in tongues. It's a straightforward question.

One hand crept up.

"Kazia," said the teacher. "Finally, a brave soul. What's the answer?"

"Well," said the girl, "science is real and metaphysics is—"

"Oh, be very careful how you finish that sentence, child," said the teacher, her face clouding.

Kazia retreated into a head shake and silence.

"Marya?" snapped Mrs. Kaliszek. "You generally have an opinion. How would you answer the same question?"

"Well, ma'am," Marya began, though there was a nervous tremolo in her voice, "science is what we can prove and—"

"Prove *how?*"

"Um . . ."

"And never say 'um,' girl. If you aren't sure what to say or how to phrase it, then allow for silence while you collect your thoughts. Otherwise you'll sound as if you are about to make something up. Be *sure* of your knowledge, but also have faith in your opinions. Now, try again."

Marya nodded and took several seconds to line up her thoughts. "Science is about measurements," she said. "Science requires us to strive to understand things in their exact way. Their shape, their nature, their reality. It is based on what can be proven and . . . what can be duplicated under laboratory conditions."

Mrs. Kaliszek studied her. "That's very well said. Are you quoting?"

"No, ma'am."

"Good. Quotes are for papers and speeches. Less so when expressing an opinion or an insight." She sniffed. "Besides, too many of the handiest quotes are from men. It's refreshing to hear a woman—particularly a young one—putting it into her *own* words."

"Thank you, ma'am."

"Now, Marya, tell us all how that is different from metaphysics?"

"Well, metaphysics is *non*-empiric and—"

"No," said the teacher sharply. "Don't tell me what it is not. Tell me what it *is*."

The other girls giggled a bit, but that raptor gaze silenced the room.

"Metaphysics is part of philosophy," said Marya, going slow to give herself time to phrase it as precisely as she knew Mrs. Kaliszek liked. When the teacher just stood there with one eyebrow raised, Marya plunged ahead. "It is concerned with philosophies about how the universe works, even those parts that can't easily be seen or measured."

"Such as . . . ?"

"The . . . nature of reality. Existence. The relationship between time and space, between causality and possibility."

"Good," said the teacher crisply as she turned away and walked back to the two metal birds.

Kazia reached over and nudged Marya, grinning. Mrs. Kaliszek handed out praise the way a miser distributed pennies—rarely and without much visible emotion. Getting a "good" from her was big, and Marya felt her cheeks burning. She knew she had to be bright red. She didn't dare look at the other girls, some of whom might be jealous or angry.

Marya and Kazia exchanged a brief look.

"Before we move into the practical part of tonight's lesson," said Mrs. Kaliszek, "I'll ask a related question. She looked around the room, and her eyes alighted once more on Kazia. "Perhaps you'll do better this time. Now . . . tell me the difference between chemistry and alchemy."

Kazia almost said "um," but stopped herself. She chewed her lip for a moment and then plunged ahead. "Chemistry is a form of science, ma'am. As Marya said, it's based on what can be proven, measured, and repeated in experiments."

Mrs. Kaliszek nodded.

"Alchemy is closer to metaphysics in that it is more of a philosophic approach, I think."

"You think or you know?" demanded the teacher.

"I . . . *know*," said Kazia, though she looked pale and uncertain. "Alchemy was used in ancient times to understand how things worked. The nature of metals, the connection between the physical world and the spiritual and—"

"And that is good enough for now," interrupted Mrs. Kaliszek. "Thank you, Kazia."

The teacher opened a cupboard and removed a tray on which were dozens of bottles and flasks of various sizes. Marya recognized some as beakers and retorts, flasks, and test tubes. The teacher looked around at the students.

"Before we continue," she said quietly, "I will tell you two things."

The girls all sat attentively, their faces serious. Marya leaned forward.

"The first thing is that one of the boys who were killed . . . ? He was the nephew of one of the other teachers in our little flying school. He was a good, brave boy. He should have grown up to be a man of note, someone to be counted." She held up a hand to deflect questions. "It was a mistake to have asked him to do what he did. What he *tried* to do. If he'd had a sister, then my friend would have asked her. Some things, as you will learn, are best left to women. Before you ask, I do not mean attacking statues with a hammer. That was done because the boy could not accomplish his task with the tools given him. He tried, we know that much, but . . . well . . . we will leave it there for the moment."

Marya glanced at Kazia, who shook her head.

"The second thing I need to tell you is that I do not believe in magic," Mrs. Kaliszek said, and let that hang in the air for a moment. "However, I believe—I *know*—that there is an unseen world that surrounds us. It's larger and stranger than anything we have so far learned to measure. Note that I said *so far*. I use those words with precision, for I believe that given time and great effort, we will find ways to include all such things under the umbrella of science. Alchemy and metaphysics will have their accepted and honored place. In time."

"Ma'am," said Marya timidly, "what does that have to do with eagles or crows? Or with those bottles?"

The smile that blossomed on Mrs. Kaliszek's gaunt features was slow in forming, strange in aspect, and more than a little terrifying.

"Why . . . *everything*, my child."

Saxon Square was empty of people as afternoon blurred into evening. A spattering of rain chased the last of the strollers indoors. The rain ran crookedly down the length of the obelisk.

Below, the circle of double-headed eagles crouched in silence.

One of them slowly stretched wide its wings and fluttered them, shaking off the chilly rain. Black bird against black shadows. No human eye could have seen it.

All around the square, though, thousands of pairs of small black eyes watched from rooftops and lamp posts. Watched. Feared.

Hated.

The class was the longest and strangest in Marya's experience.

It was frightening to a level none of the girls had ever even imagined.

Terror being the point.

Part of the point.

Hope was the other part.

Marya and Kazia walked home together.

The autumn sky was overcast, and even with the gas burning in the streetlamps, it was so dark. Every shadow seemed like it opened into an infinite world of nothingness. And yet Marya felt like something watched them from each shadow, and she did not like it one little bit.

When they reached the street that opened onto Saxon Square, Kazia stopped abruptly and leaned one hand against the wall as if to steady herself.

Marya did not ask what was wrong. She felt every bit as faint.

Kazia touched the lumpy pouch of the purse that was strung slant-wise across her body.

"I . . . I. . ." she began, and then stopped, shaking her head.

"I know," said Marya. "It's all so much."

"Too much," gasped Kazia.

Marya touched the bottles inside her own purse. They felt so strange, even through the cloth. Some were oddly cold and others strangely warm.

And Mrs. Kaliszek's words echoed in her head.

"There are many armies in this troubled world," the teacher had said. "The British Empire is one of the most powerful. The French and Germans are growing stronger. We here in Poland know without a doubt how militarily powerful the Russians are. And how did these nations become so strong? So effective in warfare?" She shook her head as hands went up. "Rhetorical question. Science. They have embraced the certainty that the only way to become powerful is through science."

"But, isn't that true, though?" asked Marya. "With steam engines, ironclad battleships with long-range guns, repeating rifles . . . they've proven that science is the strongest weapon . . . haven't they?"

"They've proven that science works for them, yes," agreed Mrs. Kaliszek. "But does that prove that science is the *greatest* weapon?"

No one raised a hand to answer.

"Let me approach this from a different direction," she said. "You are familiar with old sayings like 'woman's intuition?' Yes? Of course. Just as you know that a great deal of knowledge in a variety of areas is passed down generationally from mother to daughter to granddaughter. Healing arts, though legally practiced by men, owe a great deal to what women have investigated, learned, and shared. They, of course, tend to dismiss the deeper value of this knowledge. They talk about 'old wives' tales' and label women who are steeped in old lore as witches. They burned and butchered many, many women for possessing knowledge, for sharing it, for even having the desire to possess it. And I'm not just talking about the witch-finders of old. No. Even today, the Russian occupational government tries to suppress us, to keep us from learning, to deny as much as possible any chance we have of becoming educated."

She paused and looked around again with her feral eyes.

"Education for girls ends only a few years after puberty," she said. "They want you to become only educated enough to run a house and raise children, but they do *not* want you to pursue that education further."

Marya said, "Women have just as much potential to be as powerful as men."

"Define 'powerful,'" said the teacher, smiling thinly. When Kazia's hand shot up, Mrs. Kaliszek shook her head. "I'm not talking about warrior women, girl. We know your fascination on that topic. But the truth is that pound for pound, men are, on average, stronger. That is why nature selected them to be the primary hunters and gatherers while the women mostly stayed home to raise the children and see to the overall growth of the tribe. Those men, by the way, were expendable. There was always another brute with biceps and a club to go bash dinner over the head, but the knowledge keepers were safer at home. Sharing their insights and learning."

"Our power is knowledge," said Marya.

"The thought that knowledge is power is hardly a new one," said the teacher coldly. "Surely you have more to say than that."

"Um . . . oh, I'm sorry. Yes, ma'am," said Marya quickly. "Women have been the keepers of many subjects, grand and mundane. Healing in natural ways, the making of things, the art and science of growing and preparing foods, the science and practice of bearing and raising children, and more. They share the information between them—between *us*—because writing it down and teaching it in schools isn't always, as you say, allowed or encouraged. We do it anyway."

"And . . . ?" prompted the teacher. "What you've said so far is obvious. Give me more and give me insight. Remember—and this is for all of you—our greatest weapon is our knowledge."

"Yes," agreed Marya, "but we have to be careful with that knowledge."

"Oh dear," said Mrs. Kaliszek, and then gave a wicked little smile. "'Careful' is such a careful word, don't you think?"

"I do not mean timid, ma'am," Marya said quickly. "We need to be cautious not to be caught. Just because the witch trials, as such, are long over it doesn't mean that men don't still think of us as witches."

The teacher's wicked smile grew. "Very astute. You show promise. Continue."

"In Poland, we have three different layers of oppression," said Marya, warmed by the praise and rising to her topic. "Our families are conditioned to train us to be good girls . . . *quiet* and *demure* . . . and arrange things so that we *want* to grow up to be wives and mothers." She cut a look at her friend. "Not all families, but most."

"*Most*," agreed Kazia under her breath, and there were other echoes of that word.

"Then there is our own government," continued Marya. "We love our country, but in a lot of ways it's no different from anywhere else. So few women are allowed to reach for higher education. They train us to believe that home and babies are all that we can hope to be good at."

"Yes," purred the teacher, "they do. And the third layer?"

"Well, the Russians," Marya said frankly. "They are doing to our country what the country and traditions have been doing to women."

The teacher nodded. "Women have lived with that kind of frustration since we became self-aware."

They all thought about that for a moment, each of the girls eventually nodding.

Another of the girls said, "But we have to stay secret. Even this class . . . it's part of our flying. *Flying* because it flies from place to place. We're not even allowed to teach each other."

The smile on the teacher's face changed. It softened a bit. "That has never stopped us before. Nor will it now . . ."

That was part of it. The part that made sense. The rest . . .

God. It all became so strange after that.

And now, she and Kazia were approaching the area where the ugly, evil black eagles crouched. There was a soft sound, and the girls looked up to see a crow looking down at them from atop a lamppost. Its dark eyes seemed to blaze in the darkness.

"Come on," said Marya. "There's no one looking."

She took her friend's hand, which was cold and damp with fear sweat, and the two of them crept out into the square. The obelisk and its guardians seemed to watch them.

Waiting.

Defiant.

Challenging.

Marya pulled on Kazia's hand, but her friend did not budge. She was shivering, her eyes wide.

"What if they see us?" she whispered.

"There's no one in the square," said Marya.

"No . . . not people . . . *them*."

Marya looked at the black eagles.

"Mrs. Kaliszek said we'll be okay if we're quick," she said. "She said it would all work out if we did everything right."

"But we've never *done* anything like this," Kazia protested. "It's crazy. You know that more than anyone. Science is your religion, Marya. This, though . . . this is . . ."

She could not bring herself to say the word.

Witchcraft.

Or, even *magic.*

Marya felt her skin crawl with unease. Gooseflesh pebbled her arms beneath her coat sleeves, and the items in her purse seemed to weigh her down as if they were each bars of lead.

They hid in a bank of shadows and watched the square. The rain that had cleared the streets earlier had dwindled to a cold drizzle, and there was a biting wind out of the east. No one in their right mind would be out on a night like that.

Which is why Mrs. Kaliszek had chosen it. That's what she told the class. Everything had been planned with care. Marya suspected that the reason the teacher told them about this crazy plan on the same night it was to be put into action was to prevent any of the students from talking about it. Idle words were dangerous.

"It's clear," said Kazia, her voice fragile with nervous fear.

Marya took a steadying breath. "Then let's go."

They crept across the corner of the square farthest from the shed where the guards were stationed. Marya made sure to keep the obelisk between them and the window of the shed. It amused her to think that the ugly Russian tower was helping two Polish girls. There was some justice there.

They reached the outer circle but did not yet cross inside.

"The eagles wake up when you do that," Mrs. Kaliszek had said. "Something triggers their awareness as soon as you pass between any two of them."

"They never did anything when we spit on the obelisk," protested Kazia, but the teacher shook her head.

"Spit is nothing to stone and bronze. It rains so often that it washes away such things. If either of you girls brought a hammer and chisel with you, then neither of you would be here right now. Your parents would be laying flowers on your graves."

That fragment of conversation haunted Marya. Twice she had thought about doing exactly that—bringing something out to chisel away the leering faces of those eagles. She had never worked up the nerve, and now she was glad that her fear made her cautious; that caution kept her alive.

Tonight, though . . .

Well, tonight was different. Marya and Kazia were about to cross a very different kind of line. Between the known and unknown. A step that would take them into the larger world Mrs. Kaliszek spoke of.

Or to their own destruction if they were caught by guards, or by . . .

She shuddered at the thought.

Later in the lesson, the teacher had returned to the topic.

"The slaughter of those poor boys has taught us a lesson. Their bodies were not found *near* the obelisk. Those eagles tracked them down and killed them away from the square. That means they can travel. That they can fly. Why do you think we have those spy windows in every flying school classroom? My sister teachers are *positive* that the eagles are learning how to hunt us. Given time, they will find us. Even when we move from place to place, it's inevitable. Where does that leave us? If we close down the flying schools, then what? You girls would have to give up on your dreams of education, of becoming powerful in your own lives. If the eagles find us, then you have no futures except as slaves to a system that hates and degrades women."

"But what can we do?" asked Kazia.

Which is when Mrs. Kaliszek began telling them what the bottles were, and what the plan was.

"Alchemy and metaphysics are strange weapons for us," said Mrs. Kaliszek. "But we live in strange times, and no other weapons are allowed to us. We are left, then, with the weapons we have, and if that means that *we* have to step off the cliff of known science and take leaps of faith into the larger world . . . then that is what we must do."

The part of Marya who wanted to be a scientist one day rebelled at what they were doing. Even with what Mrs. Kaliszek had said about the possibility that the supernatural in its many forms was merely a branch of science as yet unstructured and unmeasured, the absurdity of it loomed large in her head.

"This is madness," Marya murmured.

Kazia, who was opening her purse, glanced sharply at her.

"We can just leave," Kazia said. "There's still time."

Marya thought about it. She gave it real thought. Walking away was the sensible thing to do. The smart thing.

But it was not the brave thing. Or the right thing.

Marya knew that her dreams of becoming a scientist required courage. If she walked away now, that lack of bravery would forever mark her. It would follow her.

It would mean that she accepted the Russian oppression. It meant that she did not believe she—or the women running the flying schools— were worth fighting for. Taking risks for.

She opened her bag and began removing the bottles.

"Alchemy," she said, nearly spitting the word. Even as she worked, her mind continued to rebel against the nature of what she and Kazia were doing.

Her friend met her eyes.

"Mrs. Kaliszek said it's science and—"

"I know," Marya snapped, her nerves completely frayed. Then she heard the bitterness in her own voice and said it again, softer this time. "I know."

They crouched in front of one of the eagles, and Marya was certain the thing was watching her. It did not move, but she *knew.*

"God in heaven," she breathed. "Save my soul."

They poured precise amounts of different chemicals into two beakers. The stuff smelled of sulfur and mint and hawthorn and roses. It was the strangest mixture, and there were herbs and pieces of crystal and sand and salt. The chemistry of it made no sense to Marya, but she kept working until both beakers were filled. Then Kazia produced two glass rods and handed one to Marya. They stirred the chemicals vigorously, which made the weird, mingled odor even stronger.

As they worked there was a sound. It was odd, like metal being twisted, sharp and high. Kazia gasped and paused in her work. Both girls looked wildly around at the eagles. Had they moved?

"No . . ." breathed Kazia, her face going dead pale. "They're waking up."

"Hurry," hissed Marya and stirred even faster. "Kazia, stop gaping and *hurry.*"

They finished the mixture, and each of them took a beaker and got to their feet.

There was another metallic screech somewhere on the far side of the circle.

And another to their left.

"God," cried Kazia, "they're *all* waking up. They know. Marya— *they know.*"

Another sound filled the night air. The rough and rusty cry of a crow. The call of a nightbird.

The metal sounds increased, becoming faster, louder.

"Hurry," snapped Marya. "Kazia, we need to finish this or all is lost."

When her friend did not move, Marya grabbed her by the shoulder and shook the other girl. She was not gentle about it.

"Kazia . . . *now,*" she snarled.

And the growl in her voice somehow sounded like the call of those crows. Harsh, angry.

Powerful.

Kazia stared at her, and for a moment there was nothing in those blue eyes but a blank, mindless terror. Marya shook her again, and then Kazia blinked. Again and again, and with each blink more of her friend's personality seemed to drift back. It was not much—there was so much fear there—but it was something. It was enough.

"Are you ready?" asked Marya as the metal noises filled the whole square. In her peripheral vision, Marya could see those black wings trembling, the black beaks opening. The black eyes turning their way.

The cries of the crows was louder too, but it was desperate. There was fear in that sound.

"Kazia . . . *please.*"

Kazia nodded to her, but she was unable to speak.

"Now," said Marya, and she began backing away from her friend, moving in a very slow arc around the outside of the ring of awakening eagles. Kazia moved backward too, heading around the other way. As they moved, they tilted their beakers to allow thin lines of the noxious mixture to dribble onto the paving stones.

Step by step.

The eagles were starting to swell, to rise from their crouched positions. All of them were coming awake. One stretched out a foot, and the sharp talon caught on Marya's coat, slashing the cloth as if it was tissue paper.

"Please, please, please," whispered Marya.

Above them the crows were chattering anxiously.

Each second seemed to take an hour as they used the chemicals to draw a circle around the ring of eagles. All of the metal creatures were awake now, and they hissed at the girls in voices closer to serpents than birds.

Marya looked down at the beaker she held and saw that there was very little of the mixture left. She glanced up to see how much Kazia had, but her friend was out of sight around the far side of the obelisk.

We did it wrong, she thought desperately. *They trusted us and we did it wrong. God, we're going to die here.*

Her feet kept moving even though her heart seemed to have stopped in her chest.

The eagles turned their heads toward her, the pairs of beaks snapping at the air. How soon before they were alive enough to leap from their posts and attack? Minutes?

Seconds?

No time at all?

Marya wanted to cry. To scream.

Then something hit her in the back, and she whirled, certain that this was it, that she was going to die right then and there.

"Marya," said Kazia, who stood directly behind her and had turned too. They had completed the circuit of the obelisk and bumped into one another.

They looked down at the circle of chemicals.

The ring was complete.

Complete.

Suddenly Kazia snaked out a hand and caught hers.

"They're alive," she said.

And so they were.

Not merely awake . . . but actually alive. Inside that circle, the two-headed eagles were no longer made from gleaming metal. They were flesh and bone, meat, and feathers.

Alive.

All around the square the air was torn with the furious cries of thousands of Polish crows.

And in the next moment the air was filled with black bodies hurling themselves from rooftops and lampposts.

"Run!" cried Marya. She jerked hard on Kazia's hands and hauled her away.

The girls ran as fast as they could as the squadrons of crows dove with savage intensity at the eagles.

"See them, Vjenko?" said Colonel Zhukovsky. "This is what I was tell-ing you yesterday. The younger generation have understanding. They have respect."

The major watched as the same two young girls who had visited the obelisk walked arm-in-arm across the square. They walked demurely, heads down, each holding a small bunch of flowers—an assortment of nasturtium, dill, lilac, tansy, and violets. They walked between two of the double-headed eagles and stopped in front of the tower.

The eagles lay in pieces. Their necks broken, wings twisted out of shape, eyes gouged to ragged pits. All of the eagles were the same. All ruined beyond repair.

"What are they doing?" asked the major.

"Watch," said the colonel.

The girls paused, heads still bowed, and then bent to lay their bou-quets at the foot of the obelisk. Then they curtsied, turned, and walked away, their faces pale and troubled.

"You see?" said Colonel Zhukovsky. "It's what I said yesterday, the younger generation has respect for us. They do not hate us for having won the war, nor do they resent our presence here. Clearly—*clearly*—they respect the power and order, the structure and protection Russia offers. Why else would they have come here every day to curtsy? Why else would they come here after a night of vandalism and lay flowers? It's respect, I tell you. Simple, peasant respect for their betters. And I applaud them for it. With that kind of thing in the next generation, our empire will last a thousand years. *Two* thousand."

The major nodded. "Shame about the eagles, though. And you say that no one saw anything?"

"Nothing."

"What about all that noise, though?"

"Noise?" the colonel laughed. "Nothing but a bunch of ugly old crows. The lieutenant in charge of the investigation thinks that the van-dals spread some bread or seeds to draw the birds in and use them as cover. Or a distraction."

The major looked at him and clearly wanted to say something to dispute such an absurd claim, but even though the colonel was his friend, he was also his superior officer, and so he kept his rebuke inside.

They stood there and watched the girls walk away.

"That's the future," said the colonel. "Mark my words."

All along the rooftops and eaves of the buildings surrounding the square, thousands of pairs of small black eyes watched the two old soldiers, the ruined eagles, and the retreating back of two small, slender, teenage girls.

MARYA'S
Precious Pill

by
JANE YOLEN

Not the one that years later
we could safely take
to control our eggs.
But one she made,
giving it to her daughters
and their daughters,
telling them it was one thing,
but it was another.
Something got from a Polish witch,
to ruin the death sleep of that French bitch,
who nearly killed her with accusations.
A spell from Baba Yaga, potent as radium
only slightly diminished
by crossing Slavic borders.
She had been shamed
into losing the man she loved.
But the pills she devised
would make her granddaughter
marry his grandson.
She would go to her grave laughing.
Pierre always liked her little science jokes.
She imagined him amused,
in heaven, in hell, on Ash Sunday.

RESOURCES FOR FURTHER READING

FOR MORE ABOUT MARIE CURIE:

Susan Quinn, *Marie Curie: A Life*. Da Capo Press, 1996.

Barbara Goldsmith, *Obsessive Genius: The Inner World of Marie Curie*. W. W. Norton, 2004.

Eve Curie, *Madame Curie: A Biography*. Da Capo Press, 2001.

Philip Steele, *Marie Curie: The Woman Who Changed the Course of Science*. National Geographic Society, 2006.

Julie Knutson, *The Science and Technology of Marie Curie*. Nomad Press, 2021.

Marie Curie, *Pierre Curie: With Autobiographical Note*. Dover Publications, 2012.

FOR MORE ABOUT OPPORTUNITIES IN SCIENCE FOR WOMEN:

Peggy Pritchard and Christine Grant, eds., *Success Strategies From Women in STEM: A Portable Mentor*. Academic Press, 2015.

Tonya Bolden, *Changing the Equation: 50+ US Black Women in STEM*. Abrams Books for Young Readers, 2020.

Nathalia Holt, *Rise of the Rocket Girls: The Women Who Propelled Us, from Missiles to the Moon to Mars*. Back Bay Books, 2017.

Karen Panetta and Katianne Williams, *Count Girls In: Empowering Girls to Combine Any Interests with STEM to Open Up a World of Opportunity*. Chicago Review Press, 2018.

Maria Isabel Sanchez Vegara, *Little People, BIG DREAMS: Women in Science: 3 books from the bestselling series! Ada Lovelace - Marie Curie - Amelia Earhart.* Frances Lincoln Children's Books, 2021.

WEBSITES:

https://www.nobelprize.org/prizes/physics/1903/marie-curie/biographical/

https://en.wikipedia.org/wiki/Marie_Curie

https://www.britannica.com/biography/Marie-Curie

https://www.smithsonianmag.com/history/madame-curies-passion-74183598/

https://www.biography.com/scientist/marie-curie

https://www.bbc.co.uk/history/historic_figures/curie_marie.shtml

https://www.history.com/news/marie-curie-facts

https://www.livescience.com/38907-marie-curie-facts-biography.html

EDITOR BIOS

BRYAN THOMAS SCHMIDT is the Hugo-nominated, #1 bestselling editor of twenty-one anthologies, the author of eleven novels and over forty short stories, and a screenwriter, podcaster, and musician. He lives with four crazy cats and two eccentric dogs outside Kansas City. Six previous audiobooks have reached number one on Audible. Find him online at bryanthomasschmidt.net.

HENRY HERZ's speculative fiction short stories include "Out, Damned Virus" (*Daily Science Fiction*), "Bar Mitzvah on Planet Latke" (*Coming of Age*, Albert Whitman & Co.), "The Magic Backpack" (Metastellar), "Unbreakable" (*Musing of the Muses*, Brigid's Gate Press), "A Vampire, an Astrophysicist, and a Mother Superior Walk Into a Basilica" (*Three Time Travelers Walk Into . . .*, Fantastic Books), "The Case of the Murderous Alien" (*Spirit Machine*, Air and Nothingness Press), "Maria & Maslow" (*Highlights for Children*), and "A Proper Party" (*Ladybug Magazine*). He's written twelve picture books, including the critically acclaimed *I Am Smoke*. www.henryherz.com

AUTHOR BIOS

JANE YOLEN's 400th book came out in March 2021, a lyrical picture book titled *Bear Outside*. By the time you read this, she will be on her way toward 500 and maybe more. She just loves to write. Her most popular books are *Owl Moon* and the *How Do Dinosaurs* series, and she has written poetry since she was in first grade. (She's gotten better!) Her latest adult poetry book is *Kaddish*, poems about the Holocaust. She writes a poem a day and sends them out to over 1,000 subscribers. Her books and stories and poems have won Nebulas, Caldecotts, World Fantasy Awards, Storytelling Awards, Christopher Medals and more. One award set her good coat on fire. Six colleges and universities have given her honorary doctorates for her body of work. www.janeyolen.com

LISSA PRICE's debut novel *Starters* was an international bestseller published in twenty-nine countries, with praise from Kami Garcia, Harlan Ellison, and the *LA Times*. Dean Koontz called her YA futuristic thriller "a smart, swift, inventive, altogether gripping story." *Starters* appeared on state and library reading lists, was a YALSA Quick Pick, and has been optioned for television. Kirkus called the bestselling sequel, *Enders*, "delightfully disturbing."

The Starters series has taken Lissa all over the world on book tours and appearances in North America, Europe and the Middle and Far East. She has taught workshops at SCBWI and the La Jolla Writer's Conference, and spoken at festivals including ComicCon, WonderCon, ChiCon, Wordstock, The LA Times Festival of Books, Boston Book Festival, Manila International Book Fair and Thrillerfest. Lissa graduated from the acclaimed Faber Academy in London. In addition to living in the UK, she has also lived in Japan and India, and once spent two years circling the globe, going from east to west. As an Asian woman, she supports and encourages diversity in publishing. Her home base is in the hills of Los Angeles where she's visited by coyote, deer, and the occasional bobcat. www.LissaPrice.com

New York Times bestselling author ALETHEA KONTIS is a princess, storm chaser, and Saturday Songwriter. Author of over twenty books and forty short stories, Alethea is the recipient of the Jane Yolen Mid-List Author Grant, the Scribe Award, the Garden State Teen Book Award, and two-time winner of the Gelett Burgess Children's Book Award. She has been twice nominated for both the Andre Norton Nebula and the Dragon Award. She was an active contributor to *The Fireside Sessions*, a benefit EP created by Snow Patrol and her fellow Saturday Songwriters during lockdown 2020. Alethea also narrates stories for multiple award-winning online magazines and contributes regular YA book reviews to NPR. Born in Vermont, she currently resides on the Space Coast of Florida with her teddy bear, Charlie. www.aletheakontis.com

SEANAN MCGUIRE writes things. It can be very difficult to make her stop, and people have found it generally safer to just let her get on with it. She is the *New York Times* bestselling author of more than fifty traditionally published novels and far too many short stories. Where the corn grows tall, she is there, watching from behind the rows, writing things down. May those things remain unspoken. When not keeping company with the corn, Seanan lives in the Pacific Northwest, and devotes her spare time to becoming a swamp cryptid of terrifying presence. She thinks it's going well so far. www.seananmcguire.com

JO WHITTEMORE is the author of the *Supergirl* novel trilogy (all-new adventures based on the CW television show), as well as numerous middle grade humor novels, including the Girls Who Code novel *Lights, Music, Code!*, *Me & Mom Vs. The World*, the Confidentially Yours hexology, and the Silverskin Legacy fantasy trilogy. Jo is a longtime member of the Society of Children's Book Writers and Illustrators, and she currently writes from her secret lair in Austin, Texas, that she shares with her husband and daughter. www.jowhittemore.com

Nicknamed "The Queen of Horror" by loyal readers, *MYLO CARBIA* is a former screenwriter turned bestselling author, widely known for her work in the horror-thriller genre and trademark of surprise twist endings. Born to Native American / Puerto Rican parents in Jackson, New Jersey, Carbia famously spent her childhood years writing to escape the terrors of growing up in a severely haunted house. Her paranormal experiences followed her to college at Mercer University in Macon, Georgia, where she received a bachelor's degree, magna cum laude. After years of working in the private sector and Hollywood, Carbia joined the publishing world in 2015. Her debut novel, *Ava Desantis*, hit #1 bestseller in four categories, and won several awards including the Silver Falchion Award for Outstanding Achievement in Fiction. Since that time, she has released several more bestselling titles including *Violets Are Red* and *Z. O. O.* Carbia is listed among "The Greatest Horror Writers of All Time" by Ranker.com, "The Top 10 Horror Writers Alive Today" by Booklaunch, and "The Most Influential Authors" by Richtopia.com. Today, she lives with her husband and son in Palm Beach, Florida. She continues writing exclusively for the literary world and plans to turn her favorite stories into feature films.

After years of working in fantasy game design and web development, *G. P. CHARLES* traded in computer programming for fiction writing and escaped the nightmare of missing semicolons and infinite loops. Now, instead of daydreaming about throwing the computer out the window, she finds every day an exciting adventure. When not writing, downtime is spent at home on the farm, raising horses, chickens, and two boys who are too intelligent for their own good but a constant source of joy. To learn more, check out www.gpcharles.com.

#1 *New York Times* bestselling author *SCOTT SIGLER* is the creator of eighteen novels, six novellas, and dozens of short stories. He is an inaugural inductee into the Podcasting Hall of Fame. Scott began his career by narrating his unabridged audiobooks and serializing them in weekly installments. He continues to release free episodes every Sunday. Launched in March of 2005, "Scott Sigler Audiobooks" is the world's longest-running fiction podcast. His rabid fans fervently anticipate their weekly story fix, so much so that they've dubbed themselves "Sigler Junkies" and have downloaded over fifty million episodes. Scott is a cofounder of Empty Set Entertainment, which publishes his Galactic Football League series. A Michigan native, he lives in San Diego, California, with his wife and their wee little Døgs of Døøm. www.scottsigler.com

CHRISTINE TAYLOR-BUTLER has authored more than eighty books for children, including her speculative The Lost Tribes series (Move Books). A graduate of MIT, she is known for writing compelling nonfiction for young readers. In addition, she's written a number of articles including "When Failure Is Not An Option," an essay on the need for diversity in STEM literature (the *Horn Book Magazine* November/December 2021). A fierce advocate for literacy, Christine has spoken at ALA, NCTE, and ILA, as well as numerous World Science Fiction Conventions, World Fantasy, Boskone, and the Nebula awards. She served as a judge for the Society of Midland Authors children's nonfiction award, the Walter Dean Myers children's literature award, and PEN America's Phyllis Naylor Working Writer Fellowship. Christine is past president of the Missouri Writers Guild, Emeritus Board member of Kindling Words, and Toastmaster for World Fantasy 2021. She is currently a member of the Kansas City Science Fiction and Fantasy Society and a Director At Large of Science Fiction Writers of America (SFWA).

SUSANNE L. LAMBDIN graduated from the University of Oklahoma with a BA in Journalism and moved to Los Angeles in the mid-1980s to work at Paramount Pictures. Lambdin is best known for writing on *Star Trek: The Next Generation* season four episode "Family." Author of the *Dead Hearts* YA zombie apocalypse series, of which the first book, *Morbid Hearts*, was a 2013 *New York Times* bestseller. Her strong female characters take center stage in the story, leading troops into battle or tending to a broken heart. Lambdin is adept at switching genres, as seen in her dark fantasy trilogy, *Realm of Magic*, and new military sci-fi trilogy, *Acropolis 3000*, as well as Gothic horror and contemporary romance. She lives in Kansas with her family and two lovely dogs, Shiloh and Spencer. www.susannelambdin.com

EMILY McCOSH is a graphic designer and writer of strange things. She currently lives in California with her two parents, two dogs, one fish, one tree swing, and innumerable characters who need to learn some manners. Her fiction has appeared in *Beneath Ceaseless Skies*, *Shimmer Magazine*, *Galaxy's Edge*, *Flash Fiction Online*, *Nature: Futures*, and elsewhere. More of her work can be found in her short story and poetry collection, *All the Woods She Watches Over*. www.oceansinthesky.com

DEE LEONE is the author of *Dough Knights and Dragons* and other children's books, as well as twenty reproducible books for the educational market. Her published works include more than two hundred stories, poems, plays, songs, and articles. Dee has tutored college math, taught at the elementary level, and worked with gifted students. Like Marie Curie, she enjoyed studying math, physics, and chemistry. Dee's formula for creating dark fiction is a synthesis of various elements, with dark chocolate as her catalyst. www.deeleone.com

Her anthology story, "Silence Them," was inspired by the fact that Marie and her husband Pierre attended séances together and studied them in a scientific manner. They considered the possibility that some of the phenomena they observed—the ones they couldn't explain away as trickery—could be due to physical states not yet known or understood. They even speculated that there might be a connection between the mysterious occurrences and the radiation they were studying . . .

SARAH BETH DURST is the author of over twenty fantasy books for kids, teens, and adults, including *Spark*, *Drink Slay Love*, and the Queens of Renthia series. She has won an American Library Association Alex Award and a Mythopoeic Fantasy Award and has been a finalist for the Andre Norton Nebula Award three times. She lives in Stony Brook,

New York, with her husband, her children, and her ill-mannered cat. www.sarahbethdurst.com

STEVE PANTAZIS is an award-winning author of fantasy and science fiction. He won the prestigious Writers of the Future award in 2015 and has gone on to publish a number of short stories in leading SF&F anthologies and magazines, including *Nature*, *Galaxy's Edge*, and *IGMS*. When not writing (a rare occasion!), Steve creates extraordinary cuisine, exercises with vigor, and shares marvelous adventures with the love of his life. Originally from the Big Apple, he now calls Southern California home. www.stevepantazis.com.

JONATHAN MABERRY is a *New York Times* bestselling author, five-time Bram Stoker Award-winner, three-time Scribe Award winner, Inkpot Award winner, and comic book writer. His vampire apocalypse book series, *V-Wars*, was adapted into a Netflix original series. He writes in multiple genres, including suspense, thriller, horror, science fiction, fantasy, and action, for adults, teens and middle grade. His novels include the *Joe Ledger* thriller series, *Bewilderness*, *Ink*, *Glimpse*, the Pine Deep Trilogy, the Rot & Ruin series, the Dead of Night series, *Mars One*, *Ghostwalkers: A Deadlands Novel*, and many others, including his first epic fantasy, *Kagen the Damned*. He is the editor of many anthologies including *The X-Files*, *Aliens: Bug Hunt*, *Don't Turn Out the Lights*, *Aliens vs Predator: Ultimate Prey*, *Hardboiled Horror*, *Nights of the Living Dead* (coedited with George A. Romero), and others. His comics include *Black Panther: DoomWar*, *Captain America*, *Pandemica*, *Highway to Hell*, *The Punisher*, and *Bad Blood*. He is the president of the International Association of Media Tie-in Writers, and the editor of *Weird Tales* magazine. www.jonathanmaberry.com

STACIA DEUTSCH is the *New York Times* bestselling author of more than three hundred children's books. She writes some YA, but mostly chapter book and middle grade, often for licensed characters. Her career started with her own, award winning, *Blast to the Past* series about four kids who time travel and meet famous people in history which was a result of her obsession with time travel stories! Stacia's first movie novelization was *Batman: The Dark Knight* and since then she has written many more. Most recently, she wrote the movie novel for *Boss Baby 2*. Mystery books are also a big love! She's lucky to have ghost written many mystery novels under ghost names and currently, she is launching the Boxcar Children spin-off called *The Jessie Files*. Stacia's other titles include the *Friendship Code for Girls Who Code* (Penguin), seven novels for *Spirit: Riding Free* (Little Brown/Dreamworks), and many LEGO stories! She lives on a California ranch with four horses, three dogs, and a cat that makes her sneeze. Stacia is also a reform rabbi, so if you need someone to officiate at your wedding, bar or bat mitzvah, she's got you covered. www.staciadeutsch.com

ACKNOWLEDGMENTS

Bryan and Henry would like to thank their agent, Andy Ross, the wondrously talented story authors who contributed their imaginative takes on what might have been had Marie taken a dark turn, and Rick Bleiweiss, Naomi Hynes, Diana Gill, Josie Woodbridge, and the rest of the Blackstone Publishing team who helped transform an idea into an anthology staring back at us from bookshelves.

Bryan extends special thanks also to Diana Fox, Jay Werkheiser, and Guy Anthony DeMarco for extra support above and beyond the call of duty.